FINDING THE ALPHA'S DAUGHTER

THE VAMPIRE KING'S FEEDER
BOOK THREE

BELLA MOONDRAGON

For Jeff

CONTENTS

1

MATES ON PARADE

EMORY

I make my way down the stairs, trying not to trip on the hem of the green gown I'm wearing. It's sleeveless with flowers embroidered on the bodice. I feel quite pretty, and I'm a little bit disappointed my husband won't be able to see me. I've taken extra care with my appearance, curling my hair and styling it to one side with silver clips.

The staff are busy making last minute adjustments according to my mother's orders. She's the general, and the staff are her obedient soldiers. My mother is dressed in a simple dark blue gown with long sleeves. She looks elegant and serene, and she's not letting the stress of the ball she's been planning for weeks show.

"How's it going, Mom?" I ask.

"Our guests will be arriving in half an hour, and no one has seen your brother," she replies, checking her watch for the time. "He's probably off in the woods, and he still needs to shower and put on his suit. He won't have the time if he's not back in this house in the next five minutes."

"He can get ready in ten minutes." I remind her. Ah, what would it be like to be a man and just not have to bother with make-up and styling my hair?

My mom purses her lips, her eyes narrowing in annoyance. "He's doing this to punish me."

"He's not."

"It's because I've been pushing him to find his mate ever since his twenty-first birthday, and he's going to skip out on the Ball so he'll never meet his mate and be a bachelor for life."

My mother has a habit of being more dramatic when she's stressed. The weeks of party planning are finally getting to her. I put my hand on her shoulder gently, trying to comfort her. She lets out a deep breath.

"I'll go find Colt," I assure her. "And he'll be here in time for the mating party."

"It's the Moon Goddess Ball," she corrects me.

"I know."

The Moon Goddess Ball is an old tradition for wolf shifters going back centuries. It's an event where all packs come together to celebrate the Moon Goddess. Its true purpose is to get all the young shifters in the same room so they might find their mate. Marriages within different packs help with creating and maintaining alliances.

The event is meant to be held every few years, but due to the actions of my father, the previous Alpha of my pack, we haven't been able to participate in the Ball for over twenty years. Bernard Moonraker attacking and trying to claim the territories of other Alphas hasn't endeared him to anyone. I've had to work to gain the trust of the other packs these past few years. Finally, we're not only invited to the Ball, but we've been chosen to host it this year which is the highest honor.

I make my way to the kitchen, swerving around the staff who are busy with the enormous amount of food to be served at the Ball. They look up when they see me come in, and I smile and wave them away, telling them to go back to work and not mind me. I don't want to bother them when they're so busy. I head to the backdoor leading to the woods.

The silver strappy heels I'm wearing dig into the grass, and I roll my green eyes before taking them off, holding them in one hand. My brother isn't answering my mind-link messages, potentially because he doesn't want to be found.

Colt's scent is quite familiar to me, and I follow the trail of it in the air. I end up at the pond in the woods where we spent our childhood swimming during the summers. His clothes have been left on a nearby bush.

My brother floats in the water, his skin golden from being under the sun. His red hair looks like fire in the waning sunlight. He's only wearing his boxers. Everyone is looking for him, and he's out here having a leisurely swim.

"Hey, Cinderella!" I call out. "You're going to be late for the Ball!"

Colt's eyes open, and he lifts his head, squinting under the glare of the sun. "What time is it?"

I look at the expensive watch on my wrist. It was a present from Kane for our third year wedding anniversary.

"You have less than twenty minutes to get dressed or our mother will disown you."

"Moon Goddess be damned," he yelps out, quickly swimming back to shore. He grabs his clothes and shoes but doesn't bother putting them on. "I thought I had an hour at least."

"Maybe we should get you a watch," I tell him, jokingly. "You're always on the verge of running late."

"I always make it on time."

"Barely."

He gets out and grabs his clothes. We start walking briskly back to the house. Colt is dripping when we enter through the backdoor, gaining stares from the staff at his state of undress. My brother has never bothered with modesty and would probably be a nudist if it wouldn't embarrass our mother to death. Speaking of Mom, she nearly gasps when she sees Colt.

"Why are you wet?" she asks then shakes her head. "Never mind. Go upstairs and shower. You smell like you've been swimming in the pond."

"I have been swimming in the pond."

She takes in a calming breath and commands, "Go."

Colt doesn't need to be told twice, so he goes to the stairs to start getting ready. I'm slipping my heels back on as my mom turns to me.

"I truly hope he finds his mate tonight," she says. "Let his wife take over worrying about him."

I snort at the thought. "Like you'd ever stop worrying about us. You're our mom. It's kind of what you do."

"Just wait till Mikey gets older and starts causing trouble! Then, you'll see what I had to go through."

The mention of my son makes my heart squeeze painfully. Mikey is three-years-old and back at Crimson Peak with his father. This has been the longest time I've been away from my son since he was born. Every few months, I've had to visit Moon Grove for matters I can't handle remotely. With the Ball we've had to plan. I've been in Moon Grove for close to a month now.

I already miss being able to hold Mikey in my arms and make him laugh. The thought of him growing up makes me want to cry. I know it's impractical and impossible, but I want him to be small and cute forever. I'm not ready to even think about him being Colt's age and finding a mate.

Thankfully, that's still a long way off from now.

"Mikey is a darling. He won't be anything like he's Uncle Colt," I declare.

My mother only smiles. "We'll see."

* * *

Colt

I hate wearing suits. I've always found them stifling, and ties feel like they're trying to choke me. My mom and sister insist I look my best for this damn Ball so I put on the suit and tie and hope this event ends soon. I know what everyone is expecting to happen for me, and I am sick of it already.

Music plays in the background as I make my way down to the ballroom. Several guests have already arrived. I take a deep breath and go over to where my mother is standing next to Emory. Immediately, every Alpha in attendance begins to introduce their daughters, granddaughters, and nieces to me. They're all presented to me like prized cattle—tall, short, slim, curvy. I try to be polite and smile.

Every time, we make eye contact, and I wait for that magical awakening inside me to tell me that she's my mate—blue, green, brown, gray eyes—but nothing happens. The girl knows it too, and she looks disappointed. The Alphas can never hide how visibly disappointed they are too, and then they shuffle away to give space for the next candidate.

After nearly a dozen failed attempts, I beg for a break. Emory and I stand in the corner and drink wine as she tells me about her son. My nephew Mikey is an adorable little boy, and my sister misses him terribly. Emory has decided that her son is too young for a Ball so he couldn't come with her.

"Why is Kane not with you?" I ask.

"We talked about it, but this Ball is for shifters. His presence tends to attract too much attention."

That makes sense. Not everyone was thrilled when my sister married him. The animosity between our species has lessened over the last few years, but it'll take time before we could be considered friendly. The Alphas have been tolerating Kane's presence in Moon Grove, but they've made it clear that it's Emory they trust and not him. What loyalty he can get from them is an extension of their loyalty to Emory.

"It's not fair," I point out. "Everyone gets to bring their mate except you."

"Maybe I can bring him to the next one," Emory says with a shrug. "Baby steps."

If there's anything I've learned helping my sister with her Alpha duties is that diplomacy is a delicate balance that requires a lot of careful finessing. When you're dealing with powerful people that command armies, it's better to be safe than sorry.

Alpha Gerald's booming laugh makes me turn to where he's talking to a few people. I know he's been mostly blessed with sons and grandsons, so he's not going to be part of the parade of mating prospects. From the corner of my eye, I see a figure entering the room. A petite blonde in a pink dress makes her away across the room to where he stands.

The tall man lets out a delighted sound and pulls her into a bear hug.

"Em?" I cock my head towards the group. "Who's that with Alpha Gerald?"

Emory looks over and replies, "Oh, that's his granddaughter."

"I thought he only had grandsons."

"She's the only girl. The youngest, I think."

"Have you met her?"

"Not really, but I think Mom has mentioned her. She's training to be a healer."

I'm looking around for my mom so I can ask more about what she knows. I don't know why, but my curiosity is piqued. Emory stares at me questioningly. Her green eyes search my face. "Colt, are you…?"

I don't have the chance to answer her open-ended question as Alpha Gerald is coming over with the blonde's arm tucked around his. His wife Constance is with them, and I can see the resemblance with the younger woman. They both have the same golden hair.

"Alpha Emory, Colt," Alpha Gerard says, practically beaming with pride. "I present to you my granddaughter, Lydia. She's studying to be a pack healer."

A pack healer–one of the most important members of the pack. Being a man, I can't help but glance down at how that pink dress shows off her glorious cleavage. A future pack healer with great breasts.

Emory nudges me with her elbow. "It's nice to meet you, Lydia. Right, Colt?"

I look up and finally look at her face. She has a beautiful heart-shaped face with big blue eyes, Full lips with a pronounced cupid's bow made for kissing, and all that golden hair. She's gorgeous, and my heart is practically beating out of my chest.

I stare into her blue eyes and realize they're a shade between blue and gray. There's no jolt of electricity. My sense of gravity doesn't shift. It's all rather anticlimactic compared to what I have been expecting, but something in me whispers, *"This one. This is your mate."*

"Lydia," I say her name as if I can somehow convey what I'm feeling in one word.

She smiles, having all the same realizations at me but handling it with more grace. "Colt."

I nod, dumbly. "That's me."

Lydia offers her hand. "It's nice to meet you."

I lift her hand to my lips, unable to look away from her beautiful face. "Nice to meet you too."

Emory snorts beside me. She's never going to let me forget this. Alpha Gerald and his wife are smiling like they've won the lottery. I ignore them all.

"Do you want to go get some air?" I ask, already moving to guide her away from our audience.

"I would love some air."

I haven't let go of Lydia's hand. I don't really want to. Her touch feels right. I never want to let her go.

2

IT'S NOT A CONTEST

EMORY

I've seen the mating process before, and it's always fascinating to watch. The way they stare into each other's eyes and that awareness they have of the other person in the room. It can be felt even before a shifter comes of age and meets their wolf. Years ago, when I met Kane for the first time, there was this pull between us neither of us could ignore.

If Colt and Lydia had met earlier before either of them came of age, they likely would have felt a pull. It's more subtle and becomes stronger after one meets their wolf. There's a sense of rightness deep in our bones, telling us who is the other half of our soul. I didn't expect it to be a vampire I felt that pull to, but life can be funny like that.

Things with Kane haven't been easy, but I wouldn't trade what we have for anything. We fought for each other. We fought a war against common enemies. After everything we've been through, we're stronger together than alone.

Things are simpler for my brother. His mate is a nice shifter girl. She's the granddaughter of an ally. I don't envy his easier path. I'm happy for him.

Colt has found his mate, and no one is happier than our mother. Mom has already met Lydia beforehand, so she embraces Colt's mate with open arms. Alpha Gerard is ecstatic that his granddaughter has gotten picked over the other Alphas' offspring, much to their annoyance. Everyone understands that mates aren't determined by choice, but the older Alphas have a tendency to compete over the oddest of topics.

Mom is practically gushing over Lydia. "She's a lovely girl. Pretty and smart. Colt couldn't do better than her."

"She's the sweetest of my grandkids, but we were worried she wasn't going to find her mate. She spends all her time studying," Constance adds.

"I told you not to worry," Alpha Gerald tells his wife. "I always knew Lydia was going to make a good match. And look at her. She bagged Colton Moonraker's grandson. I say we drink to that."

He waves over a server with a tray of champagne and hands all of us a flute of champagne before taking one for himself. He raises it and declares, "To a bright future between our packs."

"To a bright future," I repeat, clinking my glass against his and everyone else's.

We all take a sip of champagne. The conversation turns quickly to the wedding, and I try to drown out the talk by drinking more. Colt and Lydia are somewhere outside, and I'm not going to check on them. Knowing my brother, he's already trying to get to know his mate in more ways than one.

Besides, I've done my job. The Moon Goddess Ball is an astounding success.

* * *

Colt

"I resent that. You make me sound like a lecher," I grumble. "We just talked."

"Uh-huh." Emory raises a red eyebrow at me. "You didn't take any liberties? No hands wandered?"

I can feel the tips of my ears flushing red from embarrassment. When I brought Lydia outside for some fresh air, I fully intended to only talk and get to know her. Seeing my beautiful mate under the moonlight, with her staring up at me with those blue-gray eyes, I couldn't resist. I wanted to know what her lips tasted like. So… there had been some kissing.

Kissing led to some touching as hands wandered, but our clothes stayed on. At one point, she'd sat on my lap. Lydia was flushed and pretty after all that kissing. My erection had strained against the zipper of that damn suit. It had been difficult to let her sit there much longer, so we'd broken apart. She sat next to me, but then nothing happened after that. Just more kissing with some talking mixed in.

I pause from loading Emory's luggage into the town car so I can glare at her. "You don't get to judge me. You got pregnant before you even knew Kane was your mate."

Emory flicks me in the ear making me yelp in pain. "Don't you dare talk to me like that, Colt Moonraker. I'm still your Alpha."

I clutch my ear then point at her accusingly. "You know what you did. You can't deny it."

"I'm not denying it. I'm not ashamed." She crosses her arms over her chest stubbornly. "I wanted Kane, and I got him. What's your point?"

"Nothing! I literally just met Lydia." I give her a disbelieving look. "Do you want me to get her pregnant and then marry her within the year?"

She shrugs. "You're not getting any younger."

"I'm twenty-one!"

"And I was married with a baby when I was your age." Stunned at this turn in the conversation, I wordlessly open the car door so she can slide into the vehicle. "Just try to get married before you get her pregnant, please."

"Unlike you," I tease.

Emory sticks out her tongue, being silly. This is all an act meant to remind us of when we were kids, I have no doubt. "Call me when something interesting happens."

"I call you every week."

As much as we act like kids around each other, we take our responsibilities to the pack very seriously. I inform Emory about all the updates in Moon Grove that she's not here to see. We've had a system in place for years, and it works.

I close the car door so I can be rid of my sister and she can go back to Crimson Peak. She can go annoy everyone at Castle Graystone over me. I wave as the town car drives off. I love my sister but absence truly does make the heart grow fonder.

* * *

EMORY

It is good to be back home in Crimson Peak. I practically smother Mikey in a hug when I see him. He eventually squirms to get away and runs off to go play. Helga, who has been his nanny for years, runs after him.

My son has endless amounts of energy. He terrorizes everyone with his desire for attention. There's not a single servant in this castle that doesn't cater to his every whim. I'm getting concerned he might grow up spoiled, but it's hard to say no to his cherubic face.

His grandmother, Queen Agatha, dotes on him. Kane is the only person Mikey will listen to. It just takes Kane saying his name in a commanding tone and Mikey will cease the tantrum he's about to throw. Father and son have a special bond–Mikey fears Kane.

Scolding is the only thing that seems to work.

Kane greets me with a kiss, and the relief of being near him again makes me sigh. Even after four years of marriage, I still have a massive crush on this man. His handsome face, his dark hair, high cheekbones, and blue eyes never gets old for me. He is also a good person at heart, and that only makes him more attractive to me.

We haven't seen each other in nearly a month, so we spend some time catching up. There are stories better told in person than over the phone. I tell Kane about the Moon Goddess Ball and Colt meeting his mate. Kane is genuinely curious about the Ball, and I tell him all the details I can remember.

"How does the mating thing work?" he asks. "Is it about compatibility or proximity?"

"No one actually knows," I answer. "All we've been told is that our mate is supposed to be the other half of our soul, the perfect person for us. I don't know if it factors in proximity. Otherwise, my mate would have been someone like Darius."

Kane knows that, at one point in my life, I thought Darius, the son of my father's Beta, would have been my mate. I've been dissuaded about that almost immediately after I met Kane. The pull I feel toward him can't compare. I could only ever love Darius as a friend and nothing more.

Darius has met his mate. She turned out to be the granddaughter of Alpha Nigel of the Bluecrest Pack. They married two years ago and have a child of their own. I'm happy for them, and I'm glad everything turned out well in the end.

Kane's eyebrows furrow. "If mates are supposed to be the perfect person for you, what about couples like your parents?"

I've thought before about my parents and their marriage. I know my mother hadn't been completely unhappy being married to my father, but she hadn't been blissfully happy either. His constant infidelity and selfishness hadn't made him a good husband. She loved him, but he never appreciated her at all.

I frown before answering, "Maybe this person is meant to be perfect for you, but you can still make bad choices? Bernard made a lot of bad choices."

Kane takes my hand and guides us to the bed so we can sit. He keeps holding my hand, his thumb rubbing circles on my fingers. "I don't think Bernard was capable of really loving anyone. He was given a gift of the other half of his soul, and he took it for granted."

"He took a lot of things for granted."

I know that better than anyone. I sacrificed myself to save Lola from being sold off as a feeder to Kane almost five years ago. Bernard let it happen. Everyone was disposable to him once they no longer had any use.

"I think my parents are more of the exception than the rule," I declare, squeezing his hand. "Most mated couples I know seem happy. I'm happy. Aren't you?"

He smiles. "I can't complain."

"That's all we can hope for, really." I tell him. "I'm hoping for the best for Colt. That poor girl has to be married to *him*."

Kane laughs. "Your brother isn't that bad."

"You haven't spent enough time around Colt."

"He's not any worse compared to Lex. And Lex took his sweet time growing up."

Kane's younger brother, Lex, is now regent of Scarlett Thunder. After an exhausting war with the other kingdom, Lex married Princess Opal so their child could become the legitimate heir to the throne. We don't see Lex as much as we would like, but he never complains. The few times I've seen him, Lex has grown into a quieter but dutiful man.

I suppose fatherhood and ruling a kingdom can do that to you.

"I can't wrap my head around Colt being married and having kids," I confess. "He's the same kid who used to eat dirt."

"I heard some people grow out of that," Kane quips. "And have a little faith in your brother. He could surprise you."

"He already has."

Colt had to learn how manipulative Bernard had been. He had to step out from our father's shadow and become his own man to fight for what's right. He is one of my steadiest support systems. I can't imagine being Alpha without him there to help me.

"Colt is the least of our problems," Kane tells me. "Lola has been moodier than usual."

My little sister who used to be the sweetest little girl in the world, the one kid who never got in trouble, has evolved into a moody teenage girl who seems to hate everything.

I am included in everything.

I have become the enemy. It's as if overnight, a stranger has taken over her body and I can barely recognize this creature filled with teenage angst.

No one ever says growing up is easy.

Parenting is no picnic either.

3

SEE MY GIRL

EMORY

I knock on the door of Lola's bedroom. There's loud music playing from inside. When I don't hear a response, I knock on the door again. There's still no response.

"Lola?" I call out. "It's me. Can I come in?"

"What do you want?" she demands.

"I'm back from Moon Grove. I just wanted to see you."

There's an audible sigh. "Fine."

I open the door, and the smile freezes on my face when I see Lola. She's seated on the settee reading through a comic book. Her long dirty blonde hair has been chopped short and unevenly which makes me think she cut it herself. There's a lone streak of red that stands out against the dark blonde.

"Hey," I say, trying not to freak out at her change of appearance. "How have you been?"

She glances up from the comic book she's reading for a second before flipping to the next page. "Fine."

"And the hair?" I ask. "Is this a new thing?"

She shrugs. "I did it last week. I was bored."

"It looks... fun."

That's the word I land on? I panicked.

Lola looks up again from her comic book to stare at me. She appears to be annoyed–like I'm bothering her. "It's just hair."

"I know that, but maybe you could have had someone help you cut your hair? Nettie is great at cutting her hair. She cuts mine."

Her nose wrinkles as she stares at my hair. "No thanks."

I resist the urge to look at my long red hair. I don't think it looks bad. No one has ever said my hair doesn't look good. Maybe I should go check a mirror later.

Wanting to change topics, I question, "What have you been up to while I was gone?"

"Nothing much. Just reading and listening to music."

"What are you reading?"

"It's a graphic novel about a wolf shifter who's also a superhero."

"That sounds nice."

Lola goes back to reading. "Yeah, it is."

Did she just roll her eyes at me?

What has happened to that sweet kid who I used to read bedtime stories to? When was she replaced with this snarky teenager? Lola is sixteen now, and that means she's going to be changing and figuring herself out, but I haven't expected a whole personality overhaul. I remember being a teenager, and I don't think I became a different person overnight.

Refusing to give up, I add, "Colt found his mate. Her name is Lydia. She's from the Nightstone Pack."

"Good for him," Lola replies in a bored tone.

"We're expecting a wedding within the year. That means you could be a flower girl again."

Lola scoffs. "I'm too old to be a flower girl, Emory. I'm sixteen, not six."

"Oh. Right." I'm sputtering in embarrassment now. "You could be a bridesmaid, I think. If Lydia is good with it."

"Whatever."

I sigh, feeling defeated. Lola does not want to engage with me at all. It's like trying to talk to a wall that rolls its eyes at me. I'll try again another day.

"I'll update you about the wedding," I say finally. "If you care at all."

Lola turns up the music, and I can barely even hear myself think. I try to tell her bye, but she's not looking at me at all. Feeling like a rejected dog, I leave her room. Closing the bedroom door behind me, I can only stare at the heavy oak door in dismay.

I tell myself that this is a phase. The real Lola who is sweet and kind will return. I just have to wait out this angsty teenage chapter. This can't last forever.

* * *

COLT

I haven't had the opportunity to visit the Nightstone Pack that much. Their territory is called Nightfall and is one of the furthest from Moon Grove. It takes hours to drive to their location near the mountains. They border on the territory of one of the vampire kingdoms, Sardonia.

The Nightstone family's home is a large three-story house half-covered in ivy. The turrets and the seven-story tower attached to the house must be for defensive purposes. It looks like a fortress. My father tried to attack this pack for their territory over ten years ago, and I can see why he failed.

I stop the large black Jeep Emory and my mom gifted me for my eighteenth birthday. I decide against bringing any of the pack with me, wanting to make this a more casual visit. This is not a diplomatic trip where I have to represent my pack. I'm just a guy visiting a girl at her family home.

At least that's what I want this to be.

I glance up and can see armed men at the top of the tower watching over me. Trying not to show my nervousness, I stroll up the front door of the house like I do this every day. I ring the doorbell and wait. Standing there and waiting for someone to answer the door is nerve-wracking when you know someone is potentially waiting to jump out from the bushes and claw your face off.

Moon Goddess be damned. We're not this paranoid in our pack.

After what feels like an eternity, the front door opens, and Lydia is there dressed casually in a soft sweater and jeans. She smiles when she sees me. "Hi."

I smile back. "Hi."

There's only a second of hesitation before she moves closer to kiss me. It's short and sweet, merely a taste of things to come. She feels so good in my arms, her womanly curves wrapped in a soft sweater. My cock is already trying to say hello.

Lydia looks down and frowns at my shoes. I'm wearing my favorite pair of white sneakers. I can't stand dress shoes. I have a whole collection of vintage sneakers at home.

"You're not scared to get those muddy, right?"

Just the thought is terrifying. It would take me forever to get these shoes clean again if they got mud on them. Confused, I ask, "Why?"

"I'm sorry. I should have told you to wear different shoes," she says. "My grandpa wants you to go on a little hunting trip with us."

That doesn't sound too bad.

"Won't we be shifting?"

She nods her head. "Yes, but the rest of the family is already out in the woods waiting for us, so we'll have to walk for a bit, and they want to meet you in your human form first. They like to hunt big game, and that's usually out in the woods quite a way."

I remember Gerald bragging about taking down a grizzly bear with his brothers years ago.

"And who else is going to be on this hunt with us?"

"Just my dad and my brothers."

My stomach tries to sink to my feet. "How many brothers do you have exactly?"

"Five but only two of them are going to be here today. Jake is in class, Tyler is away on business, and George has a prior engagement."

"This is going to be you, me, your grandpa, your dad, and two of your brothers?"

She nods. "Pretty much."

I try to hide how utterly terrified I am. I've managed to avoid dating girls with older brothers. There's no avoiding this with Lydia. Family is important to shifters, and if Lydia's family doesn't accept me then my life is going to be significantly harder.

"Anything I should know?" I ask. "What topics should I avoid? How should I act?"

Her lips quirk in a smile. "Just be yourself. They'll love you."

That's easy for her to say. I can charm the pants off every woman in her family. Men are a different beast altogether, figuratively and literally. My tricks don't work on them.

"You can't walk out there in those shoes. They'll get ruined," Lydia says. "And your clothes are so nice. You won't want to ruin them. I think you and Jake are about the same height. You can borrow his stuff. He won't care."

Lydia brings me upstairs to one of the bedrooms. She picks up clothes and shoes from her brother's closet and leaves me to get changed. I wouldn't have minded if she stayed to watch me undress. And I would love to return the favor and see her undress, too.

The thought has been plaguing my dreams since I met her at the Ball. Lydia in any state of nudity is my favorite fantasy these days.

Turns out, Jake and I are the same size as his clothes fit me fine. His hunting boots are also a good fit. It's a simple outfit consisting of jeans, a plaid button down and a green vest. Comfortable and functional.

I join Lydia downstairs where she smiles over at me.. "Are you ready to go?" she asks.

"I guess so."

We hunt primarily small game in Moon Grove. I'm just hoping not to embarrass myself in front of her family. I weigh telling her the truth of my inexperience with large animals or hope I can figure out how to do this, should the opportunity arise.

Lydia leads us outside the house toward the woods nearby. Their property goes on for miles.

"Just a heads up. They can get a little competitive. You know how male shifters are."

That's great.

They're going to be competitive.

Isn't this exciting for me?

Unfortunately, I'm more than aware how competitive the men in our species are. I've been in enough fist fights during my school days to know firsthand. Male shifters have a tendency to try and work out their pent-up tensions with their fists. Eventually, they work it out with sharp teeth and claws.

It's a good thing wolf shifters heal fast, or there would be significantly less of us around. The mortality rate would skyrocket from us beating each other to death.

"There they are," Lydia says, raising her hand to wave. "Hey, guys!"

Right outside the thicker forest stands a group of men. They're all tall, muscular, and dark-haired. One of the men looks very similar to Gerald except he has a full beard. The two younger men must be Lydia's brothers. The only resemblance Lydia has to them are the blue-gray eyes.

Gerald's booming voice greets me, "Lydia! Colt! It's about time!"

"Sorry for the delay, Grandpa. I forgot to tell Colt to dress for hunting," Lydia explains. "Luckily, he and Jake are the same size."

I nod, trying my best to be polite. "Thank you for having me."

Gerald pulls me into a bear hug, patting my back before I even know what's happening. He releases me and with an arm around my shoulders, he leads me toward the other men.

"Colt, this is my son, Alcide, Lydia's father, and his sons, Scott and Tommy, her brothers. Boys, this is Lydia's mate, Colt Moonraker."

Alcide's blue-grey eyes narrow in recognition. "Moonraker? Any relation to Bernard Moonraker?"

Curse you, Dad, wherever you are.

I try to hide my wince. "He was my father."

The look Alcide Nightstone gives me could freeze my blood. He is clearly not a fan of my father.

"Come now, Al," Gerald persuades. "We can't choose who our

parents are. And I assure you, Colt landed very far from that asshole of a tree. Right, Colt?"

I nod quickly. "Right. I'm nothing like my father."

Alcide doesn't look like he believes me at all. "We'll see about that."

"Dad," Lydia's voice cuts in. She gives her father a warning look. "You said you'd be nice."

"I'll be nice, darling." I don't know how sincere he's being as he's already turned his back on us. "Let's go hunt."

Gerald slides his arm off my shoulders and follows his son. He enthusiastically repeats, "Let's go hunt!"

Lydia gives me an apologetic look. "They can be a little bit much. They're kind of protective of me?"

Kind of?

I feel like she's severely understating things. I will not be deterred. Her family is going to like me. They have to.

Lydia steps behind a tree to strip down in privacy while the rest of us men do it as a group. We shift into our wolves, and I take a deep breath.

I hope I don't get killed.

4

THE TINIEST MOVES

Colt

Colt

Alpha Gerald leads the hunting party. He moves quickly and effi-
ciently for a wolf of his age. Aside from the silver running through his
dark fur, he's as agile and healthy as his son and grandsons. I don't
know where he gets all this energy from.

I'm at the back of the group with Lydia. Because we are mates, we
can, thankfully, use the mind-link to communicate. She asks, *"Are you
all right?"*

"I'm great," I reply. *"I like being out in the woods. I spent most of my
childhood outdoors."*

*"I'm the same. I would start to get antsy if I'm cooped up inside for too
long."* She nods to a treehouse to our right. *"Dad built that for us when
we were kids. My brothers would ban me from going inside. They said it was
a 'boys only' treehouse."*

"What did they do up there?"

"Whatever boys do when they're together." She shakes her head. Her
wolf is just as beautiful as her human form. *"I always wanted sisters, but
my parents didn't have any more kids after me."*

"I have two sisters, and I've always wanted brothers instead."

"We should switch," she suggests jokingly. *"You can have my brothers. All of them."*

"What would that entail?" I ask with a chuckle.

"From what I've seen, violence and insults. I think my brothers have tried to kill each other more than anything."

"Do they ever do anything to you?"

"I was the baby, so nothing too bad except for that time they lured me into a box and taped it shut. I think they were going to try and mail me somewhere."

"We were trying to sell you off for a motorbike!" Scott chimes in. I hadn't realized she was talking to all of us, but I guess it would be rude not to include her family.

Lydia glares at the back of his head. *"I wasn't talking to you, Scotty. Buzz off!"*

"Be nice!" Alcide chides.

"Don't get rowdy!" Alpha Gerald exclaims. *"You're going to scare away the animals!"*

With all the yapping and stomping around, the animals definitely know we're coming and have run for their lives.

"Seriously, you can have all my brothers," Lydia says. I think she's just talking to me now. *"No take-backsies."*

"I think I'll pass. My sisters are not that bad."

"What are they like?" Then, she adds, *"I know of Alpha Emory, but I've never really gotten to talk to her. I've always admired her, though, since she's not only the youngest Alpha, but she's also a girl. That's pretty cool."*

I live in the shadow of my amazing older sister, and I'm not even upset about it. Emory is not only the first female Alpha of our pack but she's fought and won a war against vampires. And she managed to sneak in having a baby during all of that. Calling Emory Moonraker an overachiever is an understatement.

"She's exactly what you think she's like," I answer. *"Smart, kind, and annoyingly right most of the time. She makes me look like a demon next to her."*

"She's married to a vampire king, right?"

"King Kane of Crimson Peak. He's a good guy. A little moody at times, but I think that's a vampire thing."

"That's also kind of a male shifter thing," Lydia points out. *"Growing up, it's like my brothers were always on their period with all the mood swings."*

"Hey!" Scott calls out, turning to look at us. I guess we're back to a full-on conversation now. *"You don't have room to talk, sis. You threatened to castrate me with a butterknife!"*

"You would have deserved it!"

Tommy laughs, a loud barking sound that makes Scott glare at him. *"What? You totally would have deserved it."*

"What did he do?" I ask just to her–I hope.

"He made a misogynistic joke that women can't be Alphas because they're too emotional."

My eyes widen as I think of my sister.

"This is coming from the guy that punched a wall because his ex-girlfriend spread a rumor he has a small penis," Lydia declares, clearly to everyone.

Scott stares Tommy down. *"You know that's not true. You've seen it."*

Tommy shrugs. *"It was so long ago. I can't recall. Don't try to show us now!"*

"Do you want me to?" he taunts.

"No!" Tommy waves his hands frantically, trying to get him to stop. *"Keep it tucked between your legs!"*

Tommy moves away as Scott seems ready to whip it out and prove a point. Scott chases his brother who insists he does not want to see his penis. The display of immaturity makes me suddenly grateful I don't have a litter of older brothers. Emory is an angel in comparison.

"Did Alpha Emory ever give you a hard time growing up?"

"She dressed me up in dresses and took photos." I hope no one can hear me but her.

Lydia smiles, intrigued. *"And where are these photos?"*

I shake my head, trying to look as innocent as possible. *"Mysteriously disappeared one day. I have no idea where they went."*

"If I ask nicely, can I see them?"

She bats her blue-gray eyes at me, and she's so pretty, I have the urge to do whatever she asks.

I run a hand through my red hair. *"I may be able to unearth them if you ask very nicely."*

She moves closer to me and whispers in my ear, low enough the other men won't be able to hear, *"I can be very nice."*

The bolt of desire shoots through me. The husky quality of her voice makes me think of what she might sound like after sex. I have to close my eyes and start counting backward from twenty to stop my cock from standing at attention. I can't have an erection when her family is five feet away.

"Are you okay?" she asks, concerned.

"Little Colt just needs a minute."

She snorts. *"Little Colt?"*

"He likes you too much."

I open my eyes and see her bright smile. She says, *"I like him too."*

"He's not the only one that likes you."

Her blue-gray eyes soften. *"I'm glad to hear that."*

She nuzzles against me, her soft fur ruffling mine, and I breathe her in. She's so amazing, and I can't believe I'm with her. It's like we've been together forever.

* * *

RAINER

The library at Castle Graystone isn't a place I used to frequent often, but after marrying the castle librarian, I visit the place more than anywhere in the castle if I want to see my wife. I find Willow up on a ladder shelving books. I don't worry she'll accidentally fall as she has the grace of a ballerina while up on that ladder. I've seen her carry the heaviest books up there with no problems.

"Hello, dear," I greet her like we're an old married couple.

Three years isn't that long compared to the longevity of our species. A drop in a very large bucket. Willow and I have a tendency to bicker like a couple who've been together for decades. She would never admit it, but Willow likes the banter.

Willow looks down. "What are you doing here? Don't you and Kane have that meeting?"

"He cancelled because Emory's finally back."

"Oh. I should go see her."

Willow makes her way down the ladder. I can't help but stare at her behind as it makes its way toward me. She notices where my eyes are and rolls hers. I feel no shame.

We're married. I'm allowed to ogle at my wife as much as I want.

"We have rules about the library," she reminds me.

Willow has allowed me a few liberties while we're in the library. Deep kisses and heavy petting are as far as she's let me go in here. Anything more is sacrilege. Having sex around her precious books is a crime she will not tolerate.

I've pointed out to her that we've had sex in our bedroom which has her personal collection of books. That was a mistake. She made me sleep on the couch in the living room that night. Ever since then I've never mentioned that again.

"I know," I reply, resigned to my fate. "Even though it could be fun."

"The library is fun, just not in the salacious way you want it to be."

"What about the aisle with the books about sex?"

She purses her lips primly. "Those are for entertainment purposes. They are not an invitation to recreate them in this sacred space."

Knowing I'm beat and fearing a lecture, I pull Willow closer to me to give her a kiss. She's stiff with annoyance at first, but eventually, she gives in. Kissing Willow has always been a delight. She becomes sweet and pliant in my arms as she gives in to the kiss.

Her eyes stay closed as I pull away. I ask, "How's your day been going?"

"Nothing new." Her blue eyes open, and her expression grows serious. "But I do need to show you something."

She takes my hand and leads me to her desk. Opening a drawer, she pulls out a small stack of papers. She holds them out to me, and I take the stack. They're children's drawings in crayon.

"I found those in Bryony's room," Willow explains.

Our three-year-old daughter's drawing isn't a concern. It's the subject matter in her drawings that makes me pause. There are drawings of wolves in cages, a bloody wolf on the ground with a knife sticking out of its neck and a black sun with a smaller blue circle inside of it.

"Did you ask Bryony why she drew this?" I ask.

"I did. She said she didn't know why she drew them," Willow replies. She taps on the black sun. "She kept repeating that the black sun will devour the moon."

My eyebrows furrow as I try to make sense of this information. "Kids have active imaginations. Maybe she read something in a book or saw some kind of painting."

Willow still looks concerned. "The bleeding wolf is too violent for a child her age to be drawing."

"It could be nothing," I reassure her. "She could have overheard someone recounting a story about the war."

I put down the papers on the mahogany desk. Willow has crossed her arms over her chest. I put my hands on her shoulders. She doesn't pull away from my touch.

"Do you think we should be worried about her?" I ask. "Could it be a witch thing?"

Willow sighs. "I don't know. She's the first vampire child to be born that's not a royal in millennia. I don't know if she'll even manifest magical powers."

"There aren't really any parenting books on how to raise a vampire witch."

"If there were parenting books for this, I would have some idea of what to do."

"Even with books, parenting is still a case-to-case basis where you try your best and hope your kid doesn't grow up to hate you."

"I don't want her to be different. I want her to have a normal childhood."

"No matter what. She'll be safe and loved," I reason. "We'll figure this out. And if we can't, we'll reach out to Ivy and see if she has any idea what's going on with Bryony."

Willow keeps in touch with her niece. Ivy. who was the high priestess of Willow's former coven. Despite her young age, Ivy is a very capable witch. During the Battle of the Red Field, I watched Ivy take down several vampires with her magic. It had been terrifying and incredible to witness.

"It could be nothing," Willow says. "Just Bryony's imagination."

I nod. "It could be nothing."

"But if it isn't nothing…."

"We'll call Ivy."

"We'll call Ivy," she repeats, relaxing. "Ivy will know what to do."

5

IT'S MY PARTY

Lex

Castle Blackmoor is filled with activity as servants prepare the gardens for a party. People have been up early cooking food and decorating the gardens with balloons and streamers. Unlike their previous ruler I'm not prone to having trivial parties all year round. I try to avoid unnecessary expenses and go for more low-key events.

The nobles don't say it to my face, but they disapprove of my thrifty management and way of living. They call me practically vulgar for worrying about pennies like a commoner. I don't really care what they say about me. None of them know about the dire state of the royal treasury after the war Scarlett Thunder lost four years.

Wars are notoriously expensive, and King Peter had thrown every bit of gold at his armies all so he could punish my brother. Whatever remained in the treasury after King Peter's humiliating defeat at the Battle of the Red Field had to be given over to other kingdoms for reparations. I had to get massive loans in my first year ruling as regent to ensure Scarlett Thunder didn't collapse in financial ruin. We are in a much better place financially now with efforts to improve the economy, but we still have a few more lean years to go through before I can breathe easier.

I only spend money if I have to, but I make exceptions. My son's birthdays are one such exception. Cole is three-years-old today, and he's old enough that he understands what birthdays mean. At least, he understands what his birthday is.

A kid's birthday party isn't going to bankrupt me, so we're serving good food and having a massive cake, as well as the best blood available. Cole has been excited all week, and I've given in to his request for a petting zoo. A kid only turns three once. My son is getting a petting zoo.

I enter Cole's bedroom. Sarah has been Cole's nanny since his birth, and she tries her best, but Cole always manages to make a mess of the room. There's always a toy out of place. I pick up a turtle stuffed toy off the floor and throw it over to the open toy chest in the corner.

Sarah is busy trying to get Cole dressed which is a task easier said than done. She's managed to get him in pants, but as soon as he sees me, he abandons her.

"Daddy!" he yells excitedly.

Cole runs to me, and I kneel down so I can hug him properly. His little arms encircle my neck, and I smile. No matter what day-to-day troubles I have to fix, and the headaches they cause me, just holding my son in my arms makes everything worth it. Despite his parentage, Cole is the sweetest boy and possesses none of the faults his mother and I have in spades.

I pull back to look at Cole's round face. His pale blue eyes are bright with excitement.

"Good morning, birthday boy," I say. "How did you sleep?"

"It was good," he replies. "Can we have the party now?"

I chuckle and run my fingers through his hair. It's the exact same platinum blond as mine. His bangs are getting a little long. I should get someone to cut it soon.

"The party won't be for another hour. All your guests still have to arrive." I add in a whisper, "And the animals are still on their way."

His blue eyes are wide with joy. "Is the turtle going to be there?"

I nod. "The tortoise will be there."

"And the sloth?"

"The sloth is coming too."

Other kids might like more exciting animals like horses or elephants, but my son loves the ones that move slowly. The less they move, the better. I don't know why. Cole is a bit odd, but I love him even more for it.

"Yay!" Cole turns to Sarah who is standing behind him with his shirt. "Sarah, I'm going to see a turtle and a sloth!"

Sarah smiles fondly. "That's great, Your Highness."

I get to my feet and pat the top of Cole's head. "You be good for Sarah, and get dressed. You can't show up to your party without a shirt."

Cole runs to Sarah immediately. He lifts his hands up so she can put his shirt on him. Sarah quickly curtsies to me before going back to getting Cole dressed. I leave the room and go check on the gardens to see how things are going.

The food is prepared and ready to be served. On tables there are an array of snacks for the children such as chicken nuggets, little sandwiches, and crackers. Most of the tables are set up with goblets for blood, since that is mostly what we consume, but on a day like this, we will also celebrate with food. There's also the start of the party, the multi-tiered cake in white frosting decorated with little green turtles.

The nobles and their children should be arriving soon. While the nobles do not care for me, none of them would dare snub a party invitation. Cole is going to be their king someday, and it wouldn't look good for any of them if their kid missed his birthday party. And I know they would take any opportunity to suck up and gain more advantage in court.

The animal handlers have arrived with the petting zoo. The servants help set up little pens for the animals to be kept in. I watch as the animals are led into the pens. The selection of animals is more diverse than I expected.

I check with the servants for last minute things I need to approve, but the party seems ready. The guests will arrive soon. The noble children are dressed well in expensive garments meant to show off their parents' wealth. I should have known the nobles would rather sacrifice their children's comfort over appearances.

Cole is dressed more plainly in comparison, but no one says a word. The noble children hang on to his every word. He doesn't have to raise his voice to get people's attention. They follow his lead without question.

"Your son is a natural born leader," Queen Olga tells me, appearing by my side. "It shouldn't be a surprise considering his lineage."

I have invited the vampire royals that I thought would be amenable to come. The Queen of Sardonia is a long-time ally to my birth kingdom. And she has come with her great-granddaughters.

I look at her, trying to gauge if she's giving a compliment or an insult. It's no secret what she and the other vampire royals thought of Cole's late grandfather. King Peter didn't make a ton of friends in his lifetime. That has not been an accident.

"He's *nothing* like his grandfather."

"I meant, he takes after the Alexander kings. He has that quality your grandfather and your father had. And what your brother has."

Unlike me. I've always been the spare. I'm not meant to rule a kingdom unlike my brother. A twist of fate is the only reason the crown of a foreign kingdom has landed on my head.

The animal handler is telling the kids not to touch the sloth. Sloths aren't known to be part of petting zoos, and we only have one as a special request. Cole is listening intently to the animal handlers' instructions. He stops a boy from reaching up and touching the sloth.

Cole says something and the boy nods. They're smiling at each other. There's no bad blood. Ah, how nice and simple it is to just be a child.

"I appreciate you coming," I say to Queen Olga. "I know you don't like leaving the mountain if you can't help it."

"It's good for my great-granddaughters to get out and socialize. They'll be better prepared for their futures the more they know of the other kingdoms."

"Prepared? Aren't the twins only four-years-old?"

"They won't be four forever." She gives me a look. "I'm sure you're aware that this is not just a social visit. Every girl in this party could be the next queen of Scarlett Thunder."

There is no end to the scheming and politicking in court. Even at a children's party. I look at the children dressed in their finest clothes sitting on the grass, and I want to scoff at how ridiculous this all is. All of them are too young to already be pawns in their parents' desires for advantageous matches.

"I would prefer it that any talk of my son's future marriage prospects not be a topic for a few more years."

"Come now, Lex. It's always been the way of things. Your father had Kane temporarily engaged twice before he was even of age."

"I remember."

As a second son, my hand in marriage hadn't been as coveted. My parents hadn't bothered with getting me engaged for political purposes as a child. By the time my father died and Kane became the new king, he didn't bother using me as a pawn that way. I have been grateful as I might have ended up in a loveless marriage.

That thought reminds me that I am in a loveless marriage.--but for different reasons. This was my choice. For my son.

I look around the gardens and can't find my wife anywhere. Checking my watch, I see that she's over an hour late to the party. I hadn't bothered with trying to find her earlier as I didn't think a mother should have to be reminded about her own son's birthday.

"Will you excuse me for a moment, Queen Olga? I have a matter to attend to."

She nods, and I walk away, trying to keep my composure and not let my anger show. I make my way back into the castle and head to the east wing where Opal's bedroom is located. I open her bedroom door without knocking but stop in place as I find Opal sitting on the bed, a man between her legs.

Opal moans loudly as she grabs the man's dark hair. This is not an unfamiliar sight for me. The past four years have been like this. Fidelity hasn't ever been a part of my marriage, at least not on Opal's side.

"Opal," I bark out her name.

The man between her legs immediately gets away from her. He stands and turns so I can see his face. He's a nobleman, and I can't recall his name, but I remember he's married. His wife and child must be at the garden party.

"Your Majesty," he says, nervously.

"Go," I command.

He practically sprints from the room.

I sigh, running a hand over my face. This is not how I wanted this day to go.

"Really, Lex?" Opal says, annoyed. "Can't you give me a little privacy?"

"I give you all the space you want."

"Yes, but this only happens because you barely look at me most of the time!" Her voice rises as she grows angrier. "The lengths I have to go through for you to even notice me! You catch me with a man, and you don't even get jealous!"

I snort. "You want me to be jealous? You hate me."

"I'm your wife!" she shrieks. "You're supposed to love and cherish me! I don't even exist to you!"

I look at Opal's angry face. She's always been pretty, but her personality diminishes that fact. Any physical attraction I may have had to her withered in the unsatisfying wasteland of our marriage. What secret hopes I harbored at the beginning of our union that it could be a happy one have long been snuffed out.

"Opal, I don't care who you sleep with," I tell her. "What I care about is that today is your son's birthday, and you're missing the party."

Opal gets off the bed and goes to her vanity table. She fusses over her appearance, running a brush through her messy dark hair. "Cole probably hasn't even noticed I'm not there!"

"He will notice." I catch her gaze in the mirror and insist, "Get yourself together, and come to the party. Don't make me have to drag you there kicking and screaming."

She grabs one of the perfume bottles on the vanity table and throws it at me. I dodge and the bottle hits the wall, disintegrating into glass shards.

"Come to the party or else," I add, unperturbed. "I mean it, Opal."

"Fine!" she retorts.

I leave her to go back to the party. Opal and I may hate each other, but I'm not going to let that hurt Cole. He deserves the best. If I have to bend over backward to create a better world for him than I will.

6

AT FIRST BLOOD

Colt

I've hunted lots of times either with my pack or alone. As a wolf shifter, it's in my blood to do so. The selection of prey in Moon Grove is limited to small and mid-size prey. The largest thing I've hunted with my pack is a wild boar which is a rare occasion considering how tricky they can be to tussle with. On my own, I've mostly hunted rabbits and squirrels.

'What are we hunting?' I ask through the mind-link.

'Deer,' Lydia answers.

Gerald and the other men stop, and I almost bump into Scott. I turn to Lydia in confusion, and she nods toward her grandfather.

'It's a stag,' Gerald hisses before breaking into a run.

We follow him with no hesitation. Despite never visiting this particular forest before, I'm familiar with this kind of terrain, and I jump over tree roots and duck underneath low branches. I'm fast, but Lydia is stealthy, slipping down narrow paths and easily overtaking the men until she's running beside Gerald.

The stag has realized what danger it's in and tries to get away, running as fast as his hooves can carry him. his large, dark body is unmistakable, standing out against the greenery. We reach a river and the stag goes in, the water high enough to reach its underbelly. It crosses the body of water quickly, reaching the embankment on the other side.

Gerald is just as fast, though, and knows the terrain well. He rushes across the river and catches up with the animal as it pulls itself out of the water, sinking his teeth into its left back haunch. The stag kicks out, and Gerald backs off, not wanting to get kicked in the face. The rest of us rush across the cold water, ignoring the chill as we watch the stag take off into the forest.

I shake off the water from my fur. *'I thought you had him.'*

'I did that on purpose,' Gerald replies. *'The stag is bleeding, so he'll be easier to track.'*

'It's more fun this way,' Scott explains.

'It extends the hunt,' Lydia says. *'Cause the chase is half the fun.'*

'Come on,' Alcide calls out. 'He's getting away.'

We rush into the woods, following the trail of blood left from the bite in the stags leg. The scent of iron is overwhelming as I keep my nose low to the ground and follow behind the others, Lydia practically leading the way down the twisting, brush-covered path.

'Come on, boys,' Gerald calls back to us. *'Get to it before the stag gets too far away.'*

Gerald is one of the biggest wolves I've ever seen, easily reaching six feet and his fur flies as he cuts through the trees and around corners. His son and grandsons are smaller with fur of various shades of gray. But it's the beautiful female wolf at the front of the pack that I can't keep my eyes off as we begin to close the gap on the wounded stag that seems to understand that he's running for his life.

I'm not as large as Gerald but bigger than his grandsons. I would like to get in on the kill, but I'm behind all of them since I don't know the path. When we take a turn off the trail into the trees, I have a feeling the stag is running blind now, just trying to get away, and I might have a chance to catch up with the others and overtake them. I can track with the best of them. Maybe I can get to the stag first.

Gerald howls, throwing back his head. We answer back with our own howls and from a distance we hear howls from other wolves. I wonder if those are his pack mates back in the village or if others are out here hunting as well. Gerald starts running even faster, his large paws leaving imprints on the earth. I pass Lydia's brothers and catch up with her father.

We run through a briar patch that tugs at my fur before we come to a stop in front of a thick row of shrubbery next to a pile of stones and a thick copse of trees. The stag is backed against the dead end of trees with nowhere to go. We circle him, preventing him from moving far. The stag rears back, ready to attack with his antlers. Gerald leaps at him from behind, sinking claws and teeth into its hide.

The stag tries to shake Gerald off, and we pounce at him, attacking from all sides. He fights valiantly, managing to shake off Scott and throwing him to the ground. He can't fight forever, not as we tear at his flesh. I bite at the animal's neck, digging through muscle and sinew until I reach bone. There's a sickening snap as I break his neck.

The stag goes down, falling to the ground with a loud thud. We all step back, our muzzles bloody. We're panting, our hearts beating quickly from the exertion and adrenaline. Lydia comes over and licks at my muzzle, congratulating me for a job well done.

Gerald has shifted back to his human form. He bends down to the stag and dips his fingers to its bloody neck. He walks over to me, and I shift back to my human form as well, not caring that I'm naked in front of everyone, including my mate. The blood is still warm as Gerald paints my cheek with it.

"Welcome to the family," he says with a grin.

The rest of the family howls in agreement. Being pack animals, feeling accepted by my mate's family has me lifting my head in pride. My mate's pack has accepted me as their own. I smile back, satisfied and feeling like I'm king of the world.

* * *

EMORY

I'd just finished unpacking my final suitcase when Willow knocked on my bedroom door. I'd welcomed her in, and now, we're seated at the small dining table in my suite. Helga has brought me a small lunch from the kitchens, consisting of thick steak sandwiches and a yogurt parfait for dessert. Of course, Willow is sipping on a goblet of blood as she asks me a thousand questions about the Moon Goddess Ball and my family tradition.

I'm trying to explain the mate bond to her, but it's complicated and not something most Vampires can relate to. She asks, "Is it like love at first sight?"

"Not really," I explain. "It doesn't usually happen the first time you see the person, though it does have to do with the full moon and our age. It's very complicated, honestly. There's just this sudden new awareness of this person. You feel drawn to them, and there's this *rightness* when you're with them."

She seems to be thinking over my answer. "If Kane had been a shifter, do you think you would have known he was your mate sooner?"

"Maybe. I really don't know. I also hadn't shifted and met my wolf yet at the time we met so I have no idea how that would factor into it."

"What was it like for your brother?"

"He couldn't stop staring at his mate. I think he would have thrown her over his shoulder and ran out of the room caveman style if her grandparents weren't right there."

She laughs like she thinks I'm joking, though I'm not. "Can shifters just do that?" she asks.

"Drag our mates from a crowd of people? I've heard some truly unhinged stories. When it comes to mates, shifters tend to lose it."

"You didn't."

"I had a child and then fought in a war all within the same year," I point out. "I would say I had plenty of time to get used to the idea that Kane was my mate."

Willow nods, conceding. "You're one for the history books, Emory."

I try not to think about how one day someone may be writing

books about my life and the things I've done. It could drive a girl insane from overthinking. All I want to do is take everything a day at a time instead of worrying about what future generations will think of my actions. I'll probably be long dead by then anyway.

"I shudder to think what Colt is going to be doing with his mate," I admit. "He has always been the troublemaker. I am the responsible one, and Lola is the sweetheart. Well, she used to be."

Willow, who has been close to my little sister since Lola moved here, doesn't seem surprised. She remarks, "Lola will outgrow it. She's just in her teen angst era."

"I know, but any time I'm around her, I get the feeling she's judging me." I cup my cheeks in my hands woefully. "She thinks I'm lame."

Willow doesn't disagree. "Well…"

I stare at her in shock. "Do you think I'm lame?"

"I do not think you're lame. I think you're amazing."

"But?"

"But you're Lola's primary parental figure…" she reminds me. "And that makes you lame to her by default."

"No!" I exclaim in dismay. "I'm still so young. I'm only twenty-five!"

"That's old for a sixteen-year-old." Willow reaches across the table to pat my hand. "It's not personal."

"How can this *not* be personal? This is what I get for being a good person my entire life? I should have rebelled in high school and just had fun." Willow snorts and I shoot her a sharp look and tell her, "You're way older than me. How are you not lame?"

"I'm not related to Lola. That's enough."

I frown, wanting to pout like a child from the unfairness of it all. "I hope you know that once Bryony grows up, she's going to think you're lame too."

"That's never mattered to me," Willow says. "And I don't have to worry about the mating thing with her, so I'm fine."

The reminder that Lola will be old enough to shift into her wolf form and find her mate someday makes me want to cry more than anything else. Dealing with the teenage angst is bad enough, but all the madness with mating? She's growing up so fast, and soon, she won't even need me anymore. Where has the time gone? I've been too focused on being an Alpha, a mother,, and a good wife to realize it's slipping through my fingers.

"I can't even think about Lola finding her mate," I confess. "It feels like yesterday she was this tiny baby I held in my arms. And in no time, she'll be a grown woman."

"That's pretty much what being a parent is supposed to be like."

"Well, make it stop."

Willow rolls her blue eyes. "I'll get on that."

We both giggle, but I can't help but think time is going by too quickly. I wonder if Kane thinks about that. One day, I'll die, and he'll still have a great deal of life ahead of him.

The thought makes me stop laughing. Nothing in life is fair.

7

LOVESTRUCK ALL OVER

Colt

After we bring the stag back to the house, Tommy and Scott are given the task of processing the meat so it can be eaten for dinner later. Lydia's family doesn't seem to care what we do in the few hours before dinner. She leads me upstairs to her bedroom which is very neat and organized.

It's very utilitarian with a cork board filled with dates and times. There are study guides and notes all over her desk. The room isn't flowery and instead has a minimalistic feel to it. The space still smells like Lydia—pears, musky flowers, and vanilla.

I watch as Lydia dumps all our hunting clothes covered in dirt and leaves into a hamper. I've taken off the hunting boots and am standing barefoot on the dark blue carpet. We are both wearing clothes that don't fit us well from one of the caches near where we killed the stag, so neither of us looks our best.

I see my reflection on the full-length mirror in the room. My red hair has a leaf or two in it. There's dirt all over my arms and a line of dried red blood on my cheek. I am a mess. Lydia isn't any better with her tangled blonde hair that looks like birds could make a nest out of it.

She catches my eye and smiles. "Let's get cleaned up."

I glance at the closed door of her bedroom. "Are you sure? Your family could hear us."

Lydia rolls her eyes. "With the number of girlfriends my brothers have snuck into this house over the years, it would be hypocritical of them to get mad now."

I scratch the back of my head. "I'm just trying to make sure they don't hate me and avoid any awkwardness."

She rolls blue-gray her eyes. "Since when do you get scared of getting caught by parents?"

"What do you mean?"

"You have a reputation, Colt," she says. "Even before we met, I heard about you getting caught with two girls at Alpha Nigel's house two years ago."

"I was attending a wedding. Spirits were high, and there was alcohol," I explain, sheepishly. "And it was three girls, not two." I wink at her.

Lydia's blonde eyebrows raise in surprise. "I'm impressed. I'm not even mad."

I can feel a flush overtaking my face. I don't easily get embarrassed, but discussing a foursome you had before you met your mate is a first for me.

"That was all before you," I say. "I only want you now."

"I know," she replies, easily. "Your giant cock has made me very much aware of that."

My dick wasn't so excited during the hunt, but as soon as we got back to the house, I went hard as a rock again. It could be the lingering adrenaline or just seeing Lydia look so disheveled like she got fucked in the woods. I'm definitely hard now staring at her with that hooded look in her eyes.

I glance down at my cock and see the bulge in my pants. I try to think unsexy thoughts, but that goes out the window when Lydia goes to the ensuite bathroom and beckons me over like a siren.

I stop at the doorway and watch as she turns on the shower and waits for the water to get warm before stripping off her clothes. Her body is just as I've imagined it—ample breasts and lots of curves. My mouth begins to water as she steps under the stream of steaming water. She looks over her shoulder at me suggestively, and I don't need any more hints to join her in the shower. I quickly take off my borrowed clothes and rush over to her. She giggles and wraps her arms around me.

Her hair is a dark shade of gold beneath the shower stream. Dirt melts away from her skin, and my hands can't help but trace the curve of her hips. My lips meet hers in a rush, and she opens for me, letting me know she's just fine with the direction my mind has gone. She leans into me as my hands explore her, tracing over her warm skin, cupping her large breasts, and slipping between her legs to feel the warmth of her cunt.

She gasps as two of my fingers plunge inside of her, my thumb circling her clit. I pull her back to lean against my chest, and she can only moan as my fingers move in and out of her. I can't help but nibble and suck at her neck, leaving purple welts along her shoulder.

I cup a breast in my other hand, pinching and tugging on the peak of her nipple. Her breathing becomes shallower as she can do nothing but let me pleasure her.

"Colt," she moans. "Please."

"Please what?"

"Claim me, mate," she whispers.

"Here?" I ask when she growls low in her throat. Kissing her shoulder as an apology, I say, "I'm not sure that's such a good idea for our first time, baby."

"At least let me come." She bats her eyelashes at me as I continue to finger her.

I grin and kiss her again, increasing my pace. I slip a third finger into her. She gasps, and her body begins to spasm around my fingers. Eventually, her breaths become more shallow and the shuddering finishes. I take my fingers out of her and just hold her as she recovers. My cock feels like it might explode with how impossibly hard it feels but I ignore it.

Lydia turns around and kisses me, her tongue parting my mouth to tangle with my own. Her hand trails down my abdomen till she's grasping my cock. Her grip is tight as she tugs on my dick with her fist. It feels so good, I lean into her, ready to follow behind her and cum all over her belly. It doesn't take much until I'm grunting, spurting between us. I groan into her kiss in relief.

She kisses me back, her hands on either side of my face now. I can't help but think I've found myself the perfect mate. I never want to leave her side again.

* * *

Emory

I've just finished breakfast a couple of days after returning home when one of the maids lets me know I have a phone call in Kane's office. Alarmed, I rush in to take the call. It's not the appointed time for Colt to call me, and Mother doesn't usually call this early in the morning.

"Hello?" I say into the receiver.

"I'm going to marry her!" my brother declares.

No longer worried, I let out a chuckle. I knew he was planning to visit Lydia in her pack lands. I'm not surprised he wants to marry her. More amused than anything else. "When?" I ask. "Are we hoping for a wedding in the winter or early next year?"

"I want to marry her now. As soon as possible."

"Slow down now, brother." There's the impulsive, annoying Colt again. "Have you even proposed to her?"

"Not yet, but I will."

"And have you gotten her family's blessing?"

"I'm working on it."

"Are you aware that weddings take time and preparation? Or are you just going to drag Lydia toward the nearest officiant?" I picture that and laugh again.

"How hard can it be to plan a wedding?" I hear the sarcasm in his voice.

"It's pretty much like planning a Moon Goddess Ball which you would know nothing about since you left that to me and Mom to work on while you fucked off in the woods."

"I helped you in the way I knew best," he claims. "By getting out of your hair so you could plan the Ball and not waste time trying to kill me."

"You know, technically, Darius is my Beta. I could get rid of you, and I'd be just fine," I warn him.

He snorts, not believing my threat for a minute. "You would miss me. Darius is too nice. You'd be bored within days."

"I would get so much done because Darius would actually be dependable and not chasing after every hot girl he sees."

"Darius is married with a kid. He shouldn't be chasing any girl at all."

"Exactly. Darius would never be caught having an orgy in another's Alpha's house."

"It wasn't an orgy!" He sounds defensive about something he used to be proud of.

"What else would you call it?"

"A foursome with willing adults."

"I'm surprised Alpha Nigel didn't threaten you at gunpoint to marry his granddaughter since she was part of that."

"Sally is not ready to settle down yet. She just needed a release from all the stress of school."

"And you were just being a good guy and offering that release?"

"What can I say? I'm very altruistic."

"We should have a statue of you built next to the one of the Moon Goddess in Her temple," I mutter sarcastically.

Colt laughs for a moment but then continues in a more serious tone. "I didn't know it would be like this. People always say finding your mate is wild and messy, but this is…"

"Peaceful?"

Colt's voice softens as he agrees, "I always felt like I was running from girl to girl trying to find something I kept missing, and now I have it."

"Home."

"Yeah, it feels like home."

I smile, completely understanding what he's talking about. I look down at the framed photos on Kane's desk. There's a family photo of me, Kane, and Mikey. Our wedding photo where we both look so happy and content hangs on the wall behind me.

"I'm glad you found your mate, Colt," I say sincerely. "It's about time you settled down."

"I'm glad too," he replies. "I was scared for a time that finding my mate would be like what Mother experienced with Father."

"Our parents aren't the norm. Father was the problem. He couldn't love anyone. Even the magic of mating wasn't going to change him."

Our late father had been a selfish man. He'd been unfaithful to our mother, always taking her for granted and she stayed with him throughout all the hell he had unleashed on our family and our pack. Our mother wasn't happy, and she was never truly free until his death. Now, she's content with helping us run the pack, but there are times when I wonder if she's longing for something more in her life.

"I know, but I'm still worried that maybe I'm more like him than I thought."

"You're nothing like him. And you could never could be," I assure my brother. Colt is quiet for a moment. I wish I could see his face so I could try to gauge what he's thinking. "Colt, listen to me," I persist. "You are nothing like Bernard. He never cared about anything but himself. Anyone can see how much you care for our pack."

"Do you think he started that way? I don't think he was born like that and somewhere along the way he turned into a monster."

"He made his choices. There's nobody else to blame. It's his actions and his unwillingness to face the consequences that defined him in the end. You could never be like that."

"I'd like to think not," he replies, softly. "When we were kids, he was everything I wanted to be."

"You wanted to be like the person he was pretending to be. And I wanted to be like him too. He was my hero too, Colt," I tell him. "And we made a promise, remember? That we would be better than him."

"I can't imagine treating Lydia the way he treated Mother."

"I don't know Lydia that well, but she doesn't seem like the type to stick around if you treat her badly—mate or not. And Alpha Gerald would kill you if you ever hurt his granddaughter."

These past few years I've gotten to know the Alphas of the other shifter packs, and despite Alpha Gerald's more jovial predisposition, he isn't the kind of man a person crosses. There are stories of his unforgiving nature and steely determination when it comes to his enemies. When my father tried to take over his territory, the Nightstone Pack stood strong and unbreakable against the attack. Our pack suffered a crushing defeat that sent Bernard running away with his tail between his legs.

"Not only would Alpha Gerald kill me. Lydia's father and five brothers would help him," Colt says.

"You always wanted brothers," I point out. "And now you're getting a whole litter of them. Aren't you happy?"

"I'm ecstatic. Brothers are way better than annoying sisters."

"I resent that."

"Cry me a river, Emory," he quips. "I have to get back to work. You have a great day."

"Bite me, Colt."

"Make Kane do that instead. I heard he likes biting."

I grimace in disgust. "You are so gross."

"I'm not the one with the biting fetish. Bye, Em!"

Colt hangs up, and I glare at the phone, wishing he were here in person so I could give him a wedgie, like we did when we were kids. I'm glad he's getting married so another woman can deal with him. Little brothers are the worst--but they're also the best.

8

THE HARDEST QUESTION

Colt

I tell myself I shouldn't be nervous. Other shifters will be able to smell it on me like blood in the water. There's no real reason for the Nightstones to object to me marrying Lydia except for any lingering bad blood because of my father. Alpha Gerald doesn't seem to be holding my father's sins against me which assures me that he'll be supportive toward the union.

Lydia's brothers are loud and like to mess around, but they're receptive to discussing guy stuff like cars and sports. They shouldn't be hard to win over. It's Lydia's father I'm not sure about. Alcide seems not to like me, though he hasn't been unwelcoming. He's been more aloof than anything else. I'm hoping he won't be an obstacle.

There's a knock on my bedroom door. I'm in the middle of getting dressed, sliding a gray sweater over my head, but I call for whoever it is to come in. It may be summer, but I've learned that the weather is always colder over at Nightfall, so the sweater will be needed.

My mother enters the room, smiling when she sees me. "You're still here," she says. "I thought I might've missed you."

"I'm on my way out," I reply. "Did you need something?"

"Since you're going to propose to Lydia, I couldn't let you show up there without a ring."

She moves closer to me and slides her engagement ring off her finger. The marquise cut emerald is set in between bouquets of small diamonds on a golden band. She hands it to me, and I stare at it apprehensively.

"Mom, I can't," I tell her. "That's your ring."

"My marriage might not have been the best match, but it's not this ring's fault," she explains. "This was your Grandma Emory's ring, and she and your Grandpa Colton were very happy together. Your great-grandmother owned this ring before her, and she also had a good marriage." She takes my hand and places the ring in my palm, adding, "Your father and I might have been a fluke. I'm sure you and Lydia will have more luck with it."

I stare down at my mother. I've been taller than her since I was sixteen, and she looks almost brittle to me. Her strength is something I've witnessed and admired for years, but the damage Bernard has done to her isn't something she can hide completely. There must have been a time when she'd been young and hopeful about marrying her mate only for her to be bitterly disappointed.

"Are you sure?" I ask. "I can get Lydia a new ring."

"I'm sure, Colt. The ring should stay within the family." She reaches up and kisses me on the cheek. "I just want you to be happy, my son."

Her love for me almost feels like something physical, wrapping around me like a warm hug. Despite what my father has done, my mother's love is a constant.

"I will be, Mom. Thank you."

The drive to Nightfall feels longer than usual as I try to keep myself calm and focus on the task at hand. Lydia isn't home, I know. She's out hanging out with her friends celebrating passing an important test at school. She'd been giddy when she'd informed me over the phone that she'd passed. I haven't told her that I'm coming over to her place to talk to her family because, in the small chance this all goes badly, I'd rather she doesn't know about it until she has to.

That, and I'd like to have her father's permission before I surprise her with the ring.

The fortress of a house comes into view, and I park my vehicle in the driveway. I wave to the guards who I know are watching me from the tower as I make my way to the front door. A blonde woman that looks a lot like Lydia opens the door. She's more plump and shorter, but the resemblance to my mage with the golden hair and full lips is unmistakable.

"You must be Colt," she says. "I'm Amanda, Lydia's mom."

"It's nice to meet you, Mrs. Nightstone."

"Call me Amanda." She opens the door wider to let me in. "We're going to be family soon enough." She gives me a warm hug, and I like her already.

I follow her inside the house, listening for any other voices to gauge who else might be home. I mostly hear loud music from the second floor. It could be one of Lydia's brothers. The lingering scents in the house make it hard to guess who is here now and who has been here recently.

"Lydia isn't home. She's out with her friends," Amanda explains.

"I know. I'm actually here to talk to Alpha Gerald and Alcide, if they're home."

"Alcide is chopping wood in the back with Tyler and Georgie. I'll go get him."

"I don't want to intrude. I can wait till he's done."

"He can leave the wood chopping to the boys. He always complains about how sore his back gets after doing that chore anyway, but don't tell him I told you that."

I mime zipping my mouth, and she smiles. She leads me to a room on the first floor which turns out to be a study.

"Gerald is just taking a nap in his office. We have to peel him from his chair for dinner each night."

"I heard that, Amanda!" Gerald calls out as she opens the door. He doesn't look mad when we enter the study, his gaze alight with amusement. He's seated in front of the fireplace in a large leather chair. A huge fur blanket covers his lap. He does look very comfortable.

When he sees me, he adds, "And you caught yourself a young one. Where did you find him?"

"Outside. He wants to speak to you and Al."

"This should be interesting." Gerald gets up from the huge chair and goes to his desk to take a seat. "What do you want, Colt?"

I probably should've called ahead of time so they were expecting me. Lesson learned.

Amanda has left us, closing the study door behind her. I cautiously step forward so I'm standing across the room from the Alpha. "I would rather wait for Alcide to be here for this conversation."

Gerald raises his dark eyebrows at me. "This must be something serious then."

I can't deny that, so I nod, not trusting my mouth not to betray me and show how nervous I feel. We don't have to wait long for Alcide who enters the study wearing a flannel shirt stained with sweat. He glances at me warily before moving to stand beside the chair, forming a united front with his father. My heart begins to beat faster despite my attempts at trying to remain calm. We remain pleasantries, but my hands are shaking.

"Go on then," Gerald urges. "What's your important business?"

"My business here involves Lydia." I clear my throat and continue, "I'm here to ask for your blessing to marry her."

Alcide chuckles, crossing his arms over her chest. Her father is a few inches shorter than me, but he's more muscular, his biceps large and intimidating. Despite being middle aged, he clearly still works out. As he stands next to Gerald, he looks like a younger version of his father. I can't tell if that's a happy chuckle or if I should be worried.

"Shouldn't you be asking Lydia if she wants to marry you instead of us?" Alcide retorts. "You should know by now, my daughter hardly needs my permission to do anything."

"Yes, but I also know that this pack is traditional, and I wouldn't want to disrespect either of you by not asking for your input."

Most shifter packs are traditional and old-fashioned. No matter what age or gender, we always look to the Alpha for approval and permission. My pack is progressive by most standards as having a female Alpha is very rare. It's happened before but usually with a female Alpha sharing the power with her mate in an equal partnership.

Emory is more the exception than the rule. I provide support but I don't hold equal power with her in any way. I'm more of a glorified manager than anything else. I hold a higher position than her Beta, but I'm still not the Alpha.

Alcide looks to his father who merely shrugs. Gerald says, "I have no objections."

"Dad," Alcide chides. "At least try to think about it first."

"What's there to think about? Lydia likes him. I like him. They're fated mates. Why would I say no?"

"He's…" Alcide glances at me before hissing, "he's Bernard Moonraker's son. It hasn't been that long since his pack attacked us and tried to take our territory."

"That's ancient history, Al. It's been over twenty years since all that happened. Let it go." He opens a box on the table next to his chair which contains cigars. "We should be celebrating. Our Lydia is getting married!"

Gerald stands up and takes out three cigars from the box. He hands one to his son and one to me.

"Do you smoke, Colt?"

"Uh, sure." I don't smoke, but he doesn't know that, and I'm not saying no.

I move closer to take the cigar, and Gerald lights them with a silver lighter. The Nightstone Pack's coat of arms is engraved on it, a full moon surrounded by three wolves.

The first inhale of smoke makes me cough.

Gerald lets out a barking laugh and pats me on the back. "Inhale slowly, boy. You're supposed to savor it."

I follow his instructions, but I can't say I enjoy it. I don't complain as my pride won't let me. Gerald goes to the side of the study where he has a decanter of brandy and glasses on a table. He pours us all a glass, and we drink by the fireplace like we do this all the time. Maybe they do.

"I thought at least Tyler would be married by now," Gerald says. "I didn't think Lydia would be the first to go."

"She doesn't have to go yet," Alcide mutters, glaring at his glass of brandy. "We don't even know if she'll say yes to the proposal."

"Now, Al…." Gerald puts an arm around his son's broad shoulders. "Let bygones be bygones. Colt hasn't done anything against us, and your little girl has to grow up eventually. You weren't that much older when you and Amanda got married."

"Amanda wasn't about to go to healer school. Lydia has worked so hard for this, and she'll be too busy to plan a wedding…." His gray-blue eyes stare into me. "You're not going to elope, are you? Lydia deserves to have the wedding of her dreams."

He says 'elope' like it's a dirty word. I'm right that their family is very old-fashioned and traditional. If I skipped trying to get their blessing, I would have offended them greatly.

I nod quickly. "Of course. Whatever she wants."

"Lydia won't have to plan the wedding on her own. Amanda will help and I'm sure Colt's mother will want to give her input. Right, Colt?" my mate's grandfather ads.

"My mom loves planning events."

Gerald smiles. "See, Al? Everything will be fine."

Alcide still looks unsure as he takes a sip of the brandy. He looks me straight in the eye and declares, "If you hurt my daughter in any way, I'll make sure you pay. I'll have a plan and an alibi."

I gulp, feeling with certainty that Alcide Nightstone will gladly kill me if I ever give him a reason to. "I'll never hurt her, sir," I say, trying to gather all my courage. "I just want to spend the rest of my life with her."

"Stop threatening the boy," Gerald tells his son. "Lydia will kill him herself if it needs doing. She's going to be a healer. She'll be very efficient at knowing how to kill someone."

That makes Alcide smile.

9

FOOLS RUSH IN

EMORY

Mikey is always hungry. His stomach is a bottomless pit that never seems to be full, no matter how much he eats. Whatever food is within his vicinity, he runs toward it with relentless determination, and when he's not allowed to eat when he's hungry, he erupts into loud tantrums that don't stop until he finally gets his way..

Mikey follows me into my office, begging me for a snack. I have a phone call scheduled with Colt, and I can't put it off because I want to hear how his meeting with the Nightstones went. My son runs past me, making a beeline for my desk. The bottom drawer always has snacks inside which used to be for me as I have a tendency to forget lunch when I'm swamped with work.

The drawer is Mikey's now. Nellie keeps it filled with packets of cookies, crackers, and candy. Helga always chides her about Mikey's teeth rotting out of his skull, but my son is apparently immune to cavities. I don't know if it's from the shifter or vampire side.

He pulls open the drawer, struggling with the heavy oak but too determined to be deterred. Once it slides open, he grabs a packet of cookies triumphantly and pulls open another drawer to grab a juice box. Willow has spelled that drawer to always remain cold for drinks. It beats having a mini-fridge in my office.

Loot in hand, He runs to the soft green couch and climbs up to settle with his bounty. He's going to get crumbs all over the upholstery; he always leaves messes wherever he goes. Nellie never complains about having to clean up after him. Her patience never ceases to amaze me.

Mikey tears the packet of cookies open with his teeth, and I leave him to devour his snack. Taking a seat at my desk, I grab the phone and call my brother. He answers after a few rings.

"Hello?"

"Hey. How did it go?"

"As well as could be expected."

"Meaning?"

"Alcide Nightstone does not like me," he answers. "He really didn't care for Father."

I grimace. "I'm sorry to hear that."

As much as Colt and I try to do good and work on making a better world for our kind, our father's sordid history can never really be forgotten. It's going to take a long time to make up for the things he did, and even so, we don't expect everyone to forgive and forget. Most people have been gracious enough to give us the benefit of the doubt and judge us on our own merit. Others aren't as open-minded.

"On the other hand, Alpha Gerald does like me, and he's given me his full support."

"That's great, Colt!" I can't help but smile, even though my brother can't see me. I'm relieved. While it's not good that his mate's father doesn't care for him, the Alpha still gets the last word. As long as Gerald Nightstone is giving this union his support, there's very little anyone else can say about it.

Over the years as I've gotten to know the older Alpha, Gerald has always been upfront with me. He's been someone I can easily trust to give me the truth and not the runaround.

"When are you proposing to Lydia?" I ask.

"Soon. She's coming over to Moon Grove this weekend, so I plan on popping the question then."

"Where are you going to do it?" My excitement continues to grow as I imagine a beautiful proposal by my brother, with tears in his eyes.

"By the pond."

"Scenic. That's a great choice."

"I want to sweep her off his feet," he admits.

Giggling, I glance up to watch Mikey struggle to stab his juice box with the straw. He finally manages to get it, but the pause allows me time to think through the seriousness of my brother's situation. Tentatively, I ask him, "Do you think things are going a little too fast, Colt?"

He scoffs. "Fast? You're the one who made fun of me because you got married and had a child within a year."

"I don't regret how things went with Kane. I wouldn't trade my life for anything, but that time was also hectic and full of danger. Having a child during a war was very stressful."

"Do you wish you could have waited? Taken your time with every-thing?" he asks me.

"I don't know. Maybe? It was a little different for me because I wasn't pregnant nearly as long as I assumed I was going to be. I'm just worried that you're rushing things because I did." It's hard for me to admit to my brother, but it's true.

"Knowing you, Em, you would have been so impatient if you had to wait the whole nine months to give birth." He chuckles under his breath, lightening the mood.

My pregnancy hadn't been a fun time. I was ill for most of it and bedridden. Being stuck inside for months made me increasingly rest-less. Nine months of that would have driven me insane, so he's not wrong.

"I just want you to enjoy your life. Don't rush into something because of what other people are doing it."

"I'm not rushing anything," Colt reassures me. "Alcide has made it very clear he does *not* approve of eloping. I'm going to have a big wedding or nothing."

That makes me smile. Who doesn't love a big wedding? I look up to check on my son and see that Mikey has given up struggling with the juice box and has jumped off the couch. He runs up to me and holds out the drink and straw, wordlessly demanding I do this task for him instead of just asking. Holding the phone with my neck and shoulder, I take the items from him and quickly stab the juice box with the straw, shaking my head. He grabs it with a toothy grin and immediately begins to slurp from the straw

Ruffling his dark hair, I smile at him. When he's quiet, he's so cute. I almost forget what a hellion he can be. He looks more and more like Kane every day.

"Hello?" Colt calls out.

"Sorry. Mikey needed my attention," I reply. "So, when are you going to have this big wedding?"

"I don't know yet. I'll have to ask Lydia when she wants to have it. If it was up to me, we'd be married within a week, but Mom told me that planning a wedding within that time frame is impossible."

"It's not impossible, just unreasonable."

"How is it unreasonable?" I hear a tone of sarcasm in his voice.

"There's securing the venue, the vendors, the guest list, wedding attire…"

"Stop, stop," he interrupts me. "I get it. There's a lot that goes into planning something like this."

"You can get Mom to help you."

"She already volunteered. Lydia's mom also wants to help. Apparently, she and mom already know each other pretty well, so they're overly excited to be planning a wedding together."

"That's nice. You've got a whole team."

From what I remember about my own wedding and planning the Moon Goddess Ball, it takes a village to get anything done. Luckily, shifters believe in the strength of numbers. We know that we're stronger together than we are apart. The lone wolf dies, but the pack survives.

"I guess it's nice." He sighs. "I'm beginning to wish I can just elope with Lydia."

"You can still elope. Your future in-laws will just hate you even more. Mom will, too."

He snorts. "Thanks for the advice, Em. What would I ever do without you?"

"Fail miserably?" I quip. "Face it, little brother. You need me."

He chuckles. "I do need you–but you need me, too. Don't you ever forget it."

"I won't," I promise him. We may bicker at one another, but he's still my little brother, and I love him.

I'm also very proud of the young man he's become.

* * *

COLT

The weekend comes, and Lydia arrives in Moon Grove early in the morning. She is almost never late, arriving at least half an hour early to everything. While I was visiting her house, she showed me the thick blue planner that details out her schedule for weeks ahead. She uses different colored ink and sticky notes to organize everything. I'm thankful she is so on top of everything because I am often unorganized and chronically late.

Arranging time with Lydia consists of her opening up that massive planner and scheduling me in for times that she's free. She's assigned a specific ink color for me—red—for my hair and also so the bright color catches her eye when she's flipping through the planner.

I know what's in her planner for this weekend. She told me she's already jotted down 'WEEKEND WITH COLT' in bright red for the next two days. I'm going to have her all to myself. I'm practically beaming when I see her silver car pull into the driveway.

Lydia steps out of the car with a small leather bag. She smiles at me as she walks up, the sunlight hitting her blonde hair forming a halo. For a moment, I think to myself how lucky I am. My fears of being doomed to a loveless marriage like my parents seem so silly in the reality of who the Moon Goddess chose for me.

"Hello, handsome," she greets me coyly.

"Hello there, gorgeous."

I pull her close to me for a kiss, and her strawberry lip balm tastes almost as good as she does. I know the staff can see us from the windows of the house, but I don't mind them. I nip Lydia's bottom lip, and she opens her mouth, letting me tangle my tongue with hers. Her breasts are pressed against me, and all I want to do is undress her.

My mind immediately goes to the gutter when Lydia is around. My hands wander from her waist down to her ass. Lydia is blessed in that area too. A man could get lost exploring her.

"Colt!"

We freeze, and I pull away from the kiss to see my mother standing by the open front door. Her blue eyes glare daggers into me. My hands drop from Lydia's ass, and I felt like a guilty schoolboy. I've been cockblocked by my mother.

Lydia is flustered. "Good morning, Luna."

Mom smiles. "Good morning, Lydia. How was the drive?"

"It was good." Lydia looks between my mom and I and says, "My mom sends her regards."

Mom shoots me a significant look, and she ushers us inside the house. She insists on giving Lydia a tour of our home, all four floors, and it ends with the guest room Lydia is going to stay in. Of course, it has to be the guest room furthest from my room. As if that would be enough to deter any hanky-panky from happening this weekend.

I don't even know why my mother is insisting on some idea of celibacy before marriage. I've done the math between her wedding anniversary and Emory's birthday. Mom had to be at least four months along with my sister when she got married. I don't point out the hypocrisy to her because I want to live. It would be a shame if I missed my wedding to Lydia because I'm dead.

Lydia puts her bag down on the bed, looking around the guest room. It's one of the larger rooms since it's at the end of the hallway. There's a bay window with a reading nook that she's drawn to. She moves to the window and takes in the view of the woods.

"It's warmer here," she declares. "Does it get colder in the evenings?"

"It's usually colder at night, but it depends on the time of year," I explain.

"How can you sleep if it's hot?"

"I sleep naked." I grin. She shakes her head at me. Thankfully, Mom has left us alone. "You want to see my room?"

She nods, almost shyly. I take her hand as she comes to the doorway, closing the door behind us. I lead her down the hallway to my bedroom, and she looks around the space curiously. I cleaned up before she got here. I didn't want her to think I'm a slob–even though I am. Decorating isn't really an interest of mine, so the busiest part of the room are the trophies and medals from my school days.

The old memorabilia sit on top of a dark mahogany dresser next to a few framed photos of my family and friends. Lydia picks up a photo frame of Emory and I as kids. We're dressed in pajamas and opening presents for the Winter Solstice.

"You were a cute kid," she remarks. "Your hair used to be more orange than it is now."

I rub the back of my neck, feeling some slight embarrassment for my younger self. "My hair darkened as I got older."

"Were the kids mean about it?"

"Not really," I say with a shrug. "My father was the Alpha, after all. Besides, after I hit a growth spurt, I was bigger than most of them."

She places the photo frame back on the dresser and gestures toward all the medals and trophies. "Clearly, you were quite the jock."

I shrug. "I've always been athletic."

"Were you popular?"

"Sure."

Lydia considers me thoughtfully. "We totally wouldn't have dated in school."

My eyebrows furrow in confusion. "Why not?"

"I was a nerd who took school too seriously. You wouldn't have noticed me at all."

"That's not true. Who could miss someone like you? With an ass like that?" I drop my eyes and make a noise that lets her know I like what I see.

She grabs the baseball on the dresser and throws it at me. Her aim is so bad, it hits the wall and doesn't even graze me.

"I'm just being honest," I reply, laughing. "And accurate. I thought you liked accuracy."

"You're ridiculous."

I know she's not really angry because she's smiling. I come closer to her and take her hand again.

"I want to show you something." I waggle my eyebrows at her, and her smile widens.

"I can't wait."

10

DON'T BREAK TRADITION

COLT

The woods feel like home as much as the house. I've spent equally as much of my childhood out there climbing trees and exploring nature to my heart's content. Camping out here had been a regular event when Emory and I were kids. Our father would stay up late with us and teach us about the stars.

It's the quiet memories that only my sister and I share now that remind me that Bernard hadn't been a purely evil entity. Those moments where he was a good father to us made his betrayal even more painful to swallow. If he had only been a monster, it would have been easier to merely forget about him. As much as I despise the person he became, I still hold some affection for the father he was sometimes in the past.

Both versions of the man have shaped me into who I am no matter how I might try to deny it.

I try not to think about my father. Looking back rarely serves any purpose except to make me feel melancholy. I want to focus on the present and my future. Having Lydia with me as we walk through the woods feels like I'm on the path to where I've always meant to be.

Lydia dressed for the weather in a white sundress with blue flowers. It's long and almost reaches her ankles. The neckline is low enough to give me a nice view of her cleavage without being too revealing. The white tennis shoes she's wearing are sensible for the walk. It's easier sometimes to stay in our human form and stroll along slowly rather than rush around as wolves.

She bends down to pick up a flower, and I see a bit more of her breasts. She's mostly covered up, and it just makes me imagine her wearing less. There goes my mind in the gutter again.

We finally reach the pond. Emory is right that it's scenic. With the live oak trees surrounding us and reflecting off the water, the cool breeze ruffling our hair relieving us from the heat, and the cicadas buzzing in the air, it's peaceful and calming. This is our own little world away from everyone else. Untouchable and unknowable.

"It's beautiful," Lydia says. She closes her eyes and tilts her head back.

"This is my favorite place," I tell her. "My sanctuary from everything. Whenever things get to be too much, I come here."

"What are you hiding from?" She gives me a sympathetic look and places her hand gently on my arm.

"How much do you know about my father, Bernard?" I ask tentatively.

Her gray-blue eyes widen. "I've heard stories, but I never met him."

"The stories are pretty accurate, unfortunately. He wasn't a good man," I continue. "He took out a loan from King Kane of Crimson Peak so he could wage territorial wars with other packs, including yours." I pick up a stone and skip it across the surface of the water. It glides for a moment before sinking in.

"Oh," she says, and I can tell she doesn't know what else to say.

"Then, when that failed spectacularly, he ended up at war with Crimson Peak because he couldn't pay back the loan. When we were on the verge of losing the war as we were running out of resources, he tried to pay back the loan by selling off my sister as a feeder."

Lydia seems to be taking this all in, trying to digest the awful story. "He sold off Emory?"

I shake my head. "He tried to sell Lola. She was twelve."

Her eyes widen in horror. "How could he do that? To his own daughter? She was a child."

"The only thing my father has ever truly cared about is himself. We were all disposable," I explain. "Emory volunteered to be Lola's replacement, and my father did nothing to stop it. That's the kind of man he was."

Lydia doesn't say anything. She looks helpless, like she's trying to figure out what to say to make me feel better. Finally, she settles on, "I'm so sorry that happened to you."

"I'm not the victim. I had everything to gain from it all. Emory was gone, and I was going to be the Alpha." I pick up another stone and throw it. It skips thrice before sinking. "I didn't know what to think at first about what had happened. Bernard tried to frame it as King Kane's fault for not being merciful and taking Lola as he offered. All I knew was that none of it felt right. I didn't want to be the Alpha. That was always Emory's birthright and not mine."

"You felt guilty?"

I nod. "Every day. I'd come here and try to forget, but I know deep down that my father was wrong, and I was a coward for not speaking up."

"How old were you when all this happened?"

"Seventeen. Old enough to know better."

"Still young enough to make mistakes," she points out. "And young enough to correct them. Didn't you come through for Emory in the end?"

I pick up a rock, rubbing my thumb on the smooth surface. "She was only twenty, and she overthrew our father and became the Alpha. She's my hero, and she never blamed me for not speaking up sooner."

"The important thing is you did the right thing before it was too late."

I throw the stone, and it skips almost all the way to the middle of the pond. "Better late than never."

"Exactly." Lydia turns me to face her, and she wraps her arms around my neck. "That scared young man stepped up when he had to and he became the man you are today. And I like who you are now."

Her sweetness and understanding unmoors something in me, the last vestiges of shame from my callow youth cracking and disintegrating.

"I know it's only been a short while since we met, but I need to say this," I tell her. "I want to spend the rest of my life with you."

Her eyes widen slightly, and she smiles. It reminds me of the dawn after a long night.

"That's good," she replies. "Because I want to spend the rest of my life with you."

I take her arms away from my neck so I can get down on one knee. She freezes in shock. I pull the right out of the pocket of my pants. The emerald ring shines in the sunlight.

"Lydia Nightstone, will you marry me?"

"Yes!" Lydia exclaims, knocking me to the ground with a lunge.

We end up on the soft earth with her on top of me. Her pretty face is alight with excitement. "Oh Moon Goddess, yes!" she continues. "I would love to marry you!"

Lydia kisses me all over my face—my lips, my cheeks, my chin, my nose, and even my eyelids. All I can do is close my eyes and smile as I take in her affection. Her apparent enthusiasm in marrying me brings me relief and joy. She only pulls back and gets off so I can slide the engagement ring on her finger.

She stares at it in awe, her hand raised so she can admire the ring from different angles. "It's so pretty."

"It's a family heirloom."

Lydia drops her hand and stares at me alluringly, her eyes half-lidded. "How many people in your family do you think consummated their marriages here?"

"A lot, probably," I reply. "I wouldn't be surprised if I was conceived around here."

"We shouldn't break tradition then."

She pulls off her sundress, leaving her only in her bra and underwear. Dropping the dress to the ground, she reaches behind her and unhooks her bra. I've seen her breasts before, but they never fail to leave me in awe. Her bra joins the dress, and she cocks her head to the side, wordlessly urging me to do something.

I don't need more hints. I undress like my clothes are on fire, tossing away my shirt, pants, and boxers in record time. This kiss is different, fueled by days of yearning and anticipation. It's been too long since we shared that moment together in the shower, and I need her desperately.

Lydia lies down on the ground, and her perfect breasts look enticing with her erect nipples. I join her, and her breath hitches as I suck on one of her nipples, cupping the other breast. The midday sun heats my back, but I don't care. I kiss my way down Lydia's torso until I'm between her legs, tugging her panties off and discarding them.

She spreads her thighs, giving me easier access. I lift one of her legs and rest it on my shoulder, opening her up wider. Her eyes plead with me, and I oblige, licking her slit in slow and deep strokes. She lets out a loud moan as I take her clit between my lips and suck until she's moaning louder.

I slip my fingers into her, coaxing her to readiness. The last thing I want to do is hurt Lydia and past experiences have taught me that the wetter she is for this the better it'll be for us. Her hips buck as she begins to come instinctively chasing pleasure. I don't let up with my mouth and fingers until she feels impossibly wet, moaning out her release.

Lydia has covered her face in her hands, her chest rising and falling with quick breaths.

I rest my cheek on her thigh. "Are you okay?"

"Yes," she replies almost incoherently. "Don't stop."

"Are you sure?"

Her hands drop from her face so she can stare me down. "You have my full consent, Colt. Please continue."

Satisfied with that answer, I drop her leg from my shoulder and turn us over so she's on top. Her breasts look even larger from this view, and I guide her with a hand on her hip and my other hand on my cock. She lowers herself slowly, taking the tip of me inside her. Gravity does the rest of the work, and I slide into her halfway.

Lydia bites her lip, her blonde eyebrow furrowing. "I can't go any further."

It takes a bit of maneuvering with my hands on her hips and getting her to arch her back the right way until she's taking the rest of me in her. My vision practically goes white with the wet tightness of her squeezing me like a fist. I think I might actually die.

"Colt," Lydia pants. "What's wrong?"

She tries to move and I desperately hold her hips in place. I'm in danger of coming like it's my first time having sex. That would be embarrassing. That is not how I want this to go.

"One minute," I groan. "I don't want to finish early."

Lydia complies, her hands resting on my chest as she waits. I have to close my eyes as the sight of her naked is too enticing. Eventually, after what feels like an eternity, I open my eyes and encourage her to move. Her hips rotate hypnotically in an ancient rhythm, pushing me in and out of her like we've been doing this for years.

I thrust up to meet her as she's coming down, and we move faster. She keeps herself steady with her hands on my chest, nails digging into my skin. I cup one of her breasts, pinching and playing with a nipple. My other hand rubs her clit, encouraging her to come before I do.

"Colt," she gasps, her face flushed. "I love you."

I'm already so close to coming, but her confession takes me by surprise, and I'm bursting within her. I don't stop moving, fondling her clit with my fingers until she cries out. She's squeezing me so tight I don't know if I'll ever be able to get out of her. Wrecked with pleasure, she falls forward and rests her head on my chest.

I hold her in my arms, moving her hair away from her sweaty back so I can caress her skin. "I love you too."

11

SAFE AND SOUND

Colt

That weekend blurs together in a hazy dream. I can't stop touching Lydia. We spend hours having sex and sharing stories in between. The stories range from funny and silly to sad and sincere.

This isn't just having another body to get lost in. I'm getting to know Lydia and all her little quirks. She asks me an endless amount of questions, trying to learn as much about me as she can. I could listen to her talk for hours, discussing the most mundane of subjects.

The pillow talk gets more and more random. We're lying in my bed under the covers. Lydia is resting on her stomach, leaning on her elbows and her face propped in her hands. I'm on my back and trying not to stare at the swell of her breasts.

"I would clearly be the one to survive in a natural disaster," Lydia declares. "A healer would be invaluable and I would be able to help so many people."

"*If* you're a healer by then. I do love that you like to help people, though," I told her.

She rolls her eyes. "I'd still more valuable than you. What skills are you bringing into a catastrophe?"

"I'm strong, tall, athletic, and I can help find people. I know how to fix cars, too. Mechanics are invaluable during certain kinds of disasters."

"Vehicles would eventually become useless since gas is a finite resource if we couldn't get any into our villages. You know what never runs out? Healing knowledge and expertise."

"What about combat skills? Who's going to protect you from harm if there are riots when resources start to run out?" We are just being silly now. I drag a finger across her cheek.

"I can fight." She juts her chin out. "You've gone hunting with me. You've seen me in action."

I have had the chance to see her hunt in her wolf form. While she was in the front with her grandfather in the pursuit of the stag, she wasn't a heavy hitter during the actual fight. Her dad and brothers caused most of the damage to the stag. She did a good job avoiding the stag's horns and landing a few bites and scratches.

"You're fast, but not that strong. You'd have a better chance running away instead of trying to take someone in a fight."

"I could take someone in a fight," she argues. "You and me. I could take you."

I stare at the ceiling, knowing this will not lead anywhere good. If I tell her she can't take me, she'll insist on fighting, and I could end up hurting her by mistake. If I agree with her that she can take me on, she might continue to be less than realistic about her physical short-comings. This isn't even about ego. It's plain biology.

Lydia pokes me in the stomach. She's just trying to get a rouse out of me.

"Agree to disagree?" I suggest. "You don't have to be the strongest, babe. You could still outrun me any day."

"You're just bruising my pride here, Colt."

She tries to poke me again. I grab her hand and push her down till she's on her back on the bed. Climbing on top of her, holding both of her wrists I trap them above her head, preventing her from moving. She jerks her hands lightly trying to free herself.

"You are beautiful, smart, and very capable," I tell her. "But I am bigger than you and stronger. It's not an insult. It's just facts."

She narrows her gaze at me mischievously. "Let go of me."

I pull away from her wrists, but she doesn't push me away. Instead, she kisses me roughly. Her teeth nip my lower lip. I can practically *feel* the annoyance in her kiss. I've learned something new about my mate—she hates to lose.

In just a moment, I have Lydia on her hands and knees as I take her from behind. I can see her reflection in the mirror on the wall and watch the play of emotions on her face as I thrust into her. Lydia pushes back to meet my thrusts, desperate to come.

She rubs her clit, and her expression grows more needy, almost pained. I gather her loose blonde hair in my fist and pull her back, forcing her to lean back as I thrust deeper and harder inside of her. She's completely at my mercy. I watch my reflection as I fuck her, and I never want it to end. Eventually, she comes, and watching her face, I can no longer hold back, and I spill my seed into the condom I'm wearing.

After a few days, we have to go back to real life. We can't stay in our little love nest forever. Duty comes to call. When Monday rolls around, I kiss Lydia deeply in the front driveway wishing she could stay longer.

I pull away, resting my forehead against hers. "I don't want you to go."

"I don't want to go either, but my mom has called at least a dozen times. She's excited to plan the wedding."

"We could just leave the planning to our moms and just show up at the wedding."

"*Our* wedding," she corrects me. "We're only getting married once. We might as well make sure we do it right."

"I would elope with you this very second if I could."

"My parents would never forgive you."

"I know, so that's why we're having the biggest wedding of the decade."

I cup her face in my hands and kiss her one more time. I pour all my longing and disappointment that we have to be apart into the kiss. Lydia looks dazed when I pull away. My cock is still insatiable; even after a weekend of sex, it's half-erect.

"I have to go," Lydia says despondently.

"I know. I'll see you soon, babe."

She slips into the driver's seat of her silver car and waves. I wave back and then turn behind me to see my mother standing by the front door. My mom waves back as Lydia turns on the engine of her car and drives off.

I watch the silver car drive out of sight. A sinking feeling of yearning blooms in my belly. No wonder everyone says finding one's mate is so intense. Having her leave me is hell.

Trying to shake off the desire to write long letters to Lydia like I'm a soldier off at war, I turn to go inside the house.

My mother cocks an eyebrow at me. "Did you have a good weekend?"

Confused, I reply, "I did."

"I wouldn't know. I barely saw you or Lydia."

I shrug, smiling glibly. "It's the early days of our relationship. You know how it is."

Mom doesn't dignify that with an answer, and she walks away.

* * *

Emory

News of Colt's engagement has my mother buzzing like an overexcited bee. Not only is it the wedding of her only son, but she gets to help plan the event. Mom really does enjoy planning parties, and she's good at it.

I'm less passionate about event planning than her. Planning the Moon Goddess Ball wasn't that enjoyable for me. It's more of a necessity than an actual fun activity for me. At least she'll have Lydia's mom to help her this time so I won't have to.

I tell Kane about the little updates about the wedding. He listens attentively while we walk through the rose garden. Mikey is running around, and Helga watches nearby.

"How long has he known this girl again?" Kane asks.

"A little more than a week."

"And he proposed and got her to agree in that short amount of time?" Kane shakes his head in disbelief. "What is your brother's secret? It took me *months* to get you to agree to marry me."

"First of all, the circumstances were completely different. I was pregnant, and we were at war with Scarlett Thunder. A wedding was the least of our priorities at that time. Second, you're more of a gentleman than Colt. You respected my desire to delay our wedding. Colt would grab Lydia and elope with her if he thought he could get away with it. Besides, it wasn't as clear that we are mates as it is that they are."

"He's still more efficient than me."

"Only because he's an asshole."

Kane raises his dark eyebrows at me. "I thought you loved your brother."

"I do, but he's still an asshole," I reply. "We used to argue all the time when we were younger. Now, we just jab each other whenever we get a chance, even though it's sometimes childish."

"And I thought Lex and I were bad. The worst thing I've done to him is ignore him."

"That's worse because that's passive aggressive. Colt and I argue, but at least we're talking."

"Have you ever tried to kill him?" he jokes.

I think about that and chuckle. "No, but I have put the fear of the Moon Goddess into him a time or two."

He chuckles. "Did it even work?"

"He still gets nervous when I'm holding a pair of scissors so I would say yes."

"You're insane," he says fondly. He wraps an arm around my shoulders and pulls me closer so he can kiss my temple. "I'm so glad you don't direct your bloodthirsty tendencies toward me."

"I fought a war to keep you safe. It seems counterproductive to kill you now." Placing a hand on his cheek, I reach up and kiss him. The kiss quickly deepens with Kane pushing me against one of the gazebo pillars. After almost four years of marriage, the castle servants are used to seeing us kissing. We stopped trying to keep our affection toward one another private a long time ago.

Someone clears their throat.

I open my eyes and see Nellie standing there. She looks uncomfortable and apologetic. I lightly push Kane away, and he ends the kiss. Undeterred, he doesn't let me go and kisses my neck.

"You have a phone call, Alpha," Nellie explains, trying to look anywhere but the display Kane is making of us. "It's your brother. He says it's urgent."

Colt, as much as he enjoys a good joke, knows better than to use that kind of wording for small things. If he says something is urgent, it means it really is something very important. I push Kane away and he obliges. I kiss him on the cheek as a goodbye before leaving the garden to head back to the castle.

I rush inside and head straight for my study. Reaching my desk, I answer the phone, "Colt, what is it?"

"Something has happened, Em," he replies, the worry in his voice unmistakable. "It's Lydia."

A sinking feeling in my stomach has me taking a seat on the desk chair. "What happened to her?"

"She was driving back from Moon Grove to Nightfall. She never made it home. Her family went looking for her, and they found her car abandoned in the middle of the road."

"Did her car break down?"

"The car has no damage. There was a tree across the road, but Alpha Gerald says it looks like it was carried there on purpose, like someone wanted to stop someone–possibly her," he explains. "There were signs of a struggle. Whoever took her, she didn't go with them willingly."

"Oh Moon Goddess," I say. "I'm so sorry, Colt."

"I shouldn't have let her leave. If I asked her to stay longer, this never would have happened."

"This is not your fault. We'll find her and whoever did this and bring them to justice."

Colt lets out a frustrated sigh. "I just found my mate, Emory, and I've already lost her."

"We'll find her, Colt. You have my word. I'll do whatever it takes to get her back to you safe and sound."

"I..." He pauses, his breath heavy. I know he's trying to keep it together but I know my brother. He's always been the more emotional one of us.

"It's going to be okay," I assure him. "We'll figure this out like we always do."

"I need you, Em," he admits, his voice breaking. "I need you to help me."

1 2

THE BLOOD TAKERS

Emory

The drive to Moon Grove feels longer than ever even though Rainer is driving as fast as he can without putting our lives in danger. Willow is seated on the passenger side, and she doesn't chide him for driving so fast. Kane has not let go of my head since I told him what happened to Lydia. He's giving me his silent support and allowing me to take strength from him.

We arrive at the house, and Rainer parks the vehicle. We all silently leave the car and make our way inside the house. My mother and Colt are in his study. Colt is pacing back and forth in the room as Mom is trying to persuade him to sit down and drink the tea she's made in an attempt to calm him.

"I don't want tea," he snaps, refusing to look at her.

"Colt," I say and he turns around, his green eyes lighting up with relief. I go to him and hug him close, trying to reassure him with my touch. "We came as soon as we could."

Colt's shoulders shake as he tries to hold in his emotions. He swallows and answers, "There haven't been any updates."

"Where on the main road was she taken?" Rainer asks, going straight into business.

Colt pulls away from me and goes to stand in front of the desk, leaning back against it. "The car was not far from Red River."

I don't know all the vampire kingdoms, but that certainly sounds like one. I look at Kane who confirms, "That's King Matthias' territory."

The name sounds familiar to me. "Is he the same King Matthias who sided with King Peter during the war?"

My husband nods, his expression blank. He's told me who, among the vampire royals, does not support our marriage. King Matthias has been one that does not care for me. I've never met him, but he's already made up his mind exactly where he thinks I belong, and it's certainly not with Kane.

"Could you go talk to him and see if he knows anything?" my mother suggests.

Kane shakes his head. "We're not allies, and he has no reason to want to help me, especially if it's for a female shifter. He thinks shifters are beneath him."

"We just sit here and twiddle our thumbs then?" Colt scoffs. "Can't you two just kiss and make up? Lydia's life is on the line here."

"I've known Matthias for many years. He's always been overtly proud. Even if I tried to make amends with him, he will refuse to help us due to his own prejudices against your species."

Colt pinches the bridge of his nose, his annoyance visible. He grumbles through his teeth, "And yet again my life is upended because of a vampire elitist with a stick up his royal ass."

"Colt," I try to coax him. "This isn't Kane's fault."

"I fucking know that. I was talking about Matthias." He goes behind the desk and opens the bottom drawer to pull out a bottle of scotch. "I can 't deal with this right now. I'm going to get fucked up, and hopefully, I get some actually good news when I'm conscious again."

Colt leaves the room, slamming the study door behind him. I wince and look around apologetically at everyone.

"He's just stressed," I try to explain. "They got engaged a few days ago. This was supposed to be the best week."

"And now it's the worst," Rainer adds. "I don't blame him. If anything happened to my wife, I wouldn't be in a good mood either."

Willow, who has been silent this entire time, asks, "Is there any way to get the information out of King Matthias? If he won't speak with you, maybe somebody else can do it instead? He may know quite a deal more than we think." She's implying what I've been thinking all along–that Matthias had something to do with Lydia's disappearance.

Rainer runs a hand through his curly hair. "It can't be me. He also hates my guts."

"He hates shifters, so it can't be me," I tell them.

Kane looks contemplative. "Red River sided with Scarlett Thunder during the war. He might be willing to speak to Lex."

"That sounds like a sound idea," Mom agrees. "Any help will be useful in the search for Lydia."

"Why would she be taken to begin with?" Willow questions. "Is it because of her engagement to your brother?"

"The only ones that might care about their engagement are any of the Alphas, and we've been getting along pretty well these past few years," I explain. "And considering Lydia is the granddaughter of an Alpha, this could cause a war amongst us. I can't see any of the Alphas doing this without risking the health and safety of their pack. Besides, we're all still recovering from the last war."

Four years is not a long time to replenish resources spent on wars. Expensive wars that could go on for years. Before the war with Scarlett Thunder, my pack was at war with Crimson Peak for nearly two decades. We're not destitute by any means, but we aren't swimming in gold either.

Rainer looks somber. "It could be the Blood Takers."

That's not something I've heard of before.

I ask, "What are the Blood Takers?"

Kane, Willow, and Rainer all share uncomfortable glances.

"The Blood Takers traffic shifters and humans to be feeders for the vampire kingdoms," Kane explains. "It's highly illegal, but there are vampire royals who, like King Matthias, do not see shifters as anything more than animals. Food."

"The Blood Takers ensure the vampire kingdoms don't have to bother with willing feeders," Rainer adds. "It's barbaric and not many kingdoms allow it."

I'm not completely surprised. When I was a child, I was warned not to go off on my own or to talk to strange people on the main road. Young shifters sometimes disappeared without a trace, never to be seen again. My father always played it off like it was not a big deal, but now I might know why. The confirmation that all the warnings were for a good reason is chilling.

"Where would the Blood Takers bring Lydia?" I ask.

"The Blood Takers' biggest client is King Myenas," Kane replies. "He was King Peter's biggest ally during the war. I suspect Lydia could've been taken to his kingdom."

* * *

LYDIA

My head hurts. A pounding at my temple makes me wince as I try to open my eyes. I'm lying on something hard and cold. Nausea has me swallowing back bile in an attempt not to puke.

It takes me a second to realize it's not the headache that's causing the nausea. I'm in a moving vehicle. I force myself to open my eyes. It's dark, and I have to wait for my eyes to adjust so I can see better.

My hands are tied together. There's tape on my mouth. I peel it off quickly, not minding the sting as it's ripped from my skin. Panic begins to creep in as I realize what's happened to me.

I was on my way home from Moon Grove. While driving on the main road, I noted a fallen tree blocking my way. When I got out of the car to check the tree, I saw that it hadn't fallen down on its own. The cut on the tree was too clean.

Somebody chopped down the tree and left it in the middle of the road. Before I could get back in my car and find another way home, another vehicle came by. I was attacked. I remember clearly now the fear that bubbled up inside of me when I noted those large males were all vampires.

I might have been able to take one vampire on my own, but half a dozen was too much for a shifter of my size. I fought as hard as I could. I tried to scratch, hit, and bite them to keep them off me. One of them hit me in the temple with his stone like fist.

Even bleeding from a head wound, I hadn't given up, but before I could shift into my wolf form and run away, one of them pierced me with a needle to the neck. My limbs went limp, leaving me unable to shift. They grabbed me by the hair and shoved me toward their car. My vision blurred and then there was only darkness.

Now, I'm in an enclosed space. My hands make contact with a low ceiling. I'm in the trunk of a car. I start banging on the hood of the trunk, trying to make as much noise as possible.

The car stops.

My heart is beating fast as I ready myself to fight my way out of this. Colt is right that I'm fast. If I can shift into my wolf form, I can get away. I just need the element of surprise.

The hood of the trunk lifts, and moonlight bathes the face of a pale, muscular man. He sneers at me, his blue eyes cold and ruthless. He's short and has a sparse goatee. He grabs me by the arms, dragging me from the trunk.

"Stupid wolf bitch," he hisses. "You're not even worth the money. The other bitches didn't put up much of a fight."

"You just hate putting any effort into anything," a taller male vampire says. His smile is greasy as he looks over my body. "I personally like it when they have fight in them. It makes breaking them way more fun."

"Hands off the merchandise, boys," a bald male orders. "The more untouched and undamaged they arrive at their destination, the better paid we'll be."

The tall vampire runs a hand down my back, cupping my ass. It makes me shudder in disgust. I try to kick him away, but he just laughs. The muscular man drags me forward by the other end of the rope causing me to almost stumble.

"Can't we spare one, boss?" the first man asks. "This one's got a great ass and tits. And she's blonde too."

The bald man smacks him on the back of the head. "Hands. Off. The. Merchandise."

"You're no fun," he declares, walking off.

The muscular man tugs on the rope, forcing me to come along with him. He's moving so fast that I don't have the chance to even try to break free from the rope. With my hands bound like this, I can't shift into my wolf form without injuring myself. I frantically look around my surroundings, trying to place where I might be.

I'm in a forest, but even with the moonlight, I can't make out where I've been taken to. This place doesn't seem familiar to me at all. Another road comes into view. There's a large semi-truck with men talking to each other. They're all wearing black.

With their pale faces and blue eyes, I can tell they're all vampires. The bald man is talking to one of them. One of the men standing by the truck hands him a duffle bag. He unzips it and checks whatever is inside before zipping it back again.

He shakes hands with the other vampire. "Pleasure doing business with you."

The bald man nods to the man holding onto me. The other vampire is plain-looking with a pale blonde mustache. His hair is cropped short. He opens the back of the semi-truck, and I can see what's inside.

There are mostly young women huddled inside. From their scents, I can tell they're shifters aside from a few human women. There are a few boys, mostly teenagers. From the state of them, they could be runaways or homeless people that happened to be at the wrong place at the wrong time.

"This one's a fighter," my first captor says. "Almost bit my fucking ear off when we tried to grab her."

Mustache Man nods. "That's good to know."

He pushes me toward the semi-truck. I try to dig in my heels, knowing any escape attempts will be harder once I'm inside the vehicle. He grabs me by the waist and throws me inside. I bang my head against the wall of the vehicle..

The previous head injury hasn't begun to heal, and fresh pain almost makes me black out. The pain makes my eyes tear up. I look up at the guy who's closing the doors, trapping me inside.

"Stupid bitch," he grumbles.

13

THE MAGIC TOUCH

WILLOW

While we are at Moon Grove, I try to cast a locator spell on Lydia to pinpoint where she's been taken. Emory talks to her brother and manages to get a personal item of Lydia's from him. She accidentally left behind her hairbrush from when she was here over the weekend. There's a large map on the wall of the study that Rainer takes down and places down on the desk.

I take out a bundle of white sage and a box of matches from my bag to clear the space of unnecessary energy. Emory opens the window in the study to let out the smoke. I borrow a metal bowl from the kitchen and place it on top of the map. Pulling out hairs from Lydia's hairbrush, I drop them into the bowl. I keep small vials of dried herbs in my bag, and I throw in some mugwort and sage into the bowl as well.

Lighting another match, I throw it into the bowl. The mixture of herbs and hairs spark into a purple flame. I reach for the onyx pendulum I wear as a necklace and unclasp it. Dangling the onyx pendulum over the purple flame, I wait till the onyx glows purple absorbing the magical essence.

Slowly, I swing the pendulum over the large framed map in

counter clockwise circles, letting the magic guide me where to stop. The times I've done this locator spell in the past, there has been a tugging and the onyx will stop at a specific location on the map. I swing the pendulum for a few minutes, but the onyx continues to move without wanting to stop. Closing my eyes, I try to concentrate on the pull of the magic, but that tug isn't there.

"*Invenire locum.*" I chant the spell clearly. "*Invenire locum.*"

My magic feels like it's hitting a brick wall, preventing me from moving any closer. I open my eyes and see Rainer, Emory, and Kane's expectant looks. I hate to disappoint them, but there's nothing else I can do at the moment. I drop the pendulum on the desk and shake my head.

"Something is blocking me from locating her," I explain. "I don't know what it is."

"Has that happened before?" Kane asks.

I extinguish the purple flame with a flick of my wrist. "It doesn't happen often. There could be some kind of concealment spell on Lydia or at the location where she's at."

Emory's eyebrows furrow in concern. "You can conceal an entire place?"

"It takes a lot of magic. Usually, more than one person has to be casting it. Ivy and the coven were able to do it with their village. I was only able to find the place from memory and using my own magic to break down the wards."

"Are the Blood Takers witches?" Emory asks. "Or are they working with them?"

"The Blood Takers are vampires. As far as we know, they've never worked with witches before," Rainer points out.

"There's more than one coven. Maybe a smaller one has been employed by them," I offer. "They could also be working with them through force. Most witches are still terrified of vampires, and they could only be trying to survive."

"Regardless of the reasons, if the Blood Takers are working with witches, we'll have a harder time locating Lydia," Kane points out.

"This is a lot of effort for only one feeder," Rainer remarks. "They might be moving a whole group of feeders."

"That makes it even more vital that we locate the Blood Takers and save the people they've taken," Emory declares. "I don't like this practice, and I want it stopped."

Kane moves closer to his wife and puts a comforting hand on her shoulder. "I agree with you. We will work on banning the trade, but our priority at the moment is finding Lydia."

I look down at the map, feeling useless at not being more helpful. I have to be missing something, a spell or a ritual I can use to locate Lydia.

"I'm going to Ivy to see if she has a stronger locator spell," I say. "I'll look at the grimoires. I'll also ask the other High Priestesses for advice."

Rainer nods. "I'll go with you."

"Is there anything else we can do?" Emory asks. "I hate to just sit here and wait."

I quickly start packing my things back into my bag. "It's best that you stay with your brother and wait for any updates. We'll call you when we have something."

Rainer and I turn to leave the room. Kane's voice stops us as he asks, "What happens if you can't find a spell to locate Lydia?"

I look back at Kane's serious expression and Emory's worried face. I know I can't promise to find a solution if there isn't one. Even magic has its limits, after all, but I'm not willing to give up that easily. Not when people's lives were at stake. "We'll find something," I promise them. "There's always a loophole."

"And if there isn't a loophole, we'll make one," Rainer adds with a reassuring smile. "Need I remind all of you that we've had worse odds than this before and won? Have a little faith that we'll find Colt's girlfriend, and everything will be all right."

I look at my brave and kind husband who sees light and hope where others can only see doubt and despair. It's one of the reasons I fell in love with him. Rainer refuses to accept defeat, especially in mind and spirit. He's laughed at death and walked away triumphantly.

Emory smiles, taking comfort in Rainer's promise. "Please stay safe, both of you."

Rainer shrugs. "You know us; we like to live dangerously."

His hand on the small of my back gently ushers me from the study. He closes the door behind us, and I can see the shadows of doubt on his face.

"Rainer…"

He shakes his head. "No bad thoughts, Willow. At least not until we talk to Ivy."

* * *

RAINER

Willow and I have visited Ivy regularly over the years. While Willow's relationship with the rest of the coven is strained due to the century of bloody history between vampires and witches, Ivy is the last of Willow's family in the coven. She is the great-granddaughter of Willow's younger sister, Bryony, whom our daughter is named after, and she cherishes that connection.

Ivy and I aren't exactly friends, but we're cordial enough. She's good with my daughter, and Bryony adores Ivy, following her around the cottage and gardens to ask her about magic. If my daughter is able to use magic one day, Ivy's guidance will help her to learn how to use it responsibly. Of course, Willow will help with that, too, but sometimes parents don't have as much luck teaching their children as other adults do.

Ivy and I have quietly resigned ourselves to being in each other's lives and that's the best it's going to get.

The witch is in the middle of tending to her garden when we arrive at the village. At the back of Ivy's cottage is a large garden of herbs and vegetables for both food and magical purposes. She wears a large straw hat and has a wicker basket tucked to her side as she collects herbs with a pair of pruning shears. When she sees us coming, she waves.

Willow greets her niece with a hug. "Sorry for coming without notice. We have an emergency on our hands."

Ivy's eyebrows raise in alarm. "What kind of emergency?"

"We'll tell you inside," Willow suggests. "We need you to cast a locator spell."

"Haven't you tried casting it yourself?"

"It didn't work. I was hoping you knew a stronger variant," my wife admits.

Ivy nods. "I'll see what I can do." She drops the pruning shears into her basket and heads toward the cottage. I move out of the way because she's on a mission. I watch as she performs the same locator spell as Willow using the hair from Lydia's hairbrush and an amethyst pendulum. She adds more herbs to burn in her little pewter dish and swings the pendulum over an old map.

"*Invenire locum,*" she chants. "*Invenire locum.*"

The purple fire in the pewter dish flickers and grows bigger, but the pendulum does not stop at a location, which is exactly what happened with Willow. Ivy frowns and drops the pendulum necklace on the kitchen table.

"You're right. There's something blocking my magic," she says. "I'm guessing it's some powerful protection wards."

"I could tear apart the wards, but I need to find the place first," Willow tells her. "Is there another spell we could try?"

Ivy looks contemplative then goes to the bookshelf in the living room. It's filled with books so old the pages are old and delicate. There might even be a few bound in human skin. The sweet smell of magic that lingers makes me think these books are all grimoires.

Grimoires are books where witches write down all their spells and potion recipes. Since Ivy is a High Priestess of her coven, the grimoires are ones that she inherited from her predecessors. Generations of magical knowledge are all jammed unto the same old bookshelf.

She pulls out a heavy grimoire bound in cracked black leather. A heavy iron lock prevents it from being opened. The witch brings it to the kitchen table and drops it on the surface. Reaching into a kitchen drawer, she pulls out a silver knife—an athame as Willow once explained to me—and slices into her forearm. The smell of fresh blood has me holding my breath as drops of ruby drip on the cracked leather.

"Why is the blood necessary?" I ask, knowing this has to be some kind of witch thing I don't understand.

"This grimoire is all about blood magic," Ivy replies. "It wants blood in order to be read."

I'm reminded I have not eaten in a while. Willow notices my discomfort and takes my hand offering me support. I've gone hungry and without blood for longer periods of time. I know I'll be fine.

"And why does the book want blood?" I try to distract myself with questions.

"Because its previous owner was a witch who dabbled in some dark arcana. I don't usually use this grimoire, but there is a specific spell that can be useful to us," Ivy explains, not bothered at all by the cut on her arm.

There's a click as the lock on the grimoire gives way, and Ivy opens it without a problem. She flips to a page and points to the yellowed parchment. The ink has faded over time.

"There is a locator spell, but we'll need the blood of a relative," Ivy explains. "Does this Lydia have any family?"

Willow and Ivy both look at me for answers, and I reply, "She's from a big family, actually. She has five older brothers."

"That's great. I'll need some of their blood," she continues. "Preferably a full vial of it. The fresher the blood, the better it'll be for the spell."

"I've got an even better idea. I'll bring one of her brothers here. I'm sure any of them will be happy to help us with this," I explain.

Ivy flips to the next page and pauses before adding, "The spell has to be performed during the waning moon. It'll also require cooperative magic."

"And the waning moon is when exactly?"

"Tomorrow," Willow answers. "As for cooperative magic, Ivy and I can cast it together. If we need more witches, we can ask the coven for help."

Ivy nods. "I'll need some other supplies for the spell, but I can handle that on my own. I need you to bring the girl's brother here tomorrow after sundown."

14

LEX'S SOLUTION

Lex

I have never cared for King Matthias of Red River. We first met when he visited Crimson Peak soon after Kane's coronation. He'd recently been married, and the couple were already being unfaithful to one another. I found this out when I came back to my suite to find King Matthias's wife waiting for me, naked, in my bed.

I'd been young and reckless, seeing no need to deny sleeping with a willing body, especially since she was beautiful. It should have been a forgettable fling–a night I can barely remember–but the young queen decided to rub it in her husband's face to make him jealous. I almost ended up in a duel with King Matthias after I told him his wife wasn't even a good lay. Kane had to be the one to calm down the other king and talk him into forgiving and forgetting my rakish ways.

I would prefer to never see King Matthias ever again, but when my brother calls me asking for my help, I can't say no to Kane. A young woman's life is on the line, and I'm not heartless enough to look away when I have the power to do some good. When I'd been a useless young prince with no real purpose in my life, I chased only my own whims and pleasures. Becoming a regent and a father has shaped me into someone who cannot stand idly by when an evil needs to be stopped.

I invite King Matthias to visit Scarlett Thunder, hinting at a lucrative business proposition. The other king arrives quickly with his entourage of sycophants, and we exchange small talk like we don't despise each other. Politics is not for the weak. The number of fake smiles alone could kill a man's spirit if he doesn't have the stamina for it.

"How is your wife and child doing?" I ask as we take a stroll through the gardens. "Your son is fully grown now, if I recall."

Matthias nods, sidestepping the landmine of his wife. "Andreas is well. He's an accomplished swordsman."

"That's nice to hear."

"And how is your little boy?"

I smile, the thought of Cole genuinely bringing me joy. "He's the light of my life. I didn't know I'd take to fatherhood so well."

"Fatherhood surprises every man with the things we are willing to do for our children."

I never thought I'd agree with King Matthias about anything, but in this regard, we are in agreement. We pass by the antique statues the previous kings of Scarlett Thunder had commissioned or stolen from other conquered kingdoms. The gardeners don't tend to them, leaving them covered in moss and vines. I think about how Cole keeps trying to climb them, and poor Sarah has the hard job of trying to deny him anything. It makes me smile so I'm in a lighthearted mood as we continue our chat.

"I'm surprised you've invited me here," King Matthias admits. "If I may be blunt, I don't think we've ever cared for each other."

"We were young and foolish then. Are we not better men now and able to move past old bygones?"

"That will depend on your reasons for wanting to speak to me." He narrows his eyes.

I look around us to see if anyone is eavesdropping on our conversation. His entourage has stayed back, allowing us privacy. The gardeners have made themselves scarce. I turn to the other man to see his expectant face.

Matthias is shorter than I am by a few inches. With his high cheekbones and curly brown hair, he might have been considered attractive if a person isn't aware of his personality. He holds himself with the arrogance of a man who's always been catered to and expects nothing less. In some ways, he reminds me of my wife's late brother, Prince Jacob.

"I'm sure you're aware there's been a shortage of feeders," I begin. "It's becoming difficult to find fresh blood to sustain us in the castle."

"Difficult for you, perhaps, but I have no such issues." King Matthias smiles wickedly. "Although I know you've been your brother's dog since he won the war with King Peter and have to abide by his rules."

I bristle at the insult. "I am not my brother's dog."

"Do you not bark when he commands it?" he retorts. "Roll over? Play dead? Be a good boy?"

My fists clench in anger. I need to calm myself and not rise to his baiting. He's doing this on purpose. I will not give him the satisfaction of winning by letting him get to me.

"I am not Kane's puppet. I am my own man, and that's why I invited you here," I tell him briskly. "I know you have access to the Blood Takers, and your kingdom gets a supply of feeders from them frequently. I want the same deal with them."

He crosses his arms over his chest. "What makes you think I associate with the Blood Takers?"

"The tales of people going missing as they pass through your kingdom is well-known."

"All hearsay. The roads are dangerous. People go missing all the time. They could have been taken and eaten by the werewolves for all you know."

"Even when it's the shifters that are going missing?" I shake my head.

He sneers. "Do you think the werewolves are above cannibalism? I wouldn't put it past them."

I'm not in the mood for his games. He's trying to run circles around me and avoiding directly answering my questions.

"All I want is more blood, and all I ask is that you connect me to the right people," I explain. "It shouldn't be too difficult, should it? For a man of your influence and skill?"

King Matthias stares at me, trying to gauge my intentions. "You have a silver tongue, Lex. I can see how you managed to seduce my wife."

I don't point out how she was already lying naked in my bed. "Are you going to help me or not?"

"Of course, I can help you, but not for free," he replies. "I should be getting something in this deal besides flattery."

I still, hoping he doesn't ask for gold I do not have to give. I might have to ask Kane for the money if that's what Matthew wants since I won't be able to provide it. "What do you want?" I ask cautiously.

"I made a deal with King Peter during the war. His daughter, Princess Opaline, was pregnant with your son at the time. We had an agreement that King Peter's grandson would marry any future daughter of mine."

I have not been made aware of this deal. I haven't seen any documents where it's bene recorded. Would they even be legally binding since this was set up by my predecessor who has been dead for almost four years? More importantly, would I break this contract without repercussions?

As if he can read my mind, King Matthias continues, "I have the signed documents.. I can show them to you."

"Why haven't you informed me about this deal before?" I ask.

"It wasn't relevant before, but my wife is pregnant again. We're expecting a girl in a few months, and it's never too early to ensure your child's future."

His daughter isn't even born yet, and he's already brokered a match for her. Cole has only just turned three. He's way too young to be used like a political bargaining tool. It's been the way of our people for millennia, but it doesn't sit right with me.

"I was promised my daughter would be queen of Scarlett Thunder someday," King Matthias continues. "I'm holding you to that promise, and I'm even willing to help you find a steady supply of feeders as a gesture of my good will."

Guilt and defeat sit heavily in my stomach. I feel cornered, trying to find a path out of this, but finding myself trapped on all sides. "They're only children," I try to reason with him. "They're too young to be betrothed."

"My wife was in the cradle when she was betrothed to me," he returns. "Are you really that naïve to think your son would be the exception?"

I narrow my eyes at him. Is it worth it when I don't even need any more blood to feed my people?

I'll have to think about it.

* * *

Rainer

George Nightstone is a tall, muscular man that hovers over Ivy while she is trying to read the grimoire. Ever since we brought the male shifter to Ivy's cottage, he's been watching her like a bird of prey. Willow and I exchange looks, wary about this development. Ivy seems to mostly ignore him as she prepares to cast the locator spell.

She grabs a can of salt and pours it to the ground in a circle. The other witches in the coven who are here to help with the spell light candles and place them around the area.

When Ivy almost bumps into George as he follows her around, she rolls her hazel eyes. "Could you stop doing that?"

George is much taller than her and stares down at her with narrowed eyes. "Doing what?"

"I don't know if this is a shifter thing you're doing, but I don't like people hovering over me," she explains

His face flushes, and he pulls on his ear. "Sorry. I've just never met a real-life witch before."

"Rule number one when meeting a witch: stop being odd, and stand over there."

Ivy points to a corner furthest from her. George complies, standing at the edge of the garden as Ivy and the witches continue preparing for the spell. When they're ready to start casting, Willow joins them and stands around the salt circle. Ivy beckons George to come back, and she asks him to step into the salt circle without breaking it.

I watch all of this from the back porch of Ivy's home, trying to stay out of the way. Ivy pulls out an athame strapped to her belt and reaches for George's arm. He doesn't flinch when she slices into his forearm, catching the ruby red drops in a small bowl of water.

"*Sanguis in sanguine,*" the witches chant together. "*Invenire hominem.*"

They continue to repeat this chant. Willow dips a clear quartz pendulum into the bowl of blood. When she pulls it out, the quartz is now a bright blood red. She holds it up for Ivy to inspect.

"Did it work?" Willow asks.

"The only way to find out is to use it," Ivy replies. "Someone has to wear it. and it should guide them to where they can find Lydia."

"I'll do it," George volunteers quickly. "Lydia is my sister. I should be the one to bring her home."

"If the Blood Takers catch you, you'll both be in danger and end up as feeders. It should be a vampire that goes to get her," I cut in, approaching the salt circle. "I'll have a better chance of finding her and getting out with both of us alive."

"They'll recognize you," Willow points out. "You're too well-known."

"Isn't there some kind of spell you can use to change my appearance?" I ask her.

Ivy nods and offers, "I know a few glamour charms. They won't change your appearance drastically but enough that they won't know it's you."

"Do it," I tell her. "We don't have any time to waste."

"The charms won't permanently change his appearance?" Willow asks. "Are they reversible?"

"I can reverse them easily," Ivy explains. "Another witch could reverse them if they try hard enough so I suggest you don't get caught."

"I don't plan to," I agree. "Now, what are we waiting for?"

Ivy glances at Willow as if asking for permission. My wife sighs and nods at her niece who moves closer to me, stepping away from the salt circle so we're only a foot apart. Her delicate hands touch my face, moving over my lips, nose, and over my eyelids.

Her magic feels warm and comforting like a blanket. The sweet smell of berries tickles my nose as she transforms me into someone else.

15

DEAL WITH THE DEVIL

Kane

Lex calls me after his meeting with King Matthias. My brother has gone above and beyond and was able to get the information we need. King Matthias is aware of the Blood Takers abducting people that are passing through his kingdom. It's an operation that's been in place for a while now.

"King Myenas is the head of everything," Lex says. "The Blood Takers came to be because he got sick of having to make deals with the Alphas."

"He found a way to get blood on his own, without anyone's monitoring," I conclude, feeling sick to my stomach. "It's no wonder the shifters think we're monsters when we have people like King Myenas."

"King Myenas has always had a questionable reputation. Mother said that Father never could trust him."

"And with good reason," I agree. "Is there any way you can confirm that Lydia is in the latest batch of feeders?"

"Unfortunately, no. There's also the chance they will get suspicious about me asking for a specific shifter woman," Lex explains.

"King Matthias told me that the latest batch of shifters is headed for Carmine Falls. They should reach the castle in days."

Carmine Falls is King Myenas' kingdom to the east. King Matthias has been vague about what other kingdoms are part of the operation, so tracking the Blood Takers will be difficult.

"Can't you ask them to send you that batch of feeders instead?" I ask.

"I tried, but King Myenas told me I have to wait my turn, and he won't be sending me even one feeder until I pay up."

"How much is he asking for?"

He tells me all the specifics, and it seems feeders bring in quite an impressive amount these days. Women and children are worth more than men—and I probably don't want to know why.

I close my eyes, rubbing my brow as I try to take this in. This is despicable business. I'm not completely shocked at the actions of those in power, but it's still hard for me sometimes to understand how anyone could be so cruel.

From where I'm seated at my desk, I look at the study doors. Mikey often bursts through when he wants my attention. Regardless of how busy I get with my work, I always make time for him. The reminder that not all children in this world are so well protected is a stark reminder of the dark brutality that hides in our society. That people's value can be quantified in money makes me feel hollow.

"I don't have enough right now, so I have to wait," Lex adds.

"I will send you the money," I promise him. This is my problem, after all, not his. My wife's family is my family.

"Don't bother. They're sending me the next batch of feeders which won't have the shifter girl you're looking for, so it won't matter."

"Could we offer them more money for the current batch of feeders?"

"I tried that, but Myenas isn't budging. He wants a fresh batch of feeders because he's almost through the last one."

"How much blood does he need? Is he gorging himself on it?"

"He has the resources for it." Lex sounds annoyed.

I tap my fingers on my desk. "Where in Red River are the Blood Takers now?"

"They should be reaching the village of Rouge Curve by tomorrow," he tells me.

Rouge Curve is half a day's drive from Crimson Peak. There's a chance we could reach Lydia before she ends up in Carmine Falls. Getting her away from King Myenas will be more difficult. Castle Redbone is situated at the edge of a cliff beside a waterfall. It's a remote location that's hard to escape.

"I'll tell Rainer," I say. "He should be in Rouge Curve by the end of the day."

"You sent Rainer?" Lex seems surprised.

"He's going undercover as one of the Blood Takers. Willow's niece cast a spell so he can track her down easier," I explain.

Lex gasps. "Do you think it's safe for Rainer? What if someone recognizes him?"

"He won't look like himself." This is difficult to explain to someone who hasn't spent much time around magic.

"What does that mean?" he asks.

"Rainer's wife used a spell to change his appearance."

"Are you sure this is a good plan?" Lex questions. "I know that Rainer is capable, but he's one man. The Blood Takers are mercenaries who will have no qualms about killing him if they discover who he is."

"Rainer has infiltrated enemy territory before," I remind him. "This will not be his first time in dangerous territory."

In the latter part of my father's reign as king, he saw the potential in Rainer as a spy and sent him off on covert missions to other kingdoms. Rainer never speaks about this time in his life, but from what I could piece together, he doesn't enjoy it. My father hadn't been displeased with his work, so I know he did well at the job. Despite that, Rainer has been happier serving me in the castle as my advisor since I ascended to the throne.

"I wish him the best of luck," my brother remarks. "May he get in and out of there before anything bad happens."

"I'll tell him you said that. Before I go, what did you give Matthias for him to allow you access to the Blood Takers?"

There's a pause before Lex answers, "He wants my son to marry his unborn daughter someday."

My eyes widen in shock. "You betrothed Cole to Matthias' daughter?"

"Technically, King Peter did that before Cole was born. Turns out Matthias has signed legally binding contracts and has no desire to break the agreement."

"But Cole is only a child." I shake my head. I can't believe Lex would do something so drastic.

"Is this dissimilar to what happened between you and Opaline? It's a common practice," Lex points out. "We're aware most of these betrothals never last long enough for a wedding to take place. I'm prepared to wait for King Matthias to break the contract."

"What if he doesn't break it?"

"That will be a problem I will have to deal with in the future but my son is only three. He's not coming near an altar any time soon."

I take a deep breath and thank Lex for his help again. I'll do what I can to help my nephew when the time comes, but for now, I need to help my soon-to-be sister-in-law.

* * *

Rainer

Kane informs me that the Blood Takers will be in Rouge Curve by tomorrow. I have no time to spare as I have to make my way from Crimson Peak to Red River within the day. I don't take any personal items with me that can point to my real identity. I pack a small bag of clothes, a supply of blood, and a few weapons that I can conceal on my person.

Willow watches me from the doorway of our bedroom, her expression concerned.

Trying to lighten the mood, I quip, "How does Ivy feel about marrying a shifter? George Nightstone seems sweet on her."

"Ivy doesn't really care for shifters," Willow replies. "She thinks George Nightstone is annoying."

"Stranger pairings have happened. Look at Emory and Kane."

"Emory and Kane are mates. From what she's told me, George would know almost immediately that Ivy is his mate. Since she's not, he'd just be wasting his time with her until he finds his real mate."

I take out a gun from the drawer where I keep the few weapons I have on hand just in case and slide it inside the pocket of my jacket. "I never considered how unique that mating thing is with shifters. Vampires don't have anything like it."

"Vampires do tend to want to sleep around and have wild orgies."

I snort. "You're thinking of Lex. Not all of us are that depraved. Kane was practically a virgin before he met Emory. He was more concerned about taxes than trying to get laid."

"Why is that? He's king. He could have anyone he wants."

"It might have been the influence of his parents. King Michael and Queen Agatha were devoted to each other, and Kane has always been an old soul. He left the pursuit of pleasure-seeking thrills to his brother instead."

Willow leans against the doorframe. "How do you even end up in an orgy? Do you get invited, or do you just stumble into one by chance?"

I laugh. "Why are you curious? Are you interested in an orgy?"

She shakes her head quickly. "I just don't know who organizes these things and how it's supposed to go."

"I could ask Lex if you really want to know."

She grimaces. "I'm good." A somber look takes over. She plays with the ends of her brown hair. I move closer to her. We are well-acquainted with each other's bodies and our preferences. We've spent years learning how to give and receive pleasure from one another.

Even with the familiar pull of desire, that's not what I focus on. Willow keeps looking down and refusing to meet my gaze. I know the warning signs of her trying to hide something from me.

"Everything will be fine," I assure her. "I'll find Lydia, and we'll be back here before you know it."

She doesn't say anything. I know that when she's stressed, she tends to retreat into herself. She tries to hide her fears and insecurities deep within her. Even after four years of marriage, it can be difficult to get her to open up.

I place my hands on her shoulders. "I'll be okay. I promise."

"You have to come back," she says. "I can't raise Bryony on my own. She adores you, and you can't leave me to do everything by myself. Not to mention, I kind of like you."

"I know." I smile, reading between the lines of what she really wants to say. "I love you too, and I will be back. I promise."

Her pale blue eyes stare deeply into mine. "Don't you dare die on me, Rainer. I will find a way to bring you back just so I can yell at you."

"I would deserve it." I dip down to kiss her, but she pulls away, avoiding the kiss. "What is it?"

"It's just a bit strange to kiss you when you look different."

Ivy's glamour charms work like a dream. The changes are minimal but effective. My lips are thinner, my jawline more rounded, my eyes a bit further apart, and my nose is wider. My hair is even a shade of dishwater blond.

The small changes make me look like a different person entirely. It feels odd to look at my reflection and see a different man.

"I don't know how long I'll be gone," I persuade. "I'd like a kiss from my wife."

Willow closes her eyes. "I'll picture your actual face."

I kiss her with the familiarity of having done this dozens of times. Willow relaxes as she kisses me back, recognizing me despite the glamour charms. I would like nothing more than to continue to kiss my wife, to make love to her, but I can't linger for long. She sighs when I pull away.

"I love you," I declare. "Tell Bryony I love her too."

Our daughter is asleep in her room, and I don't want to startle her by having a stranger appear before her out of nowhere. I regret not being able to say goodbye directly. She likes me to come see her before I have to leave for trips. I've been consistent in doing that, but I have to break the streak this time.

Willow shakes her head. "You can tell her when you come back."

Smiling at my beautiful, and stubborn, wife, I kiss the top of her head. "We've got a deal.."

I grab my bag to leave, and Willow follows me as I make my way to the door of our suite. I glance at my wife once more and take in her pretty face with her short dark hair and her blue eyes. She's changed over the years in slightly different ways, and I learn to love each new version of her I get to meet. Coming home to her is my favorite thing in the world.

I open the door and I slip into the shadows. I have a long journey ahead of me.

16

THE CRUSHING NEWS

EMORY

I'm not expecting Colt to show up at Castle Graystone. It's early in the morning, and I've just finished getting ready when he barges into my suite, followed by the castle guards. He looks furious, his eyes like emerald fire. I gesture toward the castle guards that everything is fine, and they can leave us alone.

The guards leave quickly. Nellie glances at me worriedly before following the guards out of the room.

"Colt?" I say. "Is everything okay–"

He cuts me off, "Could you tell me why I had to find out from George Nightstone that you've found Lydia, and you didn't tell me?"

"I tried to call you, but no one answered," I reply. "Willow's niece, Ivy, cast a locator spell, and Rainer is on the way to find Lydia as we speak."

"Why are you sending Rainer?" he demands. "I should be the one going to find her. Lydia is my mate!"

He's upset, and I can understand why. Colt has always led first with his mouth, speaking before thinking. He's managed to escape consequences for his impulsive behavior through charm and luck. As an adult, it's an incredibly annoying trait to still have.

I try to keep my calm. "I know this is stressful for you–"

"Oh fuck off, Em! I've been waiting two days for any updates." He begins pacing around the room. "All I've been able to do is worry about Lydia, wondering if she's hurt or in pain. You should've sent someone to tell me when I didn't answer!"

I inhale and exhale deeply, trying to bite back my annoyance. "When I spoke to Mom the other night, she said you were passed out drunk," I explain. "And yesterday, Kane and Rainer spent the whole time trying to track down Lydia through any means at our disposal. I didn't leave you in the dark for no reason. I was doing everything I could to help you get Lydia back."

Colt stops pacing. He looks guilty, his anger melting away, and I can see the exhaustion and worry replace it. He runs a hand through his hair. My annoyance evaporates as I can see the source of his anger is his concern and fear." I just want to get her back," he says. "Each hour waiting to hear anything feels like an eternity."

"I know, Colt."

He goes to the chair against the wall and takes a seat, slumping against the wooden back of the chair. "Where is she? Tell me, Em. Please."

"She's in Red River," I answer. "I'm not telling you exactly where because Rainer is on his way, and you can't blow his cover. He has to be careful about this. He can't afford to make mistakes if he has any chance for him and Lydia to come back alive."

"You can't expect me not to do anything!" he argues. "I'm supposed to just sit here and have breakfast while Lydia is in danger?"

"That is exactly what you need to do."

He looks at me in disbelief. "What the fuck, Em? You want me to pretend everything is normal? That's what cowards do!"

"You are stupidly brave and honorable. I love that about you, but that kind of behavior is going to get you and Lydia killed if I let you run after her."

"I wouldn't get us killed–"

"The people that took her are mercenaries, Colt. They will kill you without hesitation. Kane sent Rainer to save Lydia because Rainer knows how to be discreet. And he's a vampire who will always be stronger and faster than us. That's just a fact."

Colt looks defeated. "You can't expect me to just sit by and do nothing. We made a promise to do good and be better people."

"Doing nothing doesn't mean we're bad people. We're just making sure Lydia comes back alive," I reason. "Kane told me about the Blood Takers and how much they sell the feeders for. I am sickened and disturbed about these people, and I would want nothing more than to have them locked away for good so they can stop abducting people."

I grab a chair and drag it closer to where Colt is seated so we're right beside each other. I look into his emerald eyes so he can see I mean what I'm saying to him.

"I want to run to Red River and free every feeder who must be terrified about what's about to happen to them," I continue. "But I also know doing that will do them no good. Instead, I have to wait for Rainer to come back with Lydia. I know that in order for this fucked up operation to get shut down is if I trust Kane to help me navigate this."

"I don't understand this world, Em," Colt admits. "These vampire kings are doing horrific things and no one is doing anything to stop it."

He might sound naïve but Colt has always had a big heart. He genuinely cares about people, and it's why I left the care of Moon Grove to him, knowing there is no one else better for the job.

"We're going to stop them, Colt. I promise you that," I declare. "You, me, Kane, and all our friends–we're going to stop them. This has gone on for far too long. It has to end."

Colt looks troubled. He takes my hand and squeezes it. "It feels like I'm seventeen again, and I'm helpless to do anything," he says. "Everyone else makes the big decisions that actually affect things, and I'm just in the background. I'm nothing."

"You're not nothing," I assure him. "You do more than enough. You *are* enough."

Colt bows his head. "If something happens to Lydia, and all I did was sit back and wait, I'll never be able to forgive myself."

I don't have the words to make him feel better. They remain trapped in my throat. I pull Colt into a hug and hold him until he begins to shake in my arms. He's bigger than me, but I don't complain as he rests his weight against me and lets everything out.

Rainer has to bring Lydia home–he has to.

* * *

WILLOW

I'm distracted as I reshelf books in the castle library. My thoughts are far away while I move the book trolley to another aisle and rearrange the books. I can't even be annoyed at whoever put the books back in the wrong order. There are even books from a different section of the library here, and I don't care.

All I can think about is my husband who is heading directly into enemy territory without any backup. I know what Rainer is capable of in combat, but he's still one person against a group of mercenaries. No one even knows how many Blood Takers there actually are. Rainer could be facing dozens of mercenaries.

Footsteps coming closer make me turn and I see Lola with a book in her hand about horticulture. We're in the romance literature aisle. I glance at the poorly arranged books and back at her. Despite the heavy eye makeup and red streaks in her hair, I can see the guilt on Lola's face clearly.

"Have you been moving books around?" I ask.

Lola shrugs, trying to act nonchalant. "Why would I?"

"Because you're the only other person besides me who spends so much time here, so you'd know how to mess up my arrangement system."

"That would be stupid and childish. Why would I waste my time doing that?"

I put my hands on my hips, giving Lola my best Mom glare. "Are you going to confess, young lady? Or should I go tell Emory what you've been doing?"

Lola immediately gives in. "Don't tell Emory! She nags and guilt trips me."

"Maybe she has a reason to nag you if you're rearranging my library books for your own amusement."

"I did it to amuse *you*. You've been distracted all day, so I thought I'd give you something to do except sit, stare, and look sad."

"I don't look sad," I argue.

"Yes, you do. You act like your husband's gone off to war."

My husband has gone off into his own little war, but Lola doesn't know that. It's not my place to tell her. "I appreciate the thought, but you're going to rearrange the books. No buts. You did something you shouldn't have, and now there's going to be consequences."

Lola lets out a bratty whine but does as she's been told. Between the two of us, we get the books in the right order quickly. But when we finish, I find myself sitting at my desk, staring into space. I have a book open, but the words on the page aren't penetrating my brain. I keep thinking about Rainer, wondering if he's doing okay.

"You haven't flipped a page for ten minutes straight," Lola points out from a nearby table. She has an open notebook in front of her.

"Maybe I just read slowly."

"You read the fastest of anyone I know. It only takes you a few seconds to get through a whole page."

I chuckle. "I've been reading for a really long time."

"That's how I know you're full of bullshit with that slow reading thing."

I practically gasp when she swears. "Lola! Language!"

"Everyone in this castle swears all the time except for Queen Agatha," she counters. "And I'm sixteen now. That's practically an adult, so I can swear if I want to."

I'm beginning to understand Emory's despair at realizing the sweet little girl who reads all the books I recommend to her at age twelve is no more. A new version of Lola is here, and she swears and rearranges my books for fun.

"Just because other people are doing it doesn't mean you have to do it too," I remind her.

"I'm not swearing cause you're all swearing."

"Then why are you?"

She shrugs and changes the topic quickly, "Where's Rainer?"

"He's on an important trip for King Kane. He had to leave early last night."

"Why didn't he take you with him?" she questions. "You go with him sometimes, unless it's a dangerous trip."

We've all agreed not to involve Lola in the situation with the abducted feeders, so nobody has told her anything. However, I've always known, since I met her, how observant she is.

"He went somewhere far away, and I couldn't leave Bryony behind." I shrug, trying to play it off.

Lola's gray eyes narrow at me suspiciously. "You know I'm not dumb, right? I know something is going on, and all of you are keeping it from me."

I look down at my book, trying to appear unaffected with this conversation. "Why would we keep you from anything? But if we are, it's probably for a good reason."

"Let me guess. I'll understand when I'm older?"

"Time is a great teacher. It helps put things into perspective."

I can practically hear Lola's eye roll. "Whatever. You used to be cool, and now you're just like every other adult around here."

I catch her gaze and reply, "I never pretended to be anything other than what I am, and one day, you'll be an adult too, just like everyone else."

"I won't!" she argues, pouting. "I would never suck the fun out of everything like Emory."

"I don't think she sucks the fun out of everything. She's just responsible."

"She's boring."

"She's basically your mother while you're here, so watch your mouth." I narrow my eyes at her.

Lola actually looks sheepish. "Emory's not boring. She's just different now."

"Of course, she's different. Her life has drastically changed in the last few years. No one would be left unaffected with what she went through."

"Yeah, and everybody loves her," Lola points out. "Do you know how shitty it feels to have an older sister that everyone says is amazing? What am I in comparison? Chopped liver?" Insecurity practically burns in her like a neon light.

Poor thing. I can't imagine growing up and feeling inadequate next to a sibling, though I didn't have that experience myself. "You're Lola. You're your own person," I assure her. "You don't have to be like Emory. All you need to be is yourself."

Lola rolls her eyes and starts gathering her things. "I don't know who that is, so thanks for the advice."

She stomps out of the library, and I can't even be bothered to scold her for all the noise.

17

AN ESCAPE PLAN

Lydia

My head fucking hurts.

While shifters can heal fast, head wounds take longer and slow down healing other injuries in the process. Cataloguing my injuries, I have a sprained wrist and bruises all over my body. besides the concussion Sleeping in the semi-truck is uncomfortable. All of us, human and shifter, are crammed together like sardines.

The truck stops a few times a day. We're traveling slowly with the men who have taken us only bothering to feed us once a day. Bathroom breaks are only allowed in groups. One of the men is always standing nearby in case we try to make a run for it.

Today's meal is canned beans, and we're expected to share with each other. Meanwhile, the Blood Takers have hunted a boar for themselves and are roasting it over a bonfire. The smell of the meat cooking makes my stomach growl with hunger. I haven't eaten anything substantial in a few days.

I shake my head when a brunette shifter offers a tin can to me.

"You need food to heal," she insists.

"I'm okay. You need it more."

I don't know how much longer it's been since they've eaten a meal.

A lot of the people look malnourished, probably from living on the streets before they were taken. It makes me feel guilty for spending an entire weekend at Moon Grove having my every whim catered to. I can survive hungry for a little while.

My empty stomach is distracting. I try to look around the forest to pinpoint where we are, but all forests look the same to me at night. During the day, we're in the back of the truck with no windows. Trying to follow a familiar scent is useless when all I can smell is the boar on the bonfire.

My stomach growls again. I glare down at it as if it's to blame for my predicament.

The brunette offers me the tin can again. It's half-empty now.

"Just take a few bites," she says. "Please."

I accept the can from her and raise it to pour the beans and the tomato sauce into my mouth. Hunger makes anything taste amazing. I finish the can quickly, licking tomato sauce from my lips and wishing there was more. I'm unsatisfied and use my finger to scoop tomato sauce from the can so I can lick it off.

"I'm Jesse, by the way," she says.

"I'm Lydia."

"What pack are you from?"

"Nightstone Pack. How about you?"

"I used to be part of the Moonraker Pack, but I ran away during the war with Crimson Peak. Then I lived in the north for a little while. I've been kind of wandering around from town to town until…." She glances to where the Blood Takers are cutting into the boar with a knife. "And now I'm here."

I lean closer to her and whisper, "Why are they even eating? They can just survive on blood, right? You think they're trying to just make us jealous?"

Jesse bites back a smile. "Maybe."

I stare at Jesse's face and try to gauge how old she is. She's skinny, probably underweight, but her face is round which makes her look younger. She has a smattering of freckles across her nose and cheeks that match her dark brown eyes. It's hard to guess her age, but I'm guessing it could be anywhere from eighteen to twenty-two.

Glancing back at the Blood Takers, I see they're busy eating. They're having bottles of blood with the meat. I've heard the vampires sometimes mix blood into wine to preserve the blood for longer periods of time. It's not as good as fresh blood but enough to survive on.

"Hey, Jesse," I whisper to her. "I need to go to the bathroom. Could you come with me?"

She looks warily at the Blood Takers then nods at me. I place the can on the ground and stand up slowly, trying not to be noticed. Jesse follows me, tucking her hands in the pockets of her jacket. Both of us avoid making eye contact with anyone as we walk to a secluded crop of trees.

As soon as we're far enough, I turn to Jess and ask, "Do you have any idea where we are?"

She shakes her head, her brown eyes wide. "I-I don't..."

I grab her by the shoulders. "Jess, this is important. When we were in the truck, did you hear or smell anything that indicated we're in Red River?"

"I really don't know. I think we might be in Red Rives considering how slow we've been traveling–"

"Hey! What are you two doing here?"

We both turn around, startled as one of the Blood Takers has followed us. He sneers at us. Instinctively, I push Jess behind me wanting to keep her out of harm's way. His red eyes watch the movement.

"What are you two doing here?" he repeats. "If you're trying to escape, I'm going to have to punish you, and you won't like that."

"We're not," I reply, trying to remain calm. "I just needed to go to the bathroom."

"Well, get on with it then." He gestures at me. "I'll watch to make sure you're not going to make a run for it when I turn my back."

Embarrassment makes me swallow hard. I'm angry, but I know

better than to pick a fight with a vampire. They are stronger and faster than me. All I've gotten is injured when I've tried.

"You don't have to watch me," I say, persuasively. "I promise I won't try to run."

He glances at Jesse and points at her. "If you run, it'll be her neck on the line. It'll be your conscience, blondie."

"I understand."

He turns around, and it's a good thing I really do need to pee. I give Jess an apologetic look, and she turns away to give me privacy. I walk closer to a tree and pull up my dress and pull my panties out of the way. Squatting down, I think about how to escape this mess I'm in.

* * *

Lex

I don't bother knocking as I enter Opal's chambers. She wouldn't have stopped if I walked in on her with another man again. I know from experience. Thankfully, she's alone this time.

Opal sits at her vanity table and applies her make-up. I watch as she powders her nose. Her hair is in a complicated updo with dark curls framing her face. She carefully applies a blood red lipstick that makes her lips look fuller.

My wife has always been beautiful. Opal looks like a porcelain doll with her fair skin, blue eyes, and long black hair. When I first met her, I'd been attracted to her for her looks and the forbidden quality of her being my brother's fiancée. I didn't even care about her personality or how she treats anyone she thinks is beneath her.

Four years of marriage have wiped away any illusions I had of her being a good person. I've seen the brittle, selfish little girl Opal is deep down, always craving love and attention. It's too similar to how I felt as an insecure boy. The difference between us now is that I've grown up.

Fatherhood forced me to be a better man. Cole deserves better than to be an extension of my inadequacies. I don't want him to grow up and bear the weight of my failures. I set aside the boy I had been, and I don't look back.

On the other hand, Opal has not taken to motherhood with the same mindset. She adores Cole and showers him with affection when she wants to. Feeding him little pieces of her affection like a puppy with treats, but Cole is still too young to understand the difference.

"Opal," I say. "I need to talk to you."

She rolls her eyes as she fusses with her hair. "What do you want now, Lex?"

"Did you know about the deal your father made with King Matthias?"

"What deal?"

"The one where he brokered a betrothal with Cole and King Matthias's future daughter?"

"I don't know. Maybe?" She shrugs. "You know these royal betrothals are mostly temporary. I'm sure my father didn't even intend to keep the deal, and I doubt King Matthias will even bother collecting on that deal."

I lean against the vanity table, hovering over her slightly. "He is."

"He is what?"

"King Matthias is collecting on the deal. That's why he was visiting the castle. His wife is pregnant, and he wants the betrothal to go through once the baby is born."

Opal pauses, her blue eyes staring up at me in shock. She tries to regain her composure and picks up her hairbrush to run it through the ends of her curls.

"Well, this isn't a bad thing. King Matthias could be a good ally."

"I don't trust him," I tell her. "And I don't want Cole involved in any of this. He's only three. He shouldn't be betrothed yet."

"This is how it is with royal children. Cole is no different."

I stare at her in disbelief. "Cole is our son. Your father decided his future before he was even born. How can you be so unbothered about this?"

"I don't see why you're so pressed about this, Lex. Cole was always going to be married for the benefit of the kingdom. It's how things have always been."

"Not always."

She scowls, her pretty face turning ugly in her contempt. "Just because your brother decided to marry that werewolf slut doesn't mean he's setting the norm."

"Don't call Emory that."

"I'll call her whatever I want. She stole my life!" she argues, slamming the hairbrush down on the vanity. "I was supposed to be married to a king! Instead, I ended up married to his brother who doesn't even have his own throne!"

Over the years, Opal has continued to blame Kane and Emory for the war and the death of her father and brother. She can never assign blame to her father and brother for their own actions. She certainly can never take blame for the things she did that led to the war. These beliefs are what fuel Opal's hatred and her inability to grow and change.

I'm secretly relieved about her disinterest in being a mother and letting me and the servants take care of Cole so she can't whisper poisonous lies into his ear. She would take all his sweetness and replace it with her bitterness.

"Believe what you want, Opal," I say. "But I will not raise Cole in the same way we were brought up. He gets to be his own person and make his own choices."

She scoffs. "What are you going to do? Let him marry whoever he wants? You can't be that naïve."

"Maybe I am." I turn and walk away, wanting to distance myself from her. Solitude is my only reprieve from my marriage. The less we see of each other, the better my life is. Fighting with Opal is repetitive and draining.

I head to the nursery where Cole is drawing with crayons. He looks up and smiles brightly when he sees me enter the room. He abandons the crayons to run up and hug me. Bending down, I welcome him with open arms, and for a moment everything feels right in the world.

"Daddy!" he pulls away and tugs at my hand to follow him.

I comply, and he takes me over to his drawings. He shows me his artwork and smiles at the incomprehensible scribbles. He points to a stick figure with yellow hair. "This is you, Daddy."

"Great job, son. You've captured my essence."

"What's es-sens?"

"What makes me myself." When he looks confused, I kiss the top of his head. "Never mind. It's a big kid word."

He shrugs and points to the other drawings, telling me about them. To be a child and so unbothered is a blessing.

"Hey, Cole, do you remember when I told you about Uncle Cyrus? He lives by the sea."

Cole's eyes brighten and he nods.

"How about you and I visit him for a few days? It will be a fun trip."

"I get to go to the beach?" When I nod, he shouts, "Yay!"

I grin as he hugs me again, his arms around my neck.

18

BY THE SEA

Lex

I haven't been to Cerise Port in years. Fatherhood and running a kingdom can keep a man busy. I've always felt a kinship with Uncle Cyrus who I've always been able to talk to easier than my own father. When my mother used to bring Kane and I to her birth kingdom, we could breathe and just be ordinary kids without having to watch how we act all the time.

I have very fond memories of visiting Cerise Port in my childhood, and even through my adolescence, when I would visit their red district. I've gotten in trouble more than a few times in the kingdom, but Uncle Cyrus got me out of trouble and watched me over to the best of his ability.

I want Cole to enjoy some of the freedom I'd been able to experience in Cerise Port, and my son is truly never happier than he is collecting seashells at the beach. Sarah carries a small bucket as she helps him. I watch from afar, walking with Uncle Cyrus. We've discarded our shoes so we can walk barefoot on the sand.

"He's a sweet kid," Uncle Cyrus remarks. "Reminds me of you when you were his age."

"Everyone says I was a hellion." I chuckle.

"When you were older, you definitely tried to turn your parents' hair gray," he agrees with a smile. "But when you were little, all you wanted was to laugh and play. You and your brother would beg me to take you to go watch the whales."

I smile as I remember watching whales from a boat and listening to them sing. "I thought the noises they made were funny."

"You used to ask me if I could get you your own whale. Just a small one that you could keep in your bathtub at home." He laughs and pats my back.

"I didn't understand they wouldn't stay small," I reply, bashfully. "I thought they wouldn't get big if they weren't in the ocean."

"Ah but like children, no whale stays little. They all have to grow up."

The words make me contemplative, and I look at my uncle as I think over his words.

He had been an important part of my life growing up, the kind uncle who tried to understand me better than my own parents. He always seemed so tall, strong, and dependable. I can't help but notice how he's aged in little ways with the graying hair at his temples and the laugh lines around his mouth. He even seems shorter as I'm taller than him by a few inches now.

Vampires live such long lives, but we all eventually age and died. We just take our sweet time getting there.

"Uncle!" a familiar voice calls out.

We both turn to see my nephew Michael running toward us. With his dark hair and blue eyes, he looks like a miniature version of Kane. He hugs Uncle Cyrus first, grabbing him around the middle. The top of his head only reaches the king's abdomen.

"Michael." Uncle Cyrus pats his head. "You're early."

"It's beach time," the little boy replies. "I'm going swimming."

"Of course. But where are your parents?"

Michael points to where Kane and Emory are walking over. They're dressed more casually for the climate in lighter fabrics for the hot weather. Emory is wearing a large hat and a sundress while Kane is in a white polo and khaki pants.

I walk over to meet them, pulling Kane into a hug. "What are you two doing here?"

"Things are tense at the castle," Emory replies. "We thought we should all have a beach day to cheer ourselves up a bit."

"I thought the exact same thing," I admit.

"Great minds think alike," my brother replies.

I pull her into a hug, and she accepts it. Over the years, whatever bad blood there once was between us has been tossed under the bridge. With kids and running kingdoms, old mistakes seem trivial. Besides, we're family, and we have to stick together.

"Is Cole with you?" Kane asks.

"He's collecting seashells." I point to where he's walking with Sarah in the distance.

We all look to see that Michael has joined Cole and the two cousins are enthusiastically looking over the seashells in the bucket. Déjà vu makes me blink at the mirage of the two boys looking so much like Kane and I as children.

"Sorry that we missed Cole's birthday party," Emory tells me. "I was just so busy with the Moon Goddess Ball, and Kane had other matters to attend to."

"There's always next year, and I don't even know if Cole will remember any of his birthdays yet." I shrug. I wish they could've been there, but I understand.

"I heard there was a petting zoo." Emory smiles.

"There was a sloth. Cole was ecstatic." I laugh at the memory.

"He's definitely going to remember it then," Kane points out.

I nod, agreeing that he's probably right.

I look past Emory and Kane to see that she's brought her siblings with her. The little blonde girl looks older, around sixteen or seventeen. There's also that hulking redheaded brother who looks like someone just shot him dead. Neither of them look happy to be here.

"I take it not everyone came here willingly?" I quip.

Emory and Kane share a look before she replies, "I'm being told it's teenage angst and my sister will grow out of it eventually."

"If you ask her, soon isn't coming soon enough," Kane adds conspiringly.

"And your brother? How is he?" I nod in the man's direction.

Emory looks sad. "Colt is trying his best, but things are difficult at the moment."

I know from my discussions with Kane that Emory's brother lost his mate recently to the Blood Takers, and they're working on getting her back. I don't know a lot about shifter culture, but do I know that mates are sacred to them. I've personally witnessed the power of it through Kane and Emory's relationship. I can't imagine what Colt Moonraker is going through.

"We're doing what we can to get Lydia back to him," Kane explains. "Right now, it's a waiting game, though, and he's having problems being patient, as we all would be."

I nod. I can't imagine what it would be like to love someone and have her stolen from me.

Honestly, someday I hope I know the first part, but not the second.

Never the second.

* * *

Lᴜᴅɪᴀ

The movement of the semi-truck makes me woozy. Jesse lets me rest my head on her lap as it's more comfortable than the metal floor of the truck. She and I have been leaning on each other. Having someone I can talk to makes this experience more bearable.

"What's it like in your pack lands?" Jesse asks. "I've never been."

"It's cold there. Lots of trees. We're on the border with Sardonia," I answer, getting lost in memories of my home. "Winter lasts longer than most places, but I love it. There's nothing like running through the snow and hunting buffalo with my brothers."

"I'm an only child. What's it like having brothers?"

"They're the worst—and the best. I wanted to kill all of them so many times growing up, but I know that they would kill for me, and I would do the same for them."

"Do you miss them?"

"Yes." I look up at her youthful face and ask, "Do you have any family?"

"They died during the war with Crimson Peak. My dad was a warrior. After he died, my mom got sick and never recovered. I didn't have anyone else, so I left Moon Grove to find a new home elsewhere."

She looks so sad, her dark brown eyes glassy. She swallows, and I take her hand to squeeze it reassuringly.

"After all this is over, you should come home with me. We'd welcome you with open arms."

Jesse smiles softly. "I'd like that."

The semi-truck stops, and the door opens. One of the Blood Takers calls out, "Get up, you lazy mongrels! We don't have all day!"

Sleeping in the semi-truck isn't comfortable for anybody, so it takes a while for us to shuffle out with our lack of proper rest and food. It's midday, and the sun makes me cover my eyes, it's so bright. They lead us off into the forest where there's a stream. The others rush over to scoop water to drink. Others try to wash off days' worth of grime from their faces and bodies.

People strip down to their underwear to take a bath. Shifters aren't naturally shy about being naked, but the humans among us are. They fidget amongst each other before eventually joining the shifters in the water. Jesse slips out of her jacket and jeans until she's only in a sports bra and her underwear.

I notice one of the Blood Takers nearby watching her, his red eyes admiring her petite frame. I urge her to go into the water quickly and glare at the vampire. He grins lasciviously and waits for me to strip. I don't give him the satisfaction and keep my dress on.

I kick off my tennis shoes and leave them on the bank before stepping into the river. The water is cold and refreshing. After days of sweating in a semi-truck, feeling clean again is amazing. I hold my breath and duck my head underwater to get my hair wet.

When I emerge, I can see the same vampire is still watching from the riverbank. I try to ignore him and swim closer to Jesse. The water is neck deep and covers our bodies from unwanted gazes. She's trying to wash her curly brown hair in the water, but without any shampoo, it won't matter much.

The stream provides enough natural sound that covers our voices. I still get close enough to whisper to Jesse, "We have to find a way to escape."

She stills, her expression like a terrified deer.

"If we reach our final destination, we'll never get to escape," I tell her. "All the stories about the Blood Takers say that no one is ever seen again once they're sold off."

"Where do you think they're taking us?" she whispers.

"I don't suspect they're selling us for cheap, so probably one of the vampire royals," I surmise.

Her lips begin to tremble. "We're going to end up as feeders."

"Probably–or worse," I admit.

All shifters are brought up with the knowledge of what happens to us when we're taken by vampires. We become their living blood bags until they drain us dry. Few people ever recover from being a feeder, but those that do are in such misery, they beg to die. As a child, I always heard the stories, which were used to deter us from disobeying. Only bad shifters that don't behave end up as feeders, they said.

That's clearly not true. It doesn't matter if you're good or bad. Anyone can become a feeder. Feeders are sometimes taken for unpaid debts, and many are prisoners of war. Even the feeders that volunteer for the job for various reasons regret their choices.

Only one thing is sure: Once you become a feeder, death is inevitable whether you die quickly or slowly. So for us, surviving is out of the question once we reach our destination.

"How are we going to escape?" Jesse asks. "They're always watching."

"We'll find an opportunity to run. Once we reach shifter territory, any of the Alphas will help us once we're within their borders."

The Blood Takers have to let down their guard eventually. They're sleeping as little as we are. They have to be tired. I just need them to look away at the right time. Once I start running, I won't stop, no matter what happens.

"What if we get caught?" she whispers.

"We won't," I assure her. "We'll shift into our wolf forms, and we'll be fast enough. Once we're safe, we can send help for the others."

Jesse still looks worried. "I'm scared, Lydia."

"It's going to be okay." I get behind her blocking the view. "My grandpa says there's always something we can do. We can't give up."

Jesse doesn't say anything else.

I don't know if she believes me or not.

I remember what they said about taking it out on Jesse if we're caught, and I hesitate. What if I'm wrong?

19

CALL IT MAGIC

Kane

While it's true what Emory says about us wanting a beach day, there is another reason why we're in Cerise Port. My uncle is one of the few people whose opinion I value. His experience and wisdom as a ruler cannot be discounted. When I first ascended to the throne, his guidance had been invaluable.

Emory has gone into the water with the boys, still keeping near the shore as she and Cole's governess Sarah assist the boys as they try to swim. Helga and Nellie are nearby on the shore, setting up a tent and table for food and drinks. Lex is helping them set up the tent. Uncle Cyrus and I walk along the shore so we can have privacy as we talk.

"What's bothering you, nephew?" he asks.

"We have a problem. My brother-in-law's mate was taken by the Blood Takers," I explain to him.

"Are you sure?" He raises an eyebrow at me.

I nod. "We found her car near Red River. Lex talked to King Matthias and pretty much confirmed that the Blood Takers abduct people in that area."

My uncle shakes his head. "I've never liked Matthias. I didn't like his father and grandfather either."

"Why is that?" I ask.

"They're always grasping. His great-grandfather, Quincy Alinac, took the throne from the Bancrofts, the original royal family that ruled Red River, but didn't do it through conquest. They had the aristocrats turn against the Bancroft king and had him and his whole family executed, even the children."

I've heard some terrible things royals have done to each other over the years, but this is especially vicious. "That's brutal."

"The Alinacs have tried to rewrite history and make themselves be the heroes. I've personally never bought their special brand of bullshit."

"I don't care for Matthias either, but he's not who I'm worried about," I explain. "I've been told the person behind the Blood Takers is King Myenas."

That makes my uncle swear, running a hand through his salt and pepper hair. "Now that's a real problem."

"Is he truly as bad as everyone says?"

"You don't gain a reputation like Myenas has without reason. He's not just a prick. He has no conscience. Matthias looks like a puppy dog next to him."

"How do you think I should handle this then?" I ask.

"I'd say get the girl back without Myenas realizing it was you behind it. He keeps a grudge, and he will make sure to get his pound of flesh."

Uncle Cyrus is making King Myenas sound like the Bogeyman. "I've fought against difficult kings before and succeeded. How bad is he compared to King Peter?"

"King Peter was petty. He ruled with only his pride and ego in mind, but he isn't nearly as ruthless as Myenas. The evil Peter caused was just an unfortunate byproduct of the action he takes for personal gain.

"And King Myenas is a sadist?" I shake my head.

"Some people find pleasure making others tremble with fear and suffer. That's what drives Myenas--his need to destroy everyone around him."

"Why?" Anger boils up inside of me.

"Power. It's the most intoxicating thing in the world," he replies. "Imagine a lifetime of never being told no and getting away with whatever heinous act you commit."

I shake my head and thank the gods I'm not like that.

* * *

EMORY

After hours of playing at the beach, the boys are tired and are taking a nap as we have lunch. King Cyrus has a full spread of fruit and seafood for my siblings and I to enjoy. He and his nephew sip on blood in wine glasses as we all talk idly at the outdoor dining table. With the cool sea breeze moving around us, making the palm trees sway, Cerise Port feels like its own tropical paradise cut off from the rest of the world.

Kane and I have come to visit a few times over the years. His uncle's support of our marriage had helped us sway over some of the vampire royals to our side. There are royals that would never support the union between our two species, and that is a change that I will never see in my lifetime. Change takes a long time to actually happen, a gradual journey at a snail's pace, so we are lucky a few of them have changed their minds.

Baby steps.

Looking around the dining room table, I don't think any of us would have guessed we'd all be dining together so casually someday. Change might take time, but it all starts somewhere.

"Where's Samuel?" Lex asks. "And Miranda? I thought we might see them."

"My children are both out of town. Samuel is negotiating a business deal with Sardonia, and Miranda is busy with her studies. She's preoccupied with this ancient text that King Basil has in his collection, and she's not coming home till she's finished translating it."

Kane smiles. "We could never get Miranda's head out of a book."

"She used to read at the beach," Lex agrees with a snort. "She never wanted to play with us."

"She stopped reading at the beach after you threw her book in the ocean."

"It was a joke!" Lex reasons with a laugh. "And Miranda forgave me."

"She did?" King Cyrus questions. "I'm surprised she didn't try to poison you for destroying one of her precious books."

"Miranda can't stay upset with me. I'm her favorite cousin."

"I'm right here," Kane pipes up, getting a chuckle out of everyone.

"And I'm still her favorite cousin," Lex emphasizes, eagerly antagonizing his brother. "Even after I committed a grave sin against our bookworm cousin, she still likes me more."

I smile before I take a sip of white wine. I've met their cousins before, and Miranda has always seemed rather strict and introverted. Her being charmed by Lex is both surprising and amusing. While Lex has grown quieter since he became regent, it's nice to see the old Lex while we're in Cerise Port.

Kane decides to ignore his brother's behavior and asks, "When will Samuel be back?"

"Soon," King Cyrus replies. "I don't know if he'll be back in time to see you, but I can call him to let him know you're here."

"I've missed Sammy," Lex declares. "We always had such fun together."

"If by 'fun' you mean you kept getting yourself into trouble...." Kane gives him a look. "The two of you together were a menace."

Curious about that statement, I ask, "What did they do?"

King Cyrus laughs. "Where would I even begin with that question?"

Kane scoffs. "What didn't they do?"

"Hold on. You make it sound like we're degenerates," Lex cut in. "We were boys just having a good time."

"'Degenerates' is a good word for what you two were," Kane counters. "The pranks you two pulled together. If it wasn't for Uncle Cyrus and I, you two would have had to serve a prison sentence in Sardonia."

Wide-eyed and intrigued, I asked Lex, "What did you do?"

"We stole Queen Olga's carriage and crashed it into a tree," Lex answers. "In my defense, we were drunk, and it seemed like a good idea at the time."

Colt who has been silent for the entire meal, finally speaks, "You thought that was a good idea?"

"Are you telling me you never did stupid shit when you were young?"

Colt looks him straight in the eye and declares, "I never got caught. I was too smart for that."

Lex sputters. "Well, good for you, shifter man. Some of us aren't as gifted."

"My father was an evil bastard, and he would have kicked my ass if I got in trouble. You were too spoiled to fear for your life."

"Now that's just a gross misinterpretation of my character. I am not spoiled-" Lex began.

Kane interjected, "You are most definitely spoiled, brother."

Lex looks stricken with his brother's swift betrayal. "Whose side are you on, Kane?"

I cover my mouth to stifle my laughter. Colt and I share a look, remembering our shared childhood of harmless pranks and silly jokes. It's nice to see him smile even if it's a momentary gaiety. It hurts me to see my brother down and depressed about losing his mate, but I understand.

Unlike him, my own mate sits across from me, safe and sound. Kane is within reach. I don't have to fear turning away and losing him. My mate gets to sit around a table and tease his brother while his is a captive.

I move an inch closer to my brother and whisper, "I'm glad you're here."

"I still feel guilty," he admits quietly. "I'm eating the best seafood in my life. And Lydia is…"

"On her way to being rescued. We just have to wait and have faith in Rainer."

"Can Rainer hurry it up a bit? I'm getting impatient."

His tone indicates his joking so I roll my eyes and shove his shoulder. "Don't be an asshole, Colt."

"Yeah, Colt, don't be an asshole," Lex cuts in. "We're younger brothers. We should be sticking together and fighting the real enemies–our evil older siblings."

Colt looks contemplative. "That is true. Our older siblings are evil."

"Entitled."

"Snooty."

"Too serious."

"Wet blankets, really."

"They never miss the chance to martyr themselves."

"They love being the martyr so much. *Too much* some would say."

Kane and I share a look across the table, amused and annoyed at the same time. At least Colt isn't so melancholy. For now.

* * *

Lex

It feels nice to spend time with family. Cole and Michael are having a great time bonding, running around the royal gardens back at my uncle's house. The boys are the same age, so they can easily relate to each other. The boys haven't been able to spend as much time together as we'd like because we've all been so busy.

It's heartwarming to see the boys playing together. Their governesses stay nearby talking to each other as they watch over the children. I try to relax and not think about all my responsibilities back in Scarlett Thunder, but that's easier said than done. I usually try to avoid being gone for too long lest the aristocrats in the castle rise up and take over.

Opal wouldn't even try to stop them. I can see her organizing an orgy over trying to keep things in order. The reminder of my wife makes me scowl. I haven't even bothered inviting her to come to Cerise Port as she won't ever want to come. If she did, it wouldn't be for spending time with our son.

The sweet scent of berries catches my attention. The wind carries the scent over to me. I can't help but follow the origin like a bloodhound and see my uncle walking with a woman with long brown hair. He points around the garden as she listens attentively.

She is beautiful, and the flush in her skin indicates she's human. She's of average height with hazel eyes framed by dark eyebrows and wears a flowy red dress that makes her look like an exotic courtesan. Her brown hair is partially covered by a red veil.

I don't move closer to them, though I want to. I wait for them to reach me.

The woman notices me first. Her hazel eyes stare at me curiously. I can't help but stare back. There's something familiar about her, but I can't place it.

"Lex, come meet our guest. This is High Priestess Ivy of the Veilholm Coven," my uncle says. "Ivy, this is my nephew Lex, the prince regent of Scarlett Thunder."

"It's nice to meet you," I tell her, trying to be friendly.

She's gone stiff after hearing my name and frowns. I don't recall meeting her before, so I'm at a loss if I've done something to offend her. It's possible I just can't remember, but I know I haven't been around that many witches in my life.

"It's nice to meet you," she replies with no emotion.

"I've invited her here to cast some protection wards around the castle. You can't be too careful these days. Fortunately, your brother has an alliance with the witch covens, and Ivy has graciously accepted my invite as a guest," my uncle explains.

"You did bribe me with the best seafood around," Ivy quips with a coy smile. "How could I resist?"

Uncle Cyrus grins. "It's nice to know I haven't lost my touch with the ladies then."

They walk away, talking amiably. I watch their backs and try to place where I've seen Ivy before. I keep drawing a blank. Who is this woman?

I don't know–but I want to.

2 0

———

A BAD OMEN

Willow

When Ivy told me she was going to be in Cerise Port, I agreed to come and see her. Kane and Emory were going for their planned visit. I haven't had the chance to visit the seaside kingdom, and I thought the change of scenery might be good for my daughter. Ever since Rainer left to go rescue Lydia, Bryony has had nightmares every night. I wasn't able to go with them because of my duties in the library, but I wanted to go as soon as I could and meet everyone there.

The frequent nightmares are not good for my daughter, so I've come to ask my niece for help.

I've just arrived a few hours ago and find Ivy working on setting up the wards around King Cyrus' castle, Brighthall, as I explain everything to her. With its sandstone walls and the domed tower that acts as a lighthouse for sailors, it's a beautiful castle. The interior is just as stunning with floor to ceiling floral tiles. Brighthall is the antithesis of the dark, gloomy castles the other vampire royals are known to live in.

"Has she had unusual dreams before all this started?" Ivy asks. "Or is this a recent development?"

"The nightmares are recent. Before that, she had been making

147

strange drawings. They're unusual for a child of her age to be imagining. Dark and disturbing."

Ivy looks at me in concern. "Do you have them with you?"

I pull them out of my leather satchel, handing them to my niece who looks over each drawing with rapt attention. The bloody one make me feel queasy. No matter how many times I see them, they always look ominous. The moon inside a black sun still confuses me.

"When did she draw these?" Ivy questions. "And do you have any idea what they mean?"

"When I ask Bryony about the drawings, she tells me cryptic things like 'the black sun will devour the moon.'"

Ivy's eyebrows furrow. "'The black sun will devour the moon'?"

"I don't understand it either," I confess. "Rainer and I thought you might know what they mean."

"Do you both think Bryony is a seer?"

"We don't know yet if she's going to be able to use magic or not. We're out of our depth with her and what comes next."

Ivy flips through the drawings again. "This could also just be a child's imagination, or she's copying something she saw somewhere. Aren't there all kinds of dark paintings in the castle?"

I shrug. She's not wrong about the paintings. "Not exactly like this. I might be more concerned if my child is just imagining these dark things, rather than seeing them from some sort of power."

"Even if Bryony is a seer, we won't be able to really test for it till she's older," Ivy explains, handing the drawings back to me. "And even for adults, the tests can be tricky. She would need to predict more than one event coming true."

"More than one?"

"We have to account for flukes. Even an average witch can guess what the future holds and be right once."

"How many would Bryony need to get right?"

"The average is three for a decent seer. We haven't had a truly talented seer in the coven for a long time. Most seers tend to get lost in the future and not really bother with the present. As a result, seers getting married and passing their gift unto their children is rare."

"Wouldn't seers want to continue passing on their ability?" I ask. I don't remember learning about any of this when I was still part of the coven.

"Seeing and knowing the future isn't all it's cracked up to be. There are seers that went insane trying to change events, only making things worse or causing the events they're trying to prevent to happen. Sometimes they create a self-fulfilling prophecy."

"Are seers not meant to warn us of the future so we can change it?" I fold my arms and lean against the wall.

Ivy shrugs. "Some seers believe that, and others believe that they're merely there to witness history unfolding before them. It all depends on which philosophy they were raised to believe.

I nod in understanding. "Which one do you believe in?"

"I've never really thought about it," Ivy admits. "When the vampires started hunting our kind, there were seers that tried to warn us and others that only kept this knowledge of things to come to themselves. They all made choices, and it didn't make any difference in the end."

"Would you rather stand by and just let things happen then?"

"If I had access to knowledge that could help me change the world for the better, I don't know what I would do with it. Maybe I'd do the heroic thing and drive myself crazy trying to change the future or I'd watch the world burn and tell everyone it's meant to be."

"I don't like either choice," I say. "If Bryony is a seer, I want her to find a middle ground."

"What if there really is no middle ground?" she challenges.

"Magic has loopholes. Its rules are malleable like clay in our hands. Why would we settle for how the generations before us did this when we can make a new path?"

Ivy looks intrigued. "I didn't know you were such a rebel, Auntie Willow."

"I'm a vampire witch. I've broken all the rules."

"That's true," she says. "What do you want to do about Bryony?"

"I think we should try to test her to see if she really is a seer. It would give me peace of mind to know what I'm really dealing with her." I let out a sigh, wishing Rainer were here to help with this.

"If she is a seer, what are you going to do?"

I carefully place Bryony's drawings into my leather satchel. "I'll prepare her as best I can to help her handle her abilities. It's not going to be easy, but I always knew parenting wouldn't be. This is just another challenge to get through."

"All right then," Ivy replies. "We'll test her."

Ivy turns away and chants a spell in our ancient tongue. The air practically shimmers with her magic as it spreads over the wall we're standing in front of.

* * *

Lydia

My body has mostly healed despite the meagre food and rest I'm surviving on. Shifter healing could do wonders especially in the direst of circumstances. With my head clear, I'm able to be alert and pay attention to our surroundings during travel. We journey through the night and set camp during the day as vampires prefer to be out at night. Unlike the myths where vampires supposedly burst into flames under the sun, the light merely annoys them, the bad ones, anyway, so they try to avoid it as much as they can.

One of them stays on guard while the others rest in a tent. They previously would lock us in the semi-truck while they would sleep before they realized how dangerous it is right now because of an unusual warm front. The unbearable heat in the vehicle in the afternoon with us all squished together like sardines results in limited oxygen supply. One of the humans almost got heat stroke, and now we're allowed to take naps on the forest floor as long as we don't wander away.

I've paid close attention to the unofficial schedule the Blood Takers have and who takes turns guarding us. The one with the brown hair and thin blond mustache is the leader. He barks orders at the others and seems to generally be in a shitty mood. He often sneers at us.

There's the stocky man who usually throws the canned food at our feet. He brings us water in a bucket to share. He doesn't talk much and mostly grunts at us. I don't think I've heard him utter a complete sentence.

The last of them has a buzzcut with the tip of his left ear missing. I've heard in passing he lost part of his ear in a fight with a shifter. He said it was a fight with an entire pack, but I have a feeling he's exaggerating. He likes to leer at Jesse, so I've taken to hiding her behind me at every opportunity.

I've grown protective of my new friend in the short time we've known each other. The other people with us keep to themselves, too terrified or paranoid to even talk to me. Jesse is my only ally, and at times, we cling to each other for comfort. It's a small harbor in this vast, terrible ocean of misery.

Stocky man is on guard duty this morning. He's the strongest out of the three, but he's slower due to his size. He's also the least observant of the vampires. I wouldn't try this plan on anyone else.

I'm hitting the can of baked beans with a rock, grunting with effort. After a few more failed attempts, I let out a frustrated sigh.

"Excuse me," I call out.

Stocky man grunts at me.

"I can't get the can open," I continue. "Can I borrow a knife?"

When he doesn't reply, I try a persuading smile and insist, "Only for a minute. I promise to give it right back."

He turns to his companions, but they're fast asleep in the tent. He squints at the sun above us, not wanting to leave the tent where he's seated.

"I could come over there if you want," I offer. "So, you don't have to step out in the sun."

He doesn't tell me to stop as I make my way toward him slowly, trying not to alarm him. When I'm standing right in front of him, I smile sweetly and offer my hand, waiting for him to give me the knife. He stares at my palm then back to his sleeping companions. Seemingly making up his mind, he pulls out a blade from his belt and places the handle in the palm of my hand. He could've just asked me to bring the can over and opened it himself, but that's why I picked him. He's fucking stupid.

"Thank you," I murmur.

He grunts.

I turn to leave.

I catch Jesse's gaze and nod at her subtly before I turn back and slash the vampire's throat. He grabs his bleeding neck, his red eyes wide in shock. He's choking on his own blood, trying to stop the bleeding with his hands. He gasps out trying to beg for help.

"Run!" I whisper fervently to the other captives.

They're frozen in shock, too fearful to immediately try to escape. I don't drop the bloody knife and run to Jesse. I cut off the ropes around her hands and then hand the knife to her so she can do the same for me. Now free of the ropes, we can shift into our wolf forms.

Jesse tosses the knife to another one of the shifters before we both rush into the woods. We shift into our wolf forms and run as fast as we can, trying to put distance between us and the camp. On all fours, we're faster than in our human forms, easily jumping over tree roots and weaving between bushes.

It feels good to let my wolf run, the wind blowing through my fur. My heart pumps with adrenaline, the prospect of freedom so near to me I can almost taste it in the air. I don't know how far we are from camp or if any of the other captives are following us. All I know is that we need to get as far away from the Blood Takers as possible and into ally territory.

We find the stream from the other day and hesitate before jumping into the water, dog paddling to get to the other side. I've reached the other riverbank when there's a loud canine yelp. I turn back to see the vampire with the shaved head dragging Jesse back to the other riverbank.

Jesse tries to fight him off, but he's stronger than her. She looks and sounds terrified, clawing at the ground to try and escape. He's careful to avoid her claws, keeping a hand on the fur at the back of her neck. She can't get away without him breaking her neck.

He catches my eye and sneers at me.

I bare my teeth in response.

Do I run for help—or go back and fight?

21

A HARD PLACE

Lydia

The vampire's red eyes glare at me. Jesse struggles to escape from his grip, and he pulls at one of her paws. There's a sickening crunch as bone breaks, and Jesse lets out a pained yelp. She goes limp from the pain, and the vampire holds her up with his superior strength. I'm antsy on my feet, wanting to jump back in the water and swim to the other side of the river.

"I'll break her fucking neck," the vampire tells me. "You try to run away, and I'll kill her. Don't try me."

I growl at him, angry and worried. Jesse continues to whimper in pain. She shifts into her human form, falling to her knees on the ground. She cradles her broken arm to her, trying to make herself smaller.

This is my fault. The plan to escape was my idea. I'm the one that slit one of the Blood Taker's throats. Jesse was only following my plan, and now she's hurt and in danger.

"I knew you were trouble the first time I saw you," the vampire continues. "You always get one stupid bitch in the litter. You're more trouble than you're fucking worth."

I shift back into my human skin so I can talk. "Let her go. I'm the one you really want to hurt."

"You slit Romy's throat, you stupid bitch. Of course, I want to hurt you." He kicks Jesse in the side, making her scream. "This idiot was just following your lead."

I swallow hard, trying to think of what to do or say to get us out of this situation and to safety. "Please stop hurting her."

He leans down and grabs Jesse's thick curls, making her wince from the pain. "Stop doing what?"

I remember the original set of Blood Takers that kidnapped me saying how the feeders are worth more when they come undamaged. And if there's anything these people care about, it's money.

"Don't you get paid less if we're injured when we reach our destination? Do you really want to risk it?" I try to persuade him. "If we die, you won't get your money's worth. Wouldn't this all be a waste?"

"The great thing about werewolves is that you all heal fast. You can withstand some pain. I can hurt you a lot, and you all just heal like it's nothing."

He drops Jesse's hair and moves to touch her injured arm. Jesse tries to hold her it against her and screams when he grabs her wrist.

"Stop!" I shout, unable to withstand seeing him hurt Jesse anymore. "I'll give you whatever you want. My family is rich. We have land and money. Just name it, and I can give it to you."

He scoffs, smiling mockingly. "I doubt whatever hovel your werewolf family huddles in each night can match a vampire king."

"My grandfather is an Alpha. He can match your price."

I know my family is going to do whatever they can to get me back whole. I would do the same if any of my brothers had been taken instead of me. The price won't matter. What was some gold over someone's life?

His blood red eyes widen in surprise before he smiles greedily. "You're an Alpha's offspring? Why didn't you say so? We can sell you off for twice the price now. Premium pedigree and all that."

Shit.

I have no bargaining chip here. Everything I try to offer him isn't good enough. I look around frantically for anything to help me but find no escape. No one is coming to save us.

I didn't think that my association with an Alpha would make things even worse for me. Before I was just like any other feeder to them, but now, I have a *pedigree*.

He grabs Jesse by the neck and drags her to her feet. "Now, get back here. And no funny business, or I'll rip out your friend's spleen and make her eat it."

I look behind me toward the freedom that had been so close to my grasp. Another chance at escape will be more difficult after this. The Blood Takers are going to be watching us more closely, and I've painted a target on my back. If what the vampire said is true, that I'm worth twice as much because of who my grandfather is, then they will be guarding me to make sure I can't get far.

"I won't repeat myself again, princess," the vampire calls out. "You got a date with a vampire king."

Closing my eyes, I reassure myself that I will get myself out of this. I will get Jesse and I to some place safe. It will just take more time than I anticipated.

The alternative is unthinkable.

* * *

Lex

Magic has a pleasant natural smell. It's a mix of the forest with the woody scent of trees and the sweetness of berries. The smell lingers around the castle and grounds as the High Priestess sets up the wards around the area. I watch as a canopy of light is built in the sky only visible during the night.

I haven't had the chance to be around a lot of witches in my lifetime, so seeing magic so openly used is new for me. I can't help but watch the High Priestess as she moves around the castle. Her magic lingers in the air like an exotic perfume. Her pretty face is just an added bonus.

Ivy is there at meal times and chatting with mostly Willow and

Emory. She's polite with both Kane and Uncle Cyrus. I'm not surprised with the former as my brother has had an alliance with the witches ever since the war with the late King Peter. My uncle has managed to charm her into enjoying his company.

I find her in the east tower of the castle and sitting by the stained-glass windows. She lights a bundle of sage with a match. The smoke moves around the room, making me cough. She doesn't turn around and continues to wave the sage to spread the smoke.

I cough again.

"Hasn't anyone told you that stalking is rude?" she asks, her back still turned to me. "You keep following me around, and I don't find it flattering."

"Who says I'm stalking you?" I try to be glib about it. "We're both guests in this castle. It would make sense we'd run into each other."

Ivy finally turns to glare at me with narrowed hazel eyes. "The castle isn't small enough for that many coincidences. Everywhere I go, you are there, watching me with your creepy blue eyes like you're planning something."

"Creepy?" I repeat. "I thought my eyes were like the ocean."

I've been called 'pretty' my entire life. I'm not unaware how my looks affect women–and lots of men. It's something that's gotten me into trouble before. That's how I ended up making Cole.

She snorts. "You really think you're charming, don't you?"

"I would like to think so." I give her my most enchanting smile. "Don't you find me the least bit amusing?"

"Not at all."

Ivy places the sage on a metal plate and leaves it on the ground. Getting to her feet, she moves closer to me. She's near enough that her flowery scent wafts over me. I can see the flecks of gold in her hazel eyes.

"I want you to leave me alone," she says, seriously. "I don't know what you want from me, but I'm not interested in whatever this is."

I can't help but lean closer to her. "Who says I want anything?"

"You're a vampire," she replies. "And I doubt you have any noble pursuits when it comes to a witch."

There are only a few inches between us. I could kiss her if I wanted to. She's right that I don't really have any noble pursuits. My fascination with her is mixed in with a budding lust I haven't indulged since my wedding.

I don't tell Ivy that. I have a feeling it wouldn't go down well if I'm too honest with her.

"I haven't really been around witches that much," I admit. "But I'm open to changing that. I would like to get to know you."

Ivy doesn't smile or laugh. Her hazel eyes sweep over my face like she's trying to solve a puzzle in her mind. I find myself drawn to the cupid's bow of her mouth. Her lips are a soft pink.

I want to know what she tastes like–but it's not her blood I'm interested in.

I lean down, moving to capture her mouth with mine.

"You used to feed on a young witch once. Don't you remember?"

That makes me stop.

Her expression is shrewd. Her words cut into me like a sharp blade.

This isn't curiosity. She knows *something*.

She's judging my reaction, waiting for me to explain.

I have a vague recollection of a young witch that became a feeder over a century ago. I had enjoyed the taste of her blood so much I began to drink her blood regularly until an incident where I accidentally turned her into a vampire. The witch turned vampire eventually became the castle librarian and married Rainer. Willow and I haven't talked or interacted in any meaningful way since then.

"How do you know about that?" I ask her. "Who told you?"

"Willow told me, of course. We are related, you know."

My shock turns into annoyance. Anger is an easier emotion to feel over shame. My history with Willow has never made me proud. It had been the only time my own father had truly been disappointed in me, and I've honestly blocked most of it out–until it was just mentioned to me again.

I had been a young and foolish man. Selfish and careless. Willow could've died when I fed on her directly, but instead it became the first time that I turned someone into another vampire. During a time when my father was trying to keep our population to a minimum, I broke his law, and he almost disowned me for it.

"I'm sure whatever Willow told you, I can explain." Again, I'm trying to be charming, dismissive. It's how I've always operated my entire life.

Ivy cocks her head to the side and she tells me, "I'll remind you that Willow is my aunt. She warned me about you."

I don't know what else to say. I look at Ivy's pretty face and can see the resemblance to Willow. They have similar eyes shape and thick eyebrows. There's a softness to Ivy's features that has been chiseled out of Willow since being turned into a vampire.

"I didn't realize she was your aunt," I admit, feeling stupid for not understanding the connection. "I didn't know Willow was close to her witch family"

One of my family's greatest shames is my father's persecution of the witches. He is the reason why the witches have such a diminished population. Even all these decades later, the witch covens are still trying to rebuild their society from what my father did to them. I had thought all this time that Willow's family might have been wiped out during the witch hunts.

"Witches are tougher than we look," Ivy declares. "I may not be as fast or strong as you are, but I'm not helpless."

She's getting feisty, and it makes her heart pump faster. I can hear her pulse beating away, and I'm distracted staring at her long, elegant neck.

"Don't you dare," she warns, noticing the shift in my focus. "I'll set you on fire if you even think about biting me."

"I wasn't–"

"*Recedite!*" She hisses out the word in a language I don't recognize, and I fly across the room, hitting the wall hard enough it knocks the breath out of me.

I lay on the ground. Looking up, I can see Ivy's angry face. She raises her hand, and I know she's casting another spell.

"*Exire!*"

The door opens on its own, as if yanked by invisible hands. I fly through the air again and out the door. I'm dumped on the ground like a marionette cut from its strings. The door closes and locks itself in front of my face.

I guess Ivy *really* doesn't like me.

22

HEADS WILL ROLL

Bryony's nightmares prevent her from getting a lot of restful sleep at night, so I encourage her to nap when she can. When she's awake, she often draws disturbing images. If my daughter is a seer, then she's seeing troubling visions of the future. It's a lot for a three-year-old girl to have to process.

Bryony is taking a nap in her room when Ivy comes to see me after lunch. She's contacted the coven about testing my daughter for seer abilities. I will need to take Bryony to the coven for the tests, but right now, she's too tired to travel to another location again. She misses her father dearly, and I haven't heard from Rainer in a few days. Having to do all of this on my own is not ideal.

"I found a simpler test. It's not as comprehensive as the tests the coven will make Bryony go through, but this is just a way to check for clairvoyance," Ivy explains. "Minor divination. A lot of witches can do this."

Divination has never been something I'm drawn toward as a branch of magic. My little sister Bryony had been fascinated with it, so it would make sense that her namesake might inherit it.

"Are we going to ask her to do tarot cards and tea leaf reading?"

"Those are a little too advanced for a three-year-old."

Ivy pulls out a butterfly broach from her pocket. It's made of gold embedded with emeralds. From the design, I can tell it's an antique. Ivy has other items with her, like a plain gold diadem and what looks to be a small brass bell.

I watch her move around the suite and place the items in different locations. When she's finished, she tells me, "There are objects that belonged to previous High Priestesses. Bryony has to find the item of the High Priestess we mention to her."

"Like she's a magical bloodhound?"

Ivy shrugs. "It's simple but effective."

I can't argue with that, and this is a test that has a zero chance of harming my child. I'm about to go wake up Bryony when she exits her room. Her hair is messy with sleep, and she's rubbing at her eye., letting out a small yawn.

"Is it test time?" she asks.

I look at her startled. "How did you...?"

She just looks at Ivy. "Test time?"

Ivy nods, smiling. "It's test time. We need you to look for objects around the suite. It's like a treasure hunt."

Bryony stops rubbing at her eye. "Okay."

I crouch down so I'm at eye level with her. "You don't have to get everything right. Just trying is good enough."

"Okay, Mommy."

I stand up and take Bryony's hand, leading her to Ivy. The High Priestess has something in her hand. She offers it to Bryony, and it's a clear quartz stone the size of her thumb. Bryony doesn't hesitate to take it and puts it in the pocket of her dress.

"Clear quartz is good for amplifying magic," Ivy says. "Are you ready, Bryony?"

She nods. She still looks sleepy, but she doesn't complain and ask to be brought back to bed. With her droopy blue eyes and messy brown hair, she looks absolutely adorable. I can't help but try to smooth out her hair with my hands.

"The first item we're looking for belonged to High Priestess

Ygritte," Ivy begins. "Can you find the right item? Take your time. We're not in a rush."

Bryony immediately heads to a side table, opens a cabinet, and reaches into it to pull out the gold diadem. She brings it over to Ivy and hands it to her.

"That's correct, sweet girl," Ivy tells her with a smile. "Good job."

Bryony doesn't really react and just asks sleepily, "Next one?"

Ivy nods. "The next item belonged to High Priestess Morgana."

Bryony goes to the kitchen area, and we follow her. She reaches under one of the chairs where Ivy has magically glued the brass bell. The item unsticks from the chair when Bryony touches it. She brings it to Ivy who is grinning now.

"Right again, Bryony. You're doing so well."

Two in a row. That's looking very good.

Bryony rubs both of her eyes, looking even more tired. "Last one?"

I catch Ivy's eye, and she looks excited and pleased. "The last one is an item that belonged to your Aunt Bryony."

My daughter heads back to the living room. She picks up one of the throw pillows on the couch and unzips the cover. She pulls out the gold brooch with emeralds. Ivy looks delighted and claps her hands.

"You got everything right," she exclaims. "Good job, Bryony!"

My daughter hands her the brooch. "Uh-huh. Nap now?"

Ivy looks at me, confused at my child's reaction. Bryony doesn't seem that enthused but what does she expect from a cranky child running on little sleep?

I place my hands on my baby's shoulders and guide her toward her bedroom. "Back to your nap now, Bryony. You did really well."

"Okay, Mommy."

"Mommy is very proud of you. I'm sure your daddy will be too."

"Uh-huh. Love you, Mommy."

"I love you too." I kiss the top of her head and place her on the bed. After tucking her in, she's out like a light. I leave her to rest and return to Ivy who is waiting for me on the couch.

"Well?" I prompt.

"She got everything right. It was so quick. There was no hesitation. She's definitely clairvoyant at the least."

"Is this conducive enough to show she's a seer?"

"Not quite. She can't really be called a seer until she predicts an actual future event."

"How will we even know if the event has come to pass?" I ask.

"Seers always know. They can sense it," Ivy explains. "The reactions tend to be noticeable–"

An earth-shattering scream reverberates from the bedroom. We both gasp and jump up from the couch.

I run to my daughter, her audible distress calling to me like a beacon. I turn on the light in her room and see Bryony twisting and turning in her bed. Ivy stands back and watches as I try to shake my daughter awake.

Bryony's blue eyes open wide in distress.

"What's wrong?" I ask her, trying to stay calm. "What's happening?"

"Dead, dead, dead," she keeps repeating. "Heads, tails, dead.."

I grab her and hold her to me, looking at Ivy who is slowly shaking her head in shock.

* * *

Lydia

The vampire with the shaved head brings Jesse and I back to camp dressed in some ill-fitting clothes he had with him in a backpack. The vampire I attacked lies on the ground, blood soaking the front of his shirt. The earth beneath him is a dark red, almost black. I'm shocked that he's still alive. I thought I'd killed him. The other Blood Takers are trying to get him to drink blood, but he can't keep it down because of the wound in his throat.

"How's he doing?" the vampire with the shaved head asks. "Can you patch him up?"

"This isn't an ordinary cut. We have to get him to a physician," one of the Blood Takers says. "He can't heal properly like this. The medical training I have isn't enough."

The vampire with the shaved head pauses, staring down at the wounded vampire. "We can't go get a doctor. We're on a schedule."

"Romy will die if we don't get him help, Toman." The other vampire stands and folds his arms.

"He knows the risks of this job. We all do." Toman glares back.

Another of the Blood Takers speaks up, "Come on, Tom. You're not going to really let Romy die, are you?"

Toman pushes Jesse out of the way so he can move closer to Romy on the ground. He crouches down, and the injured vampire looks up at him pleadingly. Vampires are already very pale, but Romy looks as white as chalk. He tries to speak, but all that comes out is garbled noises.

"It's all right, Romy," Toman tells him. "It'll be all over soon. You can rest now."

He pulls out a knife from his pocket. Before any of the Blood Takers can react, Toman plunges the knife into Romy's neck, right in the same spot where I stabbed him. He begins to saw. Romy jerks, and Toman keeps him down with his free hand. The other vampire becomes less combative as Toman saws, his face turned to the side. Just before the head comes off, I see his expression go slack.

He's definitely dead now.

"Holy fuck, Toman!" one of the Blood Takers exclaims. "Why did you do that?"

"I had to put Romy out of his misery," Toman replies nonchalantly. He wipes the blood off the knife on the end of Romy's shirt. "He was either going to die on the way to our destination, or we would get off schedule to find him a doctor, and it would've been our asses on the line. This was for the best."

"You didn't have to kill him. We could have found another way–" the Blood Take who'd called for the physician begins.

"There is no other way. I had to do what needed to be done." Toman shrugs, putting his knife away.

"Come on, Toman!" the other Blood Taker shouts. "We're supposed to stick together. We're not supposed to do shit like this!"

"Calm down, Ludwig."

"I'm not going to calm down! Romy died for nothing! We looked away for one second, and one of those wolves attacked him! They need to pay!" Ludwig shouts, looking at Jesse and me.

Toman gets to his feet. He sighs and glances at Jesse and me, too, his expression contemplative. His calmness is more unsettling than when he's angry and yelling at us like he was when he found us in the water.

Anger is more predictable. I could find a way to weather that. This calmness cannot be trusted. I know whatever he's thinking is not going to be good for us.

"You want some blood? Eye for an eye, Lud?" he asks. "I can make sure Romy is avenged. Will that make you happy?"

The Blood Taker glares at me, his expression full of hate. "You're going to hurt the werewolf bitch?"

"I'll do more than hurt her."

Toman moves toward me. He grabs me by the back of the head, his fingers digging into my scalp and pulling my hair. He forces me to my knees and stands over me. I have to bite my tongue to keep quiet as he's hurting me.

"One of these bitches is the reason Romy is dead," he declares. "One of them slit his throat."

Another of the Blood Takers asks, "If you kill them, what about the money? Werewolf women are worth twice as much as humans."

Toman shakes his head. "Our rules have always been that we kill those who try to escape. Someone has to pay"

My heart starts beating faster as the realization of what's about to happen to me sinks in. Toman's other hand wraps around my throat. Fear has its grip on me. I consider reminding him that my grandfather is an Alpha, but I can't speak. I can barely breathe. I refuse to cry or show any emotion. If this is meant to be my last moment, I'm not going to spend it whimpering and begging. I refuse to beg. I'm not going to let them win.

Does this mean he'll kill Jesse, too? I could've fucking gotten away, went for help, and now I can't do anything.

Toman addresses the other feeders. "Let this be a lesson to all of you. If any of you try to escape like these two idiots, you'll end up with the same fate. None of you are special. And no one will come to save you."

He leans down and whispers in my ear, "Normally, I would kill you, but you're too expensive to just throw away. Thank your lucky stars your grandpa is an Alpha, princess. This should have been you."

He drops me to the ground, and I break my fall with my hands. Nettles dig into my palms. Jesse screams, and I turn around to see Toman grab her. She tries to push him away with her good arm, clawing at him in a desperate bid to keep herself alive.

Before I can get to my feet to help her, Toman has his hands on her head. With a sickening crunch, he twists her head at an unnatural angle and breaks her neck. Jesse goes still. He tugs at her head and it pops off her neck.

Jesse's body falls to the ground. The vampire tosses the head behind him, and it lands in front of me. Jesse's head rolls until her face frozen in shock is staring up at me. Her brown eyes are wide with terror.

I let out a scream.

2 3

THE NEW BLOOD TAKER

Lydia

Jesse's death has left me numb with shock. I can barely sleep and eat. The memory of her being decapitated replays in my mind nonstop. The scent of her blood lingers, refusing to leave me alone. I don't know what the Blood Takers did to her body, but my best guess is that they dumped it somewhere in the woods.

The thought of her body rotting out in the elements or animals feasting on her remains makes me feel sick and diminishes my already non-existent appetite. My stomach growls, and I'm feeling lightheaded, but I ignore the can of sardines one of the teenage boys offers me.

"You should eat," he says. "You'll need your strength."

I look up at him from where I'm seated on the ground. He's of average height with brown hair. There's some baby fat still clinging to his cheeks and acne on his chin. He can't be older than seventeen.

"Don't get too close, Jim," one of the women tells him. "Look at what happened to the last person that was friendly with her."

Shame makes me swallow hard, wishing I was anywhere else. Most of the other feeders have been avoiding me like the plague. I know they blame me for Jesse's death, and I don't blame them. I am the one at fault. It's better for them to keep their distance from me.

Jim looks between the woman and me before placing the can of sardines on the ground beside me. "You really should eat."

He leaves me to go sit and eat with the others his own age. I pick up the can and look down at the sardines floating in tomato sauce. My stomach growls again, reminding me how long I've been depriving myself. A part of me wants to just give up and let myself starve to death.

The louder and more stubborn part of me that wants to survive fights against those ideas. I don't know how Jesse would feel about me giving up, but I imagine she wouldn't be pleased. She wanted us both to survive, so me giving up my life feels like a disservice to her. It feels far more shameful than the guilt I already feel about her dying.

I have to survive. I would rather die trying to escape than continue to play their games.

What other choice do I have?

I eat the sardines, not really tasting anything, chasing them with tepid water. I'll need my strength. Hunger is too distracting. I can't run without any fuel in my body.

The ropes around my wrists are tighter than before, almost cutting off my circulation. They dig into my wrists. After my escape attempt, the Blood Takers are not taking any chances. I've already shown that I can be sneaky and violent.

I've been observing the Blood Takers more closely. The vampire with the shaved head, Toman, seems to be their leader. They defer a lot of choices to him, even about some of the most benign things. The two others, Bogdan and Lazar, both give me dirty looks. They both despise me for killing their friend.

I don't know what they've done to the fourth Blood Taker, Romy, as they didn't take his corpse with us when we got back on the road. I have mixed feelings about his death. As much as I do not care for him and know that he was not a good person, he is still the first person I've ever killed. In the heat of the moment, with adrenaline and desperation driving me forward, all I could think about was getting the hell out of here.

I try to compartmentalize and pretend I was hunting an animal in the woods like I've done dozens of times before. I can't afford to mentally go down that path and assess how the act of killing someone makes me feel, not at the moment. I'll have plenty of opportunities to deal with that trauma when I get home–back to Colt–the man I love.

I can't spend too much time thinking about my mate either because he's too distracting. I have to believe he's looking for me, and so is my family. Otherwise, I'll go insane.

I've finished the sardines and discarded the can when a whisper falls over the camp. I look up to see another vampire walking into our camp as if he's just out for a stroll in the woods.

The Blood Takers are on instant alert. "Who the fuck are you?" Toman asks, his teeth elongated, and his hands at the ready to attack.

"Calm the fuck down," he says in a nonchalant voice. "I'm here to replace Romy."

"I've never met you in my life," Toman hisses. "How do we know you're telling the truth?"

"I have a letter with me from King Matthias explaining everything. It's in the pocket of my jacket. May I get it?" His eyes dart across the crowd, and I think they linger on me for a second. Maybe he knows I'm the one who killed Romy.

Toman nods to Bogdan. "We'll get it."

The other vampire reaches into the new arrivals jacket and pulls out a note. He reads it and says, "This looks legit, Tom."

The leader lowers his guard slightly. Pointing it at him as a warning, he demands of Bogdan, "Let me see."

Bogdan hands him the letter, and he reads over it, his pale brows furrowing. "This does look real unless you're ballsy enough to forge a king's signature."

The stranger shrugs, undisturbed. "I'm not stupid enough to commit a heinous crime like that. I could get executed."

Toman looks over to the other Blood Takers who also look unsure about the stranger with them. "I don't trust you, but you can stay. Any funny business, and you won't have to worry about King Matthias executing you. I'll do that myself. Are we clear?"

The stranger smiles carelessly, raising his hands in surrender. "Crystal clear, boss."

"Don't make me regret this," Toman says., eyeing him like a wild animal he can't turn his back on. "What's your name, anyway?"

"You can call me Randal."

"All right, *Randal.* You'll be on watch with Bo, and he will tell me if you do anything suspicious."

Randal gives Bo a two-finger salute. "Pleasure working with you, Bo."

"It's Bogdan. You don't get to call me Bo yet."

"Whatever you say, friend."

"We're not friends either."

Randal just shrugs that off. There's something familiar about him I can't place, and he continues to steal glances at me. He doesn't seem like the other Blood Takers to me. Toman gives him the duty of collecting the trash from the feeders and giving them more water. Everyone looks at him warily. His cheerful demeanor makes them more nervous than anything.

When he comes over to me, his blue eyes catch my own and he smiles. "I'm Randal. Nice to meet you."

I only stare at him, wondering what trick he's trying to pull on me. When I don't say anything, he refills my cup of water and walks away. He whistles as if he's done this a million times before. I watch him glide cheerfully around the camp and try to figure out what the hell is going on.

* * *

RAINER

It took me several days to track down the Blood Takers. They kept moving and seemed to travel in a pattern anyone would call confusing. They're not traveling in a straight line. They've been turning left and right into different territories, keeping to the woods and out of sight.

I finally found them through sheer luck as I intercepted a message about one of the Blood Takers dying. Through that message, I found the campsite where they buried two bodies, a male vampire and a female shifter–without a head. The request for back-up works perfectly in my favor. Even with their initial suspicion, they let me into the group, and Lydia Nightstone is within my sight.

Lydia is skittish. She doesn't trust any of the Blood Takers–with good reason. The message the Blood Takers sent involved something to do with an escape attempt and having to kill a female shifter. They want more money for the loss of their colleague and double the price for another female shifter who happens to be the granddaughter of an Alpha.

The death is too fresh for the Blood Takers, so they're not forthcoming with the details when I ask. They all blame Lydia and have alluded to wanting to get revenge but want the money for her more.

"If she's violent, shouldn't she be too troublesome to trade?" I try to persuade them. "If she attacks a vampire noble or royal you could be held accountable for being the one to give her to them." I have to be careful, or I might convince them to kill her, and that's not my angle here either.

"What happens after she's handed over to the rich assholes is none of our business," Toman says. He's the de-facto leader of the Blood Takers, I've learned. "We're here to do one job. How they want to deal with that crazy bitch once we hand her over is their fucking problem."

"But she killed your friend," I insist. "Are you really going to let that go?"

"We told you that the money is too much to just toss away," Lazar counters. "If she cost less, I would disembowel her myself. She's not even worth feeding on."

Bogdan glares at where Lydia is huddled, trying to pretend like she can't hear us talking. "I'd feed on her. Drain her dry and then set her body on fire. After I piss all over it."

I try my best to hide my disgust at their violent thoughts. I'm not surprised, but it's still disturbing to hear what they would do to the woman if given the chance.

"How much does she cost?" I ask.

"Triple what a regular wolf bitch costs," Toman explains. "Alpha blood is premium for the royals, like a good vintage wine."

"I heard that's why that king married one of them. She's an Alpha," Bogdan points out.

"I heard about that. King Karl or something," I murmur, trying to blend in.

"King Kane," Toman corrects.

I shrug. "Who the fuck knows why he married a mangy dog."

"She must be a good fuck," Lazar states. "If not a convenient blood bag."

Even with my acting skills, this conversation needs to change before I get pissed, so I ask, "When do you think we'll reach our destination?"

Toman scratches the bridge of his nose. "In another week. We have to be more careful since we have the werewolves looking for us."

"Because of the blonde girl?" I let out an exasperated sigh. "She really sounds like she's more trouble than she's worth."

"Look, if you want to feed on one of these bitches or want to get your cock wet, you can help yourself with one of the humans. They're cheap as dirt anyway," Toman says, annoyed.

"You never let me feed on anyone anymore!" Bodgan argues.

"That's because you have no self-control, Bo. You fed on three humans the last time, and they all died. I had to cut you off." He points to Lazar. "Don't even get me started on you. Remember that shipment where you fed on half of the feeders?"

As they argue amongst themselves, I get up from where I'm seated by the bonfire and walk over to where Lydia is. She's separated from the other feeders. I don't think it's her choice as I've observed them ignoring her. She doesn't seem to complain and has accepted this treatment. I don't say anything to her, even though I desperately want to let her know I'm there to help. She won't even look me in the eye.

The next morning, I learn that the Blood Takers have mostly been surviving on blood wine and whatever small prey they can hunt in the woods. Bright and early, I help them take down a bear. Bigger prey will provide us more blood and meat for the feeders. They've been giving the prisoners canned goods for nutrition, but I point out how that affects their health and the quality of their blood. It's only the possibility of them being paid less for 'subpar products' that persuades the Blood Takers to let the feeders eat the bear meat.

Bear takes a long time to cook on the bonfire and tastes very gamey, but the feeders are thankful for it when I finally begin to pass it out. I've had bear meat a time or two but don't really like it. Bear blood isn't so fantastic either, but we're all making do with what we can get in this situation.

I take a plate of roasted bear meat to Lydia. She doesn't take the plate from me and stares at it as if it's a grenade.

"Eat," I tell her. "It's not ham, but it's better than nothing."

Her blue-grey eyes bore into me, as if she's trying to figure out what all my motives are. "What are you doing?"

"I'm just trying to keep you alive" I place the plate on the ground in front of her. "Whether you like it or not."

24

THE QUEEN'S ADVICE

EMORY

I've never been to Sardonia before. Queen Olga has been asking for me to visit her kingdom for years. So far, Kane and I have managed to put off the visit as we've been busy recuperating after the war with Scarlett Thunder and raising our son. Although, I have met Queen Olga a few times when she visits Crimson Peak, and her fascination with me hasn't waned. She's always asking us to come see her beautiful kingdom. It's inevitable that I will need to do just that.

After talking to King Cyrus about how to deal with King Myenas, he points us in Queen Olga's direction for more advice. She is the longest reigning vampire monarch in history and has more wisdom to impart than anyone we know. She's seen kingdoms rise and fall and has a lot of influence amongst their kind.

So, here we are, on our way to Sardonia, which is at the top of a mountain. The castle is carved directly into the mountain itself. The area is covered in snow with freezing temperatures that deter other kingdoms from wanting to take over by force. Traveling to the mountain is difficult even with cars. We have to abandon our vehicles several miles from the castle and walk the rest of the way.

I'm trying not to shiver when we crest an incline and see a group of vampire warriors ahead of us. Kane squeezes my hand, letting me know it's all right. Queen Olga's men are waiting for us, and they help guide us. With the pine trees around us and miles of snow, we could easily get lost and never be found again. We follow along, trudging through the snow in near silence.

When we finally reach Sardonia, the sight of a picturesque town appears before us. The cottages with thatched roofs, and children running around having snowball fights, could be something printed on a postcard.

There's a large statue in the middle of the town square of a woman with the full moon as a halo above her head. Her palms are pressed together in prayer. I would recognize her anywhere. It's Selene, the Moon Goddess who my people worship.

I turn to Kane, too surprised to ask the question properly. "Why?"

He smiles and explains, "I've told you before vampires also used to worship the Moon Goddess. Sardonia is one of the few vampire kingdoms that still holds on to those beliefs. Around the winter solstice, they have a festival honoring Selene."

"I didn't know that."

"Sardonia is largely isolated from the other kingdoms, so they have different customs and traditions than the other kingdoms, which can be both good and bad." He smiles at me, looking even more pale in the cold, and I nod in understanding before continuing on.

We're escorted toward the castle, and I can't help but admire the ancient architecture. It's more rustic than Castle Graystone, and the hallways are narrower with smaller rooms. The place is not built for shifters as I can see Colt struggling to fit his larger body through some of the passageways, and yet there's an undeniable charm to the castle which has been around for thousand so of years. There are several carvings in the walls that tell stories about vampires, shifters, and even witches.

At least it's warm inside the castle, though I'm not sure how. it's so cold outside, and I don't see a lot of fire places. Maybe they are just hidden from view.

We're escorted to the throne room to wait. A mural of what looks to be some kind of creation myth sparks my attention, and I move over to look at it more closely. The Moon Goddess is in the middle surrounded by all three species. There's no war. They all seem to be living in harmony.

"You've finally made it," Queen Olga says as she enters the room. "I wasn't sure you'd ever make it up here for a visit. Welcome to Sardonia."

I give a little curtsy. "Queen Olga, thank you for inviting us." I've learned a thing or two about how to treat nobility since I've been married to such a regal king.

Kane greats her in kind, being every bit the respectful dignitary he is. He kisses the back of her hand. "Queen Olga, you look radiant as always."

She smiles fondly. "Always such a flatterer, dear boy."

Kane has mentioned Queen Olga finding him attractive as she had a crush on his grandfather back in the day. I don't feel threatened. I find it more amusing than anything else. She never acts inappropriately with Kane, just a little flirty.

She moves to stand beside me to look over the mural. "That's been here ever since the castle was built. No one quite knows who created it."

"Somebody idealistic, probably," I offer.

"Some might say delusional," she replies. "And yet, we all worshipped the same Goddess at one point in time. We may have more in common than we think."

I glance at Kane and then back at her and say, "I know that. At the end of the day, we all want similar things—safety, love, and friendship."

"You are an idealistic dreamer. I've met a few men like that over my lifetime. Your grandfather for example." She smiles at me.

I stare at her in surprise. "You met my grandfather?"

I never heard about Grandpa Colton meeting the Queen of Sardonia, so I'm quite shocked. His friendship with King Michael was unusual, but hearing he knew more than one vampire monarch is something else.

"Once, long before you were born. He had a dream that we could all get along and live peacefully together. Kane's father was almost swayed toward that vision, but Michael was too much of a pragmatist at heart."

"My father wasn't that rational by the end," Kane agrees. "For example, his paranoia led him to persecuting the witches, believing they could be a threat someday."

I know that King Michael's dark history with the witches is a source of shame for Kane. He's still trying to make up for what his father did all these years later.

"Several kings before him thought the shifters would become a threat as well, and that led to several wars amongst our people," Queen Olga points out. "Fear causes individuals to do terrible things. They see enemies where there could have been friends."

"If only more people would just sit down and talk it out," I say wistfully, "It could save everyone a load of trouble."

Queen Olga smiles ruefully. "Monarchs tend to have a hard time admitting they're wrong. They would rather hurt themselves than 'talk it out.' I don't doubt you've had to deal with this problem in your position."

I nod, knowing all too well what she means. Dealing with the other Alphas has often been a struggle, particularly when I've been trying to get them to resolve things peacefully rather than fighting with each other.

"My grandfather thought we could create a better world by working together. My father almost ruined that dream entirely," I admit. "But I think we should work toward that goal."

"It's a nice dream. I hope to see it happen in my lifetime." She smiles, and I see the truth in her words.

I can't help but stare at her. This is a woman that has lived through several lifetimes and seen the world change over the centuries. My own short lifespan is a small heartbeat compared to the length of hers. It makes me want to know more about her.

And I'm even more confused as to why she's so fascinated with me.

"Forgive me for my forwardness, but I do want to know why

you're so curious about me," I tell her. "I don't think I'm that interesting."

Queen Olga looks at me in surprise. Then, she takes my hands in hers. Her touch is soft but cold. She's wearing several rings of different designs with gorgeous gemstones of various sizes that catch my attention. I can't help but stare.

"Do you not know what people say about you, Emory Moonraker? I was intrigued to hear about you. You're the first female Alpha, and you married a vampire king. Then you gave birth to a hybrid son shortly before winning a war against a more experienced monarch. You have lived so much life, and you're still so young. I thought to myself, 'Who is this extraordinary young woman?'"

Her praises embarrass me, and I can feel my cheeks turning red. "I had a lot of help with all of that. I didn't really plan anything. It just kind of happened to me."

"Destiny may drag you toward an extraordinary life, but your actions have been your own. Don't discount your accomplishments. It is a disservice to do so," Queen Olga maintains. She glances at Kane and adds, "I also wanted to know the woman who managed to get Kane to want to settle down and have children. He'd been avoiding it for a very long time."

Kane runs a hand through his dark hair. "What can I say? I was smitten at first sight."

"You're a romantic just like your grandfather. He was besotted with your grandmother till the day he died." She shakes her head. "While I'm ecstatic to finally have you here in my kingdom, I'm sensing there's another reason you're here?"

"We came here for your advice on a delicate matter," I admit.

"And what is that delicate matter?"

Kane sighs. "King Myenas."

Queen Olga nods as if she's suspecting this. "Shall we dine first before we tackle that problem? I'd rather not discuss Myenas on an empty stomach."

* * *

Kane

The dining room feels intimate with the short table that could only accommodate a dozen people. Queen Olga tells us that they use this dining room for family and friends only. The nobles that live in the castle dine in another more spacious room. The table is made of stone and is connected to the floor, making it impossible to move.

Newer items seem out of place on such an ancient relic.. The high chairs with the cushioned sheets and the delicate china plates and gold cutlery stand out. Sardonia is this dichotomy of old and new. They manage to blend the two together.

The food in Sardonia is hearty and gamey. Since most items being imported in could take weeks to come by, their food storages are made to last for longer periods of time. The servants present to Emory a meat stew and a side of bread. Queen Olga explains that the stew is made with mutton.

She takes a bite. "It's delicious," Emory remarks with a smile.

I'm served a large goblet of blood. It's not warm but not undrinkable. Queen Olga explains that they can make their blood storages last longer here due to the cold. Most blood isn't served fresh, but it's not terrible. Getting new feeders up the mountain can be difficult, so they put in the effort to treat their feeders well so they last longer. They collect their blood in the same manner we do and freeze as much as they can to save for later.

"Have you heard of what King Myenas is doing with the Blood Takers?" I ask, taking a sip from my goblet.

"I've heard things in passing, but I try not to involve myself with Myenas. He's from a bloodline of upstarts. 'Bad blood' as my father would have said." Olga signals for a servant to refill her blood.

Emory looks confused. "What do you mean?"

"His family got their royal title through conquest. The mountain clans around that area were known for their barbaric practices even by the standards of the time. Myenas' ancestor, King Priam, united the clans so they could take over the surrounding land. If you ask me, every king that's sat on that throne has been a raving lunatic."

I catch Emory's gaze, and she looks even more worried.

"Why are you asking about Myenas?" Queen Olga asks. "Has something happened?"

"His operation with the Blood Takers has put someone we know in danger. We are trying our best to rescue her without King Myenas' knowledge," I explain, purposefully being vague.

"But you're also preparing for the possibility that you'll end up in conflict with him anyway?" I can't fool her.

I nod. "My Uncle Cyrus believes you might know how to handle King Myenas."

"You can't 'handle' a mad man, Kane." She takes another sip from her glass. "There's no predicting what he'll do."

"What do you think we should do then? We're trying to avoid another war," I tell her.

She shakes her head. "This world's weary of war. So much bloodshed and for what?"

"We don't want to go to war again," Emory assures her. "Our son is only three. Rebuilding for everyone involved has not been easy."

I cut in, "Which leads us to the question at hand–how do we appease a mad man?"

Queen Olga places her ornate goblet down on the table. "You don't appease a mad man. You just kill him before he can cause more trouble."

FRIEND IN NEED

Lydia

I watch warily as Randal comes over with a plate of food. His smile is wide and friendly like we've known each other for years. His overall niceness is unsettling compared to the usual treatment the feeders receive from the other Blood Takers. I don't know what to make of this man.

"Hello, Lydia," he greets me. "How are you today?"

"I'm great," I respond sarcastically. "Never better."

He snorts, finding me amusing, and hands me the plate. I take it reluctantly. Ever since he showed up, the feeders have been eating more. The better food has ensured I've healed from my injuries, and I feel stronger.

This would be an ideal time for another escape attempt except I don't feel like trying again. After Jesse's death, I'm afraid of what the Blood Takers will do to the feeders. They've shown themselves to be vengeful and ruthless. I would be dead if they didn't think I'm valuable in some way.

If I do nothing, and we reach our destination, I won't get another chance to escape.

Damned if I do, damned if I don't.

"You got a boyfriend where you're from?" Randal asks as he fills up a cup of water. "You look like a relationship kind of girl."

I stare at him suspiciously. "Why are you asking?"

"I'm just trying to get to know you."

"Why do you want to do that?"

"Prickly." He cocks his head to the side. "I can work with that. You and I are going to be friends."

I scoff before taking a bite of roasted deer. "You're delusional."

"Oi, Randal!" Bogdan calls out. "Stop flirting with the merchandise!"

Randal raises his hands in surrender. "I'm not flirting, Bo. Just trying to be friendly."

"Well, stop it! I already told you to go fuck the humans, not the wolf shifters!"

Randal gives me an apologetic smile. "Forgive Bo. He doesn't think men and women can be friends without sex being involved."

I roll my eyes. Randal seems to enjoy annoying the other Blood Takers. A part of me finds it amusing. Even with my distaste of him trafficking people across borders, I can't deny he's a funny guy.

The other feeders find him funny too. They stifle their giggles when Randal sasses the other Blood Takers. He's the most popular of our kidnappers, but the bar is already low, so it's not much of an accomplishment. There are no awards for being the most likable mercenary around.

"He's being annoying again, Tom!" Bogdan complains.

"I'm annoying all the time," Randal quips as he comes over. "It's part of my charm."

Toman sighs, already sick of the bickering. "Can you two idiots shut your mouths for the rest of this trip? If I have to listen to this for days on end, I'll kill one or both of you."

Bogdan points to Randal. "He always starts it."

Randal shrugs. "I can't help it. I have a compulsion to tease Bo and Laz. Sue me."

Lazar pipes up. "Don't drag me into this."

Toman points to all of them. "All of you can shut the fuck up."

I'm listening to their bickering half-heartedly when the other women leave to go pee in the woods. I follow them, not knowing when I'll get a chance to relieve myself again after this. We aren't allowed to go into the woods alone, especially after my escape attempt. I keep to myself as I find a spot further from the other women as they still don't like me.

When I finish relieving myself, the others are all gone. I'm not surprised none of them bother waiting for me. I have to hurry back before any of the Blood Takers notice, and I get into trouble again. I hesitate and turn around to look at the path away from the camp.

I could run off while everyone is distracted. I don't know how far I would make it before I get caught. This time, getting caught would mean death. Staying also means death.

"I wouldn't try that," a voice says quietly. "Not yet anyway."

I turn quickly to find Randal leaning against a tree. I've been caught.

"Are you going to punish me?" I ask. "Like what they did to Jesse?"

"No. I don't want you dead, Lydia."

"Because of the money."

He pauses before shrugging. "You can believe what you like."

Annoyance makes my voice sharper as I demand, "What does that even mean?"

"It means I don't want you dead. That's all you need to know for now."

I glare at him, trying to understand his motives. The other Blood Takers are easier to read in comparison. They're greedy assholes. Randal seems to enjoy being cryptic and infuriatingly cheerful.

"I don't trust you or a single word that comes out of your mouth," I declare. "You can stop whatever bullshit game you're trying to play because I'm not interested in playing it with you."

His cheerfulness drops, and he looks more serious than I've ever seen him before. "This isn't a game, Lydia. This is life and death. You know that."

"Then what are you trying to do?"

"Believe it or not, I'm trying to help you."

"But why?"

He looks around then puts a finger to his mouth, instructing me to keep quiet.

Lazar walks into view. He glares at both of us.

"What are you two doing here?" he questions. "Toman told you to keep your hands off the merchandise, Randal. You can't fuck the she-wolf even if you want to."

Randal shakes his head. "I'm not touching her. She just had to use the bathroom, right?"

I raise both eyebrows at him, confused as to why he thinks I'll corroborate any story he makes up.

Lazar comes closer to me, and I stiffen, wanting to back away. He's right in front of me and asks menacingly, "Did he try to fuck you?"

With wide eyes, I shake my head and reply, "He didn't touch me."

Lazar's red eyes bore into me as if he's trying to uncover all my lies. "Get back to camp. Now."

I scurry away, knowing better than to disobey. I don't even look behind me as the two vampires begin to argue. This isn't my business. They can kill each other for all I care.

* * *

Colt

I haven't been back to Nightfall since Lydia's abduction. I try to keep in touch with the Nightstone family, as we're all in this crisis together, but the guilt has made it difficult. It's easy to blame myself for what happened to Lydia, and I can imagine her family blames me too. I'm more than surprised when they're not hostile toward me when I arrive at their ancestral home.

Lydia's mother, Amanda, pulls me into a hug. "How have you been?"

"Hanging in there," I reply. "How are you holding up?"

She pulls away, unable to hide her worry but trying to stay strong. "We're hoping that we can get Lydia back soon."

"Me too."

There's a somberness and anxiety in the house since my last visit, but the family stays close to each other. They're leaning on one another for strength. I feel like an imposter amongst them. They've known Lydia her entire life and I've only recently met her.

My right to worry over her feels so deficient next to theirs. I tell myself that I'm Lydia's mate. I have the right to worry about her as much as anyone else. We all want the same thing here–to get her back to us safe and sound.

Alpha Gerald comes over. "It's nice to see you again, Colt. I just wish it was under better circumstances."

I'm reminded that Lydia and are I supposed to be planning our wedding. We should be together, spending our time choosing the caterer and the flowers. This should be a happy time we share with our families. Instead of that, I'm losing sleep at night, wondering when I can have her back in my arms.

Life kicked us all in the teeth.

"It's nice to see you again too," I answer. "I have some news from Alpha Emory about the rescue efforts."

The Nightstones all perk up when they hear me say that. They lead me to the living room and all listen intently as I update them on the rescue mission. I take a seat on a chair while the Nightstones gather on the couches. I try not to squirm at being the center of attention.

My main message to them is about Rainer and his progress in tracking Lydia down and rescuing her from the Blood Takers.

Alpha Gerald stands by the fireplace. His large form is illuminated by the firelight behind him, making him look like an avenging archangel. His anger is almost palpable. I'm reminded that he fought many battles before I was even born.

Alcide gets up from the couch and begins pacing back and forth on the carpet. "I don't like this. We're leaving Lydia to be rescued by a vampire? This isn't right."

"A shifter trying to infiltrate the Blood Takers would be suspicious. Rainer is our best bet."

"Rainer may be skilled in being a spy, but he's just one man," Alpha

Gerald points out. "If things were to go wrong, I doubt he'll be able to get my granddaughter to safety."

"He's a skilled and experienced warrior from what I've heard," I reason. "He fought with us in the war with Scarlett Thunder. He led Crimson Peak's army."

"It's hard for us to trust any vampire," Alpha Gerald explains. "There's centuries of bad blood that's hard to forget. Even if Alpha Emory trusts this Rainer, we are not as assured."

"I trust him," I insist. "And I would never trust Lydia's life on somebody who I don't think could get the job done. I believe he'll be the one to get her home."

Alcide scoffs. "You have a lot to learn about life, pup. You can't fully trust a vampire. It's in their nature to be duplicitous."

Scott speaks up. "Which is why we can't trust a vampire to get Lydia home. We should be looking for her ourselves. This is pack business."

"We should be calling on our allies now and getting the numbers we need. Sitting around here on our asses will not help anyone," Tyler agrees.

"Enough!" Alpha Gerald exclaims. "You're speaking of another war. Our people are still rebuilding since the last one."

"But it's Lydia, Grandpa," George reminds him. "They have Lydia. We can't just do nothing."

"Maybe war is what we should be planning on," Tommy adds. "After all our kind has endured from the vampires, are we really going to let them get away with this?"

My heart begins to pump faster as I take in what is happening. What Lydia's brothers are suggesting doesn't seem to be about a specific vampire kingdom. They want to go to war with all of the vampires. I know how dangerous and futile that would be.

I fought in the war against Scarlett Thunder and saw how fierce vampires are in a fight. Another war would decimate our already depleted numbers. My pack has gone through two wars in the last four years. We might not survive another one so soon.

I can't let this go further than it already has.

Alpha Gerald turns to me, his gaze somber. "Are you sure about this Rainer, Colt? Lydia is your mate. Are you certain she'll be safe in his hands?"

"A vampire's hands," Alcide adds.

I don't know Rainer. I don't think we've ever had a real conversation, but Emory trusts him. And I trust my sister with my life. I trust her with everything.

"I do. I trust him," I reply. "Lydia will come home to us. We just have to have faith."

"I trust Colt's judgement," Amanda speaks up, her expression steady but kind. "And I trust Alpha Emory's judgement. We will wait and have faith."

A REAL PHONY

Lex

I know Willow is around Brighthall. I've seen her with her daughter and Ivy on the castle grounds. They seem to take their meals at separate times than me as I'm usually dining alone with Uncle Cyrus. I know that Ivy doesn't care for me due to my history with Willow.

Ivy's connection to Willow comes as a surprise to me. It doesn't seem to be a secret, so either someone forgets to tell me, or I wasn't paying attention when people talked about it. Looking at the two women from afar, I can see the resemblance. They have hair the same shade of brown that looks reddish under the sun and the stubborn eyebrows. It seems preposterous that it slipped my mind for a time that they were related, but Ivy reminded me of that in a not-so-gentle manner.

I haven't talked to Willow in a very long time, not since I accidentally turned her into a vampire over a century ago. Shame made me avoid her in Castle Greystone. In a large castle with that many servants, she blended in amongst them, and we managed to never have to interact with each other. When I heard she married Rainer, I was mostly surprised, but I've never gotten along with him either, so I didn't have any reason to find out the details.

Now that I'm the prince regent of Scarlett Thunder, I have even less chances of running into Willow until we ended up at the same castle. Meeting her long-lost niece reminds me of why I've been avoiding Willow. Even after all these years, the guilt I have for how I treated her as a feeder has never gone away. It's one of the things I've been running from, not wanting to acknowledge the worst parts of myself.

It's seeing my son playing with Willow's daughter that makes me want to confront my past. What example will I be for my son if I'm unable to make amends for a wrong I've committed? I strive to teach him to be a better man than the one I've been. It's my true purpose in life.

My nephew, Michael, is playing with them. His parents have left to go deal with the crisis with King Myenas while Michael is safe to be a child here in Cerise Port. The trio of children are playing tag, giggling as they run around the castle grounds. Cole is "it" and chasing them as fast as he can on his little legs.

The sight makes me smile. The innocence of children is something sweet and wholesome to watch. Willow sidles up beside me. I don't say anything, waiting for her first to speak.

"Cole is a darling," she says. "Sweeter than his cousin."

"Kane and I said that it's the universe balancing itself since I was a hellion as a child, and Kane was so responsible. Our children have to be the opposite. It might be unfair to Kane, but I wouldn't trade Cole for anything."

"It's not like he turned out like his mother," she says in a tone that lets me know she's well aware of Opal's antics.

I chuckle. "Not at all. Opal is a fucking nightmare I don't know where Cole gets his sweetness from."

Willow's blue gaze watches me with consideration. "The servants at Castle Greystone said you were sweet when you were a kid, always clinging to your mother's skirts for attention."

If I could blush, my whole face would be red from embarrassment.

"Hearsay. I was a demon as a child. A clingy demon, maybe. Mostly to annoy my mother."

She snorts. "Queen Agatha has the patience of a saint. I doubt you were able to rattle her."

I smile. "Nothing can rattle my mother, not even an earthquake."

"Therefore, she must have just thought you were sweet and not annoying."

"I could have been both," I concede. "Kids are often both delightful and tiresome."

"Maybe other people's kids. Mine is perfect." She smiles at her daughter in a loving fashion.

I laugh, and I can't help but look at her fully. Her hair is shorter than I remember it being, and there's a calmness to her I don't remember. She's a woman that has found her place in the world. "I didn't know you were funny."

She looks me in the eye and declares, "You've never really known me at all."

That brings to mind memories of a dark dungeon and a young witch pale and nearly lifeless on a cot. I wince.

"About what happened between us years ago, I need you to know that I'm not proud of what I did. You deserved better than how I treated you. I truly am sorry for what happened…." I try to go on, but I'm not sure what to say.

Willow shakes her hand, looking away from me as if she's done with the topic. "That was a long time ago. We're different people now."

"Please let me do this," I insist. "I need to apologize, and I have a feeling we both need to hear it."

She swallows then nods. She keeps quiet as I manage to find a way to continue..

"It's no excuse, but I was a stupid prince who only cared about myself. I didn't even care about what would happen to you when I fed on you directly. It didn't occur to me that you might die or become a vampire, something you might not want for yourself. I was too over-come by lust for blood. Now, you're trapped this way forever. This life isn't for everyone, and I am truly sorry for any pain I've caused you."

Willow doesn't say anything. She watches our children play together. Her blue eyes are lost in thought. I try to keep still, knowing this moment is hers and not mine to dictate.

Eventually, she turns to me and says, "There was a time when I hated being a vampire. I would have done anything to be just a witch again. And there was a time I hated you and what you did to me, but I don't feel that way anymore."

She nods towards where her daughter is now the one chasing the boys around the garden. "I wouldn't have my Bryony. I wouldn't have Rainer. It all worked out in the end, Lex, so I forgive you. For all of it."

I let out a deep breath. I can't put into words the gratitude and relief I feel. Deep down, a part of me thinks I don't deserve forgiveness. I also know that sometimes forgiveness isn't for the person who did the wrong–it's for the victim.

* * *

Lydia

I'm falling asleep in the back of the semi-truck, being lulled by the swaying of the vehicle when it abruptly stops. Everyone jolts forward from the inertia, colliding against each other. The ones nearest to the wall have to catch themselves from hitting their faces on the metal. People rumble as they right themselves, wondering what is going on.

"Fuck!" Lazar yells.

"That's a flat tire," Randal says, calmly. "Do we have a spare?"

The metal doors open, and Bogdan appears. He moves people out of the way to get to the spare tire. He jumps out of the truck with it in his arms and yells, "Get out of the truck!"

We all shuffle out like sheep following an angry shepherd. We sit on the ground as we watch the vampires change the tire. There's not much to do in the forest. This is the most entertainment we're going to get.

The vampires squabble amongst each other.

"It'll hold, Laz," Bogdan tries to reassure him. "Just until we can get a new one."

Toman taps the spare tire. "It's too soft. This doughnut won't get us far, especially not in this terrain."

"It just needs to get us far enough," Bogdan reasons

"Maybe we should go get a new tire before we go," Randal suggests. "There has to be a repair shop nearby."

"In the fucking woods?" Lazar retorts. "Where in the woods are you going to find a repair shop, Randal?"

The newest vampire shrugs. "Check the map for one, then."

Toman sighs and takes out a large paper map from his pocket. The vampires all huddle around it, grumbling to each other.

"There's a town nearby," Randal says. "Two of us could go and get the tire while the other two stay here with the feeders."

"You just need one person to go get a tire," Bogdan points out.

"We can't ignore the buddy system, Bo. Safety in numbers." Randal folds his arms across his massive chest.

"That's the dumbest thing I've ever heard. We don't need the buddy system for a fucking tire!" Lazar exclaims.

"If not for safety, then for the company. That's a long walk to go on alone without anyone to talk," he reasons with a smile.

Bogdan and Lazar are both glaring at him, too annoyed to even speak. I've watched them steadily lose their patience with Randal. I have to admit, it's amusing. Randal is either unaware of what he's doing or is just a madman who enjoys making his co-workers suffer.

They all turn to Toman to determine what to do. The leader of the Blood Takers looks exasperated as he runs a hand over his face. He sighs and declares, "I'll go with Bogdan to get the tire. Lazar and Randal, you're on watch duty."

Randal grins and wraps an arm around a disbelieving Lazar. "Looks like we're buddies!"

"Get your arm off me, or I will cut it off," Lazar hisses menacingly.

Randal slides his arm away and takes a few steps back, still grinning like a fool. Maybe he really is a madman.

"Let's get a bonfire going," Randal suggests. "Don't go too far now. Just gather up the sticks that are nearby."

Gathering sticks for the bonfire gives us something to do. We walk around, looking for fuel, while Laz and Randal keep an eye on us. Eventually, we have enough, and Randal starts the blaze. I know it's for our benefit and not theirs. I've never heard of a vampire getting cold.

We take seats and Randal begins an attempt to amuse us by telling us stories, each story more fantastical than the last. He's moved on to trying to get Lazar to talk to him which the other vampire clearly does not want to do.

"Where are you from, Laz?" Randal asks.

Lazar is glaring at the bonfire, refusing to look at Randal who is feeding sticks into the fire. I'm guessing it's been a couple of hours since the other half of the Blood Takers went to get a new tire.

"All right. I'll start," Randal says. "I'm originally from Red River. My parents worked at the castle. Dad was a guard and mom worked as a maid. They were nervous about having a human child around so many vampires, but that was a pretty safe group of vampires to be around, compared to others."

Lazar doesn't say anything. He keeps his focus on the bonfire, hoping maybe he could ignore Randal away. That unfortunately doesn't seem to work on the other vampire. Randal seems to have no issue holding both sides of the conversation.

"How did I get into this line of business?" Randal continues. "Dad died during one of the wars with the other kingdoms, and mom decided it was safer to move us further east. We ended up in a small village near Cerise Port and she found a job working in an inn. I was still a human boy at that point."

"And then what happened?" one of the teenagers asks.

"Thank you for asking." Randal gives him a grin, letting us know he's enjoying telling this story. I'm not sure it's even real, but I listen anyway. "Mom died one winter, and times were hard for a while, so I started in petty thievery. That's how I got turned. Some bastard noble in a dark alley. After that, I made my way as a mercenary in Cerise

Port. Turns out I'm really good at being a mercenary. The lack of a conscience really helps with that right, Laz?"

"Bullshit."

Randal pauses. "What?"

"There are no mercenaries in Cerise Port," Lazar says. "King Cyrus outlawed that two hundred years ago. He has his own league of assassins that works exclusively for him."

The silence is heavy and oppressive. The feeders all are holding their breath as the two vampires stare each other down. My heart beats faster in anticipation. It's no secret that Lazar doesn't like Randal, and things have been steadily boiling for a while and are ready to spill over.

"I look younger than I really am," Randal explains, finally. "I was a mercenary before King Cyrus outlawed it, and then I had to move to Scarlett Thunder to find jobs again."

"You look too young to be over two centuries old, even for a vampire."

Randal shrugs. "Lots of vampires in Scarlett Thunder are better looking than others. It's probably something in the blood there.."

"Bullshit." Lazar shakes his head. "Ever since you showed up, that's all I've been thinking. Everything about you doesn't add up. You stink of bullshit."

Randal's eyebrows raise. "Is that really what you think, Laz? That I'm a phony?"

Lazar leans forward and declares, "Bullshitting phony."

Randal grows quiet. I watch the play of emotions on his face. The congenial mask he usually wears melts away to something more neutral. The sharpness of his features looks more stark without his sunny smiles.

"I'm sorry to hear you feel that way, Lazar," Randal says, indifferently. "I thought we could be friends."

"Well, you fucking thought wrong.. We were never going to be friends, you stupid–"

Something flings through the air so quickly, I can barely see it.

I look at Lazar and realize he has a knife in his chest–a silver blade protrudes. He begins to gasp for air. Blood drips down from the wound. His face is frozen in shock, red eyes wide. He slumps forward and falls on the bonfire, his body quickly ablaze.

Randal stands up and brushes his hands off.. He turns to us and says, "Well? Aren't you going to run?"

27

FROM ASHES TO FLAMES

Rainer

The feeders stare at me like sheep, confused and scared. They don't move. I don't think they're even breathing. I step around Lazar's burning body and make a shooing motion at the feeders.

"Go!" I exclaim. "What are you waiting for?"

One of the female shifters is practically shaking. "We can't go. Once the other Blood Takers come back, and we're not here, we'll be punished."

"Only if they catch you," I reason. "Which is why it is very prudent for all of you to get out of here!"

Still, none of them move. I bite back a groan of frustration. I go to where Lydia is seated a few feet away from the crowd. Pulling her up by the arm, I drag her with me not wanting to waste any more time.

"Hey!" Lydia tries to fight me off, digging her feet into the dirt. "Get off me!"

I'm stronger than her, and I don't let go. I drag her into the forest away from camp.

"Toman and Bogdan we'll be back any minute. The last thing you want to be is at that camp where a dead vampire is cooking on the bonfire," I tell her. "Why does nobody seem to grasp this?"

"Stop!" she yells loud enough for me to turn around and look at her. Her eyes are wide in terror. "I said stop."

"I heard you." I let go of her arm and point to my watch. "Time is a ticking, blondie. We don't have any time to spare."

She looks behind us frantically. "What about the others?"

"I told them to run. If they're smart, they'll be trying to get as far away from here as possible. Like we should be doing."

"Their hands are bound. They won't be able to shift."

"There are some blades in the truck amongst the Blood Takers' things. They just need to grab one. They'll be fine, blondie. We need to go-"

"My name is Lydia, not 'blondie'."

"Lydia." I pray to any deity above who will listen for patience. "I know your name. We *really* need to go."

"Why did you grab only me?" she demands, her expression untrusting. "Are you going to sell me off? Is this what this is about?"

"No. I have no plans to sell you off." I can't explain everything to her right now. We really need to get the fuck out of here.

"Are you going to…" Her eyes are wide in fear. "Are you going to make me your personal feeder?"

"No!" I grimace in disgust. "I would never."

"Then why take me with you?"

I place my hand on her shoulders, resisting the urge to shake her. I'll have to tell her something to get her damn feet to move. Sure, she has no problem running away before, but now I can't even get her to take a step in the right direction. "Listen to me. My name is not Randal. I'm Rainer of Crimson Peak. Alpha Emory sent me to come rescue you. Your mate's sister."

Her blue-silver eyes look like they're trying to read my soul. "How do I know you're telling the truth?"

I shake her a little, unable to help myself. "Would I really go out of my way to mess with mercenaries for no good reason? Lydia, please. I'm begging you. We have to go. Now."

"We can't leave behind the feeders," she insists. "They're not going to get far on their own, especially the humans."

"They're not your problem, Lydia."

"We can't just leave them! You know what will happen to them if they get caught, and they get delivered to whatever vampire royal wants them!"

"We'll send help for them, but getting you home is my priority."

"Helping those people is *my* priority." She lifts her chin into the air stubbornly. "Even though I killed one of the vampires, and they should've abandoned me, they didn't. I'm not going with you unless you help them escape too."

I groan and go to a tree, resting my forehead on the bark of the trunk. So many shifters are the same. Stubborn fools who would chew off their own tails if it meant proving a point. I'd hoped Lydia Nightstone would be different, but that would be too easy for me.

"Randal–"

"It's Rainer."

"Rainer, we have to help them. *Please.*"

I turn back to her, and her big pleading eyes are too much for me. I can't say no to this. I really want to even though I really want to.

"Fine," I acquiesce, unhappily. "But if things go south, and they probably will, I'm grabbing you and running."

She looks both hopeful and in disbelief. "You're going to help them? Really?"

"I'm a bleeding heart. Always have been. It's my fatal flaw besides being too handsome for my own good."

I head back to the camp, and Lydia follows me. She's pleased. I'm unhappy.

This will not end well.

* * *

EMORY

It's nice to be back from home. Sardonia has its charms, but it's ultimately too cold and isolated. Kane and I give ourselves a moment of reprieve before we have to go back to dealing with King Myenas.

Against Queen Olga's advice, Kane wants to try to have a talk with the other king.

The old vampire king isn't known to leave his kingdom except for when he's invited to a good party. Kane and I have to put together a party quickly that will entice the old king to come and have a chat with us. After having to put together the Moon Goddess Ball, I'd been hoping not to have another party for a long while, but at least I don't have to plan this alone. Kane has been throwing parties in Castle Greystone since before I was even born.

He leaves most of the planning to the staff who already have a system in place for these occasions. He defers most of the decision making to the senior staff aside from the few things he absolutely has to give his opinion on. I'm impressed and jealous. I wish this staff had been helping me plan the Moon Goddess Ball.

When I tell Kane this, he says, "You could have asked them for help. They would have been happy to oblige."

"But they would have had to travel to Moon Grove. I don't want to inconvenience anyone."

Kane looks amused. "It wouldn't have bothered them, Emory. Planning a party is more fun for them than catering to the courtiers. Actually, they jump at any chance to get away from the courtiers."

"I still wouldn't have asked. The staff at Moon Grove probably would've been uncomfortable."

While relations between our two kingdoms have improved in the past few years, there is still a lot of history that's hard to forget for most people. I understand it's going to take some time to mend bridges though I wish the mending would go faster at times.

There's a knock on the door, and one of the senior staffers, Thomas enters. He says to Kane, "The birds have arrived, Your Highness. You told me to come get you once they're here."

I turn to Kane in confusion. "Birds?"

Kane gets up from his desk and explains, "King Myenas has a long-standing interest in birds. I've asked for exotic birds to be brought to the castle for an exhibit. In case the party isn't enough to entice him…"

"Maybe the birds will," I finish his thought. "I have to say I wasn't expecting King Myenas to be into birds, of all things."

"He's not into sweet, little birds." Kane leads us from the study down the hallway to one of the rooms which is now filled with dozens of caged birds. "He likes birds of prey. The ones that feed on sweet, little birds."

A thin, bald man with a pointed, bird-like nose is waiting in the room. He bows to Kane. "Your Majesty."

"You must be Sir Gavin." He turns to me and explains, "Emory, this is Sir Gavin. He's a collector of exotic birds."

I look at Gavin who bows as well. "My Lady."

"Oh, I'm not–you don't have to. You can just call me Emory."

I know some vampires are still very formal and tend to call me titles around the castle. I usually tolerate it, but I could never get used to it.

Gavin's forehead crinkles for a moment before he nods. "Lady Emory, then."

Knowing I'm not going to win this battle, I concede. Gavin shows off his little menagerie. There are birds I've seen in books, and there are birds I've never even heard of. They come in all sorts of colors from black to a rainbow of feathers.

"And over here is the rarest in my collection, the Firebird. There are known to be less than fifty of them in the world."

Inside the cage is a bird with feathers that look like flames. Its feathers are a mix of reds, yellows, and oranges. Its beak and eyes are obsidian black. Something about its face looks sickly and old.

"Is it sick?" I ask.

"Not quite, My Lady," Gavin replies. "She's ready to die."

"What? The Firebird is dying?"

Gavin nods. "Any day now. I've been waiting."

Kane's dark eyebrow furrow. "Sir Gavin, why would you bring a dying bird to the castle? Wouldn't it have been better to be left behind at your estate?"

"The Firebird dying is the reason why I brought her to the castle. I thought it would be a spectacular show." At our confused expressions, he explains, "The Firebird is known in some places as the phoenix. It dies and resurrects in a gust of flames. There's nothing like it in this world."

I stare more curiously at the bird. "It can come back to life?"

Gavin nods. "Some cultures believe that the Firebird can live on forever if she chooses to. Like vampires."

"We're not truly immortal," Kane says. "Only long-lived."

"I believe the Firebird is the same. She's been with me for over three centuries. I don't know if she'll outlive me, or I'll outlive her. I suppose time will tell."

I move closer to the cage to stare at the bird. Unlike the other birds of prey that look like they might peck or scratch me if I got too close, the Firebird only cocks her head at me. From the side profile, it's a majestic creature. Staring at it head on, it looks almost confused.

"Hey there, old girl," I coo. "What things have you seen?"

"Quite a lot. I believe she was already over five hundred years old when I found her," Gavin tells me. "She's lived a long life and probably has seen more than most."

"Aside from being able to resurrect themselves, what else are Firebirds able to do?"

"Their song is hypnotic. It can leave you in a trance for days. And their tears are able to heal wounds. Some say their tears can heal any wound and cure any poison."

"Can their tears really do that?" I ask skeptically.

"I'm unsure. I've used her tears to heal a few scrapes on human staff members over the years," he explains, "but I've never tested it on anything more substantial. Being a vampire, I've never needed to."

"Would you say she's magical?" I can't believe I've never heard of this before.

I wouldn't have asked that a few years ago, but after meeting Ivy and her coven, and seeing what magic is able do, I'm aware of just how fantastical and bizarre our world can be.

Gavin shrugs. "It is said that the first Firebird was a familiar to a witch from a long time ago. I cannot attest to the validity of that as witches can be secretive about their history. They certainly wouldn't tell me anything."

Kane and I share a look, wondering what happened with Gavin and the witches he tried to talk to. They probably didn't trust him at all.

"The Firebird is certainly a magical thing to behold," Gavin concludes. "Her rebirth will be nothing like you've ever seen."

I smile, looking forward to the spectacle.

2 8

SAFETY IN NUMBERS

Rainer

The feeders are still at the camp, trying to untie the ropes around each other's wrists. They haven't thought about raiding the truck for anything sharp and were making do with whatever they could find around the camp. They all look surprised to see Lydia and I return. I make a beeline for the truck and find the knives the Blood Takers left behind and hand them over to the feeders.

"Lydia insisted that we don't leave you behind," I tell them. "I'm giving you the option to follow us, or you can go on your own. The choice is all yours."

"Where are you headed?" one of the women asks.

"Burgundy Bay. King Basil's kingdom is to the east from here. I suggest getting out of Red River and somewhere where the leaders aren't allies of Carmine Falls and King Myenas."

One of the humans, a teenage boy, asks, "Will we be welcome there too?"

"You'll be free to return to human territories once we reach Burgundy Bay," I assure him.

"If they catch us, they'll punish us," a woman points out. "Just like what they did to Jesse."

211

"If you stay here, you're as good as dead," I remind them. "Once you reach Carmine Falls, they'll be no coming back. No feeder has ever left King Myenas' castle alive."

"We can trust him," Lydia adds. "He's an ally of Alpha Emory of the Moonraker Pack."

Emory's name has the shifters whispering to each other. The humans aren't as familiar with her name and look confused.

"Is that true?" someone asks. "You know Alpha Emory?"

"I'm the godfather to her son. We're good friends." I gesture toward the woods. "Now, could we please get a move on? Toman and Bogdan will be back any minute now."

The shifters all decide to come with us. The pack likes to stick together, and they feel more comfortable in larger numbers. The humans decide to go off on their own, not fully trusting either shifter or vampire to truly help them. One of the teenage boys decides to drive the truck away as it'll help give them some distance before they have to go on foot.

I hand one of the boys the keys to the truck. "Good luck."

"You too," the boy replies. "Run fast."

Most of the shifters shift into their wolf forms as they'll be able to run faster on all fours. A few of them are too weak to shift, and no one is strong enough to carry anyone else, so they will slow us down. There's not much I can do about it but hope we are fast enough. Like a shepherd leading my flock, I guide them in a frantic run to the woods trying to be speedy enough to put a distance between us and the Blood Takers but not too fast to leave people behind. We've crossed a good distance until we reach a ravine.

"We have to go around," I say.

Lydia shifts back into her human form. "We can climb down. It's not that steep. In wolf form we'll be able to go down easier."

"It's too dangerous. You could fall to your deaths." I know terrain better than anyone else, so I have to make them listen to me.

"Isn't Burgundy Bay right there?" She frantically points to what looks like the castle from the distance. "This is the fastest way."

"What about the people that are too weak?" I counter.

"We have spare cloth," one of the women suggests. "We can make slings and tie them to us so they'll stay on. The stronger people can carry them for a little while."

I look down at the few weak members of our group. They look small enough to still fit in a sling. I agree to the idea, and the stronger people help each other with the slings. In their wolf forms, the shifters scale down the ravine carefully. Their paws dig into the dirt as they slide down the large stones. As for me, I would have had an easier time if I had a rope, but I left that back at the camp, so I have to follow the shifters example and take my time scaling down the ravine.

I mostly have to press my butt against the stones and dirt to keep my balance. I slide my boot down until it reaches a large stone that I can step on. My other boot follows. I slide my butt over the stone and repeat the process.

We are all completely covered in dirt and grass, and by the time we reach the bottom, my legs are chafing. Add ravine scaling to the list of things I never want to do again. Lydia is the last shifter to reach the ground as we've both been keeping watch over the others.

When she reaches the bottom, she relaxes a little. She does a little shake to as much lingering dirt and little grass out of her fur as she can. I look at my ruined pants and know they are a lost cause. The shifters need a minute to catch their breath as many of them are panting wildly, especially those carrying the weaker members of our group.

I look at my watch. It'll be sundown soon. We can't stay here long. I'm about to tell them this when there's a shout from above, "Randal!"

It's Bogdan. We all look up to where he's standing above the ravine. He looks like he's contemplating jumping down to get to us. Even for a vampire, that's a high fall and he'll break his knees.

"You fucking traitor!" Bogdan yells. "I knew you couldn't be trusted!"

I look at Lydia and the other shifters. I can see the fear and panic in their eyes. Freedom is so close. It's just within grasp.

I try to think of a plan. "Look, Bo, it's not what you think!"

"Think what, you greedy asshole? You killed Lazar and went off with the feeders so you can get all the money for yourself!"

At least my cover hasn't been completely blown yet. I can work with that.

"It was Lazar that was the traitor, Bo!" I explain. "He tried to kill me and wanted to make off with the feeders! I was only defending myself!"

"Bullshit! If that was true, then why are you all the way here with then feeders?"

"During the fight with Lazar, the humans ran off with the truck! I was trying to bring the feeders somewhere we could hide them till we found another vehicle!"

"I wasn't born yesterday, Randal! You're clearly the traitor here!"

"You've got to believe me, Bo! I would never do this to you and Toman!"

"My name is Bogdan, you filthy lying piece of shit!"

Bogdan pulls out a crossbow. The shifters tense, their fur rising and they growl. Lydia bares her teeth. I raise my hands up in surrender.

"You don't want to do that, Bogdan!" I tell him. "You could shoot any of the feeders by mistake!"

"Fuck the wolves! I'm going to blow your head off!"

Lucky for me, Bogdan is a bad shot. He fires the crossbow, but it misses, the arrow hitting the ground beside me. The sound makes several of the shifters burst into tears. Most of the group turns tail and runs, their survival instincts pushing them to run as fast and far away as they can.

Lydia grabs the edge of my jacket with her mouth and pulls me toward where the others are running. I don't need to be told twice and follow them. I have to keep a slower pace not to leave the shifters behind. Several arrows are fired behind us, and I'm almost hit more than a few times.

The sun is beginning to set. The sky looks like a blood-soaked field as the shifters run for freedom. They know this is their last chance to get away. If they get caught again, there will be no other chances.

Most of them are malnourished from a diet of canned food and perhaps from living a hard life before their abductions. Those carrying the others are even slower, so Lydia stays in pace with them, encouraging them to keep going. The sky is darkening, but I can still see the castle in Burgundy Bay in the distance. We've managed to scramble up the far side of the ravine, away from Bo, or so I think. A few more miles and we'll reach its border.

I hear the sailing sound of an arrow darting past me, and Lydia slumps forward, hitting the ground. I stop. One of the slower shifters stops too, her expression terrified and dismayed. I glance past her to the border of Burgundy Bay where they will be vampire guards that will prevent us from coming in without an explanation..

I reach into my pocket for a piece of paper with the Alexander family coat of arms and hand it to the shifter who takes it in her mouth gingerly. "Show them that. They'll know to let you in, and that you're affiliated with Crimson Peak. Go!"

She doesn't hesitate and runs forward, following the other shifters toward Burgundy Bay. I go to Lydia who is on the ground. She's bleeding in her side, crimson blood staining her blonde fur. She stays on the ground, her breath shallow.

Bogdan appears in the distance. He sees what he's done and exclaims, "Fuck! I didn't mean to shoot *her*!"

I look over Lydia frantically, trying to see if the arrow hit any of her major organs. "She's losing blood. We have to get her to a doctor."

"The nearest doctor will be in Burgundy Bay!" Bogdan retorts. "I'm not letting her get away when all the other fucking wolves are gone!"

"She's going to die, Bogdan! You're not getting a payday if she arrives at Carmine Falls dead!"

"This is all your fault! I was trying to shoot you!" Bogdan points the crossbow at me. "Ever since you showed up, everything has gone tits up!"

I glare at the end of the crossbow and look back at Bogdan. Like

Lazar, he's hot-tempered and led by his emotions. I don't show any fear of him shooting me, knowing that's what he wants. These sorry excuses for mercenaries are all just big bullies.

"If you're going to shoot me, Bo, do it already. I haven't got all fucking day to listen to your whining."

Bogdan snarls and presses on the trigger. The crossbow goes off with a click, but nothing else happens. The arrow he's loaded isn't placed correctly. I can see it from here. Before Bogdan can fix it, I grab the end of the crossbow and pull it away from him.

He tries to take it back, but I turn the crossbow around to hit him in the face with the stock. There's a sickening crack as his nose breaks, blood spurting down his chin. I aim for his temple and knock him out. He slumps down to the ground like a discarded marionette.

Throwing the crossbow aside, I return to Lydia who has shifted back to her human form. "Are you okay?"

"You have to… get the arrow out," she says. "I can't heal while it's… still inside me."

"I have to get you to a doctor."

"Burgundy Bay is still miles away. I won't… I won't make it if you don't get the arrow out now."

I look to the castle in the distance and swear. Why does everything have to be so difficult all the time? I unbuckle my belt and take it off, offering it to Lydia. She looks confused.

"This will hurt. You could bite your tongue off, so bite this instead."

Lydia doesn't question this and grabs the belt. She bites into it as I look over where the arrow is protruding from her side. I take out the flashlight in my pocket to give me better light aside from the moon. There's so much blood.

"I'm sorry."

I hold the flashlight with my mouth to keep my hands free. I have to be careful because I could break the arrow off inside her. I know there will be a lot of blood when the arrow comes out.

I grip the arrow as close to the wound as I can, and Lydia screams in pain, muffled by the belt in her mouth. It's hard to pull out the arrow with all the blood. It's wet and slippery as I try to avoid causing more damage.

Lydia is in immense pain, having to do this all with no anesthesia. She tries to crawl away, but I hold her down with one hand to her ribs to keep her still. She lets out pained cries as I continue to fide the slippery surface. Finally, I grasp the shaft tightly enough and pull it out.

29

AN UNFAMILIAR BED

Lydia

I wake up in an unfamiliar bed. After being on the road for so long, sleeping in the back of a semi-truck, or on the hard forest floor, a mattress feels like heaven. My head rests on a pillow that might as well be made of clouds, I feel so comfortable. I open my eyes reluctantly, not eager to part from the best sleep I've had in weeks.

The harsh fluorescent lights sting my eyes. I reach up a hand to block the lights. Looking around my surroundings with the white beds and the sterile scent in the air, I surmise I'm in some kind of infirmary. It's a small room, and each bed is separated by cubicle curtains. I sit up and hiss. My side aches from the movement.

Pulling up the hospital gown I'm wearing, I see that my abdomen is covered in bandages. I suddenly remember Bogdan shooting me with a crossbow as we were trying to escape the Blood Takers and get to safety. Rainer had to pull out the arrow so my body could heal itself, or I would have bled out. I lost consciousness as soon as he finished. It was an excruciating and grim experience.

A nurse comes over, pulling back one of the curtains. She's dressed in pink scrubs. She's a vampire. I can tell because her eyes are that eerie pale blue.

I pull down the hospital gown to cover myself.

"You're awake," she says, cheerfully. "We didn't know how long before your body would heal itself. We don't get a lot of wolves- I mean, shifters in Burgundy Bay."

I decide to ignore the nurse's verbal slip. While relations between our two species have somewhat improved over the years, a lot of vampires still refer to us as wolves or werewolves. The latter is an offensive term,, but I don't have the energy to deal with that now. I'm recovering from a wound for the Moon Goddess's sake.

"I'm in Burgundy Bay?" I ask. "How did I get here?"

"Your friend brought you in. A tall male vampire with curly hair."

She must be talking about Rainer. That makes sense.

"How long have I been asleep?"

"A little over a day. Doctor Montgomery cleaned the wound and sewed it up, but after that, your body began to heal itself and just needed rest."

I nod. "And where's the vampire that brought me in?"

"He's been busy helping the other shifters get home. He should be around somewhere."

And that is when Rainer appears as if he's a spirit that's been summoned to the land of the living. He enters the room with a bright smile that seems to leave the nurse in an awed daze.

"Hello again, Janie. How have you been?" he greets her.

Nurse Janie smiles then clears her throat, remembering her professionalism. "I'm good. Thank you for asking. How are you?"

"I can't complain." He turns to me and smiles in relief. "I'm glad to see you're awake. You had me worried there. How are you feeling?"

"I'm a little sore, but that's to be expected." I straighten up my blankets.

"What did the doctor say?"

"Doctor Montgomery is on his lunch break. He should be back in half an hour," Nurse Janie tells him. "If you'll excuse me, I have to get back to work."

The nurse walks away briskly. We both watch her leave the room. I turn to Rainer and remark, "I think she has a crush on you."

He shrugs. "We can't blame her. I'm a very likable guy."

I roll my eyes. "Didn't you mention you have a kid?"

"I do. I have a four-year-old daughter. She means the world to me."

"And what about her mother?"

"My wife is alive and well," he replies. "And happily married to me."

"What does she think about other women crushing on you?" I can't help but snicker a little.

"She's aware that it's beyond my control. My charm cannot be contained, and all that matters is that I don't flirt back, and I come home to her."

I stare at Rainer, trying to imagine him with a wife and child and having a hard time believing it. This man just seems incapable of being serious if it's not a life and death situation. I won't dwell on that. He's his wife's problem at the end of the day.

"The nurse says you've been helping the shifters get home," I say. "Are they all gone?"

"I've been securing transport for them, making sure they end up in the right places. I can't contact packs directly as they won't trust a vampire, so I have to rely on Emory to talk to them on my behalf. As you would expect, this causes things to go slower than I would like, but we're getting there."

Even vampires and shifters aren't immune to bureaucratic red tape. Shifters are stubborn by nature, and Alphas can butt heads more often than necessary. Growing up seeing my grandfather argue with other Alphas for the most mundane things has made me grateful I'm not in line to be an Alpha. I'll happily leave that responsibility to somebody else.

"Where are the shifters staying?" I ask.

"At a cottage near the castle. King Basil has graciously let the shifters stay there until I can get everything sorted," Rainer explains.

"Have you talked to my pack?" I take a deep breath, wondering how my family has reacted to hearing that I'm alive.

He nods. "I informed Emory as soon as I could where we are. She's talked to your grandfather, and they're headed here to come get you."

Tears well up in my eyes from relief. I'm finally safe, and I'll be reunited with my family and my pack again. I can't even let myself think about being with Colt again. It seems unreal. The shifters are also safe, and none of us will be forced to be feeders. The nightmare is over.

I turn away, not wanting Rainer to see my cry.

"Hey," he says, softly. "It's okay. You've had a rough time."

My shoulders begin to shake. My voice trembles when I try to speak. "I know. It's just I–I thought for a moment that I wouldn't be able to get out and… and I'm just relieved. I can breathe again."

"You were brave and noble. You refused to leave behind the others even at the cost of your own life."

"I was terrified. I didn't have a plan. All I knew was I couldn't leave all those people to such a horrible fate." I swipe at my tears.

"You kept going despite your fears. That's what bravery is." He gives me a reassuring smile.

I wipe my tears with the back of my hands again. Rainer hands me a box of tissues from a nearby table. I take one from the box and wipe my cheeks.. Rainer doesn't say anything and takes a seat on a stool as I try to compose myself.

"Do you think the humans were able to get away?" I ask, remembering how they drove away in the semi-truck to get to safety faster. "I didn't see Toman."

"I don't know what happened to the humans. They might have gotten away…" He shrugs, but I can tell he's worried, too.

"Or Toman found them?"

Even alone, Toman is a vampire that's stronger and faster than a whole group of humans. If he found them, they would have no chance against him. I don't know what Toman would have done to them for trying to escape, but I hope they were able to get away and are safe now. Jesse's death still weighs heavily on my heart.

"I wish I could go help them, but you're my priority." Rainer reminds me. "And I'm doing what I can for the shifters."

"I'm not more important than anyone else."

"You are to Colt Moonraker. They had to stop him from running after you."

I take a deep breath, knowing what he's saying is true. "He would have gotten himself captured or killed."

Colt like most shifter men can be impulsive and hot-headed. If he managed to find the Blood Takers, he would have fought them to his dying breath. An image of one of the mercenaries ripping his head off like they did with Jesse deeply disturbs me. I know it wouldn't have been something I could have survived.

"That man is in love with you. And all he wants is to get you back," Rainer reminds me.

My heart melts. I have tried to avoid thinking of Colt and how much I've missed him. Having only recently met my mate, being parted from him has felt painful, like I imagine missing a limb would feel. The blissful week we spent together at Moon Grove feels like a lifetime ago.

"I want to get back to him, too," I say. "Is he coming to Burgundy Bay with my family?"

Rainer smiles. "From what I know of Colt, he's on his way here as we speak."

I smile back, feeling lighter and vibrant with hope.

* * *

KANE

Emory and I both agree to have Mikey stay at Cerise Port while King Myenas is in Crimson Peak. We feel better knowing Mikey is far away and safe from any nasty surprises the old king might bring with him. Call it paranoia, but we'd rather be safe than sorry. My mother has met the vampire king a few times, back when my father was the king, and she does not care for him at all.

Nevertheless, Dowager Queen Agatha helps with setting up the party. She's better at these things than me, and I have always left the planning of balls and soirees in her experienced and capable hands. Emory doesn't enjoy party planning either, so she's glad to let my mother take the lead. The bird exhibition was Agatha's idea as she knows about King Myenas's obsession with birds.

"How did you find out about his bird obsession?" I ask as we enter the ballroom and watch the staff decorate.

"Your father took up falconry for a time. He and Myenas bonded over their shared interest but were ultimately too different from each other to form a lasting friendship."

"Is that all they did? They just talked about birds?" I can't help the face I'm making.

"For hours. I was almost scared your father loved his pet falcon more than he loved me. Can you believe that? I was competing with a damnable *bird*."

I almost snort. Few people are aware of how funny my mother can be at times. Lex inherited his predilection for drama from her, no doubt.

"I'm sure he couldn't love a bird more than you, Mother," I assure her. "And I don't remember my father having any pet birds when I was a child."

My father never seemed the type for pets, unless one counted his horses as my father enjoyed a good horseback ride on the lands. My mother is the same, and I recall seeing them riding off on their horses away from the castle. I always wanted to join them, but it had been my parents' thing. And by the time I was old enough to ride my own horse, I would rather ride with boys my own age.

"He outgrew falconry by the time you were born. He would rather go hunting with his friends up north. That's why there's that hunting lodge."

I have never been much for hunting myself. I still remember my father bringing Lex and me hunting with him. Lex didn't have the stomach for it. I tolerated it and never complained. Neither Lex nor I have gone hunting since our father's death.

Thomas comes over with the guest list. My mother takes it from him, and I look over her shoulder to see it also has the seating chart for dinner. She takes a pen from Thomas and makes some corrections before handing the guest list and seating chart back to him. My mother has the patience to remember which royals and aristocrats cannot be seated together. It's a trait I have not inherited from her.

"For a man with his reputation, King Myenas' fondness for birds is sort of strange," I point out. "Even if he prefers birds of prey."

"Why would it be odd for Myenas to like birds? Birds are cold, and they only care about themselves. Myenas can probably relate to them." Mother shrugs and goes to the next task. I consider her point and trudge along behind her. I'll be happy when all of this is over.

We know that Rainer has been successful in his task, and Lydia will soon be on her way home, but we have to end this blood trading once and for all.

30

A COMMON INTEREST

Kane

Emory stays close to me, holding my hand as King Myenas enters the ballroom. His entourage of guards and favored courtiers are with him. He's an imposing figure, tall and muscled at six feet five inches. Some might consider him handsome, but there's a wildness in his blood red eyes that's unnerving. He hides it in icy calmness that doesn't allow anyone to relax around him.

King Myenas stops in front of me and bows his head slightly. "Kane, I am pleased to finally see you again. Last time I was in your kingdom was when your father was king and you were a small boy."

I nod back at him. "I'm pleased to see you, too. I've heard that you and my father used to have common interests."

He raises an eyebrow at me. "I had the utmost respect for your father, though we never had much in common."

"I heard that you both have an interest in birds. My father used to enjoy falconry," I remind him.

King Myenas genuinely looks surprised. "That was such a long time ago. It seems like ages ago now."

My mother is at my side, and I look to her for help. She looks to the ceiling as if asking for divine strength before stepping forward. This grabs King Myenas' attention, and he smiles widely.

"Agatha!" he says, pleased. "You have not aged a day. Still the most beautiful woman in the room."

He's taking my mother's appearance in with relish. I have to stop myself from making a face. I hadn't anticipated King Myenas trying to flirt with *my mother*. She doesn't even smile at him and just inclines her head in the slightest nod.

"I would love to catch up," King Myenas continues, unperturbed that my mother has not said a word. He offers her his arm. "Shall we, Agatha? I hope you don't mind, Kane."

My mother sighs but doesn't decline. She takes his arm, her blue eyes looking everywhere but at him. Before I can protest, he walks away with her. Emory and I are left watching him as he talks *at* my mother more than anything.

"I don't trust that bastard," she whispers. I look at her, and she continues, "He didn't even acknowledge me," Emory tells me. "It's like I don't exist. Is it because I'm a wolf shifter?"

I wrap a comforting arm around her. "It could have been worse. He could have called you terrible names."

Emory frowns. "I still don't like him."

I kiss the top of her head. "Don't let him hear you say that."

King Myenas avoids me for most of the party. He keeps my mother near him, constantly whispering things in her ear when he's not loudly boasting to her about all his riches. She keeps quiet, and occasionally, I catch her eye. I owe her a long overdue vacation after this.

After dinner, she leads King Myenas to the room where the bird exhibit is being held. She makes some excuse and escapes out of the room through a hidden passageway behind a large painting of my great-grandfather. This gives me the opening to finally talk to the old king one on one. He stops and looks at all the birds in the cages.

King Myenas spends most of his time observing the Firebird. She looks even sicklier this day. She's in the middle of a nap and has her eyes closed. A lot of her feathers have fallen out making her look like a half-plucked chicken.

"It's a Firebird," I explain, stepping beside the older king. "According to Lord Gavin, she's about to die."

King Myenas frowns and looks closer into the cage. "Is he not doing anything to help this poor creature? Anything to ease her situation?"

"You have a soft spot for such creatures?" I'm surprised to hear this.

"Only for birds. They can be fiercely intelligent. They are hunters that cannot be contained to one location. They rule the skies. How could I not admire them?"

What I'm about to say is interrupted as the Firebird awakens, her black eyes glowing a bright golden yellow. She spreads her wings as wide as she can in the cage and bursts into flames. King Myenas and I are stuck watching as the bird self-immolates, her flesh and bones burning into a pile of ashes at the bottom of the metal cage.

"It's dead!" King Myenas looks shocked.

I urge him to look at the pile of ashes as a tiny bird's head pops out. Her black eyes stare up at us, new and inquisitive. She makes chirping noises.

"The Firebird is also called the Phoenix. She dies and is reborn from the ashes," I explain. "She's the rarest in this collection. I thought you might like to see her resurrection." I'm overjoyed that our timing was so perfect. I look to her owner and see a delighted look on his face as Sir Gavin has finally witnessed what he's been waiting for.

"I have never seen anything like her," King Myenas states, watching the little bird with curious and greedy eyes. "I would love to add her to my collection. What is the price for her?'

"She's not for sale. She's only here as part of the exhibit," I explain.

King Myenas looks back at me, his expression mocking. "Everything has a price. Introduce me to the Firebird's owner. I will persuade him myself."

"Sir Gavin adores every bird in his collection. He will not part with them for anything." I'm sure he can hear our discussion, but I am trying to protect him the best I can.

King Myenas's face darkens. "I am not a man that accepts no. I want the Firebird, and I shall have her."

Or else... what?

I don't ask him that, knowing it will not lead to anything good. Instead, I say, "I'm sure Sir Gavin can be persuaded with a lighter touch. I would be glad to assist you in acquiring the Firebird."

"And what will be the price be for your help, Kane?" he questions, his blood red eyes sharply assessing my face. "I'm sure you didn't invite me to this party just to show me exotic birds. What is it you truly want from me?"

There's a pause, heavy with anticipation.

I look him right in the eye and answer, "I want you to stop the blood trade."

"The Blood Takers don't belong to me."

"But you are affiliated with them, and they follow your orders. I have heard from trusted sources about how you're able to get so many feeders at Carmine Falls," I continue. "If you stop buying, they'll have to stop the trade."

He doesn't look pleased. "These are all rumors and none that can be proven true. And even if they were, what is your interest in saving random shifters and humans?"

I shrug, pretending to be nonchalant. "Does it matter?"

"It matters to me why it's important to you. And do not lie to me, I know it's important because you would not go through all this trouble for some ordinary feeders."

I try to keep my face neutral, hiding all my emotions behind a brick wall in my mind. Lydia isn't out of the dark yet, and the truth of her identity could complicate this situation and make it much worse, so I opt for a lie that will sound convincing.

"One of the feeders belongs to me. She's my own personal feeder. I am not pleased that she's been taken and that somebody will be feeding on my property."

King Myenas smiles mockingly. "Finally tired of that slut you married then? I always thought it a shame that you sullied your family line for some werewolf bitch. Her blood must taste amazing, but every man gets bored of eating the same meal every day."

I clench my fists, fighting the urge to punch him for talking about Emory in such a foul way, but I have to remain calm. Too much is on the line for me to lose my temper even if this bastard deserves it.

"Tell me, do you fuck this feeder too?" King Myenas asks. "Is she both your feeder and your mistress?"

I swallow the disgust I feel at his words and answer, "The details don't matter. I want her returned to me immediately. I don't want anyone else touching her, and I want the blood trade ended once and for all for what they've done."

King Myenas looks at the Firebird then back at me. "It looks like we both want something badly. Let's find another room to sit and negotiate our terms."

I feel like I'm about to make a deal with the devil, and maybe that's exactly what this is. "Follow me. Let's talk in my office." I'll bring Gavin in later, after I've worked out the details.

* * *

RAINER

Dr. Montgomery is an interesting man. He's a bit kooky, a bit unorthodox, but as I'm wandering around the castle after most of the other shifters who weren't wounded in the escape have left, I find myself carrying on lengthy conversations with him just to have something to do. During one of my talks with Dr. Montgomery about Lydia's recovery, and he tells me that Lydia should be cleared for travel in a few more days. Now that she's resting in the hospital and eating better food, she's healing quickly. The doctor doesn't ask any questions about what my relationship to Lydia is. Having a group of shifters suddenly appear one night in their kingdom has attracted enough attention, and I'm trying to keep a low profile.

I am looking forward to getting home myself. I miss my wife and daughter, and honestly, I miss my face. I wish I would've asked

Willow to give me some sort of a potion to drink to change me back into my old self once I didn't need to look like this anymore. Randal is a good looking fella, which is why Nurse Janie and many of the others keep flirting with him, but it's not the same, and every time I accidentally look into a reflective surface, I have to do a double-take. I'm looking forward to having my old mug back, sooner rather than later.

I'm also quite concerned about my daughter. Leaving when she was starting to have those bad dreams wasn't ideal, and I wonder if Willow has gotten any answers as to what in the world is going on with her. I hope that Ivy or someone will be able to give us more information and assure us that it's nothing to worry about, but I won't be at ease until I can hold my baby girl in my arms again. I never thought I'd be able to have children since it's usually just royal vampires who are blessed with having children naturally, but thanks to me marrying a witch, we were able to have such a perfect little girl. I hope I don't do anything to screw it up. I have to help her, and I can't do that while I'm here in Burgundy Bay watching over Lydia.

Burgundy Bay is a smaller kingdom with fewer resources. They rely heavily on trading with other kingdoms to sustain themselves. I know that the shifter packs will be open to trading with King Basil after his help, so I'm not surprised when the Alpha of the Nightstone Pack arrives in the kingdom with an entourage. King Basil greets the Alpha himself at the western gates of the castle.

King Basil is about the same age as Kane. He looks young next to Gerald, with his salt and pepper hair. Gerald is taller and still fit due to staying active. His son and grandsons are built the same which makes me realize Lydia is the runt of the litter.

"Alpha Gerald," King Basil says. "Welcome to Burgundy Bay."

Gerald nods. "It's nice to meet you despite the circumstances, King Basil. I appreciate your assistance with not only my granddaughter but with all of my kind that you've given refuge."

"I didn't know your granddaughter was amongst the group."

The king glances at me, silently blaming me for not telling him about this fact. I merely shrug. I've been busy trying to play telephone with Alphas. Informing King Basil about who Lydia was seemed like a risk not worth taking.

"She's hard to miss, my Lydia. Blonde, pretty, and clever. Takes after my wife in temperament." Gerald looks around the castle courtyard. "Where is she?"

"Lydia is recovering in the infirmary wing," I answer. "I told Alpha Emory about Lydia's injuries."

The Alpha's eyebrows furrow. "That tidbit might've gotten lost on its way to me. What are her injuries?"

"She was shot with an arrow, but fear not, a doctor has patched her up, and she's almost fully healed," I explain.

"An arrow wound? I have to see her now. Sorry to be rude, King Basil, but I haven't seen my granddaughter in weeks."

"I completely understand, Alpha Gerald. I'm going to leave it to Rainer to show you the way to the infirmary wing." King Basil steps away. "I will see you later. We've prepared a small feast in your honor."

The older shifter follows me from the courtyard into the castle. On his way, he explains that the rest of the family and Colt are also on their way, but he was closer, visiting another pack in hopes of looking for the missing shifters together, when Emory let him know I'd gotten Lydia to safety.

The castle, called Burgundersee, sits next to a large lake called Lake Nett. It's an ancient castle with eight towers, timber roofs, and turrets. It's not nearly as large as Castle Graystone, so it doesn't take long to reach the hospital wing.

I open the doors and see Nurse Janie making her rounds. She stops when she sees me and smiles shyly. Lydia isn't wrong about the nurse having a small crush on me. I have no intentions of entertaining her infatuation but try to stay polite.

"Hello, Janie," I greet her. "This is Lydia's grandfather, Gerald. Is she awake?"

Nurse Janie's smile drops. She looks between the two of us, and her eyebrows furrow in confusion and she replies, "She's not here. A man came earlier and had her discharged by Dr. Montgomery. He said he was a friend of yours."

I freeze as the shock of the news hits me. Before I can ask, Gerald cuts me off, "Who was this man? Was he a vampire?"

Nurse Janie nods. "He said his name was Tom."

I let out a curse that makes Janie wince.

"Rainer," Gerald's voice grabs my attention. "Do you know this 'Tom'?"

I run a hand over my face, knowing the nightmare isn't really over. "His name is Toman. He's a Blood Taker."

31

THE BAD MEWS

Kane

I can't hide the irritation I feel as I'm told that Rainer has sent a telepathic message back to the castle through several of our allies to let me know there's been a problem with Lydia. She's gone-back with the Blood Takers. That changes everything as I begin to deliberate with Myenas.

Damnit, I thought we had her out of harm's way at least.

King Myenas follows me into my office, and I close the door behind us. I don't lock it. I have guards right outside the door, ready to come to my aid should the old king try anything nefarious. Emory is in the next room so she can listen in on the conversation.

I turn around, and King Myenas is standing by the window where a view of the gardens can be seen. I walk to my desk and take a seat, waiting for him to join me so we can begin this negotiation. He doesn't move. I stay put, refusing to come to him like a dog begging for attention.

"What happened to the mews?" he asks.

"Pardon?"

"A mews is a birdhouse designed for birds of prey. Your father had one for his falcons. It used to be kept near the rose garden."

"I don't remember having one. My mother might know what happened to it."

"Pity." He finally turns to me, walking slowly toward my desk. "You didn't inherit your father's interest in falconry?"

"My father had moved on to hunting by the time I came around. We either hunted or went horseback riding together."

"That's a shame." He takes a seat on the chair across from me. "None of my children have ever cared for birds. My sons care more for horses, and my daughter keeps those tiny fluffy dogs for company."

"Tiny fluffy dogs?" I repeat. "What kind?"

He snorts. "The ones with the high-pitched yapping. More fur than brains. Useless little things, not even good enough to feed on."

"I'm sure your daughter is relieved you don't want to eat her pets."

"We all have our preferred pets," he says. "And yours seems to be a peculiar choice in lovers. I never thought Michael's son would be so enamored with wolf women. What do you think your father would say about this fetish of yours?"

I give a bland smile, not liking the topic of conversation. "Shall we discuss terms for the trade?"

There's a knock on the door, and Thomas enters, hurriedly coming over to my side. He has a clipboard and pen ready to take notes of this conversation. He's doing his best to hide his nervousness which I appreciate. King Myenas doesn't pay attention to Thomas's interruption and leans back his chair like we're merely there to have a casual conversation.

"It's simple, Kane. I know your true target. It's not the blood trade in general you have a problem with, though you pretend it is. I know we have that girl back in our possession, the one you called a personal feeder. " I stare at him before giving a small nod. He smirks. "I want the Firebird, and in exchange, I'll give you your little feeder back."

"I want her back immediately and unharmed." I keep my teeth clamped together as I speak.

He shrugs. "The feeders tend to get a little roughed up in travel. She will be brought back to you mostly unscathed."

"I don't want anyone to feed on her."

King Myenas's red eyes focus on me, trying to look for any weakness. "You sound really concerned for someone that's just a feeder. Is she important to you beyond being your property?"

I keep my face neutral, trying to hide my disgust at his wording. "No one else gets to have her."

He smiles smugly. "I want more then. Since she matters so much to you, I want the Firebird and gold. Double the amount a regular feeder is sold."

I glare at King Myenas. "This is extortion. The deal is you get the Firebird, one of the rarest birds in the world, in exchange for the feeder. That is more than enough."

"The Firebird is a magnificent creature, and I am delighted to have it in my collection, but I'll still be out of pocket with your feeder. And if you truly care for her, then you shouldn't hesitate to cough up the gold."

I bite back a curse, annoyed. King Myenas is one of the wealthiest vampire royals. He doesn't need more gold. He's doing this for his own amusement. It'll cost me a fortune to buy the bird from her owner, if he'll even agree to sell.

"I'll pay the regular amount of gold for a female shifter. Nothing more, nothing less."

King Myenas sighs dramatically. "Maybe she doesn't matter that much to you then. What is the name of your little feeder?"

"Lydia," I answer through gritted teeth. "And I do care about her, but I will not let you extort me. You don't need the money."

"I don't *need* the money, but that doesn't mean I can't have more of it. In fact, I'm going to want triple the amount of gold now. If she's managed to enchant you, her blood must be worth it. I could auction her off to the highest bidder for a hefty price."

Panic flares in me. "You wouldn't."

King Myenas's dark grin widens. "I would. I'd love nothing more in this world."

"You won't get the Firebird if you auction her off."

He shrugs. "It's a sacrifice I might be willing to make. I'm sure I can get my hands on another Firebird again in the future. I'm a very patient man."

Thomas stops writing and stares at me in concern. I weigh my options. I don't know if King Myenas is bluffing or not. He's never been someone I can read easily.

If I had more time to think, I would come up with other solutions to make sure I don't lose greatly on this deal. Extortion and exploiting a situation to my benefit has never been my way. King Myenas has been playing this game far longer than I have, and he has no scruples. To him, winning is everything.

I lock my hands together and rest them on the desk. "I'll pay double the regular rate. You'll get half now and the other half along with the Firebird once Lydia is back in my care."

King Myenas seems to think this over, taking his time by looking at his fingernails. I'm left to wait, trying to hide how anxious I am for his answer. The sick bastard. Eventually, he looks up and meets my eye.

"I agree to your terms."

He offers his hand, and I take it, shaking it and resisting the urge to crush his fingers or punch him in the face. "Deal."

Thomas writes a contract for us to sign, detailing more of the terms of our agreement. We both sign it with Thomas acting as a witness. Once King Myenas finishes signing the contract, he gets up from his chair to leave. The ink is still wet, and it glistens like black blood.

"It's a pleasure doing business with you, Kane," King Myenas says, pleasantly. "We should do this again."

He walks through the door. I glare at his back and feel like I've lost a battle.

* * *

RAINER

Alpha Gerald is furious when we both realize that Lydia is back in danger. Toman has managed to kidnap her right under our noses.

Nurse Janie is profusely apologetic when she realizes the mistake she's made by letting Toman take Lydia from the hospital wing. The nurse looks like she's on the verge of tears, not that vampires can easily cry.

"I didn't know," she says. I notice how badly she's trembling. She's gone from the fun, flirty nurse to a ball of nerves in a matter of moments. "I am so sorry. If I had any idea who he was, I would have never--"

"It doesn't matter," Alpha Gerald cuts her off. "What we need to do is get my granddaughter back before this Blood Taker gets her to Carmine Falls. How near is that kingdom from here?"

"If he has a vehicle, he could be in Carmine Falls in a couple of days." I go over the math in my mind, trying to figure out which path he would take, how secretive he would be, whether or not Lydia will try to fight him, if she's strong enough or even awake.

A semi-truck of feeders takes longer because they have to be kept hidden. Only back roads and out-of-the way routes would suffice. Toman is alone and has only one person to move across borders. He will have an easier and faster time in reaching his destination now.

Alpha Gerard looks like he wants to rip my throat out. He bares his teeth in rage. "How could you let this happen? She was supposed to be safe here!"

"I don't know how he got into the castle," I reply. "But Toman is an experienced mercenary. He's used to being able to go into places he's not welcome." I still can't believe any of this has happened. How in the world did I let this bastard back in when we fought so hard to get away from him? I can't believe he had the nerve to sneak in here and take her right from out of my grasp!

"He was dressed up like one of the servants," Nurse Janie explains. "I thought that he might have been a new hire. We usually get new people coming in around this season."

"You didn't bother to check if he was who he said he was?" Alpha Gerard barks at the poor nurse.

I push Nurse Janie behind me, shielding her from the Alpha's wrath. "She didn't know, Alpha Gerald. Your anger is understandable, but taking it out on her will not help the situation."

"What do you want me to do then, Rainer? Smile and say thank you for fucking up?" He picks up a clean bedpan on one of the hospital beds and throws it at the wall. "She was right here! I was supposed to bring her home tonight!"

"We will get her back," I say. "Toman couldn't have gotten that far yet. Even if he has a vehicle, the terrain around the castle isn't forgiving for driving."

"Then what are we waiting for? We need to catch him before he gets away."

Alpha Gerald moves toward the door, but I stop him with a hand on his muscular shoulder. He turns and growls at me low in this throat. His silver blue eyes flash gold. I drop my hand but don't get out of his way.

I may be stronger and faster than Gerald Nightstone, but this is a man that's worried for a loved one. Shifters are by nature fiercely loyal, and Alpha Gerald is no different. If he considers me a threat to Lydia, he will die fighting me tooth and nail. Even if I win, he's not going to go down lightly.

"I have to go on my own. You're too conspicuous," I reason. "If you are captured, they'll kill you on sight or throw you in the dungeons to be another feeder."

"That's my granddaughter in danger. My only granddaughter, Rainer," he retorts. "I let you try to rescue her once, and you managed to lose her just when I was about to take her home. Why in the Moon Goddess's name should I let you try again?"

I wince but I don't back down. "If they reach the castle, I can get in without being noticed. I'll get her out alive. You won't be able to do that. Even an Alpha can't fight off a castle full of vampires."

He doesn't look convinced. He turns away, running a hand through his salt and pepper hair. "If she dies…"

"I swear on my daughter's life, I will get Lydia home," I continue. "I'm not going to fail you again, but you need to let me do this. Alone.

That means, when the rest of your family shows up, you keep them back, too."

He turns back to me, his expression torn. "I'm going to regret this."

"I'll make sure you won't regret it."

"Fuck." He shakes his head. "This is what I get for trusting vampires. Go!"

Alpha Gerald yells the last part, and it makes Nurse Janie jump. She's teary-eyed but keeps quiet, terrified of the shifter. He's an intimidating figure, tall and muscled. There's a ferocity to his anger that can't be overlooked.

When I don't immediately move, he exclaims, "Get the fuck out of here, Rainer! Get her back!"

I don't hesitate this time. I turn away, running as fast as I can out of the hospital wing. I run through the halls of the castle, past the servants doing their chores. When I reach the courtyard, I run past Alpha Gerald's family and pack members. I have no time to explain to them what has happened.

My only focus is getting out of this castle and finding any trace of Lydia. Her scent leads me outside of the village and back into the woods. Her scent is in the wind guiding my way. I can't fail her a second time.

32

BAD TO WORSE

EMORY

We hear the news about Burgundy Bay from Alpha Gerald. A collective dismay clouds over us all as we realize how close we have been to getting Lydia home. The news devastates Colt who has shifted into his wolf form and refuses to change back. He's been sleeping in the forest, avoiding everyone in the pack including our mother.

Colt has tried to go after Lydia and had to be stopped by our male staff at Moon Grove several times. Eventually, we hauled him back home, and now, my Beta, Darius, is staying out in the woods with him to keep an eye on Colt and prevent him from doing something foolish. Darius keeps me up to date on what's going on in Moon Grove. We're both worried about my brother.

I had to go home to the castle. I hate that we weren't able to get to Lydia, but I can't stay away from my son when there are so many people looking for her. And I trust Rainer. He'll get her back, I just know it.

Darius and I talk on the phone so I can keep him updated on how things are progressing on our end. Kane's deal with King Myenas is our last resort. The other king is enjoying forcing Kane to bend to his infuriating whims. I have a burning desire to punch the old vampire in the face and damn the consequences.

"I wish there's more I could do for him," Darius tells me on the phone. "Every time I catch a glimpse of him in the forest, he turns tail and runs."

"Where is he sleeping?"

"He probably found an empty den. It's getting colder, and he won't be comfortable sleeping in the open like this."

"Is he eating?" I ask, not able to imagine my brother refusing food.

"He must hunt as we find remains of his kills around the forest." Darius sounds as worried as I feel.

"Great." I sigh. "He probably smells horrific."

"I've gotten a whiff. He's beginning to smell ripe."

"Maybe you should hose him down." His smell is the least of his worries, I know, but he's got to get himself back together. He's not helping anyone in his present state.

"Your mother said we should all drag him into the house and force him into the bathtub for a bath."

"He'd fight you. Colt always tried to escape bath time when we were kids." The memory lightens the mood for me for a moment–but only a moment.

"I'll make sure to remember that." There's a pause then he continues, "I can't imagine what he's going through. If anything happened to my wife, I'd go insane too."

"We're supposed to be planning a wedding, not plotting against an old vampire tyrant." I feel a tear slip down my cheek.

"Well, plotting against tyrants is your specialty, Emory," Darius reminds me. "Historically, you're very good at it."

I smile despite the circumstances. Darius is an old friend of mine. Through the years, we've learned that we work well together, and I don't regret choosing him as my Beta. He's a good man, and I'm glad he's there to watch over my brother while I can't.

"Thank you," I reply. "And please keep my brother from doing anything stupid. He's the only brother I have."

"I'll do my best."

The call ends after that, and I hang up the phone. I rest my head in my hands, feeling like the weight of the world is on my shoulders, and there's no easing it. This reminds me too much of being in negotiations with Scarlett Thunder all those years ago before King Peter died. Each day is filled with anxiety and waiting for the next fire we have to put out.

Kane enters the study, looking as tired and anxious as me. Closing the door behind him, he leans against the door with his eyes closed. He unbuttons the collar of his black shirt as if he's overheated. He hasn't been sleeping well as he has had to convince Lord Gavin to part with the Firebird.

Lord Gavin hasn't made this an easy task as he believes no money in the world is worth parting from the rare bird. Eventually, there is an amount that even Lord Gavin can't decline along with land and jewels.

"That bird is the most expensive animal in the world," Kane says. "At this rate, our son will inherit only a cabin and a spoon."

"They'll call him the Pauper King. It'll be sufficiently tragic," I quip, trying to make him smile. "The Pauper *Hybrid* King."

Kane scoffs. "That's awful."

I get up from my desk and move closer to Kane. He meets my halfway, and we seek comfort in each other's arms. The weight of the world isn't so unbearable knowing that I have someone to share it with. Kane's heart in my hands is both salvation and strength.

"Do you have any updates?" I ask, looking up at him.

He nods. "I have good news and bad news."

"Good news first."

"Rainer has sent word that he's tracked Lydia, and he knows where she's being kept."

Whatever relief I feel I know is temporary. I close my eyes, knowing what comes next is going to be terrible. "And the bad news?"

"Lydia has been brought to King Myenas's territory, Carmine Falls. She's in the castle."

Dread makes it hard to breathe. The worst we've feared has happened. Lydia is in real danger now.

* * *

LYDIA

I'm woken up by water being thrown at me. I gasp and wipe it from my eyes and look up to see Toman with an empty pail. I look past him and realize I'm in a dungeon. There are vampires in the room dressed in guard's uniforms.

I try to remember how I got here. The last thing I can recall is resting in the hospital wing at Burgundy Bay. Rainer assured me that I was safe. How have I ended up back in this terrible nightmare? Escaping to Burgundy Bay couldn't have all been a futile dream, could it?

It couldn't have been a dream. I'm wearing a hospital gown. That means Toman must have taken me from the hospital wing while I was unconscious. I look around for an exit in the room, but the door is blocked by the two guards.

"All this trouble for one feeder, Toman?" one of the guards mocks him. "We thought you were bringing a whole truckload of feeders."

"I was, but the shipment was sabotaged by some stranger. He claimed that he was sent as back-up, but he was lying." Toman spits on the ground. "He murdered my crew and let all the feeders escape."

"You got scammed?"

The guards all laugh, enjoying humiliating Toman who scowls.

"I didn't get scammed. I don't know who this man is working for, but he's more dangerous than he looks," Toman says. "He might be one of King Cyrus's assassins."

"Why would the league of assassins care about your feeder operation?"

"I don't fucking know! All I know is that he wants this bitch in particular!" Toman snaps. "He was always sniffing around her. I know she has to be valuable."

One of the guards bends down and touches my wet locks. "I don't know, Tom. She's got some nice tits, but I wouldn't pay more for her than the usual rate unless her blood tastes like fucking ambrosia."

I slap his hand away, and the guard glares at me.

"Feisty, huh?" he snarls, reaching for my hospital gown. "Let's rip this off and see how much you're really worth."

I slap his hands away. His red eyes darken with fury, and he back-hands me. I taste blood in my mouth as pain rips through my cheek. I have to ignore it, so I turn to glare at him. Before he can hit me again, there's a commotion as the door in the dungeon opens.

A tall man appears. He has dark hair and blood red eyes. The guards all go quiet, and with a fist on their chest, they bow reverently. Toman bows low, his nose almost touching the ground.

The tall man stops before the Blood Taker. "Where are my feeders, Toman?"

Toman gets down on his knees. "I-I am sorry, my Lord. I lost this shipment-"

The punch is swift and brutal. Toman is thrown to the side, his skull slamming against the cold dungeon floor. The impact would have killed a human. Toman's temple is bleeding as the tall man walks over and stares down at him imperiously.

"What happened to the feeders, Toman?" he asks. "How did you manage to lose all those feeders? Such a simple task I gave you, and you managed to fuck it all up."

Toman sits up but keeps his gaze on the ground. "Apologies, my Lord. We were sabotaged. A stranger, who I believe to be an assassin, infiltrated our crew and killed them all one by one. He escaped with the shifters and brought them to Burgundy Bay."

"An assassin?"

Toman nods. "It makes sense, my Lord. He's very clever."

"Clever?" the man scoffs. "Something you're not."

The man reaches down and grabs Toman by the throat. He lifts him up until his feet are dangling in the air. Toman struggles against the strong grip on his windpipe which is preventing him from breathing. The man doesn't seem to be fazed by Toman's weight.

"I gave you a chance, Toman. You were a guttersnipe some fool turned into a vampire. You should have never been allowed to receive the eternal gift. All you've ever been is vermin, a rat pretending to be more than he is."

"M–My Lord, please," Toman begs. "One–one more chance."

"I don't give second chances. And even if I did, you would only disappoint me. It's in your nature. The most merciful I could be is if I ended your miserable existence right here."

"P-Please!" Toman is almost hysterical in his desperation. "I'll–I'll make up for the lost feeders! I'll get–I'll get you more blood!"

The man shakes his head. "Oh, Toman. Do have some dignity before you die."

"I brought you an Alpha's girl!"

This makes the man pause. The guards all look intrigued at the revelation. They all turn to me, and I try to shrink myself, backing away until I'm pressed against the cold dungeon wall. The man's blood red eyes look directly at me, and I shiver, feeling goosebumps erupt all over my skin.

There is something about this man that makes me feel like I need to run and hide. He's a predator amongst predators.

"Who is this, Toman?" he asks, his voice almost cooing. "What have you brought me?"

Toman grunts as he's dropped to the ground, discarded like a broken marionette. He still scrambles to answer quickly. "She's the granddaughter of an Alpha, my lord. Gerald Nightstone is her grandfather."

"Nightstone?"

The man looks amused. He steps over to me, and I try to crawl away, but there's nowhere else to go. He leans down until we're seeing eye to eye. His red eyes take me in like he wants to devour me whole.

"I fought your great-grandfather back in the day," he tells me. "I tore him to pieces and let my kin lick the blood off the floor."

My grandfather never likes to talk about how his father died, only that it's a bloody and disturbing tale. Looking at this man, I can't tell if he's telling the truth or not. I don't know what to say. My hands clench into fists, nails digging into the palms of my hands.

"By any chance, is your name Lydia?"

I freeze at the mention of my name. A chilling smile appears on his face as he catches the movement. I don't know how he knows my name, but I can see this can't be good for me. He looks even more intrigued.

"I knew Kane had to be hiding something from me," he says. "He never said you were related to Alpha Gerald. That makes you more valuable. I'll need to renegotiate."

He stands up and gestures toward the guards. "Have the servants clean her up and bring her to my room. I want her looking and smelling pretty."

Two guards grab me and pull me to my feet. They start dragging me from the room. I turn around to see the tall man move toward Toman. He rips the vampire's head off his neck in one quick pull, blood spurting in a red fountain everywhere. There's red all over the floor and walls.

He throws away Toman's head like it's garbage, and Toman's body collapses to the ground.

3 3

CASTLES AND CAVES

RAINER

It takes me time, but I'm able to get into Castle Pestera. The castle is named for the fact that it's built into a cave. Nearby is a waterfall which the kingdom is named after. During the summer, the water turns red due to the algae. Some people call it Blood Falls. It's fitting territory for a vampire king.

In the olden days, humans used to think the waters turned into blood because of dark magic and evil rituals. Whether any dark magic has ever been performed in Castle Pestera is merely hearsay. King Myenas's ancestors committing evil acts in the castle is more believable, but the Blood Falls take on the red hue due to mother nature. The falls look normal during this time of the year, and they do a good job of insulating noises from coming in or out of the castle.

The only way into Castle Pestera, other than the front door, which has a huge drawbridge and a mote, is through the cave which is heavily guarded. I show up with a new identity and forged papers about being hired as a new guard. The guards look over my documents skeptically before one of them escorts me through the caves. The caves are steep and half-filled with water.

We have to walk on suspension bridges to be able to travel toward the castle. According to the guard that's escorting me, the suspension bridges can disappear when the water gets too high during the rainy season making it impossible to arrive at the castle or to leave there at times using this route. If the mote is also overflowing because of the heavy rains, they are unable to use that route either. People become completely isolated in the castle for weeks or even months. Most of the people in Carmine Falls are used to being isolated from the other kingdoms due to their location, but King Myenas takes it further by isolating himself from his people.

"You can swim, right?" the guard asks. "We got a few men that have died because they slipped or the suspension bridge broke. A few got caught in the current and went down the falls, crashing into the rocks and eventually having their heads twisted off by the rocks."

"I can swim," I tell him. "But that probably doesn't matter if one goes over the falls." I swallow at the image of terrible deaths, easily able to imagine those scenarios as I walk on the suspended bridge. The water looks dark and foreboding beneath me. The cave is completely dark except for the torch that the guard is holding. If he leaves me behind, I'll be blind and unable to find my way out.

"This is insanely dangerous," I mutter.

He just laughs at me.." One of the guys managed to survive his trip down the falls but he developed a fear of being in water. I heard he doesn't even take baths anymore."

"Poor guy. Does he still work here?'

The guard pauses before answering, "Look, first thing you have to learn if you're going to work here is that you do your job no matter what it is. If His Majesty tells you to swim down the falls, you'll do it. Otherwise, it won't end well for you."

I stare at the back of his head warily. "He sounds like a great guy to work for," I say sarcastically.

"I'm warning you, buddy. Anyone that pisses off the boss doesn't get a nice retirement plan. You do your work and stay out of trouble. Be a very efficient ghost."

"Thanks," I reply biting back my sarcasm. "What are the job benefits?"

He tsks. "You'll get yourself killed by talking like that. I tried to warn you. It's your funeral, man."

I bite my tongue knowing my wit isn't appreciated in my present company. We reach the end of the cave, and I can see the falls. The suspension bridge is close to the cave wall, but there is a point where a person could easily fall off the bridge and down the falls if they don't watch their step. I'm not afraid of heights but, turns out, I'm very afraid of falling down a waterfall.

I'm more than grateful when we step off the suspension bridge and onto the grass. The land around the castle is slanted, making it easy for someone to slide down into the dark waters below. I don't know whose idea it was to build a castle here, but I'm not a fan. I keep a hand on the cave wall as we climb up the stone stairs toward the castle.

In comparison to the frightening journey to get there, the castle is small and spartan in comparison. With its limestone walls and turrets, it looks like a toy castle that's been enlarged. We enter through a side door. The hallways are narrow, giving a claustrophobic feeling of entering a tomb. Or a prison.

"I'm bringing you to the head guard, Sergei, and he'll check if your papers are all in order," the guard tells me. "By the way, what's your name again?"

I don't hesitate in answering, "I'm Roman."

* * *

Lydia

The guards drag me out of the dungeon and through a series of labyrinth-like hallways, making it difficult for me to remember the path. They walk quickly, forcing me to jog to keep up with them. They don't slow down, but I manage not to trip as we go upstairs into what I'm assuming is the first floor of the castle. The hallway is dark and lit only by torch sconces on the walls.

The walls are made of a dark gray stone, and there are several portraits of vampires that look like the tall man from the dungeon. They all have the same dark hair and red eyes. The cruel curve of their mouths practically mocks me. They're all wearing simple circlet crowns.

I'm dragged through more hallways until the guards stop and open a heavy oak door. They push me inside of what I quickly determine to be a bathroom. The walls and floors are made of dark marble. There's a large sunken tub in the floor with several bronze faucets on one end of it. The lack of windows in the room makes it feel cold and uninviting.

The guards leave and close the door behind me. There are no exits, but I only wait a short moment before two vampire women enter the bathroom. They close the door behind them. They're dressed plainly in thick grey and brown wool dresses with their hair covered in beige kerchiefs.

They must be servants. One of the women turns on the faucet to fill up the tub with hot water. The other woman urges me to take off the wet hospital gown. When I don't comply, she turns me around and starts to untie the hospital gown from the back.

"Please," I whisper. "I need to get out of here."

The woman doesn't say anything. Once the hospital gown is untied, I have to keep it up with my hands. She turns me toward the tub which is now half-full. The other woman tests the heat of the water with her hand, and when she's satisfied, she gestures for me to come closer.

"Could you help me?" I ask. "I shouldn't be here."

The servant who undressed me nudges me toward the tub. When I refuse to move, she grabs my arm and drags me forward. When we reach the edge of the tub, she grabs the edge of the hospital gown and yanks it away from my body. Now fully naked, I try to cover my body with my hands.

I'm not shy about being nude, as most shifters aren't, but I'm in a strange place with vampires who do not respect my personal space and keep dragging me around. I don't feel comfortable without clothes on. I feel vulnerable and exposed. The castle is also drafty, and I shiver as the cold marble bites into my bare feet.

"Water's not too hot," the other servant says. "Get in, please."

It's the 'please' that makes me comply. I have a feeling I will be pushed into the tub if I don't comply. Gingerly, I step down into the tub, and the water does feel nice. I've always preferred searingly hot showers, so the tub makes my muscles relax.

After weeks of bathing in rivers and rainwater, having an actual bath should be a pleasant time, but the servants don't leave me to bathe on my own. They scrub my skin with soap that smells like roses. The rude servant uses a wooden brush with rough bristles to scrub a layer of my skin off, leaving me feeling raw and red. The nice servant massages oils into my hair with a gentler touch.

It's an uncomfortable time all around with neither woman caring for what I say or do. They work on me for what feels like hours before finally deciding they're finished. They tug me out of the bathtub and dry me with large towels. I smell heavily of roses.

When I'm sufficiently dry, one of them steps out for a moment and then is back with what appears to be some clothes and other items they'll need to get me presentable. They dress me in a long blood red gown with long sleeves. It's too tight around my chest, and one of the servants has to unlace the front of the dress to accommodate my breasts. Most of my chest is still left exposed. The rest of the dress covers me decently and reaches down to the floor. I step into a pair of red slippers.

The nicer servant brushes my hair with a comb before arranging my hair into a braid. There's a large mirror in the bathroom, and they move me over to it when they're finished so I can see my reflection. I don't look like myself with the old-fashioned clothes. I don't get a say on what I'm wearing, clearly.

The women open the bathroom doors, and the same guards from earlier reappear. They grab my arms and drag me from the bathroom, seemingly still not trusting me to be able to walk on my own. I'm led down a series of more hallways before they stop at a set of oak double doors. There are more guards in this hallway and they stand guard against the walls like statues. The guards open the double doors and push me inside a large bedroom.

It's what I would expect a medieval king's bedroom to look like. There are crimson curtains framing large windows. Next to the windows is a large ornate fireplace with the head of a gray wolf hanging above it. There're two dark mahogany chairs around a table near the fireplace and a large dresser across from the bed.

The canopy bed is huge and could easily fit half a dozen people. Thick crimson curtains and a black and red comforter make it look imposing. The wolf's head has my heart race as I move closer to it. The deadness behind the eyes disturbs me.

The oak doors open behind me. I stay still, too terrified to move. Heavy footsteps come closer until warm breath tickles the back of my neck. The scent of leather and copper pennies makes me shudder in recognition.

It's what the tall man in the dungeons smelled like.

"Little wolf," he whispers in my ear. "Do you recognize who's on my mantle?"

I say nothing, my stomach turning, and my mouth filling with bile.

"That's your great-grandfather. I kept his head as a trophy."

I close my eyes in horror, my hands clenching into fists. The pain of my nails digging into my palms keeps me from crying. I never met my great-grandfather, and the revulsion of knowing how he'd been defiled beyond his death makes me sick. I have to hold my breath to keep myself from vomiting.

Large hands grip my shoulders and force me to turn around. The same hands move to cup my face, forcing me to look up. My eyes open reluctantly, and I stare into those cold, red eyes. This must be the last thing my great-grandfather saw before he died.

"Ironic, isn't it?" he continues. "You'll be mine too—in the end."

Before I can even scream, he opens his mouth showing two sharp fangs. He pulls me closer quickly, his teeth digging into my neck. The pain is excruciating as I can feel his teeth tearing through muscle and skin. My nails dig into his arms, trying to get him off, but he's too strong.

Eventually, fighting seems impossible. I feel too tired. All my panic and fear melt away as dark spots appear in my vision. Oblivion beckons, and I'm unable to resist it.

3 4

PROMISES AT DAWN

Lydia

I wake up in a dark room. I'm lying on something soft. Opening my eyes, I realize I'm on a bed with a fur blanket. My neck aches. I touch it gingerly to find dried blood.

I try to get up, clinging to a bed post for support. Moving makes the world start spinning around me. Lying back down on the bed, I close my eyes. My limbs aren't cooperating and feel heavy like they've been filled with cement.

The memories come in flashes. Blood red eyes, sharp teeth, pain, and a wolf's head mounted above a fireplace. I touch my neck again and find the wounds have scabbed over but haven't fully healed. Disgust crawls all over my skin like ants, and I want nothing more than to take a shower and scrub layers off my skin.

My body refuses to cooperate. I've lost too much blood and need time to recover. I don't know how much blood the vampire took from me, but I know it's more than a mouthful. He didn't drain me, obviously, but I still feel like crap.

The door opens quietly and footsteps come closer. I try to open my eyes and see a dark figure coming toward me. Memories of pain make me try to get away. Attempting to crawl backward brings a wave of nausea, and I turn over to get to the edge of the bed as my stomach dry heaves.

I haven't eaten anything in a couple of days, so there's nothing in my stomach. My body gives up realizing there's nothing to purge. A hand hesitantly touches my back. I push them away with one hand, not wanting to be touched.

"Go… away…" I say as I close my eyes, my cheek resting on the fur blanket.

I'm too weak to fight off whoever it is. I just want to be left alone. Maybe if I go to sleep, I'll wake up back in Nightfall, and this will all have been a terrible nightmare. I could forget a bad dream and never think about it again.

Reality isn't as kind.

"Lydia," a familiar voice hisses. "It's me."

"Who?"

I'm so tired. I want sleep and the freedom of being unconscious.

"It's Rainer. I'm here to get you out."

The familiar name makes me turn around. I blink and let my eyes adjust in the dark. There are windows in the room, but they're covered by thick curtains. These evil vampires seem like the type that hate sunlight after all.

There's the brown curly hair and pale blue eyes. It is Rainer.

I get up too quickly and nearly fall forward. Rainer catches me, his hands on my shoulders. The relief of seeing a friendly face has me hugging him. I barely know Rainer but him wanting to save me–again–makes me feel closer to him.

Someone here cares for me and wants to help me. I'm not alone.

Rainer pulls back and gingerly touches the bite marks on my neck. I wince and move away from him, not wanting anyone to touch me there. I shiver as I keep remembering the sensation of teeth on my skin. I desperately want to take a long shower and wash the feel of that monster's hands off me..

"Who did that?" Rainer asks. "Who fed on you?"

"I don't know who he is. He killed Toman after I was brought here. Everyone follows his commands in the castle. And he…" I hesitate before I continue, "He said he's the one that murdered my great-grandfather. He keeps the head mounted in his bedroom. Who is he?"

"Listen to me carefully. This is Carmine Falls, King Myenas's kingdom. We're in Castle Pestera. He's the one who fed on you, and he's in command of the Blood Takers."

"This is where we were headed all this time?" I ask.

Rainer nods. "No feeder has ever escaped Carmine Falls. That's why Emory sent me to come save you before we got here. Unfortunately, Toman was able to sneak into the hospital wing at Castle Burgundersee and take you."

"How did Toman get into Burgundy Bay?" I know that he's the one that took me, but it's all a hazy mess in my mind right now.

"I don't know. Maybe he had false documents or someone helped him, but he was able to get in and out before anyone noticed."

"People just turned a blind eye to him sneaking me out as I was unconscious?"

"He could have paid someone off to help him. It doesn't matter now."

"It does matter. Burgundy Bay was supposed to be a safe place for us," I argue. "If Toman could just take me without anyone noticing, then what's stopping other Blood Takers from taking the other shifters?"

Rainer looks away. I'm realizing in the short time we've known each other that he has a tell. His blue eyes can't hide what he's feeling. And I know I saw suspicion in them.

"Tell me," I insist. "What do you think happened?"

He sighs. "I think that Burgundy Bay isn't as secure as we thought it would be. I'll have to inform Kane and Emory to get the shifters out faster. Your family was there, but I sent them home, so I don't know if they can be of help."

"Does King Basil know?" I ask, hoping everyone else is okay and wondering just how close I was to being back with my family. I can't think about that now.

"I don't know. I'll have to leave this for others to take care of," he replies. "Right now, you are, and have been, my priority for all this time. I'm going to get you out of here as quickly as I can."

"What are we waiting for then? Let's leave now."

He hesitates. "We're in a verified fortress, Lydia. There are guards everywhere in this castle. If we get out without being noticed, we'll have to go through the cave. Did you get a look at it on the way here?"

"I was unconscious the entire time. Toman must have drugged me."

"Well, it's very easy to die from falling down a waterfall over here if you don't drown in the cave."

"Better that than staying here to die," I tell him. "He–King Myenas–he takes too much blood. I don't know how long I'll survive if he keeps feeding on me."

Rainer nods grimly. "All right then. We'll leave. It's morning. It won't be easy for us to get across enemy territory in the daylight, but most people are asleep in the castle, so this is our best chance."

I try to stand, but the world is spinning again. Rainer gently lies me down on the bed. I cover my face with my hands, feeling useless and hating myself for it. My body is too weak to even stand.

"You need to recover," Rainer says. "I'll bring you food and water. As soon as you can walk, I'll get you out of here."

"Promise?"

"I promise you, Lydia. I'll get you out of this castle."

I'm holding Rainer to this promise, or I will haunt him as a ghost for the rest of his long vampire life.

* * *

KANE

Lord Gavin reluctantly hands over the Firebird in its cage to Thomas. He does seem regretful at having to lose such a rare bird in his collection, but he's hardly at a loss. I've given him enough land and gold to keep his descendants in the lap of luxury for centuries to come. This Firebird has to be the costliest animal on this continent.

"You will take the very best care of her, won't you?" Lord Gavin asks. "She's a delicate creature and very selective of what she eats and drinks. I only fed her special water from a spring I have imported from Maroon Moors. And she will not eat mice or larvae."

I resist the urge to roll my eyes and nod at Thomas to take the bird away. He bows to me then leaves the room with the Firebird in hand. Lord Gavin looks forlorn as his former pet disappears. I would almost feel sorry for him if my wallet hadn't been so diminished.

Lord Gavin sighs. "Forgive me, Your Majesty. I have had the Firebird for so long that it feels like a part of me is missing now that I have to part from her."

"That's understandable," I reply, trying to make this go as smoothly as possible. "Who could blame you for feeling that way?"

"My wife says I'm too attached to my birds, but they do bring me joy. More joy than anything else in the world, to be honest."

That's too much even for me. Wanting him to just leave so I never have to hear him wax poetic about his pets again, I say, "I truly appreciate you selling the Firebird to me. I assure you that it will be taken care of."

He nods. "I suppose if the Firebird must go somewhere that it should be in the care of my king. You have the resources to make sure she'll be treated accordingly."

Lord Gavin doesn't need to know that the Firebird is not staying with me. It's no longer his business. That overpriced bird is mine now. And I'm taking it from one bird fanatic to give it to another.

Lord Gavin takes his leave, and once he is out of the castle, I look for Emory who is waiting in a town car outside. The Firebird is beside her in the backseat. I get into the front seat, and Thomas starts the car. I have guards in another car following us.

The drive to Burgundy Bay is long and quiet. We're all focused on this upcoming meeting with King Myenas. We're to meet him on neutral ground, and King Basil has graciously agreed to let us meet on his land. The meeting place is a plot of land not far from Castle Burgundersee.

We're not the first to arrive. King Myenas's entourage has set up tents in the area. Thomas parks the car, but no one leaves the vehicle immediately. I meet Emory's gaze, and we stare at each other warily, wondering if we're walking into a trap.

"King Basil should be able to see us from the castle," I reassure her. "If things go south, I want you to get to Castle Burgundersee. King Basil will give you refuge there."

"If things go south, I'm not going to leave you alone to deal with King Myenas. We stick together. Always."

I sigh. "Emory."

She gives me a look. "Kane."

"Should anything happen to me, Mikey will need you. I don't want our son to grow up as an orphan."

A stubborn look appears on her face. I know that look. When Emory is determined to get something done, she doesn't stop. This trait of hers has only gotten stronger with age.

"If anything should happen, I will drag you back home with me. No buts. Mikey deserves to grow up with both of his parents alive."

I stare at my wife. I never get sick of her beautiful face. Her red hair is long and almost reaches her waist now. Her emerald eyes are like green fire. This woman has gone to hell and back for me and with me.

"I love you," I tell her, unable to say anything else.

Her gaze softens. "I love you too."

Thomas, who has been doing his best to pretend like he's not there, clears his throat. "Sorry to interrupt, but King Myenas seems ready to speak to you, Your Majesties."

We all look outside the car to see King Myenas stepping out of a tent. Knowing there is no delaying this, we all get out of the car. Thomas carries the bird cage, a white sheet over it to hide the Firebird from view. I reach for Emory's hand, and she grasps it reassuringly. Our guards follow behind us, ready to fight to the death for us.

King Myenas waits outside of the tent, his entourage of guards and courtiers behind him. From an outsider's perspective, it would look like they're in the middle of a party that we're interrupting. King Myenas is in his full regalia, wearing a gold circlet crown and an ermine coat.

"Kane," he greets me. "I'm so glad you could join us."

"Myenas," I reply. "Shall we get down to business?"

He looks to Thomas who is holding up the birdcage. "Is that my bird?"

I look around him and find no sign of a blonde shifter. Aside from Emory, I can only smell vampires in the air. Either Lydia's scent is being masked, or she isn't here at all. I'm going to hope my suspicions aren't true.

"Where is Lydia?"

King Myenas has the gall to look confused. "Who?"

"The shifter woman I want you to return to me. We had a deal. The Firebird for her. Where is she?"

"Ah, yes. Your werewolf mistress."

He looks directly at Emory, enjoying trying to publicly humiliate her. Emory doesn't react as I've told her everything about the lies that I let King Myenas believe.

"About that..." King Myenas continues. "I recently learned more about your mistress. And from the new information I have about her, I'm going to have to renegotiate the terms of our agreement."

TERMS OF AGREEMENT

Kane

I'm speechless with fury. I want to slam my fist into King Myenas's smug face. It's not surprising that he would try something like this. Everyone has told me there is no use trying to reason with this madman. This is what I get trying to resolve all this without having to spill any blood.

I grit my teeth, acidic words trying to escape me. Emory keeps an iron grip on my hand, preventing me from lunging forward and beating the crap out of King Myenas. All the trouble I went through to get him this damn bird and he can't even hold up his end of the bargain. My wife places her other hand on my arm, shackling me to her so I can't move without dragging her along.

"You…" I take a deep breath, trying to swallow every curse I know. "We had a deal. I would give you the Firebird, and in exchange, you would return Lydia to me. I even gave you gold on top of that. What more do you want?"

King Myenas looks at his nails, seeming bored. "You seem upset. Maybe you should take a moment to calm yourself before we can continue negotiations."

"We already did negotiations," I counter, every word coming out stilted. "What has changed that you think this is reasonable for you to do?"

"I learned who your mistress is. You never told me she's descended from an Alpha. If I had any prior knowledge that she was a Nightstone, I wouldn't have agreed to the previous terms so easily."

"Why does it matter who she's related to?"

"It matters because I have a long history with her family. And it would pain me to have to let her go."

I have no idea about this long story between King Myenas and the Nightstones. No one in Lydia's family has said anything about it. Surely, they would have told Emory at least. And for all I know, King Myenas is making all this up as an excuse not to lose his only bargaining chip.

"It makes sense now why you chose her as your mistress. Those Alpha bloodlines just taste different. Delicious like a good vintage wine."

I look at Emory whose emerald eyes are wide in shock.

"You fed on her?" she questioned. "You weren't supposed to do that."

"Kane wasn't supposed to withhold information about his mistress either, but here we are," King Myenas returns. "This is all on you for trying to cheat me."

"I wasn't trying to cheat you."

If anything, he's trying to cheat me.

"I'm willing to let it go, which is very generous of me. I usually kill anyone that lies to me. Here are my new terms. In exchange for the return of your mistress, I want the Firebird, the rest of the gold I was promised, and..." He looks at Emory as he continues, "I want a steady supply of werewolf feeders every month."

I stare at him in disbelief. "You can't possibly expect me to agree to this. I don't have a way of providing feeders to you. You're the one with the underground operation of kidnapping people to be feeders."

"I don't expect you to do that, Kane," he replies then points to Emory. "Your wife, on the other hand, I've heard is well-respected amongst the other werewolves. I'm sure she and your mistress's family can get something going."

Emory glares at him, her jade eyes burning in anger and loathing. "I am not going to do that. I will not hand over my people to you."

King Myenas doesn't even acknowledge her. He turns to me and says, "You should muzzle your bitch and train her to do what she's told. I thought she would be better behaved than this."

Emory lets out a low growl, baring her teeth. Her eyes flash gold. I keep my arms around her to pull her back. As much as I think King Myenas deserves to have his face ripped off, I know that this will not end well for us if we physically try to fight him.

"I'll give you three days to think over the new terms of our agreement," King Myenas concludes. "We'll meet back here on the full moon. Hopefully, your mistress can last till then. She was already beginning to fade the last time I fed on her."

King Myenas smiles smugly, knowing he has us where he wants us. He walks away, and his entourage follows him. Emory struggles against my grip. I know she wants to shift into her wolf form and attack the older vampire.

"I want to kick his ass too," I tell her. "But that won't solve anything. We have to regroup and find a way to fix this."

"How?" Emory asks, her brow furrowed in frustration. "The Firebird is all we have. I'm not going to hand shifters over to him."

"We won't," I reassure. "I will do everything in my power to ensure that it'll never come to that."

* * *

Emory

Later that evening, I sit down in my office and pick up the phone to dial Alpha Gerald. He'd much rather speak to me than Kane since we are the same species. Kane has locked himself in his office and hasn't come out since we got home from Burgundy Bay. I'm sure he's trying to come up with a plan to get Lydia back and end the feeder trade once and for all.

I have the unfortunate job of informing Alpha Gerald about what's happened to Lydia. He sounds exhausted and at the end of his rope.

"If this goes on any longer, I'll storm into Carmine Falls with my men, and I will get my granddaughter back myself," he says, his voice thick with emotion. "I can't let that... that *thing* feed on her like a leech. This was never supposed to happen. I was supposed to keep her safe."

"Rainer has infiltrated the castle. He's working on getting her out as quickly as he can." I try to assure him, but I'm not sure it even works to make me feel more calm.

"I don't have as much faith in vampires as you, Emory. I can't even believe I let Rainer talk me into letting him be the one to rescue her. None of this is right."

"It's a complicated situation." I try to appease him. "King Myenas is a powerful man. Brute force will not work for this problem."

"Brute force is how our kind has survived for this long."

"That's what my father believed, but our greatest strength as a species is that we look out for each other. We hunt and live together. We protect each other. That's why we live in packs."

"J failed Lydia. I was supposed to protect her. I wanted to make sure she and her brothers never went through what I did. What my father had to go through."

"King Myenas said he has a history with your family. Is that true?" I ask, hoping he'll tell me what's gone on in the past.

"There used to be a pack near Carmine Falls called Silverlake. My mother, Elena, was from that pack. When Myenas tried to take the territory, my mother's father called on his allies to defend themselves. My father, Gabriel, went to fight for the pack, and he was captured and killed. Aside from my mother, the Silverlake pack was wiped out."

"I'm so sorry," I tell him. "I didn't know that happened. I've never even heard of the Silverlake pack."

"It's not something people like to talk about. I was barely a year old when all this happened, and I had to grow up without a father because of Myenas. I vowed that my pack would never go through what happened to the Silverlake pack." His voice is full of emotion as he talks about an event he clearly wishes had never happened.

That explains how fiercely the Nightstone pack fought off my father when he tried to take over their territory. Alpha Gerald has already gone through a great loss that shaped him into who he is today. It does make me wonder why this shared history matters to King Myenas.

"It doesn't make sense that he'd be holding onto Lydia so tightly after all these years if he was victorious," I say.

"I honestly don't know. I was of the understanding that we'd just leave one another alone. I've dreamt of going there, to his castle in that fucking cave, and killing him, but I didn't want to bring my people to war. If he doesn't return Lydia soon, or Goddess forbid he harms her, I will do just that."

"I can't blame you," I admit. "I wanted to kill him today. It took all I had to restrain myself from doing so. But we are working on an alternative plan. Hopefully, we can get Lydia out and end the blood trade.'

"I wish you the best of luck, Emory. If anything changes, let me know. In the meantime, I will be talking to the other Alphas to see if they are willing to unite with us."

With that, he hangs up, and I take a deep breath, trying to calm myself. It doesn't work.

Since Kane is dealing with the new terms that King Myenas has demanded, I decide to take the town car to Moon Grove. There are things I don't want to say over the phone. I have to do this in person. Thomas parks the car, and I step out of the vehicle.

It's late at night, and my mother and the staff should be asleep in their beds. I enter the house and find it dark and quiet. I make my way upstairs to the bedrooms and go straight for Colt's room. It's empty like I expected it to be.

I head downstairs and toward the kitchen, exiting the house through the backdoor. The familiar scent of the woods greets me. There's nowhere like the woods around my childhood home—good or bad. Memories flood back over me. Some make me want to smile. Others are bittersweet and tragic.

When I'm in these woods, I think of my late father before I learned about the kind of man he really was. I remember playing in the woods with Colt. I would bring Lola here to escape from the rest of the world. And this is where I finally met my wolf, unlocking an integral part of myself.

I'm not surprised this is where Colt chooses to hide. These woods are as much part of my concept of home as the big four-story house. I know that I'm safe here. I am in control of myself despite being at mother nature's mercy.

I don't shift into my wolf form because I don't want to bother with taking my clothes along with me. Instead, I rely on my superior senses to find Colt. I find paw prints in the dirt and trace the lingering scent in the air. There's a den underneath an old willow tree. It must have once been the den of a coyote or some other animal.

I kneel on the ground and peek inside the den. Colt's golden eyes stare back at me in the darkness. He doesn't come out, and I don't ask him to. Guilt makes it hard for me to look at him, and I stare at the ground.

"I have some news, Colt," I tell him. "It's about Lydia."

There's rustling as Colt's head pops out of the den entrance. His wolf ears perk up to listen. I know he wants good news. I wish I could tell him that I succeeded in getting Lydia back to him, and he can be with her again.

Guilt gnaws me from the inside out like a desperate animal wanting to escape.

"I'm so sorry, Colt," I continue. "I failed you. Lydia is at Carmine Falls. She's become a feeder."

Colt lets out a pained whine. He growls and digs his paws into the ground. He's furious and devastated. I watch as he shakes his head, trying to deny what's happened.

"We're doing what we can to get her back, but it's going to take more time. Rainer is there with her, trying to get her back. You just have to be more patient..."

Colt doesn't want to listen to my excuses anymore. He turns tail and runs, bursting past me, and almost knocking me over as he rushes from the den. I can only watch helplessly as he disappears into the trees. I could chase him, but what good would that do? He doesn't want to see me at this moment.

"I'm trying," I whisper to no one. "I'm trying my best."

BLOOD AND WATER

Lydia

Rainer managed to sneak me some food from the kitchen, and I'm feeling better after getting some rest. I'm able to walk without feeling nauseous which I can contribute to that fast shifter healing. He also took a dress from the servants' quarters for me to change into as the heavy velvet gown I'm wearing is going to be difficult to move in, especially if it gets wet in the cave. From how Rainer describes it, it sounds like an obstacle course in the dark, and I need to be able to move unencumbered.

"When will King Myenas come back?" I ask.

"He's left the castle to meet with Kane," Rainer explains. "The guards think he'll be gone the whole day."

"Where is he meeting with Kane?" I wonder if that has something to do with me.

"They're near Burgundy Bay. That should give us a head start once we're out of the castle and the cave."

"Good."

I look up at him expectantly and gesture to the plain gray dress on the bed. He gets the hint I need privacy to get dressed and steps outside the room. The bedroom I'm in is not the same one that belongs to King Myenas. The guards moved me not long ago. It's smaller and sparse, only containing a bed, a chair, and a half-empty wooden bucket of water.

I'm unlacing the bodice of the red dress when Rainer knocks lightly on the door. "Lydia?"

I move closer to the door and ask, "What is it?"

"I just heard the guards talking to each other. The king is back."

Panic hits me like lightning. We didn't count on King Myenas and his entourage being back so soon. Rainer told me that traveling that distance should take most of the day. He must've come through the other entrance of the castle and not the cave. That makes sense since he is the one who owns the damn place.

We need more time.

"We're supposed to have more time than this," I say, fear making it hard to breathe.

"I know. I don't know why he's back so soon," Rainer tells me. "I can hear him coming down the hallway. I have to go."

"Don't leave."

I can't bear being left alone with King Myenas again. Rainer is my only lifeline in this hellhole. I just want him to take me away from here. I hate this place, and I never want to see it again.

"I'll come back later. I promise."

"Rainer, he's going to-"

"I'm sorry," he whispers. "Hang in there, Lydia."

His footsteps are light, but I know he's gone. I understand he's just trying to keep up the ruse of being another guard going through his rounds at the castle, but I can't help but feel resentful for being abandoned. He knows what's about to happen. Neither of us can stop it.

I step away from the door as heavy footsteps come closer. My heart thuds quickly in my chest as hazy memories of pain and blood flash quickly through my mind. My body tenses from the memories. I look around the room for a weapon, anything to defend myself with.

I can't turn around and look as the door opens, and King Myenas steps into the room. There's the scent of leather and copper pennies. I grab the chair and toss it to the wall where it breaks on impact. I take one of the chair legs and turn around, brandishing it like a sword.

"Go away," I say, trying to hide how afraid I am. "I mean it."

King Myenas grins, amused and not at all worried. He closes the door behind him. He's blocking the only exit, and I reluctantly take a step back. This is a mistake as King Myenas stalks forward like a predator knowing its prey is trapped.

"Do you think that can hurt me, little wolf?" he taunts. "I've fought Alphas and kings. I've slaughtered whole packs of your kind. And do you really think that little piece of wood will be what kills me?"

"I can certainly try."

Vampires, for all their longevity, are not truly immortal. They can be killed by decapitation, being stabbed in the heart, or fire.. They bleed like everyone else. Their superior strength and speed just make it harder to kill them.

I kick the wooden bucket at him, trying to use it as a distraction. The water splashes his legs, the bucket hitting his knee. He frowns in annoyance. I lunge with the chair leg, aiming the sharp edge right above his heart.

He grabs the chair leg before I can plunge it between his ribs. Blood red eyes stare down at me, looking more bored than anything else. He pulls the object out of my hands and breaks it in half, tossing the wooden pieces across the room. Before I can make a move for the door, King Myenas grasps my shoulders.

My eyes widen in fear. I try to get out of his iron grip, but I'm unable to. "Please don't–"

"Hush, little wolf. It's over now."

"No, please–"

He pulls me forward, his sharp teeth biting into my neck. I scream as loud as I can while clawing at his wide shoulders, trying to make him let go. He holds on, pulling me close as he feeds on me.

Dark spots cloud my vision. My knees feel weak. I'm being pushed toward the bed until my back is resting on the soft furs. King Myenas is on top of me, pressed close to my body like an unwanted lover as he drinks from me.

My hands clutch the furs beneath me, and I wait for it to end. How much blood is even there to take? My body feels like it's sinking into the bed. I stare up at the canopy as the darkness lulls me to suffocating nothingness.

* * *

RAINER

I walk quickly down the hallways, trying to be as unnoticeable as possible. Unfortunately for me, Castle Pestera being a smaller castle has a more limited number of guards and servants, so it's harder to blend in. The guards all talk and joke around in between their shifts as there's really not much to do. Even staring at the waterfall outside can get boring after a while.

"Hey, new guy," one of the guards calls out. "Where are you going?"

I hold up the metal pitcher I'd taken from the kitchens. "I'm just bringing water to the king's new feeder."

"Who put you on feeder duty?"

I shrug, letting them try to work out whether I'm lying or not on their own. "I don't have time to chit-chat. If I let the feeder die of dehydration, it'll be my head on the chopping block."

The guard steps into my path, blocking me from moving forward.

"Look, new guy, if Sergei finds out you're not really assigned to the new feeder, and you're just trying to get some ass or blood on the side, he'll cut off your balls before pushing you down the waterfall. I've seen him do it before."

I grimace, disgusted at the imagery of castration and also the implication I'm trying to take advantage of Lydia.

"I'm really just bringing the feeder some water. That is the *only* thing I'm doing."

The guard continues like I didn't say anything, "Unlike other places, we're very strict about who can touch the feeders. Unless you're the king or someone close to him, you don't get to feed directly. You only get the extracted stuff like the rest of us."

I nod, agreeing more to get him to shut up and leave me alone. "I'll keep that in mind."

"I'm serious, new guy. Sergei can be an asshole, but the king will not show any mercy. Some of the punishments he's inflicted on those who have displeased him in the castle would make your curly hair straighten from fear." He shudders. "He doesn't believe in second chances. You mess up once, and you're done for."

More annoyed that he's deterring me from what I'm trying to do, I nod again. Arguing will only prolong this, so I try to be as agreeable as possible. "Thank you for the warning. I appreciate it."

He pats my shoulder. "We have to stick together over here. We only got each other to rely on."

"Right."

"What's your name again, new guy? Something with an R?"

"I'm Roman."

"Right, right." He gestures to himself. "I'm Grigor. It's nice to meet you."

"It's nice to meet you too, Grigor." I raise the pitcher again. "I really have to get this to the feeder. Nice talk."

I swerve quickly around him, determined to get away before he can stop me again. I walk briskly down the hallway until I finally reach Lydia's bedroom. Unlike other feeders, she's not kept in the dungeon. King Myenas insists that he wants her to be closer to him so she has her own room.

I wonder if he wants her to be separated from the other feeders so no one else will try to take blood from her. From what I've heard from the castle servants, it's a common practice for King Myenas to have his personal feeders only for him to feed on. He doesn't like to share, and he would find it beneath him to even have to. He sees Lydia as nothing more than his property.

I knock lightly on the door, but there's no answer. I wait for a moment before twisting the doorknob to enter the room. It's dark inside. There's no source of light, like a window or a lamp that's been left on, and there's no fireplace in the small space. I use my superior eyesight to be able to navigate the room.

Lydia is on the bed underneath the fur blanket. There's a candle on a metal holder on the bedside table. I put down the pitcher on the bedside table and open the drawer. I find a matchbox, so I light the candle to brighten the room. The smell of dried blood is noticeable, but as I look over the bed, I find blood on the sheets.

"Are you okay, Lydia?" I ask quietly, trying not to scare her. "Are you hurt?"

Lydia lets out a muffled sob. "Just leave me alone."

"Are you still bleeding?"

"No. The wounds are closing up."

"I have water here. You can clean yourself with it."

Lydia pulls down the fur blanket. There's a bleakness in her blue-gray eyes I haven't seen before. She glares at me, but there's no real heat to it. She sits up and reaches for the pitcher. She pours water into her hand to wash neck and down her chest where blood has dripped and dried.

Water splashes onto the sheets and blankets, but Lydia doesn't care. I turn away to give her some privacy.

"What's your plan to escape the castle?" she asks. "Or are you going to wait for King Myenas to kill me first before you do anything?"

I look at her, shocked at what she just said. "What?"

She smiles mockingly. "He's fed on me twice. He takes too much. I can barely stand without feeling dizzy. I'm not going to last long here."

The sleeve of her red gown slides down, and I see yellowing bruises on her shoulders. I glance at Lydia's face and see the dark circles under her eyes and the hollowness in her cheeks. Her skin is paler than before and sickly. She reminds me of a porcelain doll that could easily break when not handled carefully.

I know that she's right. This is not a place a feeder ever comes back from. Lydia will die here if I don't get her out soon. The problem is, since King Myenas has returned and claimed Lydia as his personal feeder, the castle is heavily guarded. We won't even make the journey from the castle to the cave without being noticed.

When I don't immediately answer her question, Lydia scoffs. "I knew it. I'm going to die here."

"No," I counter. "You are not going to die here."

She stares at me skeptically. "And what are you going to do, Rainer? Do you want us to swim down the waterfall?"

"I have a plan. And I'm going to need you to trust me."

37

THE POTION SOLUTION

Willow

I receive a letter from Rainer asking for help about a spell or potion that could make someone appear dead without actually killing them. This is beyond my level of magical expertise, so I take the matter to my niece. Ivy has a nearly encyclopedic knowledge for spells and potions. When I tell her what we'll need, she quickly comes up with an answer.

"There's a potion for that," Ivy explains. "It slows down your heart rate and places your body in a deep magical sleep."

"Great," I reply. "Do you know how to make this potion?"

"I've brewed the potion once before. It's a complicated potion, and I'll need to gather ingredients for it."

"Just tell me what you'll need, and I'll get it for you," I promise her.

I need Ivy to brew this potion as we're both aware how hopeless I am when it comes to potion-making. I've melted my fair share of cauldrons. Ivy doesn't have the same problem. Being a High Priestess requires being a more well-rounded witch when it comes to the magical disciplines.

There will always be areas they naturally excel in, but an intermediate proficiency in the other disciplines is still needed to be an effective High Priestess for their coven.

Luckily for us, Cerise Port has one of the best markets as they trade with several kingdoms. We're able to find all the ingredients needed for the potion, even some obscure items. Ivy is nearly done working on the wards around Brighthall, but King Cyrus has told her she can stay longer if she wants to. Ivy has been treating her time in his kingdom like a working vacation and seems to be enjoying King Cyrus's hospitality.

The vampire king doesn't even bat an eye when we tell him we need a room to brew a complicated and highly dangerous potion. He gives us the room with no questions asked.

I may be mediocre at potions, but I assist Ivy in any way I can. I help her by grinding wormwood in a pestle. She chops up the brains of some animals on a cutting board. A clear liquid in a pewter cauldron begins to bubble as Ivy turns the heat higher on the small stove.

I watch her as she adds ingredients into the cauldron, one by one. The ground up wormwood goes in first. Ivy throws in a few sprigs of asphodel. She stirs the pot with a wooden spoon a few times before leaving the potion to simmer.

After a few minutes, Ivy takes the bloody chopping board and uses the knife to carefully slide the animal brains into the cauldron. White berries are crushed, and the juice is strained before being poured into the potion. Ivy stirs the liquid a few times before turning off the heat. She leaves the potion to cool down.

"Do you think it'll work?" I ask.

"We'll find out soon," Ivy replies. "A skull should appear on the potion when it's done."

It takes another half hour before the potion is finished. Ivy takes the lid off the cauldron, and we both look down at the liquid inside. A white skull appears before dispersing back into the potion which is a sickly pale green color. Ivy looks pleased, and she uses a ladle to transfer the potion into a glass bottle with a cork.

When the bottle is full, she hands it to me. "Six drops only. Four on the tongue and two drops underneath the tongue. This is very important. The wrong amount will cause the potion to work differently."

"How?" Now, I'm scared.

"It could be so weak that the person taking it doesn't fully go to sleep.. They would still be able to hear and feel everything while being unable to move, essentially being paralyzed. If it's too strong, they might not wake up at all and be stuck in a magical coma for the rest of their lives."

I clutch the potion tightly, wary about giving it to Rainer now. "Are you sure the potion will work?"

"It's highly effective. I've seen it used before."

I pause. "How do you wake someone up from the potion?"

"There's an antidote," Ivy replies. "It will take a whole moon cycle to brew it. I'll have to get started on it immediately if we want to wake whoever you're using this on soon."

I look at the potion doubtfully. "Actually, just getting this to Rainer will be difficult. Where he is at the moment is so isolated that any mail that goes through the castle is heavily monitored."

"Where is Rainer?" she asks me.

I hesitate before answering, "He's at Castle Pestera at Carmine Falls."

Ivy raises her eyebrows in surprise. "Your husband is at one of the most difficult castles to break into, and you want to send him a dangerous potion through the mail?"

"I don't really have another route of getting the potion to him." I sigh. I wish I could take it to him myself.

"Why don't you ask King Cyrus? He might have an idea on how to do this," she suggests.

"I don't want to bother him. He's already been so kind, letting Bryony and I stay here as guests."

"Auntie Willow," she begins, her hazel eyes staring me down, "this is a life and death situation. Your husband is going to need all the help he can get. We should be a bother. We need to bother anyone we can for this."

I can't argue with that. I would do anything I can to help my husband. He's risking his life to save Lydia. The least I can do is make sure he gets home.

Ivy and I go to King Cyrus who advises us that we have an in by getting someone to visit Castle Pestera as a guest and have them slip the potion to Rainer while they are there. Our list of candidates for that task is slim to none. King Myenas won't let a witch or anyone from Crimson Peak visit his domain so easily. It's not as simple as the king is making this out to be.

"Of course, it's simple," he says. "You can just ask my nephew for help."

"Kane is already doing whatever he can to deal with this situation-"

"I meant my other nephew. The blond one, remember?" He smirks at us as if he knows something I don't.

I blink, genuinely surprised. Ivy and I look at each other, trying to make sense of what King Cyrus just said. The vampire chuckles, amused at us. He inclines his head to where Lex is standing by the doorway of the dining room.

"It's nice of you to join us, Lex."

* * *

LEX

Ivy snorts, looking at me like I'm nothing more than a pitiful street urchin that has just asked her for spare change. "Seriously?" She shakes her head, and I know in that moment, she doesn't think I'm capable of doing anything important, anything that takes intelligence or courage.

"Lex currently has a treaty with King Matthias of Red River," my uncle explains. "He's already shown interest in doing business with Myenas. Through Matthias, Lex can get an invite to one of the monthly revels Myenas hosts for his 'friends.'"

Willow looks at me, her blue eyes almost pleading. "Would you do that for us, Lex? It could be dangerous." Unlike Ivy, Willow knows the sacrifices I've made in the past, and even though she and I haven't always had the best relationship, she's willing to ask this of me now.

I stride forward, stopping in front of Willow. "I still owe you for what happened before. So yes, I will do this for you."

She flashes me a grateful smile but then warns, "If King Myenas finds out you're helping us, you could end up imprisoned, or worse-killed. I don't want to put you in harm's way like that. You have a son to think of, after all."

"I'm no stranger to dealing with megalomaniac old vampires. If I could survive months living with King Peter, I can survive one night at Castle Pestera." I understand what she's saying, and while I agree it will be dangerous, I can't let either of these women think I'm scared.

I never talk about the time I spent in the dungeons of Scarlett Thunder, injured and left on my own after King Peter's son Jacob beat the shit out of me. I only managed to escape with help from Uncle Cyrus who sent a servant girl to get me out of the cell I was locked in. It has been the lowest point of my long life so far, and it definitely changed me in different ways. There are times I don't recognize the man I've become. All of the ideas I thought were important before I went to live in Scarlett Thunder have faded away.

If I can survive that ordeal, King Myenas isn't going to intimidate me.

"You can't go alone," Willow argues. "Even if King Myenas considers you an ally now, I don't trust him not to turn on you."

"She's right, Lex," Uncle Cyrus agrees. "You should have someone by your side who can help if things turn dicey while you're at Carmine Falls."

Willow nods. "I should go. I can use my magic to help us escape if it comes down to that."

"What about Bryony?" Ivy asks. "If something happens and neither you nor Rainer come back, she'll end up as an orphan."

I doubt that Bryony is going to be left alone on the streets to fend for herself if worst comes to worst. I have no doubt that Ivy would take in Willow's daughter. The witches take care of each other. Ivy also has a soft spot for children as I've seen her playing with Bryony and even with Cole and Michael.

Whatever distaste Ivy feels for me doesn't extend to my son, and I'm relieved for it.

"Somebody has to go with Lex," Willow reasons. "Who else could it be?'

Ivy looks conflicted. She glances between her aunt and me before suggesting, "I could go instead."

Willow touches her niece's hand. "It can't be you, Ivy. You have the coven to think about. If they lost you–"

"They'll replace me with a new High Priestess. That's how it's always been. I'm not special by any means," Ivy counters. "I'm not married, and I don't have a child waiting at home for me. I'm the best choice in case this does turn into a suicide mission."

I wince. "I don't think it's going to be that bleak…."

Ivy turns to me, her stubborn eyebrows furrowing in annoyance. "Let me be clear, I don't like you. I will probably never like you. The only reason I'm doing this is to protect my aunt and my cousin. But mark my words, I will drag you out of that castle alive if it's the last thing I do."

I'm momentarily stunned. Staring into Ivy's hazel eyes, I realize how unfairly pretty she is. I've never seen a woman look like she hates me more, and yet, my stupid cock is stirring to life. Her red lips are set in a frown, and I'm thinking about what it would be like to kiss her. What she would taste like.

If this woman is as passionate out of bed, all I can think about is how passionate she would be in bed.

And this really isn't the time to get aroused. Not when we're planning to infiltrate a fortress of a castle filled with the worst vampires around. But it has also been over four years since I've been with a woman. I've been living celibate like a monk to honor my loveless sham of a marriage.

And my cock is asking me, "Why have we been doing that for all this time?"

Knowing the situation in my pants is going to be too visible to be hidden soon, I begin to back away. "I'll call King Matthias and get us the invite," I tell them. "We'll work out the rest on the way to Carmine Falls. If you'll excuse me, I'm going to make that phone call now."

I practically run out of the room, moving briskly down the hallways. I'm trying to get from point A to point B without embarrassing myself. I'm all worked up, and I have to make this phone call quickly. Then, after I successfully flatter Matthias the idiot, I'm going to have to deal with my troublesome cock—its bad timing and its incorrigible desire for women we can't have.

My tastes when it comes to sex have also had a common theme—if it's forbidden, then I want it. Damn all the consequences that will immediately come with that choice.

38

I KNOW PLACES

Lex

King Matthias informs me of a small party King Myenas is throwing for the royals he's in business with. Due to my recent alliance with Red River, I've secured an invite to Castle Pestera for the event. The invitation comes with restrictions but it's our only way to get the potion to Rainer so I can't complain. I'm allowed a plus one, but I'm not allowed to bring guards or weapons inside of the castle.

The drive to Carmine Falls is long and tense. Ivy spends half of that time going over ground rules with me. We may be keeping up the ruse of her being my mistress and personal feeder, but that in no way means I'm allowed to touch or bite her. If I cross her established boundaries, she will not hesitate to set me on fire.

The witch stares at me in a way that tells me she's being completely serious.

"If you're pretending to be my mistress, I may have to touch you," I tell her. "It would look odd if you shudder at being in close proximity to me."

Her hazel eyes narrow at me. "Fine. If your hands wander to anywhere inappropriate, your hand will explode."

"You can do that?"

She nods. "I've done it before. And not even magic can heal that kind of injury."

I realize at this very moment that Ivy might be unhinged which still doesn't lessen my attraction to her. My type also happens to fall under that category. I can't explain it. My life would be easier if I wasn't attracted to women who don't want me dead in some way.

The state of my marriage wouldn't be what it is if I hadn't been attracted to Opal when she wasn't mine to want. If I had stayed away from her, I might have avoided a lot of terrible things that happened. I don't want to linger in the past, but the consequences of it haunt me every day of my life. The only positive to come out of it is my son.

When we arrive at Carmine Falls, Ivy and I have to leave the guards and the car behind. They're not allowed to come with us. The guards of Castle Pestera are blocking the entrance to the drawbridge. It's the safest way into the castle, heavily guarded, difficult to access, and one of the major reasons why no one has succeeded in attacking the place.

It's better than the cave entrance I've heard of. That way is too much trouble. I have no desire to walk on slippery limestone until we reach the manmade hanging bridges with dark water rippling beneath us like bottomless ink. No thank you.

But once we cross the drawbridge, we don't go straight into the castle. Instead, we go down a flight of stairs to the left of the opening. It seems strange to me, almost like we're going to the dungeon, but I follow along anyway.

The stairs lead to a tunnel. It's pitch black and even with my superior eyesight, I'd struggle to see anything without the guard's torch lighting the way. Ivy isn't able to see well at all, so she's wrapped her arm around mine, terrified to be left alone in this dark place.

"Don't be scared," I whisper to her. "Everything will be fine."

Her nails dig into my arm. "If I get lost here and die, I'm going to haunt you as a ghost. You'll never be free of me."

I smile, knowing she can't see it. "Don't threaten me with a good time."

I can almost *hear* her eyes roll. "You're incorrigible."

"I prefer 'charming.'"

"Incorrigible."

Ivy doesn't let go of me as we follow the guard along this tunnel that seems to go on forever. Finally, we reach the end of it and realize we are inside the castle. We've just taken a different route, which makes me wonder if the doors at the front of the castle even open. Of course, I'm not surprised that King Myenas has some other tricks up his sleeve.

The guard leads us to a ballroom filled with people. There's a string quartet playing music in the background as royals and courtiers drink glasses of blood, talking amongst each other.

King Myenas is at the center of it all, holding the attention of all the vampires in the room. I'm reminded of the last time I saw him at King Peter's masquerade ball at Scarlett Thunder. King Myenas wore a bird mask with feathers as he and King Peter plotted war against my brother and my birth kingdom. Terrible memories of my time in the dungeons flash through my mind.

"Are you okay?" Ivy asks. She stopped clinging to my arm as soon as we reached the ballroom. "You tensed up."

"I'm fine."

"Are you sure? Because getting here was bad enough, and I can't imagine trying to escape if we have to run."

I look at her. Her pretty face does look concerned. I know she doesn't like me, but we are each other's sole ally in this room. We only have each other. Whether or not that concern is an extension of her self-preservation doesn't matter to me.

I reach for her hand, her soft palm helping ground me in the present. "I'm going to be fine. Now, follow my lead."

Ivy keeps quiet as I lead her through the ballroom, pacing by royals and courtiers who watch us curiously. Seeing me with some random woman must be odd to them. I doubt any of them recognize who Ivy is. Most vampire royals can't even bother remembering the names of their vampire servants let alone who the high priestess of a coven of witches is.

We stop in front of King Myenas. I nod in respect. I may only be regent and not king of Scarlett Thunder, but the only man I would even consider fully bowing to is my brother. Ivy does a low curtsy, knowing that King Myenas is expecting her deference.

"King Myenas," I greet him. "Thank you for the invitation. I've been looking forward to this for some time."

The old king glances at King Matthias who smiles encouragingly. "Matthias has told me of your interest in joining our business venture. I trust that your relationship with your brother will not affect such matters?"

"Of course not. Business is business."

King Myenas looks bored and motions for a servant to come over with a glass of blood. The servant offers the glass to me, and I take it. I don't immediately drink it. King Myenas raises his own glass, and several others around us follow his lead.

"To new partnerships then," he says. "And may we all prosper in this endeavor."

He takes a long drink of the blood, and so does everyone around us. I take a sip, the warmth of it making me close my eyes. This is fresh blood, taken only a few minutes ago. It's almost enough to get blood drunk on and get lost in the euphoria.

"Good, isn't it?" King Myenas asks. "There'll be more of that in the future should this go well. Come sit with me, and we'll discuss how you can join us."

I have no choice but to comply. I take a seat beside King Myenas, and we begin to negotiate. Ivy makes herself scarce and quietly slips out of the ballroom. She's just some feeder to everyone in this castle, and they won't care where she wanders off to.

* * *

Rainer

Willow tells me that Lex and Ivy will be in the castle for the little party King Myenas is throwing. I stay close to the ballroom and am able to watch as the two appear and follow Igor into the ballroom. I wait by the open doors for one of them to come out, trying to act like

I'm just doing my guard duties by standing by the wall. I'm not disappointed when I see Ivy slipping out of the ballroom.

The brunette looks around the hallway, confused and new to the environment. She doesn't know where to go next, looking for a familiar face.

"Ivy!" I whisper and frantically wave at her to come closer and away from the ballroom doors. "Over here!" I look around to make sure no one else is paying any attention to me. There are a few guards further down the hallway, but they don't even look in my direction.

Ivy looks wary as she comes closer. "Is that you…?"

"It's Rainer." I cock my head toward another hallway. "Come with me."

"How am I sure it's really you?" She pauses and folds her arms, and I feel myself getting a little agitated.

Letting out a long breath, I try to be as patient as possible. "I can prove it. Ask me something only I would know."

She looks to be thinking it over before saying, "Where did you and your wife get married?"

I don't hesitate to answer her question. "We got married in your backyard. You officiated it. There was a full moon. Kane and Emory were our best man and maid-of-honor."

Ivy looks relieved. She lets out a long breath and grabs my arm. "Oh thank the Goddess. I was about ready to shout your name there."

With a touch to her lower back, I push her toward the hallway. "We can catch up later. Follow me."

I lead her down the long and windy hallway toward Lydia's room. I open the door without knocking, knowing Lydia should be awake. The blonde is sitting on the bed, hugging her knees to her chest. She looks up with terrified blue gray eyes when she sees us.

Her eyebrows furrow at the sight of Ivy. "Wait. Aren't you a…?"

Ivy's magic smells sweet like berries. It's what differentiates her scent from a regular human's. I know Ivy and Lydia haven't met, but Lydia is able to tell what Ivy is. We're lucky there's too much alcohol and strong perfumes on other guests that no one in the ballroom seemed to notice that Ivy has the distinct odor of a witch.

The brunette tries to smile encouragingly. "Hi," she says. "I'm Ivy. I'm a witch and here to help you."

"You're getting me out tonight?" Lydia's eyes widen with hope, something I haven't seen in her for a while.

Ivy blinks. "I would love to try, but even I can't fight off a whole castle of vampires. Also, getting out of here is going to be a nightmare. That cave tunnel is horrifically long and dark from what I hear, and it's your best bet at escaping."

"They probably led you through the secret tunnel next to the door didn't they?" I point out. "Believe me. You got the nicer path into the castle." I don't think they ever open the front doors.

"Can you both focus?" Lydia cuts in. "How are you going to help us?"

Ivy reaches into the pocket of her red dress and pulls out a glass vial with a sickly pale green liquid inside. "This is an enchanted sleeping potion. It will put you into a death-like sleep. As far as anyone can will be able to tell, even vampires, you'll appear to be actually dead while just being in a nice, deep sleep."

Lydia stares at the glass vial warily. "How do you wake me up?"

"I am working on an antidote. But first things first. Rainer has to sneak you out of the castle." Ivy hands me the vial. "Listen very carefully. Six drops only. Four on the tongue and two drops underneath the tongue."

"Six drops?"

"Repeat it. Four on the tongue and two drops underneath the tongue," she insists.

"Four on the tongue and two drops underneath the tongue," I dutifully recite.

"Good. You have to follow that to the letter. If you mess up the amount, it will change how the magic affects Lydia."

I tsk. "No pressure at all, huh?"

"You heard the witch, Rainer," Lydia says. "Six drops only."

"When should we do this?" I ask.

"Let's do it now. I can't be awake when Myenas comes later. He's going to want to feed on me after the party. I need that potion now," Lydia begs.

The genuine fear in Lydia's face and voice convinces me, and I come closer to her. I uncork the bottle and realize it comes with a dropper attached to the cork. How convenient. I raise the dropper, and Lydia opens her mouth.

Six drops only. Four on the tongue and two drops underneath the tongue. I follow the directions accurately before returning the stopper to the vial. Lydia grimaces and reaches for the pitcher of water on the bedside table. She drinks from it directly and swallows a few sips of water before putting it down.

She turns to us and remarks in disgust, "That tasted disgusting. What did you put in that? Rotten fruit?"

I look at Ivy and ask, "Is the potion working?"

Ivy looks at her watch. "It should be working just about…"

"It was like rotten fruit mixed with expired milk," Lydia continues to rant. "Why can't you make your potions taste better? Aren't witches capable of–"

Lydia collapses forward on the bed and goes still. Gingerly, I turn her over on the mattress. She's gone shockingly pale, and her body is stiff. Her breathing is so shallow she looks like she's not doing it at all. Her heart is beating faintly.

"Now," Ivy concludes. "It's working now."

39

LIVING DEAD GIRL

Ivy

Once we know the potion is effective, Rainer and I go to the ballroom. He has to inform King Myenas of Lydia's unexpected death while I get Lex and use the commotion to disappear unnoticed. Lex is in conversation with King Myenas and King Matthias. He's managed to look like he belongs with them, laughing at their jokes and appearing interested in their conversation.

Rainer bows deeply when he approaches them before moving closer to King Myenas to whisper in his ear. The king immediately stands up and causes cups of wine to fall over. He doesn't say a word to the other royals and hurries off to leave the ballroom, Rainer following him. The courtiers are distracted and whispering amongst themselves about the old king's behavior.

King Matthias is still conversing with Lex. Knowing I have to keep up the ruse of being a mistress, I touch Lex's shoulder and murmur into his ear, "Hey."

Lex is a good actor. He doesn't stiffen up and visibly forces himself to relax at my touch. His hand circles my waist, pulling me closer and pushing me down to sit on his lap. His lips touch the shell of my ear making me shudder.

"Hey yourself," he croons like we've been lovers for years. "Where have you been?"

"Just powdering my nose." I can feel King Matthias watching us, and I make the effort to sound seductive. "Did you miss me?"

"Of course, I did."

Lex's half-lidded gaze is hungry like he wants to eat me up until there's nothing left of me. He moves my long hair out of the way so he has access to my neck. I always thought vampires would be cold to the touch like corpses. Instead, Lex's hands and lips are warm, almost burning.

He kisses my pulse point, making my heart beat faster. I feel my skin flushing. I'm angry that he's taking liberties and confused because I feel something else other than disgust. I don't like this man, but my body doesn't get the message.

Lex pulls away and rests his head on my shoulder. He catches King Matthias's gaze and says, "Sorry, my friend. You know how demanding new mistresses can be. She needs my attention almost constantly these days."

King Matthias chuckles as he picks up his glass and takes a sip. "You don't need to tell me, Lex. I'm sure you can find a spare bedroom to fuck her into submission."

Lex gets to his feet, forcing me to get up. He keeps his hands on me to keep me close. His hand's on my waist. His mouth leaves kisses on my cheeks, my chin, and my neck.

He avoids my mouth. And my lips feel like they're burning from anticipation. The cloud of confusion makes me irritable. I don't *want* to kiss this man. I don't want him to kiss me *at all*.

I don't fight off his plays at being two lovers eager to find a place to be alone. Guards and servants ignore us, embarrassed at our lack of shame. Lex might as well press me up against the wall and take me there with how eager he's acting. I'm getting nervous that clothes will be flying off of us until we find the entrance to the tunnel.

With no eyes around to watch us, Lex's hands drop from me, and he steps away as if I'm deceased. I glare at him. I don't know what's wrong with me. My traitorous body enjoys his touch, coming alive like a match being thrown on kindling.

If I look at Lex objectively, he is one of the most handsome men I've ever met. He's a pretty man with his blond hair and delicate aristocratic features. Some might even call him beautiful. He's what I pictured when my mother used to read fairytales to me of princes that saved damsels in distress from monsters.

I know the reality is that he may be a prince, but he's also a monster. I'm not a damsel in distress that needs saving. We're not in a fairytale. If I indulge in the impulses my body is burning for, it will not end happily for me.

"What now?" Lex asks. "Did the potion work?"

I nod. "I hope Rainer is going to meet us in the tunnel with Lydia. We have to wait for him. Getting her out through the caves will be so much more difficult"

Lex opens the heavy metal door that leads to the tunnel. He moves to the side and gestures toward the tunnel. "Ladies first."

"You know I can't see as well as you can in the dark."

Lex walks inside the tunnel and pulls out a torch they attached to the wall. It's not lit, so he hands it to me.

"*Ignis*," I murmur and the top of the torch blazes to life. The torch bathes Lex in warm light. He looks almost angelic.

He cocks his head toward the tunnel. "Well?"

With a light source in hand, I enter the tunnel. Lex follows behind me, leaving the metal door partially open behind us. The tunnel is long and narrow. I'm not claustrophobic, but the narrow space makes me uncomfortable.

I glance behind me several times to see that Lex is still there, and I'm not alone in the terrifying darkness. We don't go far. With nowhere to sit, we stand close together in the dark forced to only stare at each other. Staring into the endless darkness is far more unpleasant.

With no other distractions, I'm forced to admit that Lex truly is the prettiest man I've ever met with those long, dark lashes framing ocean blue eyes. This is the kind of face a woman could never get sick of looking at. It might even be to wake up to such a face in the morn-ings. The thought makes me frown.

"Is something wrong?" he asks. "You look upset."

I shake my head and decide that being honest with him is not an option. "Everything is perfectly fine."

"Are you sure?"

"Absolutely."

He goes quiet, looking down at his feet as he contemplates some-thing. Eventually, he asks, "Are you talented with all kinds of potions?"

"I can follow a recipe. Creating my own potions is harder. It's not something I'm naturally gifted at."

He nods. "But if you could find a particular recipe, you'd be able to make it easily?'

"Yes." I look at him suspiciously for his line of questioning. "Why are you asking?"

He hesitates before finally answering, "I need you to make me a love potion."

* * *

RAINER

I know that King Myenas might be upset with the news of Lydia's death since he's been using her as a bargaining chip with Kane. The fury he unleashed at the sight of Lydia's unmoving body on the bed is a sight to behold. He has every servant and courtier within near distance running away in fear. The meager furniture in the room is tossed around when he realizes Lydia won't awaken no matter how hard he shakes her or whatever else he does. I stand outside with a few other guards, watching.

The potion Ivy brewed is very effective. Even vampires with their superior senses can't tell the difference between Lydia in her magical comatose state and a real dead body. The castle doctor, Morrison, is called, and he examines Lydia's body before declaring that she must have died in her sleep. The blood loss from feedings overwhelms even a shifter's healings when not given enough time to recuperate, he reminds the king.

"You're saying this is my fault?" King Myenas hisses menacingly.

Dr. Morrison stammers, trying to calm down the king before he decides that the doctor is to be blamed for Lydia's death instead. "Of course not, my Lord! I was only explaining her cause of death."

King Myenas rubs a hand over his mouth. "This is unacceptable. I needed her alive!"

"I understand your frustration, but I can't bring back the dead. Perhaps if she had been brought to the clinic sooner, I might have been able to revive her-"

"Get rid of the body."

The doctor blinks. "My Lord?"

"Get the body out of my sight! She's useless to me now! Just like the rest of you!"

Dr. Morrison scrambles to get out of the room and gestures frantically to the guards watching from the doorway. We enter and gingerly pick up Lydia from the bed. Her body has stiffened and gone heavy due to the potion. I lift her by the shoulders, her head resting on my torso as we carry her out of the room. The doctor follows us out, closing the door behind him to put distance between himself and the king.

"You know what to do with her," he says before walking away and heading back to his rooms.

Glancing down at Lydia's sleeping face, I ask, "What do you do with corpses in the castle?"

"Well, we used to throw bodies down the waterfall, but the bodies just pile up in the water below, and it gets disgusting once they start decaying," Grigor explains. "Getting bodies out of the castle and cave is too much of a hassle so digging mass graves is out of the question."

"We settled on cremation," another guard continues. "We dump the bodies in the incinerator. Ashes are easier to dispose of."

"Incinerator?" I repeat. "Where is it?"

"It's in the south wing. The king said he doesn't want to see the corpse, so we need to take her there immediately."

I have no choice but to help carry Lydia toward the south wing. In a room near the kitchens we reach the incinerator. It's a large metal furnace. The room is mostly bare aside from bodies on the floor covered with a sheet.

"We can fit three bodies in at a time," Grigor says. "Let's load this in and grab two of the bodies off the ground."

Obviously, I can't toss Lydia into the incinerator. My goal here is to get her out alive, not to actually kill her. I have to find a way to stall until I can get out of this.

"What time is it?" Grigor and the other guard look confused. And I add, "Isn't it time for dinner? Aren't you two hungry?"

Grigor nods. "Well, yeah, but we have work to do."

"It's just loading bodies into an incinerator and pulling down a lever. It's not that hard." I lean closer to them conspiringly and suggest, "How about you two go and get dinner, and I'll finish up here?"

Grigor and the other guard look at each other before Grigor asks, "Are you sure?"

"I'm the new guy. I know I have to earn my stripes. And we've been dealing with those annoying royals all day. You two deserve to relax and have your dinner."

"If you're really sure…"

"I'm sure, Grigor. I've got this."

I take Lydia's body from them and place her on an old wooden table nearby. I make a show of opening the incinerator and grabbing the nearest corpse on the ground and loading it in.

When I turn to see Grigor and the other guard still there, I goad them, "If you don't hurry, Milosh is going to drink all the blood, and you'll starve for the night."

That gets them to leave. They mutter their thanks to me before leaving the room. I wait and listen to their footsteps echoing down the hallway. Once I know they're out of hearing range, I grab two more corpses off the ground and stuff them into the incinerator. I reach for the lever and pull it down, turning on the machine.

Fire comes to life in the incinerator and goes to work on the bodies inside. The smell of burning flesh makes me want to hold my breath. I grab a spare sheet from the corner of the room and wrap Lydia in it. If I run into anyone in the hallway, it'll be easier to lie and say it's just one of the feeders from the dungeon.

Lifting Lydia bridal style in my arms, I hold her close. This is our only chance of me getting her out of here. I can't mess this up. Here's to hoping Lydia's faith in me isn't misplaced.

A DARK TUNNEL

Lex

Ivy's hazel eyes stare at me in shock. Her gaze bores into me as she tries to decipher if I'm serious or not. A younger me would have laughed and made a whole production out of this situation. I don't have the same need to turn everything into a joke anymore.

"What?"

"I need a love potion," I explain. "I thought you might be able to brew up something. I will compensate you for your time. Whatever you want."

"That's not what I'm concerned with," she snaps. "Why do you need a love potion?"

"I'm married."

"Yes. I know."

I sigh, preparing myself for the embarrassment of having to admit the state of my marriage to a woman I barely know. "It was for all intents and purposes an arranged marriage. We married to secure my son's claim to the throne and to smooth things over between our kingdoms after the war."

Ivy stays silent, waiting for me to continue.

"We've been married for four years, and we're miserable together.

She constantly cheats on me, and I bury myself in work to avoid having to be around her."

"Cheating aside, have you tried working on your relationship with your wife? Maybe go to marriage counseling? Avoiding her doesn't really help things."

"I've tried over the years, but there are some things I can't fix. Opal hates me for killing her brother. You can't really get past that."

"Why did you kill her brother?"

"Her brother had me imprisoned in the castle, and I was trying to escape. I had to fight him to the death for my freedom," I answer. "Opal watched me do it. Despite how selfish they both were, they loved each other. He even sacrificed himself for her."

"Are you sorry for having killed her brother?"

"I don't feel good about it. I did what I had to do. Jacob wouldn't have let me walk away alive. Only one of us was going to survive that fight and it happened to be me."

"Surely, your wife should see that you didn't kill Jacob because you had a choice. You didn't want to do it," Ivy says with a hint of sympathy in her voice.

"That doesn't matter to Opal. She looks at me, and she sees her brother's killer. My brother killed her father in battle. There's too much bad blood between us." I shrug as if it's as simple as that.

"Then why do you need a love potion?"

"I've tried to love Opal before in my own way. It never works. I can't make myself feel anything for her," I confess. "Deep down, I know that all she wants is to be loved, so if I could force myself to love her, it might make things better between us. Vampires live for so long, and being stuck in an unhappy marriage is like a life sentence in prison."

"It won't work."

"What do you mean?"

She sighs. "Love potions don't actually create love. They only simulate a powerful obsession for somebody. It's a shallow imitation of the real thing."

"That's better than nothing," I argue.

"It isn't. You wouldn't really be happy. You'd *only* think you were," she argues. "And the love potion wears off. You'd have to keep drinking it over time."

"Would you be able to provide me with a supply of the potion long term or recommend someone who can?"

"You can't be serious." She folds her arms under her chest.

"I am."

"You'd be throwing away a chance at real love!"

"I know that, but I have to be pragmatic. I know that finding love like what Kane has with Emory or Rainer has with Willow is probably not an option for me." I tell her. "I would have been content with something like what my parents had. Theirs was an arranged marriage where they managed to fall in love. Unfortunately, I don't have that, so a love potion is my last option."

Her gaze is pitying, and I hate it, not wanting to be a sad, pathetic creature in her eyes. I also know that, despite her prickly behavior, Ivy is a big softie just like her aunt. I've seen how gentle and kind she is with children. Pity will get her to help me, so pity is a win for me.

"Please," I beg softly. "You're the only one that can do this for me."

"Fine. I'll brew the love potion for you. Even if I think you're making a terrible mistake."

"I don't really have other options. Royals don't divorce. We just stay married till one of us dies, and I don't plan on dying any time soon."

"That's good you don't want to die because if Rainer gets caught, we might have to run for our lives."

I shake my head. "He won't get caught."

"How are you so sure of that?"

I would never admit it to his face, but Rainer is one of the most competent men I know. There's a reason Kane sent him to find Lydia over everyone else. Ivy has no idea about Rainer's past as a spy. He has a proven track record with dangerous missions. And he does most of them with a smile, that cocky asshole.

"I've known Rainer for a really long time," I reply. "I know what a sneaky bastard he can be. And the man must be homesick by now after everything he's been through, including staying in this hellhole, so I imagine he has a vested interested in not fucking this up."

* * *

RAINER

Sneaking a body through a castle shouldn't be that difficult, but I have a few close calls with guards patrolling and a few guests who got lost in the labyrinth of hallways when they left the ballroom. Lex and Ivy should be waiting in the tunnel so we can all escape together. I have heard of a secret tunnel that goes through the cave without having to use the hanging bridges. I'm not sure I can carry Lydia while trying to not fall into the watery depths of death below, so I'm glad for an alternate route.

I'm near to my destination when the head guard, Sergei, appears down a hallway. I have to stop myself in time to prevent myself from bumping into the other vampire. His blue eyes look at me curiously. Then he sees the body wrapped up in a sheet in my arms.

"Roman, why are you carrying a body around with you?" he asks. "You're assigned to guard the hallway near the ballroom. Why did you leave your post?'

I think of an excuse and lean closer to explain, "I had to leave my post because there's been an incident with one of the feeders. The king isn't happy and demanded I get rid of the body immediately. I was just following his orders."

"Why wasn't I informed about this?" he barks.

"Grigor was supposed to tell you. I'm on my way to the incinerator."

"The incinerator is on the other side of the castle. What are you doing here?"

"Oh, it is?" I feign confusion. "That's my bad. I'm still getting used to the castle, and I swore Grigor said the incinerator was this way."

"Unless you're dumping the body down a waterfall, this is not the right place. Turn around, and head for the kitchens. The incinerator is further south from there."

I nod, smiling sheepishly. "Thank you for clarifying that. I would have wasted more time if I didn't run into you."

"Do you need me to come with you so you don't get lost again?"

"There's no need for that. I'll manage on my own," I tell him, turning around. "Thanks again. I have to get this thing cremated."

"Don't let any of the guests see you, Roman!" he calls out. "Corpses aren't party-appropriate!"

"I'll keep that in mind!"

I don't want to waste more time going back and forth in the castle, so I duck into the nearest empty room and wait for Sergei to pass by. Once I'm certain he's far away, I continue my path toward the north wing of the castle. The room that leads into the tunnel is small and cramped. It's completely sparse.

A heavy metal door has been left partially open which makes it easier to get through. I balance Lydia on my shoulder so I can use one hand to open the door wider. Slipping into the tunnel, I make sure Lydia's head doesn't hit anything as I readjust her weight in my arms. I pull the metal door closed behind me, and I'm left in darkness.

Even with my superior vampire vision, seeing in pitch black darkness can be difficult. It takes me a few minutes to find the light of the torch. Ivy is holding up as she and Lex stand in the endless darkness. They both look relieved to see me.

"That's Lydia, I presume?" Lex asks, gesturing to the body wrapped in a sheet.

I nod. "Let's get Sleeping Beauty home."

The path through the tunnel is long and very dark. Our only light source is the torch Ivy is holding. She has to walk ahead of us, and there are times when she hesitates. Her practically human vision makes it hard for her to decipher things in the dark, and Lex has to nudge her forward to indicate to her where to step.

"Stop poking me," she hisses at him.

"I'm only trying to guide you," he whispers back. "You said you would haunt me as a ghost if you get lost and die in here."

"You said you thought that would be a good time."

"It would be a good time for me, but would it be for you?"

She glares at him then confesses, "This has been the longest day of my life. Dealing with you on a more permanent basis would be exhausting, ghost or not."

He grins. "You can admit I'm growing on you. It's hard to resist my charm."

I have to snort at that. Lex turns back to raise his blond eyebrows at me. I shrug. I've known him too long to take him seriously.

Lex has always been a flirt. He likes attention. Why he's trying to flirt with Willow's niece is beyond me. Ivy doesn't seem to like him all that much anyway.

"Leave her alone," I say. "She's too young for you."

"I'm not trying to do anything."

"Sure, you're not. Listen to me. Little Lex is not coming near Little Ivy. Do you hear me?"

He sputters. "It's not Little Lex. It's Big Lex. Giant Lex."

Ivy laughs. "Are you seriously talking about your cock right now? Really? While we're in the middle of trying to escape?"

"Rainer insulted my manhood. I can't just let that go."

Ivy turns to me and gives me a look. It's the same disapproving stare her aunt gives me. "You shouldn't be encouraging him, Rainer. You know better."

I shrug, smiling at her in an apology. Ivy and I have formed an amiable friendship over the years. We're related through marriage, and since Ivy is important to Willow, she's important to me.. Ivy is the last remaining member of Willow's family, and my wife cherishes that connection to her former life.

There's more bickering. Our voices echo through the tunnel. Once we leave the tunnel and reach the exit, we climb up limestone steps and the entrance of the tunnel comes into view. The moon lights our way to our escape.

There is one problem—there's security at the gate who will be wondering about the body we have with us. I reach for the blade I have in my pocket. If I can't think of another way to get past them, I might have to get rid of the guards. We've made it this far, and I have to make sure we finish this mission. Before we can discuss what to do next, Ivy whispers something under her breath, *"Somnum."*

The guards collapse to the ground in a deep sleep. Ivy doesn't say anything else and steps around the guards. Lex and I exchange a look of astonishment. Even after four years of marriage to a witch, magic is something I can never get used to.

FIRE AND FURY

Ivy

Lex and Rainer both look flabbergasted as the guards abruptly collapse to the ground. A simple sleeping spell is hardly anything to gawk at, but vampires and shifters tend to be weird about magic. They are either awed like I'm performing a miracle or deeply confused about how it works. Growing up around magic, it's perfectly ordinary for me to wield it, but I try to limit it for the comfort of others.

I step around the bodies of the guards, silently apologizing for the headache they'll wake up to later. Magic tends to leave traces, and for sleeping spells, it feels like a bad hangover. Vampires heal fast, so I know the guards will be fine. As I try to step out of the cave entrance, I'm stopped by an invisible barrier.

I raise a hand and touch the barrier. Magic hums underneath my touch, a warning it will fight back if I try to unravel it. I press my fingers into it, trying to twist and tame the magic to my will. It snaps back with a hot jolt like electricity making my yelp in pain. Lex is there immediately, pulling me back and trying to look at my hand for injuries.

"What happened?" he asks. "Are you okay?"

I push him away, shaking my hand to get the residual magic off. "I'm fine. There are wards around the exit."

"What?" Rainer exclaims. "And you're only learning this now?"

"They're meant to prevent people from leaving. They don't seem designed to keep people out. That's why I didn't really feel anything when we came in earlier."

I don't mention how I'd been distracted by the darkness of the cave and having to stay close to Lex so I wouldn't get lost. Being so close to him does things to my already distracted mind. I hadn't been paying attention to any magic that's in the area. That was stupid of me as we're now trapped in enemy territory.

Rainer lets out a deep sigh, exasperated with the turn of events. "Can you get rid of the wards then?"

"It'll take me a few minutes. Wards aren't my specialty."

"Willow can unravel wards quickly," he reminds me.

"Because *she* is good at warding magic. Unfortunately for us, Aunt Willow isn't here at this moment."

"Is this going to take a while?" Rainer asks, looking like he wants to change directions and take the path that leads to the waterfall. "Should I sit and wait?"

"That might be for the best."

Rainer places Lydia by the wall, removing the blanket around her face so she can breathe better. He goes to the top of the limestone steps and has his sword at the ready in case anyone else is leaving through the tunnel soon. It's late, but the party is still going on. By my estimate, we still have a few hours before dawn which is when these vampires will probably want to go to bed.

Lex leans against the cave wall and watches me work on unravelling the wards. His blue gaze doesn't leave me, and it makes me self-conscious. Having someone's absolute attention is not a feeling I particularly enjoy. Even when I'm casting magic or brewing potions, people tend to focus more on conversation or find something else to occupy their time.

I turn to Lex. "Can you not stare as I do this? You're distracting me."

He blinks, looking sheepish. "I didn't mean to make you uncomfortable."

"You are staring at me like I might melt if you look away. I don't even think you were blinking."

"Sorry. I just find magic interesting. I haven't been around many witches, so this is all new to me."

I'm a novelty. It's not a surprise. The Moonstone fellow, one of Lydia's older brothers, had been the same way when he saw me cast magic a few weeks ago. He stuck around until the novelty wore off, and then he found some other diversion to occupy his time.

I don't put much stock in Lex's interest and concentrate on the wards, knowing this is temporary, too. I study the wards, trying to look for weak spots to unravel them. The magic is layered, cast over a long period of time. Whoever cast the warding magic took their time, ensuring the magic would hold and not deplete over the years.

King Myenas having a witch that works for him isn't a surprise. I've suspected that's the reason locating Lydia was initially very difficult. How long this witch has been working for him is the real concern. Most witches stay away from dealing with vampires due to the bad blood between our species.

A witch helping a vampire to kidnap shifters is not a good look. This could lead to our kind having problems with the shifters. Rescuing Lydia and getting her home is more important than ever for me. Some good will will help in offsetting the terrible actions of what I hope is a lone witch.

It takes me more time than I care for to unravel the wards. It's a long mind-numbing process where I have to untangle magic like tight knots. When I finally unravel the last knot, the magic evaporates into thin air. There's a ripple of light throughout the tunnel before we hear a loud blaring siren.

Rainer is immediately on his feet. "What the fuck is happening?"

"They put an alarm in the wards," I reply, angry at myself for not sensing the alarm sooner and stopping it. "It must be set to go off if the wards go down."

"Can you turn it off the alarm?"

"I can, but it'll take time."

"That's time we don't have," Lex points out. "Do you think they can hear the alarm from the castle?"

Rainer and Lex look toward the long tunnel that leads back into the castle. They must hear something with their superior vampire hearing because they both looked panicked. Rainer picks up Lydia and practically runs out through the gate. Lex grabs my hand and pulls me behind him, following Rainer into the grassy field outside.

"What are we running from?"

Lex doesn't turn around as he answers, "Half the guards in the castle!"

* * *

Rainer

The alarm in the cave is still screaming, attracting the attention of the vampires in the field. It's packed with cars. The guards of the vampire royals have been sitting in the vehicles or talking amongst themselves to pass the time. Seeing me running toward them carrying a woman wrapped in a blanket raises some eyebrows.

I recognize a familiar vehicle and rush in that direction.

Thomas, who had been taking a nap in the town car, jolts awake when I knock on the car window.

"Unlock the door!"

He immediately follows my command, unlocking the door. I slide into the backseat of the car. Lex and Ivy reach the vehicle, and Lex pushes her into the backseat with me before running around the car to get into the front seat. Thomas's eyes widen when he sees the small army of guards coming at us from the cave entrance.

"Drive, Thomas!" Lex orders, closing the car door. "We don't have all night!"

Thomas doesn't have to be told twice. He turns the engine on and slides the car out of the row of parked cars. He peals out of the parking lot and books it when we reach the dirt road, trying to put some distance between us and the guards. I watch through the rear window as the guards take the cars of the vampire royals despite the protests of the royals' guards.

Half a dozen cars are coming at us, gaining speed as their drivers only care about getting us. Thomas looks at the side mirror nervously. Lex lets out a curse. Ivy looks at me with wide hazel eyes, wondering what we're supposed to do now.

"We can lose them," I try to reassure her. "Right, Thomas?"

The driver doesn't immediately agree. He looks to our right where a car has appeared. It moves closer to us, trying to hit the side of our car. Thomas speeds up to avoid contact, the tires of the town car screeching.

Another car appears to our left as the car at our right gains on us again. We're trapped between the two cars. Thomas is going as fast as he can and can't do anything but drive as the cars move closer, boxing us in. Metal screeches as cars make contact, jolting us from the impact.

"Fuck," Lex hisses. "They're going to kill us."

I turn to see Ivy rolling down the window on her side. I'm about to ask her what she's doing when she throws a fireball the size of a grapefruit at the car on the right. The vehicle catches fire immediately. The guards scream in terror and stop the car, swerving wildly and hitting a nearby tree.

The car explodes upon impact, a loud boom reverberating through the air. I barely have time to react before Ivy is nudging me to roll down the window on my side. I lean back to give her space so she can throw a fireball out of the window. The car on our left tries to avoid it and swerves backward. It's too fast, and the car flips around, landing on the roof on the side of the road.

"Do more of that!" I tell Ivy. "Keep the fire coming."

She gives me a conspiring smile as she continues to throw fireballs out of the window. The guards try to avoid the fireballs. Some get hit immediately, the fireball hitting the engine and causing explosions. A car tries to dodge the exploding vehicle and ends up hitting another one, causing a huge pile up behind it.

The guards in the second car must not have been wearing their seatbelts, and one of the guards goes through the windshield, his body flying through the air before landing on the dirt road with a bone crunching thud.

One of the cars has front end damage, but it's still functional. The guards turn the car and return to chasing us.

"Still got one more, Ivy," I say. "Let's finish this."

She has to lean the upper half of her body out of the window. I hold unto the back of her dress with one hand to prevent her from falling out. She's about to throw a fireball when one of the guards takes out a gun. He also leans out the window to aim and shoot.

He fires and the bullet narrowly misses Ivy. I pull her back inside the car. Another bullet hits the rear window and travels out the windshield.

"Shit," I hiss, grabbing Ivy and forcing her to duck her head to avoid bullets. "Any of us have any guns?" Vampires don't usually carry weapons, but Myenas isn't known for playing fair.

"I got a pistol in the glove compartment," Thomas replies.

Lex doesn't hesitate and opens the glove compartment to take out the pistol. He tosses it toward me. Ivy grabs hold of Lydia so I can lean out the window and shoot at the guards. It's not an ideal position to be shooting a gun in, but I make it work.

I fire shots at the car, managing to hit the guard with the gun right in the forehead. He goes limp, his body hanging half out of the car. I fire at the wheels of the car and manage to get one of the front tires. This causes the car to swerve, and the driver has to step on the brakes to prevent him from losing control of the vehicle.

It stops abruptly, nearly causing the guard to hit his head on the windshield. He opens the car door and steps out. It's Grigor. He looks furious and kicks the wheel of the car in frustration.

"Sorry," I mutter. "It's nothing personal."

"What's not personal?" Ivy asks.

"I think this whole chase has felt *very* personal," Lex remarks. "I personally hate anyone who has tried to kill us today. And I feel no guilt for what happened to them. You can call me a monster if you want to."

"You're a monster," Ivy says with no real heat. She looks more amused than anything else. "But you're not wrong."

4 2

A WELCOME SIGHT

RAINER

The drive from Carmine Falls to Crimson Peak is long, but we don't dare stop anywhere except for when we have to get gas. After Lydia's abduction in Burgundy Bay, none of us know which of our ally territories have been compromised. There's no relaxing till we reach the border of Crimson Peak. Castle Graystone is a welcome sight after my long, awful adventure, especially my stay at Castle Pestera.

It's the middle of the night, so sending a message ahead through telepathy hasn't worked as most of the castle's residents are asleep, so there's no one there to greet us at the courtyard. Thomas parks the car, and Ivy exits first. She holds the car door open as I carry Lydia out. The potion Ivy brewed for her is truly effective as she has not stirred at all throughout our entire journey.

Lydia feels cold to the touch. Her limbs are stiff, and to any outside party, she appears to be dead. It's only because I'm holding her that I can feel and hear the very faint beating of her heart. The unnoticeable shallow little puffs of breath that signify that she's still alive are easy to miss.

We hurry across the grounds as fast as we can. Lex and Ivy look a little tired. The adrenaline from being chased out of Carmine Falls is wearing off, and the exhaustion from our long night is settling in. Lex opens the large double doors of the castle and ushers us inside.

I stop a passing maid who looks like she just woke up and ask her where Kane and Emory are. She tells me they are still asleep, which explains why I can't reach Kane with my mind. I ask her to relay go and wake them up and tell that we've returned, and we're headed to the clinic. After that, we head straight to the clinic to have Dr. Martin check over Lydia. Thankfully, he is awake, so I let him know we are on our way.

When we arrive, Ivy explains the potion she brewed to Dr. Martin who is looking over Lydia's vitals with a concerned expression.

"There's an antidote that I was working on. It takes a full moon cycle to brew," she says. "Willow will be bringing the potion supplies from Cerise Point, and I'll continue working on the potion here."

"Are there any lasting side effects with this potion?" he asks. "This must leave some damage to the body."

"There could be some side effects, but we won't know till Lydia wakes up," she admits.

The doors to the clinic open. Kane and Emory enter. Both of them look relieved to see us. Emory comes over and envelopes me in a hug. I hug her back then hug Kane who pats my back.

"Good job," he tells me. "For a minute there, I thought you weren't coming back."

"Me? Fail? Who do you think you're talking to?" I quip. "I haven't failed a mission yet."

Kane smiles, not even rising to my baiting. "It was a cake walk for you, huh?"

"Easy as pie." I turn to Emory who looks like she might actually cry. "You okay there, Em?"

"You don't know how grateful I am that you brought Lydia back. Colt is going to be so happy to have her back. And her family will be so relieved."

I shrug off her gratitude. "It's nothing. It was the right thing to do."

"It was not nothing. You did what everyone said was impossible and dangerous."

"It wasn't that hard."

Lex scoffs from where he's sitting on a stool. "We almost died escaping Carmine Falls."

"The important thing is we didn't die," I counter. "It doesn't matter how close we were to death because we survived, and that's all people will remember."

Lex shakes his head. "You're unbelievable."

Kane steps closer to his brother. "I'm glad to see you're in one piece, too, but I do have some questions."

"Of course you do."

"Did you get a good look at everyone King Myenas is doing business with?"

"For the feeder operation? I saw everyone's faces clear as day." Lex stands up. "I should probably write it all down for you before I forget."

"Let's go to my office."

Lex nods to Emory in acknowledgement before he and his brother leave the clinic. Ivy has finished explaining the potion to Dr. Martin and tells them she has to go call Willow about the potion ingredients. The mention of my wife makes me miss her even more. I can't wait until she returns with my daughter.

I smile at Ivy as she exits the clinic, leaving Emory and I alone. The redhead is staring over at the unconscious Lydia, looking like a weight has been lifted from her shoulders.

"Is she okay?" Emory asks. "I can't imagine what she went through with the Blood Takers and then being at Castle Pestera."

"It wasn't pleasant, but Lydia is tough," I answer. "A weaker woman might have been crushed by the situation she was in, but she kept fighting. She's a testament to the strength of her people."

"I'm sure her family would love to hear that."

"When are you going to tell them she's here? I made a promise to her grandfather I would bring her back."

"It's still the middle of the night. I'll wait till sunrise before I start making calls."

"I doubt they would care what time it was when you called. They've been waiting for so long to have her back. You shouldn't wait."

Emory turns to me. "I suppose you're right." Her green eyes look over my face. "It's so odd to look at you with this face. You have to get Willow to reverse this as soon as she's back in the castle."

"Willow chose this face. Is it bad?"

"It's not that. You just don't look like yourself which is what makes it strange."

I run my fingers through the magical hair. "I am missing my handsome face. It's a crime to deprive the world of it even for a short time."

Emory snorts. "I should go make those calls. It's nice to have you back, Rainer."

"I'm glad to be back."

It's after Emory leaves the clinic that I begin to feel the days' worth of exhaustion coming down on me. I haven't slept well since Burgundy Bay. My body is at its limits demanding rest from me. If I don't sleep soon, I will collapse.

Dr. Martin notices my fatigue and gestures to one of the empty hospital beds. "You can sleep here for a few hours."

"I might as well go to my suite."

"I still need to check you over to see if you're well."

"Nothing a little sleep can't fix," I assure him.

Dr. Martin eyes me then nods, giving in over fighting. He must think it's not worth it.

"If you're feeling worse than expected, come here immediately. I won't tolerate anything else."

I salute the doctor. Knowing that Lydia is safe in Dr. Martin's care, I leave the clinic to make my way to my suite. It's empty without my family. Bryony's toys are scattered in the living room, and Willow's growing pile of books are on every available surface. I let myself miss my wife and child, having been away from them for weeks.

I wish they were home to see me after a successful mission, but knowing they'll be here soon is a good consolation. I go to my bedroom where the bed is made and everything is tidy. Willow's scent lingers on the sheets. It's the familiar scent of parchment, wildflowers, and soap.

I don't have the energy except to take off the guards uniform I still have on, tossing it to the floor to be discarded later. That uniform is filthy, and I'll be glad to never lay eyes upon it again. In my boxers, I pull back the sheets to climb into bed. Surrounded by my wife's scent and finally able to relax, I fall into a deep, blissful sleep.

* * *

Emory

I call the Moonstones first, knowing they will want updates immediately. I get Lydia's mother on the phone who sounds relieved and happy to hear the news. They will be coming to see Lydia in the morning. I expect the full Moonstone pack to be in the castle by sun up.

The next phone call is to Colt. No one picks up the phone for a little while. It's allowed to ring for what feels like an eternity until one of the staff at Moon Grove answers. She instructs another servant to wake Colt as the Alpha needs to talk to him.

Colt comes to the phone, his voice groggy and deep from sleep. "Hello, Em. What is it?"

"Hello, Colt," I reply, trying to contain my smile. "We did it."

"Did what?"

"We got Lydia back like I promised."

Colt goes silent, then he asks, "Please tell me it's for real this time. Please, Em. Don't make me hope again only for her to be taken away from me once more."

"She's really here at Crimson Peak, Colt. We're having the castle guards watch her like a hawk. No one comes near her unless we want them to."

"It feels too good to be true. Is she okay? Has she asked about me?"

"She's asleep," I say, not wanting to explain the potion over the phone. "Dr. Martin said she has no injuries."

"I'm heading there now."

"It's nearly four o'clock in the morning, Colt."

He scoffs. "It'll be nearly sunrise by the time I get there. And what does it matter what time it is? I've been waiting for this for weeks."

"I suppose when you put it like that…"

"Like I would even be able to go back to bed knowing Lydia is so close to me," he says. "I will run there in my wolf form if I have to."

"You have a perfectly decent and expensive Jeep. You might as well use it."

"You said I could pick any car."

"I thought you'd pick a sensible car, not a monster vehicle that guzzles up gas."

"Are you seriously making fun of my Jeep the same day I get my mate back?"

"I can multitask," I return with a grin. "I'll see you later, brother."

"See you later, Em. And thank you. I really mean it."

"I know, Colt."

My brother arrives a few hours later. It's still a bit dark out, and the sun won't be completely up for a couple of more hours. I greet him at the door and pull him into a hug. He's so much taller than me, and I wonder what happened to my little brother.

Colt wants to beeline for the clinic, and I don't want to stop him. I go with him where he finds Lydia amongst the hospital beds. He doesn't leave her side, holding her hand as she lies there, appearing to be asleep. He kisses the back of her head and exhales as if he's been holding his breath for far too long.

"When will she wake up?" he asks.

"You'll have to talk to Ivy. They had to give Lydia some kind of sleeping potion to sneak her out of Carmine Falls. It's not permanent, but the antidote will take some time to brew."

"How long?" I can see concern on his face as he glares at me.

Hesitantly, I say, "A full moon cycle. Ivy's already started on it."

His eyes widen, but then he nods in acceptance. I'm glad he's not mad. "But Lydia is fine otherwise?"

I nod. "Ivy said Lydia should be just fine." That's not exactly true, but we'll see what happens. No need to worry him now. "We just have to wait for the potion." I move closer to him and place a hand on his shoulder. "I'm sorry you have to wait again to talk to her."

"What's a month?" he returns, calmly. "At least now she's safe. I know where she is, and I can see her."

"Still, I'm sure you wish she was awake now that you can finally see her again."

"We can make up for lost time later. But for now…." He looks down at Lydia, his expression full of adoration and relief. "I'm content to just watch her sleep. Is that weird?"

"A little bit, but it's kind of romantic."

"Does Kane ever watch you sleep?"

"Absolutely not."

"You're completely insane, you know?" he quips. "But you are also the best sister in the world."

My heart melts, and I'm getting teary-eyed. "Can I get that in writing?"

Colt shakes his head. "Absolutely not."

43

LOVE AND POTIONS

Emory

The Nightstones arrive before breakfast. Alpha Gerald, along with his son and many grandsons, is eager to see Lydia. They crowd the clinic where she is still unconscious under the effects of Ivy's sleeping potion. Colt is asleep in a nearby chair, slumped in a way that will most likely leave him with a stiff neck when he wakes up.

I've explained to the Nightstones about the sleeping potion and that Ivy says she should be finished brewing the antidote in a few weeks. The Moonstones are disappointed that they have to wait a little bit longer to talk to Lydia, but they're more relieved that she's finally safe.

"We're bringing Lydia home to Nightfall," Alpha Gerald says. "We can watch over her until the antidote is ready."

"She'll be safe there," Alcide adds. "No one will get close to her without us knowing."

Alpha Gerald grins knowingly. "They certainly won't be able to leave in one piece."

After what happened at Burgundy Bay, I understand their point. They don't want to risk someone taking Lydia away again. Nightfall is as good as a fortress. A Blood Taker trying to sneak in there would have a difficult time getting out alive.

Colt wakes up during our conversation and insists on coming with the Nightstones back to their territory. Alpha Gerald doesn't protest nor does the rest of his family. I take Colt away from the clinic to talk with him as they get ready to transport Lydia out of Crimson Peak. My brother looks groggy and yawns as we enter my office.

"You need to shave," I tell him. "And a shower. You're beginning to smell ripe."

He shrugs. "I'll shower when I reach Nightfall."

"That's hours away. Take a shower here. The Nightstones are going to have breakfast with us before they go anyway."

"I didn't bring any clean clothes with me."

"I'm sure Nellie and Helga can find something that'll fit you. You can shower in the guest room you always use."

Colt lifts an arm to smell his armpit. He nods and acquiesces, "You might have a point. I wouldn't want the Nightstones to think I don't bathe."

"When was the last time you took a shower?"

He looks contemplative. "Time blurs together. I honestly can't remember."

"You're gross," I remark. "Go shower. That's an order from your Alpha."

"Fine." He rubs at the thin beard on his chin. "Do I have to shave to?"

"Are you growing out a beard?"

"Maybe."

"It currently looks unkempt. Maybe trim it a little."

Colt salutes me then walks out of the office to go take that much needed shower. I go looking for my maids and find Helga. I ask her about finding clothes for Colt to change into and some shaving supplies to tackle the patchy beard on his face. I don't even know if a beard would suit my brother, but this could just be a phase. He went through a few phases as a teenager from dyeing his hair bleach blond to eating an all-protein diet.

Colt looks and smells fresh and clean at breakfast. Over the years of living at Castle Graystone, I've taken to having my meals in a small dining room that the vampire aristocrats never go into. While I generally don't mind eating in my suite, it's nice to have a meal with my friends and family, too, without the judgmental glares and whispers from the nobles.

This dining room is less formal with a smaller table. I use it when I have occasional visits from other shifters, usually messengers from other Alphas, so we can have a meal and discuss business at the same time. Since it's morning, the nobles will likely still be in their suites and won't be in the hallways. It's an ideal time to have the Nightstones over as we can all have a nice meal together without worrying about running into someone rude in the castle.

The staff has quickly put together a nice breakfast spread of meats, eggs, pastries, and fruits with the option of coffee or tea to go along with it. The Nightstone boys seem ravenous and dig into their food right away. Shifter men tend to be all the same when it comes to their appetite. They're all bottomless pits.

Lydia's mother, Amanda, has opted for a lighter meal of yogurt and a croissant. She's sipping her coffee as she asks me, "How is your son, Emory?"

"He's good, than you. Michael is currently in Cerise Port staying with his Uncle Cyrus," I reply. "He'll be coming back later today along with Willow. Willow is Ivy's aunt. They'll be working on the antidote together."

"Is there a way to brew that antidote faster?" Lydia's brother, Tyler, asks. "I don't know how magic works, but isn't there some kind of shortcut?"

"I don't know much about magic either. Ivy should be joining us soon. You can ask her if there's a way to speed up the process."

Ivy does join us for breakfast and sits near me. She answers all questions about the antidote and explains there's no rushing the brewing process.

"Taking shortcuts could affect the potency of the antidote. It's generally not advised to mess with the recipe. When it comes to potion brewing, you have to trust the process."

"Are you going to be staying here while you work on the antidote then?" Another one of Lydia's brothers, George, asks. "It might be easier if you stay at Nightfall in the meantime. We have the room."

Ivy looks at him for a moment before saying, "I don't need to be near your sister while I'm brewing the potion. There's no reason I should stay at your home for three weeks, but thank you."

George shrugs, and he gives Ivy his most charming smile. "I can think of a few reasons."

Ivy purses her lips but doesn't dignify his obvious flirting with a response. She pushes away the rest of the omelet she's eating and excuses herself. George waits a few seconds before excusing himself as well before leaving the dining room. I look at the older Moonstones who are shaking their heads and laughing in amusement at the male shifter's behavior.

"That's a Moonstone trait," Alpha Gerald says. "We find something we like, and we go after it—no questions asked."

"I don't think Ivy is interested," I reply. "Besides, if she was his mate wouldn't he know already?"

"George doesn't want a mate," Another of the brothers, Tommy, points out. "He wants a… friend in the meantime."

Amanda chides him. "Tyler. Don't talk like that in front of Alpha Emory."

"I'm just being honest." Tyler shrugs.

Amanda sighs. "We have your sister back with us. That should be all you boys focus on for now. Leave that poor girl alone."

"Tell Georgie that." Shaking his head, Tyler takes another bite.

Maybe I should have a conversation with George Nightstone. I wouldn't want to have trouble between his pack and Ivy's coven because she decided to use her magic on him. I've already got enough on my hands to deal with. Another interspecies war is more than I can handle.

* * *

Ivy

George Nightstone cannot take a hint. I walk briskly through the castle hallways and back to the guest room I've been staying in. George catches up to me quickly. He's tall and moves fast despite his beefy physique. A large hand grabs my arm, preventing me from moving any further.

I glare at his hand then direct my annoyance to his face. George isn't unattractive. He has that rugged handsomeness many shifters have with an unshakeable confidence. Having grown up as an Alpha's grandson, he's has always known and understood his place in the world.

"What do you want?" I demand more than ask. "I have things to do."

He gives me that charming smile. "There's no need to be hostile. I thought we were friends."

"We're not friends. You wanted to sleep with me, and I said no. End of story."

His dark eyebrows furrow, his blue-gray staring straight into mine. "I do actually want to be friends, Ivy," he says. "It's not just about sex."

"You want a distraction while you wait to find your mate. I don't want to be just someone's pastime until you find the person you're actually supposed to be with."

"It's not like that."

"Explain it to me, then." I push his hand away and cross my arms over my chest. "The fact of the matter is shifters don't usually mate with witches. You're going to find your true mate someday, and I'll be out in the cold."

He looks away, guilty and frustrated.

"It's better not to pursue anything between us. All this leads to is me getting hurt in the end while you run off into the sunset with your mate," I continue. "No, thank you. I don't want any of that."

I turn to leave but George holds me back again.

"What if I never find my mate?" he says. "What if I'm waiting for nothing?"

"Is that even possible?" I fold my arms beneath my chest.

"It happens to a small percentage of shifters. I could be one of them."

"Or you could be like the majority of shifters and run into your mate someday." I shake my head. "If you really want to be my friend, then you should respect my wishes. I don't want to be with you whether it's in a purely sexual way or as your temporary fun relationship before you meet your true love."

"Ivy–"

"Don't, George." I step back. "Just leave me alone."

He finally lets me go. I run away, heading for my suite. He doesn't follow me, but I don't look back until I reach the guest room. Entering the suite, I close the door behind me and sigh against the wood.

"Are you having a bad morning?"

I nearly scream at the familiar voice I'm not expecting. Lex is seated in a chair and reading a book. I don't know how long he's been in here, but he's not supposed to be in my room at all. The suite isn't locked, but I'd thought he'd respect my privacy and not come in when I'm not in the room.

"What are you doing?" I ask, annoyed. "You almost gave me a heart attack."

He drops the book he's reading on the coffee table and stands up. "I wanted to talk to you about the love potion."

That damn love potion.

Everyone is always requiring something from me whether it's a special potion or time I don't have time to spare. What non-witches don't understand about magic is that it doesn't solve everything. It can be a bandage for a problem, but it can also, at times, make things worse because they're not addressing the root of their problem. They all seem to think magic is the cure-all for all of life's issues.

"Not right now, Lex," I tell him. "I have to work on the antidote for Lydia. I need to concentrate on that."

"You said that the antidote would take weeks to brew, right? Can't you work on the love potion on the side?"

I stare at him in exasperation. "I only have one cauldron with me."

"I'll buy you another one," he suggests. "In fact, I'll pay for all the ingredients. It's the least I can do."

Realizing it'll be easier to just give him the list than to fight him on this, I quickly write down the love potion recipe I found in one of my grimoires and hand it to him. "It'll be expensive. A lot of the ingredients are rare."

He grimaces while reading over the recipe. "It doesn't look like this will taste good all brewed together."

"Taste doesn't matter when it comes to potions."

He's not wrong. A lot of potions taste awful. While there are ways to make them taste better, it's an unnecessary step to the brewing process that takes up time and energy. It's better to just tolerate the taste for a short moment than to waste time.

"I'll work on getting all these," Lex says, heading for the door.

I'm still blocking the exit, and it's only when he's a foot away from me, and I'm staring up at his handsome face, that I wonder why people have trouble falling in love with the right person. People seem to want someone they can't have or someone they shouldn't be with. Why do we complicate our lives with complex romances? I never understood the point of all the mess when it comes to love, and that's why I've always avoided it.

"Ivy." Lex's blue eyes stare down at me. "I need to go."

I move away from the door so he can open it and leave the room. He steps out, and I turn to look at him. For a second, we're on either side of the doorway. He looks at me curiously and asks, "Are you all right?"

"Yes," I reply. "I'm just thinking."

"Thinking about what?"

"Love potions."

And maybe Lex is right about this. At least he's choosing who he's going to be in love with. It seems better than whatever George is offering me. Even if the love is a manufactured obsession, isn't that better than assured heartbreak?

"Ivy...." Lex's blue eyes look concerned. "Are you sure you're okay?"

"Never better."

I close the door in his face.

44

SEE YOU AGAIN

EMORY

After breakfast, the Nightstones don't want to delay getting back to Nightfall. They carefully transport Lydia out of the castle and into one of their vehicles parked in the courtyard. Colt is going to leave with them and stay at Nightfall while Lydia is under the sleeping potion. I can't blame him for wanting to be close to his mate after being away from her for so long.

Colt has his hands in the pockets of his borrowed jacket. His shoulders are slumped as he looks down at the ground. I'm reminded of a younger version of my brother when he'd had to apologize for something that he'd done. He looks guilty.

"I know I should get back to Moon Grove," he says. "Our pack needs us. You need me there to take care of things while you and Kane work on fixing this mess with Carmine Falls but..."

"You just got Lydia back," I finish for him. "And you want to be by her side and protect her."

He nods. "I know her family can protect her. Her brothers would all die for her, but I wouldn't be able to live with myself if something happened to her again."

I place my hands on his arms. "Colt, I understand. I have a mate, too. And where you need to be right now is by Lydia's side."

"But our pack-"

"Darius is at Moon Grove. He'll hold down the fort till you can come back. He *is* my Beta, after all. I'm sure he can manage on his own."

"I already forced him to take over when I was staying in my wolf form and living in the woods."

"I'm sure he won't hold it against you," I tell him.

"Darius is a good guy."

"He is and he's also very capable so I can trust him to keep it together till you can come back home."

Colt pulls me into a hug. I'm not expecting it, and it takes me a second before I'm hugging him back. I pat him gently, smiling at our moment of brother/sister love before he pulls away.

"Thank you for everything you did to get Lydia back to me," he says. "I know I was a mess through the whole thing, but you didn't hold it against me."

"You're my brother," I reply. "I'd do anything for you–even when you annoy me."

He snorts. "I love you, too, sis."

I felt terrible when I'd failed Colt. When it's seemed that all I'd been going while trying to get his mate back to him kept going nowhere. Seeing him relieved and happy to have Lydia back has made everything worth it. His dorky smile lighting up is face means the world to me.

I'd never tell him any of that, though. There's no reason to give him ammunition to tease me with. We may love each other, but we're still siblings. We can't be too sappy without breaking out into hives.

"Take care of yourself, Colt," I tell him. "That's an order. No more forgetting to bathe. The Nightstones might think you weren't raised right."

"Alcide Nightstone already holds me being my father's son against me, so I don't need to give him any more reasons to dislike me."

"I think he might be softening toward you. He didn't say anything bad about you during breakfast." I shrug and give him a smile.

"That's cause he's not on his home turf." Colt replies. "But it's all good. Once I'm staying at his house, I just need to let the Stockholm Syndrome set in and brainwash him into liking me."

"Is that what you do with everybody?"

"Kane was able to do it to you when you moved into Castle Graystone," he reasons.

I stare at him in disbelief. "That is not what happened. We fell in love. He's my mate."

"I'm sure you two were the cutest couple in this hellscape of a castle, but you have to admit that being trapped together in a confined space played a hand in your relationship."

I'm suddenly reminded why I like my brother living long distance from me. I truly find him incredibly annoying. "You know what? Get in the car and leave," I demand, forcibly turning him around and pushing him toward the nearest parked vehicle. "Go bother someone else. I don't have to see your ugly mug till the antidote finishes brewing."

"Are you really foisting me off another family that quickly?"

"They can keep you. I have Darius as my Beta. The pack and I are going to be just fine so never come back. Have a beautiful life in Nightfall."

"You don't mean that, Em. You'd miss me." He turns and flashes me a sarcastic grin.

Alpha Gerald comes forward and takes my hand in his, interrupting our sibling squabble. "Thank you for your help, Emory. You will always have our loyalty and support in the future."

"There's no need to thank me, Gerald. I was glad to help."

"Your brother will be part of the family soon enough. And family is everything." His eyes crinkle at the edges as he smiles fondly at me.

That is something we're in total agreement about. "Family is everything."

Colt gets into one of the cars with one of Lydia's brothers. I give him a mocking smile and salute him. Colt salutes me back. The other shifters get into the vehicles and drive out of the courtyard to head home.

* * *

WILLOW

While I enjoy Cerise Port's charms, being back home in Castle Graystone is so much better. The children are glad to be home as well. After hearing that Rainer has managed to save Lydia and has returned to Crimson Peak, I rush home to see him again. Traveling with children slows me down, but we make it there eventually.

I leave Bryony with Ivy as I want to talk to Rainer alone first. I want to know how the mission went, and I have to remove the glamour spell on him. Letting my daughter see a strange man in our suite wouldn't go over well. It would only confuse her.

I find Rainer asleep in our bed. There are clothes scattered on the floor that he must've been too tired to bother putting away. It looks like he's gone to sleep naked. The sheets are only covering him from the waist down, his muscled torso exposed.

He's asleep on his child, his cheek lying on a pillow. From the back, he looks completely the same as I remember him. It's only when I get close that I can see the glamour charm at work. His features are still changed to make him look like somebody else.

I lean over him on the bed and gently touch his face. My magic pours out of my fingertips to melt the glamour spell, disappearing into the ether. Rainer's handsome face reappears–the same handsome face that I know and love.

His blue eyes blink open, staring at me sleepily. "Willow?"

"Rainer," I reply. "Welcome home." I smile and lean down to kiss him. He responds immediately. After being away from each other for so long, there's a desperate need to be close and feel each other's touch. I kick off my shoes, and we tug at my clothes, unbuttoning and unlacing my dress until it's a heap of blue cloth on the floor.

We can't stop touching each other. Rainer's large hands cup my breasts, and I straddle him on the bed. His cock is thick and large pressed against me. I feel slick and ready, having missed the feel of him deep inside of me. I move my hips, grinding myself against him, and he leans against the headboard, his expression pained and feverish from arousal.

"I've missed you," he moans. "I've really missed you, my love."

"I've missed you too."

I can't wait. Not after weeks of being away from my husband. I grasp his large dick in my hand, holding it steady as I bear down on him. He slides into me slowly, careful not to hurt me.

Rainer's fingers reach for my clit, rubbing it in soft circles to make me slicker. He takes his time with one hand on my hip to guide me down. When I've finally taken all of him, he doesn't move and gives me time to adjust. There's no feeling in the world like when I've taken all of him.

We're wrapped so closely together that we could be one being. Rainer kisses me deeply, his tongue tangling with mine. I move first, angling myself up and down. The push and pull of him inside me makes me moan. Rainer isn't immune to the pleasurable sensations, and he kisses my neck, my shoulder, and then moves on to my breasts.

He moves against me, thrusting deeper and making me cry out. It's fast and almost animalistic. He's so deep inside me, I feel my head beginning to spin. His fingers on my clit are still gentle despite our hurried lovemaking.

"Kiss me," I beg. "I'm going to come."

The kiss is hot, and I begin to fall right over the edge. Rainer moves one hand down my back, tracing my spine until he finds the spot that makes my pussy flutter around his cock. Shivers wreck my body as I come, my mind going blank. I can't focus on anything else.

Rainer pushes me until I'm lying on my back on the bed. He grabs my thighs and guides me to wrap my legs around his waist. I lock my ankles at the small of his back, and he starts to move again. Quick thrusts have me holding onto his back for support.

Rainer's warm breath fans my cheek, his head buried in the mattress beside mine. The angle of his thrusts has him hitting that spot inside of that makes me moan in pleasure. I don't think I can come again so soon, but I want to see Rainer lose control. It doesn't take long.

He groans as he finishes then almost collapses on top of me before catching his weight on his elbows. Turning over, he lands on the mattress beside me. We're both panting as we stare up at the canopy not really seeing anything.

Eventually, he turns his head to look at me, his gaze adoring. "That's the best part of coming home."

"Sex?" I tease him. "Nothing else?"

He shakes his head. His smile is pleased and soft.

"I love you," he declares. "Every second I was away, I thought of you."

"Thought of me in what way?"

He takes my hand and places a kiss on my wrist. His tongue traces the pale blue veins causing goosebumps to appear on my skin. I don't complain as he starts leaving kisses between my breasts, down my stomach, and in between my legs. He licks deeply into me, and I close my eyes to enjoy my husband's very talented tongue.

45

BAD MAN'S BLUFF

Kane

Rainer's successful rescue of Lydia should have meant that the whole mess is over. I'd been expecting King Myenas to inform me about Lydia's supposed death, but instead, he continues to act like nothing has changed. He talks like the deal is still on-going despite the fact he has no leverage on me anymore. I'm confused about his behavior and inform my council immediately about King Myenas's irrational scheming.

"Do you think he's banking on you not knowing about Lydia to still get what he wants?" Emory suggests. "You give him what he asks for, and he can claim that Lydia unexpectedly 'died' before she can be returned?"

Rainer lets out a deep sigh. "He's obviously trying to con you, Kane."

I look over their faces. Willow doesn't seem to disagree with their theory, and I have to admit it makes sense. I already know King Myenas is enough of a greedy snake to try and change deals on me at the last minute. This whole mess has been extended because he refused to take the damn Firebird in exchange for Lydia.

I shake my head. "I'm not letting him do this to me again."

345

"You'd need to get him to admit that Lydia is dead or that someone stole her out of the castle. His guards did see us making a run for it, after all. I don't know if they are aware we had Lydia with us. They could've lied to him about the whole incident to save their asses." Rainer shakes his head, and I can tell the entire ordeal was stressful for him. I'm glad he's home.

"He definitely needs to confess. Otherwise, he can say you're the one that's trying to get out of the deal," Willow points out. "We already know he has no problem going to war with us."

"He supported King Peter's crusade, but King Myenas mostly stayed out of the battle," Rainer reminds us. "I think he's less scary than he's making himself out to be. He'd probably want to avoid an actual war he has to fund on his own. Too much money and resources wasted if he loses."

"Is that why he's trying so hard to shake you down?" Emory asks. "He lost too many resources for no return during the previous war?"

"Wars are expensive," I agree. "Even if you're only supporting it with funds, it can burn a hole through your pocket that can take years, even decades, to recover from."

I would know how expensive war is. The last war with Scarlett Thunder is still hurting my pocketbook. I'm not in the red, but I'm not building another castle any time soon. If I can help it, I'd like to avoid any wars, or even short-lived battles, for the next century to give the royal coffers time to fully recuperate.

Willow tsks. "He doesn't know that you know about Lydia's death, but you can't tell him how you know because that would reveal our part in rescuing her. You're stuck in a game of chicken with him."

I groan, leaning back in my chair. "I did that four years ago with King Peter. I don't want a repeat."

The war with Scarlett Thunder had mostly been a game of posturing. King Peter threatened to attack my kingdom if I didn't give him what he wanted. I refused to give him back his son if he attacked my kingdom. Neither of us relented for months, and I might've gone gray from stress if I wasn't a vampire.

Emory reaches over and takes my hand. "You need to be more

decisive. Let him know he can't bully you into giving him what he wants."

At this point, I have to struggle not to directly tell King Myenas that he can fuck himself for all I care, but I know that won't go down well. Even if I get King Myenas to back off, it doesn't fix the root of this whole mess. His underhanded business with the Blood Takers ruins lives. It benefits him with money and power that allows him to act the way he does.

"I need to end the business with the feeders. It's how he has allies. He provides them a steady blood supply without going through the trouble with the shifter packs. If I can cut off his blood supply, his allies will not stick around," I explain.

If there is anything I know about the vampire royals after all my years of existence it's that most of them are self-serving at heart. I don't delude myself to think any of them has any genuine friendship with King Myenas. They couldn't possibly actually like him, not with the way he acts. It's simply easier to be his 'friend' than to be his enemy.

"You want to end the trafficking of feeders?" Emory asks, her emerald eyes bright with hope.

"I want to end it. No more people being kidnapped and sold off with no chance of escape." I nod in agreement.

"Not that I want to play devil's advocate here, but if you cut off the blood supply, won't the other royals just start trafficking to get their own feeders?" Rainer raises his hands in surrender. "I don't like it either, but that's the way it was back in the day."

"You cut off the head of this monster, and two more will grow in its place," Willow agrees. "You need to find a better alternative for the blood supply. If you get rid of King Myenas, someone else will replace him."

I know they're right. Creating a power vacuum could lead to more problems down the road. I have no doubt somebody like King Matthias would jump at the chance to replace King Myenas in the feeder trafficking. All it would take is one royal with enough greed and ambition.

"What do you suggest I do?" I ask. "I can't let King Myenas continue on, and I can't risk someone else rising up to build another empire on the ashes of his."

Rainer looks thoughtful. His pale blue eyes look lost in thought. I give him a look and inquire, "What are you thinking?"

"Why don't you replace him then?"

I scoff. "Me? Replace King Myenas in his feeder trafficking?"

"It wouldn't be the same operation. You already tried this with providing better care for the feeders in Crimson Peak. Why not extend this to other kingdoms? You could set up a better deal with the Alphas to provide feeders with a more humane system."

"There would be no more kidnapped feeders forced into a living hell before dying," Willow adds. "If there's enough blood to go around, feeders would be let go faster with a better quality of life."

I look at Emory, trying to see what she thinks of this mad idea. It sounds like a pipe dream, something a naïve monarch would think of and never be able to accomplish. It has taken time to create a system of more humane treatment of feeders in my own kingdom. We no longer take feeders for the rest of their lives. Rather, they enjoy much shorter stays as feeders in the castle as they're freed and replaced with new feeders at regular intervals. People repay their debts and get to move on.

"What do you think?" I ask her. "If you think this is a terrible idea, I'll drop it immediately. These will be your people affected the most."

Emory's emerald gaze stares into mine, trusting and steady. "My people are already affected. They're taken by force on the roads and never seen again. A more humane system will benefit us all. And there's no one else I can trust to be in charge of that changed system than you."

I look around, taking in their expressions. Not one of them looks like they doubt that I wouldn't be able to do this. It's humbling to have people's absolute faith in me. The pipe dream doesn't sound so unreachable anymore.

"If we do this, we'll be changing everything," I tell them. "We'll need to get all the Alphas and vampire royals on board, something that's never been done before. We'll be changing the world as we know it."

Emory smiles. "We better get started then."

* * *

Lex

Now that Lydia Nightstone is back with her pack, I'm going to head back to Scarlett Thunder. Cole and I have been away for too long, and I have a lot of work to tackle. I'm not looking forward to the paperwork, but that's part of running a kingdom. There's always an endless amount of paperwork.

Kane is in the middle of a meeting, so I wait till he's available to talk to say my goodbyes. Cole is feeling a little homesick, despite how he's been enjoying getting to play with children his own age. He and his cousin Michael get along really well. It's heartwarming to see the two boys playing together, not burdened by petty things like sibling rivalry and jealousy.

My son will never know what it's like to be the second son, being brought up as the spare to a more important older brother. It has defined who I am for so long that I tend to forget it doesn't fit me anymore like a coat that's too small. The reality of stepping up and becoming a ruler is a lot less fun in reality and more mind-numbing work than anything else.

I'm in the gardens watching the children play together, running through trees and pretending they're knights off on a grand adventure, when Ivy finds me. We haven't spoken since I asked her about the love potion again. I know she's been busy with the sleeping potion antidote. After I provided her with the items on the list of ingredients for the love potion, she hasn't given me any updates, and I've left her to do her thing.

"Hi," she greets me.

"Hi." I give her a friendly smile. "How have you been?"

She gives me a look, raising her stubborn eyebrows at me. "Not to be rude, but could we skip the small talk and get straight to business?"

I bite back an amused smile. "By all means."

Ivy reaches into the pocket of her robe and pulls out a glass vial. Inside of it is a light pink liquid. She offers it to me. I stare at it warily.

"Is that the…?"

She nods. "It's the love potion."

I take it from her carefully, terrified to drop the glass vial and break it. I hold it up in the moonlight to get a better view of the potion. The liquid inside is opaque and shimmers under the light. It almost looks like the potion is glowing.

"Will it work?" I ask. "How quickly does it take effect?"

"From what I heard, it should take effect almost immediately. The effects of it should last up to a few months. You'd have to keep retaking the potion."

"It wears off?"

Ivy nods. "There's no love potion that lasts forever. If you want the potion to wear off faster, unfortunately there's no antidote for it. You'd just have to wait it out."

"Are there side effects to taking the potion long term?"

"The potion was originally intended for human consumption. I don't really know how vampire physiology will be affected by it. I also have to warn you that I don't know how effective the potion will be for you in that regard and whether that'll affect how long the potion lasts in your system."

I give her an amused look. "I'm your vampire guinea pig?"

"I don't think a vampire has taken a love potion before. You might be the first."

I snort and look at the potion again. "If it doesn't work, will you make me a different batch?"

"Of course. I'll need a fresh supply of ingredients, but I can try again."

"I'd pay you for your time."

She shrugs, looking away. "Are you sure about this? I know that love can be messy, and you don't always get to choose who you fall in love with, but this won't be the same as real love. It's just a pale imitation of the real thing."

"I'd rather have a pale imitation of my own choosing than noth-ing," I explain.

"I've had nothing for almost four years." I pocket the love potion, conscious of its weight against my thigh. "Thank you for this, Ivy. I really appreciate it."

She nods and replies, "You're welcome."

I leave without looking back, ignoring the conflicted look on Ivy's face.

4 6

BEST LAID PLANS

Kane

As Lex is leaving to go back to Scarlett Thunder, I tell him about the plan to end King Myenas's feeder trafficking operation by replacing it with my own more humane system. My brother looks at me like I've lost my mind. Saying it out loud to another person makes me realize how unhinged the plan really is. I expect Lex to tell me this is a bad idea, and I should come up with a new plan.

Instead, my brother bursts into laughter. I can only stare at him until he stops laughing. Lex's blue eyes are bright with amusement. When I don't smile back at him, he asks, "You're serious?"

"No, Lex. I just had to tell you a joke before you left," I reply sarcastically, rolling my eyes. "Of course, I'm being serious. I know it sounds insane, but Rainer, Emory, and Willow all agree that it's the best way to stop King Myenas for good. You may think it's a bad idea-"

"Hang on," Lex cuts in. "I never said it was a bad idea. Yes, it's insane, but it's not a bad idea."

"You think it's a good idea?"

"I think it might be good enough to work."

"Then why did you laugh?"

"I was more amused about the idea that you're the one that's going to do this. I would have expected something like this from anyone else but you."

I raise both my eyebrows in disbelief. "Why do you think I wouldn't do something like this?"

"It's a big risk, and you're not the kind of person that usually takes big swings like this. You like to control every aspect of something and try to hedge your bets to make sure you win."

"That's not true. I had no idea if I would win against King Peter during the war."

"You tried almost everything to prevent that war from happening. You didn't immediately rush toward the battlefield the first chance you got." Lex frowns. "Actually, now that I think about it, having power over all the other kingdoms by controlling the bloody supply is something you'd want so you can boss everyone around."

I glare at him, annoyed at his description of me but also knowing deep down he's sort of right. I do enjoy being able to have some modicum of power over the same royals who have always looked down on my wife for not being a vampire. That petty part of me I try to ignore all the time relishes the idea of being able to stick it to the snobs. And I also know that they need someone to keep them in check. Otherwise, their greed and hunger for power turns them into monsters like King Myenas.

"Are you going to help me or not?" I ask him. "If you're going to be an asshole and detract me from getting this off the ground, I can go to Uncle Cyrus instead."

Lex scoffs. "Calm down, brother. I was just messing with you. You know I'll always have your back."

"Even if you think I'm a control freak who wants to boss everyone around?"

"If anyone should be the boss of everyone, it might as well be you," Lex replies. "You have Emory and Rainer to make sure the power doesn't get to your head. And if they fail, we'll have you executed and put your son on the throne."

I stare him down. "You're joking again?"

He shakes his head, grinning. "It's like you don't know me at all."

"Lex…"

Sensing I'm getting sick of his behavior, Lex drops the teasing and says, "I think this plan can work, but you'll need to do it the right way. You know how stubborn the other royals can be. This will be the most important pitch of your life."

"I know that," I tell him. "Which is why I need everyone–you, Emory, Rainer, and Willow–helping me do this. I can't do this alone."

There was a time when asking for help was a difficult feat for me. I was terrified to let anyone in. I saw that vulnerability as a sign of weakness. My marriage to Emory changed all that.

Emory being a shifter means she sees the world differently. The shifters believe in the power of teamwork and taking care of each other. The lone wolf dies, but the pack survives. I've seen the merit of this thinking in their society.

Vampires can be self-centered and only interested in their own gain and ambition. For centuries, I followed this way of life until it nearly cost me my kingdom. I couldn't have won the war with Scarlett Thunder by myself. I needed the help of my friends and allies to get me through the battle. I needed the woman I loved by my side to be my rock when I was at my weakest.

The war changed all of us in different ways. My brother grew up and became his own man. Our relationship became stronger. The jealousy that kept us apart for our entire lives dissipated, and only our familial love and loyalty remained.

I no longer have to wonder if Lex is secretly vying to usurp me and take my throne. Even if he isn't the king of Scarlett Thunder, Lex doesn't crave power. He leads only because of duty and necessity. My brother would choose peace over power if given the choice.

This is why I know I can trust him with the plan. He won't tell a soul, and he can help me when I need him the most.

"All right," Lex says. "What do you need me to do?"

* * *

Lex

I'm not looking forward to having guests again after Cole's birthday party. It hasn't been that long, and the expense troubles me. The royal coffers are still low on funds, but I couldn't refuse my brother when he asked me if I could host the meeting between the vampire monarchs. I'm surprised Kane didn't choose Sardonia instead, but he explained he didn't want any of the royals to try and wiggle out of attending because they didn't want to make the trip up the mountain.

Scarlett Thunder being on flat land gives less excuses to escape. This time of the year is when we have the best weather, so the excuse of not wanting to travel through a storm is also out. Kane is doing everything he can to make sure all the royals attend this meeting. He's provided funds for the blood and gold this event will cost, but I know the castle servants are not happy that they have so little time to prepare.

After a few days of preparations, the royals are set to arrive in Scarlett Thunder. I'm going over the blood supply with the servants when Opal stomps down the hallway. She's in her pink silk robe, and her hair is still messy from sleep. The servants scurry off to get out of her way.

"Lex!" she shrieks, making me wince. "Why didn't you tell me we were having guests?"

"I tried to tell you, Opal. You refused to join me for dinner, so I could explain everything to you."

"You didn't send a note!"

"I sent you several notes. The servants told me you threw them into the fireplace before even reading the letters. Why did you do that?"

"I did that because you took our son on a vacation and left me behind! Me! His own mother!"

"I thought giving us space would be good for us so we're not arguing all over the castle."

"You just wanted to escape being around me!" She pokes me in the chest. "I bet you were fucking every whore you came across in Cerise Point!"

"Believe it or not, Opal, I don't sleep with everything that moves." After a short pause, I amend, "At least not anymore."

She scoffs. "Why would I believe you? It's not like you have any reason to stay loyal to me. You don't love me. You don't even like me."

The mention of love reminds me of the potion I have in my pocket. I've kept it close since Ivy handed it to me. This is the first time I've seen Opal in person since I arrived back in Scarlett Thunder. This would be the ideal time to drink the potion so I can make sure I fall in love with her and not anyone else.

I reach for the potion in my pocket and freeze when my fingers touch the narrow neck of the glass vial. Opal stands in front of me, scowling and pretty like a rumpled flower. She looks like she's just rolled out of bed with a lover. She probably has done just that, spending her night with another man.

Opal accuses me of not loving her, but she doesn't love me either. I can picture a dismal future of me hopelessly obsessed with her because of the love potion, and all the while, she never returns my affections. She can go on hopping into the beds of other men while I suffer endlessly. The hope of the love potion feels naïve and foolish, the futile ideas of a romantic idiot.

"What?" Opal demands. "Why are you looking at me like that?"

Opal is a spoiled brat. Even if I loved her with my entire being, potion or not, it would never be enough for her. She chases what feels good for her and doesn't have regard for anyone else. I've spent years doing the same thing until I no longer have the choice to be that selfish because of our child.

"Lex!" She stomps her feet, on the verge of a tantrum. "Stop daydreaming! I'm talking to you!"

I close my eyes, realizing I've wasted my time with this love potion idea. I've wasted Ivy's time. A magically-induced love for my wife wouldn't change our marriage. It would only be creating a different kind of prison for me.

"Opal," I say, "the royals will be here soon, and your hair is a mess. You should get dressed before anyone sees you like this."

I open my eyes as Opal runs her fingers through her messy black hair. She lets out a panicked shriek and runs off. "I don't have enough time to get ready! You're such an asshole, Lex!"

When Opal is out of sight, I give myself a few seconds to mourn the hope of a happy marriage before I have to face all the vampire royals. They can smell blood in the water better than sharks. I have to hide away all my sorrows in a lead box inside of me and lock it shut. Too much is at stake here to let my own personal problems get in the way.

Kane is the first to arrive. Rainer is by his side. I watch from a window as a servant leads them from the courtyard and into the castle. I step outside my office and walk down the hallway to greet them.

The two of them stand in the foyer as I make my way down the staircase. I give them my most convincing smile. As far as they know, nothing is amiss. The servants might whisper about my latest spat with my wife, but that's nothing new.

"Brother," I say. "Rainer."

Kane nods, his expression grim but determined. "Are we ready for this?"

"As ready as we'll ever be."

Rainer shrugs, looking the most relaxed out of all of us. We've always been similar in how we hide any negative emotion. We smile and pretend like everything's going well. He'd hate it if I ever pointed that out to him.

"Let's change the world," Rainer says. "Again."

47

COUP D'ÉTAT

Kane

I don't know how much King Myenas is looking into Lydia's death. I know people have to be talking about seeing Lex flee Carmine Falls with a witch who throws fireballs at guards. Having the meeting with all the vampire monarchs at Scarlett Thunder is a way to deflect that this whole thing isn't my idea. After what happened in Burgundy Bay, I'd rather be safe than sorry.

Lex has no issues with looking suspicious. My brother has the ability to smile at his enemies and pretend to be blissfully ignorant. I couldn't look so carefree even if I wanted to. I carry my burdens on my shoulders at all times like an old coat.

While I've managed to repair my relationships with most of the vampire royals since the war, there are some I still hold no love for. Even for the sake of diplomacy, I can't fake caring for certain individuals. Emory teases me that I'm becoming a grumpy old man, but I can't help myself. The older I get, the less of people's shit I'm willing to tolerate.

How Queen Olga manages to keep so serene and unbothered with all these fools I don't know.

Queen Olga is one of the earliest to arrive. She's always punctual and thinks tardiness is one of the worst sins. Being 'fashionably late' is just plain rude from her perspective. She's wearing a white fur coat and practically glides into Castle Blackmoor.

I smile and take her hand to give it a kiss. "Queen Olga, I'm honored you could come at such short notice."

She gives me a fond smile. "You did say it was for an important business venture. I trust this is something more than a gold mine?"

"It'll be worth more than gold to us." I offer her my arm to take, and she loops her arm through mine. "We're still waiting for the others to arrive. In the meantime, you can tell me about your great-grandchildren. How are they?"

Queen Olga and I talk in the meeting room, sipping on goblets filled with blood as she tells me about her family. I leave Lex and Rainer to greet the royals that follow. They are each brought to the meeting room. King Matthias is one of the last to arrive, and I avoid looking at him. Lex seats him on the far side of the table, the furthest away from me.

Once the vampire royals have all arrived, I stand from the head of the table. "Thank you all for coming. I appreciate your time on such short notice." The curious stares from the royals have me inwardly taking a deep breath to steel my nerves. "The reason I've gathered you all here is to address the situation with the feeders. I know how difficult it is to have a steady blood supply let alone having a *quality* blood supply. I am here to provide you with a solution to this ongoing issue."

The royals whisper amongst each other. King Matthias looks shocked, and he turns to Lex. He asks him what's going on, and my brother shrugs. I raise my hands to placate the room and regain their attention.

"Please listen to what I have to say. For centuries, we have taken our blood supply by force by having feeders sell themselves or their loved ones to earn money or simply to pay off their debts. No one comes to us by choice, only through coercion. And sometimes they are not given a choice at all and are just taken on the road to never be seen again."

"What are you getting at, Kane?" King Matthias demands. "Did you gather all of us here just to talk about the plights of feeders?"

I look away from him and focus on the other monarchs. "I know most of you don't care for the feeders. You think them beneath you just because they're not vampires. And I may not be able to change your mind today about that, but here is a question I have for all of you–how expensive and difficult is it to get your feeders from one supplier?"

They whisper amongst each other again.

"I know that the majority of you are supplied feeders by Carmine Falls's Blood Takers. I am not shaming you for that as I know having a steady blood supply can be really difficult these days," I continue. "Wolf shifters are currently experiencing record low birth rates, and humans are dying from famine and diseases. Who can blame you for taking the easiest route toward supplying you with feeders?"

I pick up my goblet still half-full with blood and look at the red liquid. "Unlike the humans and the shifters, our kind needs this to survive. Every drop of it counts for us even if the blood quality isn't the best. Feeders living in squalor in dungeons just waiting to die causes poor quality blood, but we'll take what we can get, won't we?"

I carefully set the goblet down. "What if I were able to provide you with more blood? *Better* blood? I can create a new system where you get more feeders sent to your kingdoms to stay for shorter intervals. *Fresher* blood from healthy feeders."

"What do you mean by shorter intervals?" King Basil asks.

They all look intrigued. I have their attention.

"Feeders don't stay until they die. They stay a week and give you as much blood as their bodies allow in order for them to stay healthy and replenish their systems. They leave, and a new batch of feeders come to give more blood. This system ensures we can get more feeders volunteering to give blood, and there will be less bodies to be disposed of."

King Matthias scoffs. "That will never work. You're trying to create better conditions for feeders, but the shifters will never agree to this. We need to be more forceful with the werewolves again and demand they give us feeders."

"This will land us in wars with the shifter packs," I point out. "And that will drain your coffers dry quickly. Even if you win the war, it takes years for finances to recover. Right, Lex?"

My brother nods, looking exhausted. "Kane is right. Scarlett Thunder is still in debt after the last war. My advice is to avoid battle at all costs. It's just not worth it to be a warlord in this economy anymore."

"We'll take over the wolves' territories and take their resources then!" King Matthias argues. "Then we'll take their people and have all the blood we want!"

I reply sarcastically, "Good luck with that, Matthias. I'm sure you'll be able to fight multiple wars with the packs and succeed."

Queen Olga, who has been silent as she listened to my proposal, asks, "How are you going to get this steady supply of feeders? Are you going to have your own version of the Blood Takers?"

"Definitely not," I answer. "My wife, Alpha Emory of the Moonraker Pack, is negotiating a deal with the other packs to supply us with the blood donors."

"Are you competing with King Myenas or trying to replace him?"

"Well, everyone on his client list is in this room." I look over all their intrigued and slightly disbelieving faces. King Matthias looks furious. "That will depend on all of you whether you want to continue doing business with him or allow me to do a better job."

* * *

RAINER

"You son of a bitch, you did it," I say, still reeling with how Kane has managed to convince the vampire monarchs to agree to his insane plan.

"Hey. That's my mother you're talking about." Kane is smiling so I know he doesn't really take offense. "I'm surprised I got them to agree, too. I thought I could get maybe half of them to sign on, but I managed to get most of them onboard."

"I don't think those old bats have ever agreed on anything in centuries."

The vampire royals have all left to return to their kingdoms. Kane, Lex, and I are in Lex's office celebrating over our victory. King Matthias and a few of his friends have not officially agreed to Kane's new blood donor business, but they haven't rejected the idea. I'm guessing they're hedging their bets to see which side will be more profitable for them. They have no real loyalty to King Myenas, and they only want to follow where the blood and gold are going.

"Well, if the choice is between you and King Myenas, anyone with common sense would pick you," Lex says. "You're offering blood at a lower rate with a faster delivery time. No more having to sneak feeders through kingdoms."

"Does anyone like King Myenas?" I ask. "Who truly likes that man? His own people in his castle don't care for him. They are afraid of him, but no one loves him."

Lex snorts. "I heard his kids don't even like him. And his wife doesn't live in the castle. She stays in a different castle altogether."

"I never saw his wife around Castle Pestera, so I believe that." I nod.

Kane looks relieved. He's leaning back against the couch and has his eyes closed as if he's about to fall asleep. "King Myenas is going to be pissed when he finds out I sabotaged his business."

"Good," I say. "He deserves a little bit of stress after the terror he put Lydia and her family through."

"And Colt. Emory's brother was falling apart while his mate was gone. Poor kid," Kane adds.

"This is why I can't feel sorry for King Myenas. He's done terrible things, and he doesn't deserve my sympathy." Just thinking about that asshole makes me want to punch something.

Lex nods. "That I can agree with. There's nothing behind those eyes. Not a soul. Just empty."

"We're agreeing on something?" I quip. "Is the world going to end?"

"Stop being an asshole and don't ruin the moment, Rainer." Lex shakes his head at me.

I'm about to make a joke when the door opens with a bang. The door slams into a wall as Opal enters the room like a hurricane. She's dressed in some elaborate tulle dress with many layers. I haven't seen her since we've arrived, and Lex hasn't mentioned where his wife has been all this time.

I don't pry into Lex's personal life, but what I've heard through the rumor mill is that he and Opal aren't happily married. Lex hasn't complained publicly, but Opal's chronic infidelity isn't a secret. It's not a surprise, given her past behavior. She has always been remarkably spoiled and selfish.

When she sees us sitting on the couch together, her face transforms into an ugly sneer. I'm reminded of her deceased brother, Jacob. Their expressions are very similar.

"What is he doing here, Lex?" she shrieks. "You know what they did to my father!"

Lex looks exasperated and stands up, his hands raised as if he's trying to placate a wild animal. "This is a private meeting, Opal. I need you to leave and come back later if you want something--"

Opal grabs a vase and throws it at us. We all dodge out of the way, and the vase hits the wall with a loud crack. Porcelain shards fall to the carpeted floor. She isn't deterred and grabs the sword hanging on the wall as decoration.

She pulls it out of the scabbard. It looks really sharp despite supposedly only being for decoration. Her blue eyes are burning with hatred. Lex walks toward her slowly.

"Put the sword down, Opal," he says, calmly. "We can talk about this."

"No more talking!" she retorts. "The three of you killed my father! He's dead because of all of you! I'm going to make you pay!"

With the sword raised in her hands, Opal rushes toward Kane.

48

OFTEN GO AWRY

Emory

With the Nightstones all refusing to leave Nightfall until Lydia is woken up from her magically-induced coma, I decide to hold the meeting with all the Alphas at Alpha Gerald's home. His home is a fortress, and he has the room to accommodate all the Alphas and their entourages. I'll also get to have Colt with me for support during one of the most important meetings of my life. And despite not being on my home turf, I know I have the Nightstones on my side as allies.

Alpha Gerald is one of the most important allies I currently have. He's part of the older generation of Alphas who have managed to keep their packs alive and thriving through the decades. With wisdom and experience, I've come to appreciate him over my time as an Alpha. Gerald is the kind of Alpha I hope to become someday. He's well-respected amongst our peers, and they will listen to his opinion.

I'm less nervous when the Alphas arrive at Nightfall, and we all gather in the large dining room in the house. Alpha Gerald sits at the head of the table, and I sit across from him on the other end. I'm reminded of the first meeting I had with the Alphas years ago when I'd been new to the job. I'd been nervous and scared they wouldn't accept me after the damage my father had done during his time as Alpha.

Gerald had been the most skeptical, but now things have turned around. It's his encouraging gaze that bolsters me to stand up and begin the meeting.

"Thank you all for being here," I say. "I know it's been some time since we were all gathered together like this."

"Are you asking us to go to war again with you, Emory?" Alpha Nigel asks teasingly. "I hope not. The last one wasn't that long ago."

I smile as the Alphas chuckle around us. "Not quite. I'm here to ask something for all of you. I know it's going to be a big ask, but it is something that can help all of us in the long run."

"Now I'm really worried," Alpha Bastille remarks. "Does this have something to do with the vampires again?"

"Yes." I pause and look over their faces, worry and doubt creeping in. "It's about the situation with the feeders."

Alphas Silas cuts in, "We heard about what happened to your granddaughter, Gerald."

Silas's wife, Mary Claire adds, "We're sorry to hear about Lydia. She's always been such a sweet girl."

Alpha Gerald nods graciously. "There is no need to worry. We were able to rescue Lydia from the Blood Takers with the help of Alpha Emory and her husband."

"You were able to get her back?" Alpha Bastille questions. "I've never heard of anyone being able to come back once the Blood Takers have taken them. How did you manage it?"

"It wasn't easy. Dealing with King Myenas has been increasingly difficult," I answer. "It's why I've gathered you all here today. The trafficking of our people and of humans has to end. King Myenas has been taking people by force and sending them to certain death for far longer than any of us would like to admit."

There's silence as they're taking in my words, truly listening to what I have to say.

"We were able to save Lydia, but she is only one person. There have been thousands that we weren't able to save," I continue. "We must do something to end this system. Even the ones that volunteer as feeders are in living hell before they die in inhumane conditions, unable to even earn a chance at freedom."

Nigel's wife, Angela, leans forward and asks, "If you're not asking us to go to war, then what are you asking of us?"

"We need a new system for the feeders to ensure they are treated better. No more being drained dry with no chance of escaping. King Kane has a plan to ensure feeders stay for shorter times in vampire kingdoms before they are sent home to recover. They'll be provided better housing conditions while they stay in the castles."

"So, you don't want to abolish having feeders at all?" Alpha Nigel asks. "You only want to improve their situation?"

"There's no getting around that the vampires will always need blood. And it's when they're desperate for it that they allow monsters like King Myenas to do what he wants in exchange for it. There will always be someone providing blood, but what we can do is make sure we have control of how this blood is taken and distributed."

Alpha Silas frowns. "Who will be the provider then?"

"King Kane will be the new provider while one of us will be in charge on our end to make sure he is being fair and honest," I reply. "And because I'm aware how I may be biased toward him as he is my husband, the liaison can't be me. You will all have to vote on who it should be."

The Alphas whisper amongst each other. I take my seat and meet Alpha Gerald's gaze. He looks proud, and it's his lack of doubt that gets me to relax. If he thinks there's nothing to fear, then I'm going to believe him.

Alpha Gerald isn't wrong. The Alphas agree to the new system with the feeders. They have their own caveats, such as paying the feeders more and price cuts for trading with vampire kingdoms. When it comes to choosing the shifter liaison, they first try to appoint Alpha Gerald who immediately declines it.

"I have enough on my plate managing my pack," he says. "And I just got my granddaughter back. I don't have the same energy as I did as a young man. Pick someone else."

The liaison position goes to Alpha Bastille of the Silvercrest Pack. He's younger than Alpha Gerald, closer to my late father's age. From all accounts, Alpha Bastille is a good choice. He's known to be honorable and strong-willed.

Alpha Gerald has whiskey brought in, and we all have a glass at his insistence. "We should celebrate. We're creating a better world and a better future for the next generation."

He clinks his glass against mine, and I take a sip. The whiskey smells awful and almost makes me gag. I put my glass down on the table and just watch as everyone else drinks. This has all gone so much better than I expected.

* * *

Lex

Rainer moves quickly, shielding Kane with his body. The sword slices into the dark fabric of his shirt and leaves a large cut on his shoulder. He hisses from the pain and pushes Opal away with his other arm, nearly knocking her off her feet. Blood drips down from the sword, onto the carpet.

Opal's blue eyes are wild. She raises the sword again and swings at Rainer. He narrowly avoids the blade hitting his neck. Ducking, he grabs Opal by the abdomen and knocks her to the ground. The sword falls to the carpet, and Opal gets on her hands and knees to try and reach the weapon.

I've been watching all of this occur like a deer in highlights, stunned that this is actually happening.

Rainer looks at me as he tries to keep my wife from getting the sword again. "A little help, Lex?"

I run to them and grab Opal by the hips, forcing her to fall forward on her face. She lets out an angry yelp muffled by the carpet. I stand over her, basically keeping her down as Rainer crawls over to the sword and grabs it. Opal thrashes like a wild animal, trying to escape my grip.

"What is going on with your wife?" Kane asks, having moved away from the couch.

"I don't know!" I reply. "She wasn't like this earlier!"

Opal manages to roll on her back, kicking at me and hitting me in the groin. I go down, the pain bringing me to my knees. She's on her feet before I can even react, trying to grab the sword from Rainer. He pushes her away, and she hits the wall.

Rainer pushes Kane toward the door. "You have to get out of here."

"There's no fucking way I'm leaving until this is over," Kane insists. "Lex, call for the castle guards?"

"We'll be fine." Rainer practically shoves Kane toward the open doorway. "Just go!"

Kane doesn't leave the room, but he isn't moving either. I slowly get up, my groin still aching. I look to where Opal is passed out. There's blood on the wall that has me worrying about a head injury.

Even though I'm exasperated with her, I go to my wife to check for injuries. I shake her, trying to get her to wake up. If she's concussed, she shouldn't be asleep. I touch her hair, and there's wetness at the back of her head. My fingers are coated in bright red blood.

"She's bleeding," I tell Rainer. "We have to get her to the hospital wing."

I move to pick her up. I'm in such a rush to help her, I don't notice until it's too late, and she stabs a broken piece of ceramic from the vase into where my neck meets my shoulder. The sharp pain has me grasping at my neck. Blood quickly runs down my collarbone and chest. I instinctively drop her on the ground.

"Opal, what the fuck did you do?" Rainer yells.

Opal gets to her feet, and she runs toward Rainer. With the sword in his hand, he reacts instinctively and pierces her through the chest with it. Right through her heart. She goes still and looks down at the silver sword embedded into her chest before collapsing to the ground.

I pull the vase shard out of my neck and drop it to the ground. More blood gushes out from the wound. I grasp at it uselessly, applying pressure to try and stop the blood from escaping my body. Kane rushes over and tries to help, but I motion for him to stay back. Opal is lying on her side, her expression blank.

She's dead. My wife is dead.

I don't know how to feel. I know I should be devastated, but the shock numbs everything.

"We have to get you to the hospital wing," Rainer advises. "Immediately"

He puts my arm around his neck so he can support my weight. Kane grabs the other side, and they push us forward toward the door. I keep looking down to where Opal is lying. Her blood stains the carpet a dark red.

"I'm sorry about Opal," Rainer says. "I never liked her, but I know she was your wife."

The wound makes it hard for me to talk. I might choke on my own blood if I try. What would I even say to Rainer? You don't need to be sorry? We never loved each other anyway?

All of it sounds cruel and harsh. Even if it's true that there has never been any love between Opal and me, that doesn't mean she's nothing to me. She's the mother of my child, and she has given me the best thing that's ever happened to me–Cole.

Kane grows more concerned when he turns to look at my pale face. "Fuck. This wasn't supposed to happen today!"

The blood loss is making it hard to think. I'm getting weaker on the way to the hospital wing. They refuses to let me give up. Kane is basically carrying me by the time we reach our destination.

The doctor and the nurses are in a flurry when we enter the hospital wing. Kane drops me down onto a hospital bed.

"Don't let him die," he tells the doctor. "His son already lost one parent today."

Cole. My son is in his room, probably playing with his nanny. He's completely unaware he just lost his mother. He's so young.

Will he even remember Opal? If I die today, will he remember me years from now when he's an adult? Or will we be just vague ideas of what his parents were like?

"Don't die, Lex," a voice says. It could have been Kane or the doctor. It might have even been Rainer.

The world goes black, and my thoughts dissipate.

49

THE LAST DUEL

WILLOW

I never like it when Rainer comes home injured. The gashes Opal left on him have healed by the time I see him, so there's no reason to drag him to the clinic to get checked over by Dr. Martin. He tells me that Lex is in worse shape and is being treated by the doctor at Scarlett Thunder. Opal is in the worst condition of all—since she's dead.

"She's dead?" I look at him in disbelief. "How?"

"I ran a silver sword through her heart. I had to stop her. She already injured Lex and would probably go after Kane next. She couldn't be reasoned with."

"Does Kane know?"

"He was there. Since Lex is unconscious, he had to get Lex's second to take over running Castle Blackmoor in the meantime."

I've personally never cared for Princess Opaline. She and her brother murdered the librarian who ran the place right before me. When Lex had to marry her for political purposes, I didn't say anything as it wasn't my business, but I also felt bad for him. Opal always proved herself to be a selfish, and at times, destructive bitch.

I don't think anyone could be truly happy being married to her. I still feel some sympathy for her son who has to grow up without a mother now. Having a child of my own, I can't imagine leaving Bryony to grow up without me. I've seen that sweet little boy playing with Bryony and Mikey in Cerise Port, and he doesn't deserve this.

"Her son is the same age as Bryony," I say. "He's so young. Too young to not have a mother anymore."

Rainer sighs. "Opal made her choices. After she tried to kill Kane, this was never going to end well for her."

"I know. I don't feel pity for her. I pity her child."

"I pity that child too." He looks around our suite and asks, "Speaking of children, where's Bryony?"

"Lola has been a dear and is helping babysit her for me. They're outside in the rose garden."

We make our way to the gardens and find Bryony and Mikey playing together. The maids are nearby watching them run around the trees. Lola is sitting by the gazebo, sketching something on a pad. Her blonde hair looks shorter since I've last seen it.

"Hey, Lola," Rainer greets her. "How have you been?"

Lola looks up from her sketch pad and answers, "I've been bored. You all have been gone or ignoring me for weeks."

"Sorry, kid. We had a crisis on our hands, remember? Your brother's mate was kidnapped. I had to go deep undercover and infiltrate a castle in a cave."

Lola scoffs. "There are no castles in caves."

"How would you know?" Rainer challenges. "You didn't see this place. You could fall down a waterfall and die."

"You're making that up." Lola turns to me. "He's making stuff up."

I shake my head. "He's really not."

Rainer takes the seat beside Lola. "It wasn't all fun and games. Lydia got shot with an arrow and I had to patch her up. I had to help a bunch of people escape mercenaries. And then I had to escape in a car while a witch threw fireballs at the enemy."

"That all literally sounds like you had a lot of fun," Lola remarks.

He cocks his head to the side. "It's fun in hindsight, I guess."

I take a seat on Lola's other side, sandwiching her between us. "Seriously. How are you?"

She looks down, refusing to look either of us in the eye as she admits, "Having no one around was kind of lonely and made me miss all of you. Don't tell anyone, but I'm glad you're all back."

Rainer grins and pulls her into a hug. "I'm glad to be back, Lo."

She pushes him away like a grumpy cat. "Did you save Lydia?"

"Who do you take me for? Of course, I did."

"Good." She looks between us and asks, "Is it all over now? Are we back to normal?"

Rainer tsks. "Not quite over yet, but we're getting there."

"Emory left to go meet the Alphas and refused to bring me along. Is whatever she's doing there connected to all this?"

"I cannot confirm or deny that." When Lola rolls her gray eyes, Rainer grins and tells her, "Your sister and Kane are going to make things better for feeders. Emory is changing the world. You should be proud."

"I am proud of her," Lola replies. "But don't tell her that."

I bump my shoulder against hers. "Why not?"

"Because that's embarrassing."

"Speaking of embarrassing, is it true you're crushing on someone?" Rainer teases her. "Is he cute?"

Lola grimaces. "I had a crush, but I'm over it. He's way too old for me."

"Now you have to tell us who it was."

"Nope."

Lola gets up quickly. Sketchpad and pencil case in hand, she runs off before we can interrogate her more. Rainer moves closer to me and wraps an arm around me. I rest my head on his shoulder.

"Who do you think she had a crush on?" he asks.

"It was you."

"What? Really?"

"Women always know these things."

Rainer looks contemplative, mildly disturbed at the revelation that Lola previous had a crush on him. "She's like my niece."

"And you're too old for her." He pulls away to look at me like I've gravely insulted him. "You are ancient compared to Lola."

"Am I *ancient* compared to you?"

"No. You're just the right age," I tell him, kissing him softly. "You needed time to mature. To age like a fine wine."

Rainer doesn't rise to my teasing and is content to kiss me back. This is the best part—my husband coming home.

* * *

KANE

I expect the news of me sabotaging King Myenas's feeder trafficking operation to reach him quickly. His business partners being present at the meeting means they have to warn him that he's about to lose a fortune. The moment I arrive back at Castle Graystone, King Myenas is on the phone demanding to speak to me at once. I have to remind myself not to gloat even if I really want to.

"Myenas," I greet him casually. "To what do I owe the pleasure?"

"Cut the shit, Kane. I know what you're doing. You're going to ruin my business with the feeders over petty grievances?"

"You've been misinformed. I'm simply providing an alternate way for the other royals to get a supply of feeders."

"This is a hostile takeover, and you know it!" he exclaims. "This is my business! I've been running this before you were even born!"

"Times change, and you have to change with them. Your clients were not happy with the service you providing, and they're glad to take my business over yours."

"All of this over a werewolf bitch?"

"The deal was supposed to be simple. You give me back Lydia in exchange for the Firebird. You're the one that tried to extort me, so I found a better deal for myself."

"You're not getting her back. I will tear her apart before you get to see her again!"

"I heard she's already dead." There's a deafening silence on the other line. "And you were never going to inform me, right? You were going to continue to extort me in exchange for nothing, so no, I don't feel guilty for sabotaging your coffers."

"You won't get away with this! I'm coming for you!"

"With what funds?"

King Myenas lets out a series of the most vile swear words I've ever heard.

"Look, we can settle this with an expensive war you can't afford, or we can end this with a duel. Just the two of us. One-on-one."

"If you think I'd fall for such an obvious trick–"

"No tricks. Just a clean duel between us on neutral ground."

"Guns?"

"I thought you were more old school. Swords?"

"Fine," he says. "Where are we dueling?"

I can't believe he's agreed to this. There's no way he's actually going to be able to beat me. It would be nice to have him dead so I don't have to worry about him anymore. It's almost too good to be true.

Scarlett Thunder is the most ideal place for a duel. In the land where the Battle on the Red Field occurred feels right. I'm not sure if they'll bother documenting this duel. I dread to think what they'll even call it. I tell him, and he agrees to meet me there the next day.

Emory isn't home yet from her meeting with the Alphas. If she was, she'd try to talk me out of it, but I have no doubt I can beat that old bastard, as long as he doesn't cheat.

The last time I set foot on the field was with hundreds of men at my command. For this duel, I show up dressed in my armor with my sword at my hip. Emory arrived just in time to come along, even though I wish she hadn't, and our friends are here to bear witness. Willow asked Ivy to come in case I need to be healed from a bad injury.

King Myenas arrives a few minutes after us. He's in shiny black armor. His entourage of soldiers and courtiers are there to watch as well. His wife and children are nowhere to be found.

We stand across from each other. King Myenas looks determined and angry. His red eyes blaze with hatred. He sneers before putting on his helmet.

"Are you ready for this?" Emory asks, handing me my helmet. I nod to her, and she looks over at King Myenas. "Clean fight. No cheating or it's a forfeit."

"Muzzle your bitch, Kane."

I put my helmet on. "That is the last time you disrespect my wife."

"Or what?" He pulls out his sword from its scarab. "You're going to kill me."

"Is this to be a duel to the death?"

"I wouldn't want anything else."

Our audience makes sure to keep their distance. King Myenas and I stare each other down, swords drawn waiting for the other person to lunge first. King Myenas lets out a war cry and runs forward. I move to block him, but he's not aiming for me.

He's heading toward Emory. Her emerald eyes widen in shock, and I move instinctively. I block King Myenas with my body, knocking him to the muddy ground. Landing on his back, he throws a punch to my head.

My helmet takes most of the impact, but King Myenas is big and strong. I get a little lightheaded. I throw a punch down at him, and he dodges it by trying to push me off him. We slide in the mud, unable to get a grip on the earth. By the time we're on our feet, we're covered in mud.

King Myenas raises his sword and lunges at me. I parry it. He thrusts the sword, and I block it with mine. This continues for several minutes.

I knock him back to the ground. The fall knocks the wind out of him. His helmet has flown off, leaving his face exposed. I raise my sword, and he grips my hands to keep me from sinking the blade into his flesh through one of the creases in the armor. I bear down on the sword, using my strength to force the point of the blade closer to where his neck is exposed.

King Myenas is a strong man, but so am I. I'm younger but not new to battle. His red eyes are desperate as the sword lowers. I put more of my weight into the handle of the sword.

He grunts as he tries to keep the sword from moving closer. He knows the moment it's over. The blade digs into his neck. He grits his teeth from the pain.

The wound in his neck is bleeding profusely, and he begins to choke on his blood. "You are...not my...equal..."

"I'd never want to be like you," I declare. "And I'm keeping the Firebird."

His hands drop as I pull back the sword. He's unable to stop me as I raise the sword and slice his head off. His head rolls through the mud, his expression permanently shocked. He truly never thought he could lose to me.

That doesn't matter what King Myenas thinks anymore. He's dead. I've won. His reign of terror is over.

IN THE END

Lex

I don't know how long I've been asleep. I wake up in the hospital wing with a bandage wrapped around my neck. The memory of Opal stabbing me with a ceramic shard has me gingerly touching the bandage. It doesn't hurt anymore, but there is some stiffness.

I blink against the harsh fluorescent lighting in the hospital room. The sound of crinkling paper makes me look over to the floor where my son is drawing with crayons on paper. Ivy is seated on a chair nearby writing on a thick leather notebook. When I sit up, she looks over at me and closes the notebook.

"Hey," she says. "How are you feeling?"

"Like I got stabbed."

Cole abandons his crayons to run to the hospital bed. "Daddy!" He tries to climb up the bed, but it's too high for him, so I pull him up, ignoring my stiff muscles. He wraps his arms around my neck. "I missed you!"

I smile, hugging him back. Having my child in my arms gives me a sense of peace. His love for me is pure and unrelenting. I can face anything in the world because of him.

Cole's nanny, Sarah, is nearby. She looks apologetic as she tells me, "I'm really sorry, Your Grace. It's time for Cole's lessons."

Cole shakes his head, tightening his arms around me. "No! I want to stay with you, Daddy!"

I pull him back gently. "You can come see me later, Cole. You have to go to your lessons."

I would have been happy to have Cole with me and have him skip all of his lessons for the day, but there are things I want to talk about without having him overhearing. And I know Cole would never leave me and sleep in the hospital wing if I let him.

"Thank you, Sarah," I tell her. "Take care of him."

Cole pouts as Sarah picks him up. She gives me a smile and takes my son away who reluctantly doesn't fight her. Ivy has gotten up from her chair to pick up the half-finished doodles Cole made and the crayons off the ground. She leaves the bundle of paper and box of crayons on a nearby table.

"Not that I'm not happy to see you," I say. "But what are you doing here? I thought you were at Crimson Peak."

"I was, but Emory and Willow asked me to be there for the duel between King Myenas and King Kane just in case he got seriously injured and needed healing."

"Wait. What duel?"

"You've been asleep for two days," she answers. "The two vampire kings decided to settle their issues with each other in a one-on-one duel. Your brother won, and King Myenas is died."

"King Myenas is dead? Is Kane all right?"" I run a hand through my hair, trying to process this information. "Why do I always miss the epic battles?"

"Kane is fine. He has some minor injuries that will heal on their own. The duel was interesting to watch. It was very medieval."

"I'll have to take your word for it." I point to her. "You haven't explained why you're actually here."

She looks down at her feet, her long dark hair partially covering her face. "I wanted to see how you were doing with the love potion.

Ever since I gave it to you, I can't help but feel like I did the wrong thing. I know taking the potion is your choice…"

"Ivy-"

"And we're not really friends, but you deserve real love. Not something I brewed up in a cauldron. You deserve to fall madly in love with someone. I've never really been in love, but I know it's not something you can force."

"About that, I actually-"

"Then when I got here, I heard that your wife is dead, and you were injured and in the hospital wing. The doctor said you were mostly healed, and I didn't have to do anything except to sit around and watch you sleep. And that's why I'm here."

"Will you let me talk?"

Ivy finally looks up, her hazel eyes wide in realization. "I'm sorry. Was I just talking over you?"

"Kind of a lot, but I'm not really upset," I quip, giving her my best smile. When she smiles back, I add, "I'm glad you're here. It's nice to see you."

Ivy blushes. She looks beautiful even under the fluorescent lights. I know my initial attraction to her was physical, but in the little time I've spent with her, I've found I like the little quirks in her personality. I've seen how brave, loyal, and caring she can be. Those are all traits I admire in a person, and that tells me this could be a good starting point for developing something more substantial and real.

The kind of emotions you can't get in a bottle.

"I'm sorry about your wife," she says, her expression filled with sympathy. "Your son is too young to lose his mother."

"I know, but Cole is young, and I'm still here for him." Her hands reach forward as if to offer comfort, but she pulls back. I wish she didn't, but I know this thing between us is going to take time. Lots of baby steps. I add, "I didn't drink the love potion. I couldn't get myself to do it."

"Why not?"

"Because you're right. I deserve real love." I stare at her pretty face and wonder if she can get what I'm hinting at. When she doesn't run away screaming, I gesture toward the chair. "If you're not too busy, could you stay a while? Tell me about Kane's epic duel?"

Ivy drags the chair closer to the bed. She takes a seat, and I lean back against the bed to listen to her talk. I don't know if this will go anywhere, but I'm choosing to be hopeful. I can be very patient when I want to be.

* * *

EMORY

The next few months are some of the busiest in my life. With King Myenas's death, Kane had to negotiate a treaty with the heir to Carmine Falls. King Myenas's son, Aiden, is a lot more agreeable than his predecessor. He and Kane may never be friends, but they won't be enemies.

The new system for feeders isn't perfect. Even with the Alphas cooperating with the vampire royals, they'll never care for each other, but at least they're no longer trying to actively kill each other. My mother reassures me that progress takes time. The changes I'm trying to enact might not even be realized in my lifetime, but I can still hope that the next generation continues the work we've started.

Ivy learned about the Firebird's healing abilities and incorporated the bird's tears in the sleeping potion antidote. Lydia awoke from her magically-induced coma, much to her family and Colt's overwhelming joy. My brother and his mate didn't hesitate to continue with their wedding plans. They insisted on expediting the date to a mere few months, much to our mothers' combined stress.

It's all worth it in the end as I watch Lydia walk down the aisle toward my brother. I've never seen Colt so happy. Everything we have gone through to get Lydia back has led up to this moment. I have to hold back tears during the ceremony as Kane holds my hand.

The reception is a non-stop celebration. Lydia is constantly on the dance floor with one of her brothers spinning her around. Colt is dancing with our mother, who has been crying the entire time. Willow and Rainer are dancing with each other, lost in their own little world.

Lola is talking to a group of young shifters her age. My sister might finally be making friends. She's actually *smiling*. And she hasn't sulked at all during the whole event.

Ivy is seated with Lex at a table. They're whispering to each other with the giddiness of early love. I'm not sure if those two will work out as a couple, but I'm happy for them. Lex deserves some happiness in his life.

Kane offers me his hand. "Shall we dance, Emory?"

I take his hand, and he leads us to the dance floor. Kane is a great dancer, graceful and confident. I let him take the lead, knowing he will make us look good. Dancing with him is as easy as breathing.

Colt has taken his wife back from her brothers and is dancing closely with her. So close they might as well be one person. They kiss deeply, completely uncaring about who can see them. This has my mother shooing the kids toward getting some cake so they don't have to watch this display.

"They should probably get a room," Kane says. "Before they go too far and really give us a show."

"It's no surprise how he got her pregnant."

I wince as I realize I've spilled the beans about Lydia's pregnancy. Colt confided in me before the ceremony as he couldn't keep the news to himself. He's asked me not to tell anyone else since Lydia is still in her first trimester. I didn't mean to tell Kane, but we don't keep secrets from each other, and it just came out without me thinking.

"Don't tell anyone," I whisper. "No one is supposed to know yet."

Kane nods and looks over to where my brother and sister-in-law are sticking their tongues down each other's throats. "Good for them. They'll be great parents."

"With a large extended family to guide them along the way."

He turns back to me. "Your pregnancy was during a very stressful time. Do you wish you got pregnant at a later time?"

"I would never regret Mikey, but during a war wasn't an ideal time to be pregnant," I agree. "But something I've realized is that our lives are never going to be anything but bizarre. We live in a world with wolf shifters, vampires, witches, and magic. Life is always going to be interesting."

Kane smiles and pulls me closer. I rest my cheek on his chest. I can feel his rippling muscles through his charcoal suit. His familiar scent lulls me to close my eyes.

"Whatever happens, I'm glad it's you by my side. No one else," he tells me. "You are the woman I was meant to spend the rest of my life with."

I know he's right. Even without mating magic guiding us, we would have found each other eventually with the certainty of destiny and fate. There's something reassuring in that. All my roads lead to Kane Alexander.

"If younger me had any idea I'd end up marrying a king, let alone a vampire…"

"What would you have done?" He grins down at me.

"I would have thought I was very lucky to be married to such a handsome man," I say with a smile. "Good job, younger Emory. You hit the jackpot."

He laughs. "I've been very lucky, too. I'm married to a very beautiful, intelligent, strong woman."

"Look at us. The luckiest people alive. I would be horribly jealous of us if I were anyone else."

Kane kisses me, and we don't care who's watching us. I can understand my brother's exuberant joy. Love is the peace after battles fought and won. I don't have to explain that to Colt as he already knows this truth.

What the future holds for all of us, I have no way of knowing. Even if there's magic to give a glimpse on what is to come, I would rather not know and not spoil the surprise. Life is best when you're living in the moment. I want to impart that to our son and all the children of his generation.

The next generation is on their way–learning what it takes to run a kingdom or a pack, and to make this world a better place than how we found it. That's what I wish for Mikey, Cole, Bryony, and all the other children that may come into our lives.

For them, this is just the beginning.

Read the first chapter of Book 4 starting now!

BOOK 4 CHAPTER 1: THE PRINCE

Michael

Blood-red walls cloud my vision. I focus on the spiraling, floral velvet details of the wallpaper instead of the tall, dark-haired man pacing vigorously across the room, leaving tracks in the carpet.

Roses. Mom has always loved roses, and this room is a testament to her love of daylight, sunshine, and those late summer flowers that bloom in such a rich, dark red it reminds everyone of blood.

Fitting for a family of vampires, I surmise. Well, mostly vampires.

I check my wristwatch and sigh as Cole continues to mumble curses under his breath and twist his fingers through his black, slightly wavy hair.

"Shouldn't it have started by now?" Cole's ocean blue eyes meet mine. His normally handsome, chiseled features are blurred by stress as he pulls his hand over his face, pinching the bridge of his stately, regal nose.

We don't look alike, not at all. As cousins, we share the height passed down through our male line. Tall, with broad shoulders and muscular frames, we're a physical match for each other, but where his skin is bright and fair, reminiscent of a polished opal, and his hair is raven black and glossy, I'm…

Different.

I run my fingers through my dark brown, curly hair and shake my head at him. "Your incessant pacing is stressing me out."

"I'm stressed out," he echoes, throwing his hands up in emphasis. He moves with phantom grace in my direction–a vampire trait. As an adult who has known this man since we were born, essentially, I'm used to his ability to walk so quietly no one can tell he's there until he opens his fat mouth, but to anyone else, this would be completely, utterly menacing. I'm used to vampires and their ways. Probably because I am one, in a strange, distorted way.

"Don't posture at me, Cole. It's not my fault your betrothed is late to her own wedding."

"She's more than late," he growls. "She's not even here yet."

"So… she's running late. Are you telling me now that you're suddenly excited for this? You've been moping around for weeks acting like your world is collapsing." In truth, Cole's world is, in fact, imploding. Cole grew up spoiled rotten by his father, my uncle Lex, and the kind-hearted, sweet tempered Ivy, who I believed for years to be his actual mother.

At twenty-six, I've learned the family lore, however, and now understand Cole's inability to act rationally in most situations, seeing as his birth mother was the deranged Opal, who died when he was young.

Still, Cole grew up loved, spoiled by his parents, and has an infinity for women and feeders that can make even the most hardened commanders of my dad's army blush. Being forced into a political marriage is Cole's worst nightmare.

But I wouldn't mind, honestly, if I were in his shoes.

With another long, drawn out sigh, I turn toward the antique desk I've been leaning against for the last hour and pour myself a second dram of scotch, sans the blood. Cole scoffs, rolling his eyes to the ceiling as I turn to him, taking a sip.

"Enjoying your aperitif?"

"Jealous?" I grin around the rim.

"I'm starving," he growls, starting his pacing again. "It's been ages."

"Didn't you just come up from the feeders?"

He throws me a hard look and turns to pace to the other side of the room, his black tux fitted perfectly to his frame and his black shoes polished so effectively they shine like obsidian. Cole mumbles something under his breath that sounds a lot like, "Stupid, hybrid motherfucker," but I ignore him and check my watch again.

"Have you considered that maybe she's not coming at all?" I ask.

"It's not up to her. This is an alliance between my kingdom and her father's."

"But in the event King Mattias… changed his mind… you'd be off the hook."

"I'm not getting my hopes up." Cole snarls, his fangs elongating.

"Put those away," I smirk, setting my glass down on the desk just as the door to the Rose Room opens and a male servant steps inside looking weary as he scans the room. "Prince Michael, your mother needs your assistance."

"Thank the gods," I mutter as Cole gapes at the servant.

"What about me?"

"We're still trying to locate the bride," the servant replies nervously, his face going pale as Cole simmers with rage.

"So I'm supposed to stay here by myself?"

I cross the threshold into the hallway, murmuring to the servant in passing, "Will you please have a decanter of wine spiced with blood sent up for him, for all of our sakes? I really don't want to deal with him biting maids again."

The servant swallows hard as he nods and quickly shuts the door behind me, guiding me to the ballroom.

Mom is standing in the center of an elegantly decorated room. Candles that have been burning are now down to the wick, given that the ceremony was supposed to take place three hours ago. It's nearly morning, and I watch as she and my dad dismiss the last of the guests who'd gathered to watch what was supposed to be a show of faith and unity between two precariously friendly kingdoms.

"It's off, then?" I ask, coming to a step beside them and bending to give Mom a quick kiss on her cheek.

Dad narrows his eyes at the empty archways where the last guests have disappeared. "I knew this was going to happen."

Mom signs and grimaces. "No, you didn't. There's a good chance the poor girl is held up in one of the rural villages between our kingdoms in this storm, Kane."

Dad shakes his head, his blue eyes shining with displeasure. He's so much taller than Mom, whose head barely brushes the top of his shoulder as she turns into him, laying a hand on his chest. "Kane, go find Lex and talk to Cole. I doubt he'll be disappointed in the *delay*."

Dad shakes his head, his eyes sliding over mine on his way to mom's face. "King Mattias has been mum on every detail about the wedding he demanded of us–decades ago. He had no plans to actually send his daughter to my kingdom, despite months of back and forth and his insistence the wedding happen here, in our home, regardless of the fact Cole is the heir to Scarlett Thunder. You have to see that, Em. This is not a delay." His voice dips to something soft and warm as he says her name, her nickname, something he's only allowed to call her. It warms my chest as I watch them, in love after almost three decades together–a vampire and a wolf shifter.

But Dad isn't looking too happy right now as he continues. "He did this to try to embarrass us, to put us through the show of unity and togetherness with no plans to make good on his end of the bargain, that fucking bastard."

"Kane!" Mom hisses, her eyes sliding in my direction apologetically, as if I'm still a curious three-year-old who just learned a new word that I'll repeat consistently and out of context, possibly naming my imaginary friend "Bastard" and insisting he joins us for dinner. That did happen once, in her defense.

I clear my throat, coming to my father's aid, "Dad's right. King Mattias ignored several attempts to introduce Cole to his daughter before the wedding and hasn't even sent us a picture of the girl."

"We don't even know her name," Dad adds, giving me a ghost of a smile in thanks for having his back on this.

Mom, ever the optimist, tilts her chin in defiance. "Send a few guards out on the road, anyway, just in case her car is in a ditch, and she's stranded in the rain." With that, Mom turns, her crimson gown and cloak trailing behind her.

Dad and I watch her go in the glare of dozens of candles and red velvet.

"Have you given any thought to what we talked about recently?" I ask into the silence. I glance at Dad, noticing his jaw tightening as he tucks his hands in the pockets of his pants.

"You know how your mom feels about it, Michael."

I take a breath. "The odds of me finding a mate are slim, you know that. I'm more vampire than wolf."

"I know, but she's holding onto hope that you can marry for love."

"And what do you think is more likely?"

He swallows, shaking his head. "I agree with you. We need to find you a wife, a vampire, for the good of the kingdom. It'll break her heart, though."

I nod, hating the sinking feeling tightening my chest but turn for the exit. "I'm going to make sure Cole stays away from the feeders. He's a bit of a mess. I think he was secretly looking forward to this."

Thanks for reading! Book 4 will be released soon!

ALSO BY BELLA MOONDRAGON

The Alpha King's Breeder series:

Bought by the Alpha: The Alpha King's Breeder Book 1

Loved by the Alpha: The Alpha King's Breeder Book 2

Lost by the Alpha: The Alpha King's Breeder Book 3

Luna of the Alpha: The Alpha King's Breeder Book 4

Legacy of the Alpha: The Alpha Kings's Breeder Book 5

Daughter of the Alpha: The Alpha King's Breeder Book 6

Descendants of the Alpha: The Alpha King's Breeder Book 7

Shadow of the Alpha: The Alpha King's Breeder Book 8

Son of the Alpha: The Alpha King's Breeder Book 9

Spare of the Alpha: The Alpha King's Breeder Book 10

Claimed by the Alpha: The Alpha King's Breeder Book 11

Atonement for the Alpha King: The Alpha King's Breeder Book 12

Rejected by the Alpha: The Alpha King's Breeder Book 13

Abducted by the Alpha: The Alpha King's Breeder Book 14

Wolf Shifter Fairy Tale Retellings series

Beauty and the Alpha Beast

Sleeping Beasty

Tangling With the Alpha

The Luna's Vampire Prince series:

The Culling

The Kingdom

The Conquered

Pregnant With Four Alphas' Babies

Chosen As the Breeder

Mated to Four Alphas

Threats Against the Breeder

At War for the Breeder

The Stolen Breeder

Four Alphas, Four Babies

Becoming the Luna Queen

Descendants of the Breeder

Desired by the Devil series

Whispers of the Devil

Banter of the Devil

Murmurs of the Devil

The Mafia Kings series

Indebted to the Mafia King

Loved by the Mafia King

Claimed by the Mafia King

Secrets of the Mafia King

Burned by the Mafia King

Kidnapped by the Mafia King (coming soon!)

Dark Stalker Romance series

Tempted by Sin

Fated to Sin

Secret Billionaires series

Finding the Secret Billionaire by Olivia Bhelle Kildare

Falling for My Secret Billionaire by Bella Moondragon

Driven by the Secret Billionaire by ID Johnson

Wolf Shifter Alpha Kings series

Ravens and Ruins

Sundrops and Shadows

Snowflakes and Sabotage

The Vampire King's Feeder series

Claiming the Alpha's Daughter

Loving the Alpha's Daughter

Finding the Alpha's Daughter

Bewitching the Alpha's Son (coming soon!)

Writing as B. Moon

The Boy Who Died

Sign up for Bella's newsletter here.

Or get a free novella from The Alpha King's Breeder series when you sign up here:
The Beta and the Maid

Follow Bella on Facebook here.

Follow Bella on Bookbub here.